ECHOES OF
Pemberley

CYNTHIA INGRAM HENSLEY

Oysterville, WA

ECHOES OF PEMBERLEY

ISBN: 978-1-936009-19-0

Graphic design by Ellen Pickels

Cover photos by Ciobanu Alexandru Cristian © 2006 and Björn Höglund © 2010

For my mother — my hero

Acknowledgments

I would like to express a very special thank you to my husband, Douglas. By believing in me, you made me believe in myself. To Amber, thank you for reading and re-reading, and for your continued advice and input. I wish also to express my sincere gratitude to all the family and friends who have encouraged and loved me along the way. To Jane Austen, thank you for giving this world the greatest romance novel ever written. And finally, this first time author would especially like to thank my editor Mary Anne Hinz, Ellen Pickels for seeing my vision, and Michele Reed at Meryton Press for making what was only a dream a reality.

Chapter 1

Derbyshire, England

S ean Kelly pulled on to the narrow, two-lane road and drove along the wooded fringes of the estate to Ashridge. He could see the village sitting in a cove with a rocky cliff to one side and a green, quilted pasture to the other. Ashridge was a postcard village, much like those of County Down in Northern Ireland where Sean lived.

He looked for a place to park under flapping banners that welcomed people to Ashridge's Annual Cider and Perry Festival. On the crowded street, local vendors sold everything from crafts to jarred honey to visiting townies eager to pay the inflated prices. The little parish had obviously once had its heyday but now was no more than a wide spot in the road, appreciated mostly by the faithful residents who chose the quiet, simpler life it had to offer.

Nestled in what the locals fittingly called the silent valley, the ancient hamlet was first established as Kympton and seemed to possess a restrained whisper of another time. On the highroad, a waterwheel, which looked as if it hadn't turned since the Great War, loomed motionless. Nearby, the village train station sat empty and closed up, no longer bustling with passengers off to London. Kympton Way, the main street that ran through the center of town, was lined with old, stone storefronts that had traded their goods for generations. The romance of eras past was at every turn, haunting the soul and enchanting the heart.

Tractors occupied most of the parking spots, but near the end of Kympton Way, Sean finally found a space and pulled his relic of a Land Rover in between two muddy JCBs. This would be his home for the next six weeks, and it was probably for the best. What else could he and his father say that hadn't already been said? He hadn't meant to disappoint the man. Hopefully his mother was right; maybe some time apart *would* put things right between them again. Exhaling a reluctant but accepting sigh, Sean grabbed his guitar from the back seat and shut the door.

As he looked up and down the main street, the familiar reek of plowed fields and manure flooded his nostrils, a comforting whiff of home to a lad raised on a horse farm. Behind the earthy smells were the sharper scents of cider and perry, intensifying his thirst and persuading him into the throng of people in search of drink, his guitar slung over his back.

A few blocks up, Sean stopped in front of the Green Man Inn and Pub, Ashridge's only hotel. The lunch specials were written on a small chalkboard, held in place by a foliate rendition of the inn's mythical namesake, but it was the sound of a well-played fiddle rather than the promise of a meat pie that persuaded Sean inside. Music always was a good icebreaker, and he hoped to meet a few of the locals. Although he was only in England for the summer, he might as well make the best of his temporary exile from Ireland, be damned his father's bloody Irish pride.

As Sean stepped up to the bar, the bartender, a stout man wearing old-fashioned half-moon spectacles on the tip of his nose, took notice of his guitar and frowned at Sean. He pointed to a sign that read, *No singin' for yer cider.* "Sorry, mate," he said.

"A half-pint, please." Sean tossed a pound on the bar.

"Oh, come on, Bobby," the young fiddle player called out across the pub. He looked to be in his early twenties, a few years older than Sean. "Let my good mate, er… what's your name, mate?"

The question caused a spatter of laughter from the audience, and Sean had to yell over the rumble to answer. "It's Sean!"

"Jolly good name, Sean! How 'bout it, Bobby? Let my good mate Sean sing us a tune."

The crowd cheered in support of the fiddle player's request as Bobby sat a pint of cider on the bar. "I asked for a half," Sean said and pushed the glass back.

"A quid buys a full pint," Bobby countered, pushing the glass back once more. "Sing a fair chantey for the crowd and the next one will be on the Green Man."

"Thanks." Sean smiled and lifted his glass to Bobby. "Cheers."

The crowd hooted and banged their tables as he crossed the room to the slightly raised stage. There was a jukebox in the corner, but the festival and too many rounds of cider had them lively and in want of traditional music such as old sea chanteys and pub songs. Sitting in clusters around small tables, Sean saw only the faces of strangers but felt at ease. He had been singing in pubs since... well, since he *could* sing. When he was a little boy, his dad would stand him and one or two of his brothers on a bar stool in one of the pubs back home and have them sing for his ale. The memory caused a slight tightening in Sean's chest, but he swallowed it away and introduced himself to the fiddle player. "Name's Sean Kelly."

"An Irishman!" The fiddle player looked scandalized for the sake of the crowd.

"Aye." Sean grinned and played along. "But me mother's English!"

"That's all right, mate. My name's Rick Meriwether." He pulled the bow across his fiddle with a screeching mock. "And me mother's Irish!" The audience laughed heartily at their banter. Like him, Sean thought, Rick Meriwether probably grew up in the country around small village pubs and amongst the country folk who patronized them. Pulling his guitar strap over his shoulder, he nodded to Rick, and the two settled into a quick easy harmony, singing the songs they had learned as boys. Charmed by the familiar tunes, the rowdy village audience joined in, clapping and singing along to words they knew by heart.

Several songs later, the low-ceilinged room had begun to grow warm as Sean and Rick bowed to applause and set their instruments aside. They had earned their drink and, after the singing, were suddenly in need of it. In one smooth gulp, Sean swallowed the last of his cider and set his empty glass in front of the bartender. "My wages if you please, Bobby," he said to the bartender with a smile.

"You've a way with the crowd." Bobby poured two fresh ciders from the tap. "Are you going to be in Ashridge for long?"

"Yeah, six weeks." Sean slid onto a bar stool. "I've a summer job at Pemberley Estate."

"Working for the Darcys, eh?" Rick asked, nodding a thank you to Bobby for the drinks.

"Aye." Sean took a long pull on his mug. "Know them?"

"*Know* them?" Rick repeated. "Everyone in Ashridge knows the Darcys. Bennet Darcy bloody well owns just about everything you see looking left to right."

"Oh." Sean took a more cautious sip now. "A Scrooge of a landlord, is he?"

Shaking his head, Rick chuckled. "Hardly. The rents are barely more than they were when his grandfather took over the place after World War II."

"Took over the place?" Sean questioned. "I thought Pemberley was the seat for the Darcy family."

"It was…is…you know how these old manors go from hand to hand. Chap named Howell married a Darcy and ran Pemberley for awhile. Ran it right into the ground according to my grandfather, but that was before my day. Granddad says Ashridge was fortunate the Darcys got hold of the estate again. Ben Darcy's a good man."

"Really?" Sean's eyebrows lifted disbelievingly. He had met Bennet Darcy just that morning and found him to be somewhat unfriendly, to say the least.

"Met him, have you?" Rick read Sean's expression.

Sean nodded and set his half-empty mug down on the bar. Being new in town, he didn't need the cider to go to his head.

"A bit reserved, was he?" Rick continued with an obvious understanding.

"Rather."

"Don't worry, mate." Rick clapped a hand on Sean's shoulder. "He's a good chap, just the silent type. Some say it's the reason Ashridge lies in what's known as the silent valley. The Darcys of Pemberley own most of it and they have always been a quiet lot. Very…private-like." Rick looked past Sean and pointed to the door with his chin. "There's one of them now."

Sean turned and stared at the teenage girl who stepped into the pub. She was beautiful, but her beauty was cool and removed like an exquisite sculpture at the National Gallery. You could look but weren't allowed touch. It was like there were brass posts and red velvet ropes around her. She was right in front of them, yet completely separate. The low murmur of conversation fell to a hush when she closed the door behind her. Wearing a pair of crisply pressed khaki trousers and an argyle cardigan, she wasn't one of them and knew it, casting a guarded glance over their faces but never meeting anyone's eye.

"Two Cokes please, Bobby," she said, and sat down at an empty table near the door.

"Coming up, Miss Catie," Bobby said and then whispered into Sean's ear, "Close your mouth, lad. She's out of your league."

"Catie Darcy?" Sean asked incredulously, blushing faintly at Bobby's observation. Not only was Catie Darcy beautiful, she wasn't at all what he had expected. "But…I thought she was just a kid."

"Not any longer." Rick shook his head. "She's near seventeen now, grown into quite a prize with those looks and a fortune to match."

Sean turned to his new friend's smiling face and tried to regain his composure. "It's just...well, to be honest, I was expecting braces, plaits, and freckles. You know...a little girl. Not...not..."

"Don't be drawn in by the pretty face, mate." Rick took a drink and glanced cautiously at the girl. "The little miss has a reputation. Word is, when she was a tyke, she made her nannies cry and frightened away piano teachers. People say she only got worse after that daddy of hers died."

"*Great*," Sean groaned more to himself than Rick. The news made him reconsider his cider, and he swallowed another healthy gulp. His Aunt Rose hadn't mentioned crying nannies or frightened piano teachers, and furthermore, she spoke of Catie Darcy as if she were a child. Of course, to Aunt Rose she would be. He was nineteen, and the woman still referred to him as her sister's boy. He was no longer a boy, however, and Catie Darcy was certainly *not* a child.

Warily, Sean looked at her once more. It was a pretty face, prettier than any he had encountered thus far. The last one, Patricia, a graduate student who wore more makeup than his mother liked, had taken his virginity and left him smoldering in the remnants of a lust that shamed him when he came home late and met his mother's eyes over her knitting. Her disapproving looks didn't stop him though — Patricia did. She found another inexperienced undergrad plaything and shooed him away like a bothersome fly. But he had learned from it. As to *what* he had learned from it...well, he was still figuring that out.

Swallowing slowly, he looked at Catie Darcy again. It was a good job, and the wages would easily see him through next term. He would ignore the pretty face and make the most of Catie Darcy's infamous temperament. He'd been around horses all his life and had dealt with his fair share of spoiled, high-spirited fillies before. Granted those were of the equine variety, but surely there couldn't be much difference. All he had to do was to stay focused on his job, keep charge of the situation, and try not to get kicked in the head. Still, he couldn't help but wonder who the other Coke was for.

Alone at the table, Catie Darcy sipped at her Coke while she waited for her best friend Audrey, who was now officially late. She had probably stopped to chat with every other person on the street, Catie thought resentfully as her solitude grew more and more uncomfortable. The daughter of a politician, Audrey Tillman was naturally friendly and extremely talkative. She was popular at school and, like her councilman father, well-liked in Ashridge.

The door clanged open, and Catie breathed a sigh of relief. "What's the matter?" Audrey asked as she sat down. "There's a festival going on outside, and you look like you're at a funeral."

"I would've been at yours had you been any later," Catie snipped. "Did you see my brother out there anywhere?"

"He and Sarah and the twins were heading this way when I came in. Why?"

"Good." Catie looked thankful. "I'm bored and ready to go home."

"Home!" Audrey exclaimed. "But the festival goes on all day!"

"Like I said, I'm bored. Plus, I didn't get home from school until late yesterday evening and still have unpacking to do."

"Only you, Catie Darcy, would leave a village festival to unpack." As Audrey spoke, someone across the room gained her attention. "Who's the dark-headed dreamboat at the bar?"

Catie's eyes followed Audrey's just in time to see the dreamboat turn away. "I don't know — probably a tourist in town for the festival."

"He was looking at you." Audrey nudged her friend with a teasing smile.

"Everyone looks at me. Ashridge should charge a fee to gawk at Pemberley's rich orphan. Maybe the village could raise enough money to replace that crumbling war memorial they're always talking about."

"God, Catie, stop being such a killjoy. Maybe he likes your looks."

Before Catie could respond, her brother and his wife came into the Green Man, holding the hands of their five-year-old twins.

"Welcome, Mr. Darcy!" Bobby suddenly became animated. It was a long standing tradition for the master of Pemberley House to pop in at the Green Man on the day of any festival and buy a round of drinks for everyone. Clearly, Bobby was happy to have a packed house when Bennet Darcy arrived. "What'll you have, sir?"

"A cider for me and Mrs. Darcy and something a little less concentrated for my boys."

"A wee nip of the valley's cider will put hair on the lads' chests!" a patron called out from the other side of the pub.

"They're Derbyshire lads, man!" Mr. Darcy called back enthusiastically. "They were *born* with hair on their chests!" This statement generated a loud racket of clanging glasses and shouts of approval. "A round of cider on Pemberley Estate, Bobby!" he shouted over the din. "And be warned ... I don't count the five hundred heads you billed me for last year!"

Laughing with his customers, Bobby waved off the gibe. The more hubbub, the more drinks he sold. He and Mr. Darcy gave each other a friendly nod as waitresses passed out the free cider, stirring a series of boisterous toasts and cheers.

"Thought you said this was called the *silent* valley," Sean said, smiling into his mug.

"It is, mate." His new friend laughed. "It is."

Chapter 2

Pumping her legs hard, Catie brushed strands of hair from her face, careful to keep the speeding bicycle steady on the rough terrain. Recent storms had rutted the path, forcing her to avoid channels and ditches as she rode alongside the riverbank. Finally reaching the lake, sweating and winded, she let her bicycle fall and lay back on the cool grassy bank to catch her breath. The lateness of the afternoon created diamonds that sparkled and shimmered on the water's rippled surface as the sun traveled slowly towards the dam. Beyond the glittering lake, she could see Pemberley in the distance — home.

Sitting in the rise of the valley, the old manor was as much a part of the landscape as the trees, hills, and sprawling grounds around it. The park itself, a mixture of formal gardens and thick woodlands, claimed almost five miles of a rambling river, boasted several ponds, a generously sized fishing lake, and a wide stream that meandered tranquilly in front of the home. Wiping her face with her sleeve, Catie gave the hall of her ancestors an appreciative smile and started home.

A rumbling growl of hunger persuaded her pace up the winding approach road, a thigh-burning incline rewarded by an easy descent to the house. Speeding through the courtyard, she circled around to the service entrance and skidded to a stop, sending gravel flying to clank against the kitchen window. As she leaned her bicycle against the wall, she heard the sound of pots and pans banging and clamoring inside. The lingering aroma of cooking was still thick in the air. Her shoulders slumped; supper had started without her.

"You're late, Miss Catie." Mr. Johnson, Pemberley's cook, felt compelled to state the obvious when she stepped inside the kitchen.

"Thanks," Catie retorted as she tucked the book she had been reading all afternoon under her arm and turned on the tap to wash her hands.

"I'd not dally were I you. Mr. Darcy's been in a foul mood since the post came." Mr. Johnson dried his knives as he spoke but looked up when Catie abruptly turned to him.

"The post?" she questioned, not able to hide the concern in her voice.

"Yes," he replied as his usual frown grew significantly at the mess before him. "Look at my floor!"

Catie looked down and saw that her muddy footprints followed her to the sink. "Sorry." She shrugged one shoulder, giving Mr. Johnson a lopsided smile. "But I shouldn't dally...foul mood, remember." She dried her hands, kicked off her shoes, and hurried up the service stairs to the summer breakfast room where her family had informal evening meals in the warmer months.

Approaching quietly, she could see Ben and Sarah sitting in their respective seats at each end of the table, with their sons, Geoffrey and George, between them. "The post," she whispered. "Surely they haven't come already." Realizing her book was still tucked under her arm, she slid it out of sight on a hall table. She didn't need Ben seeing one of her "rubbish romance novels" as he called them, especially if her report had arrived from Davenport that morning. Although she was sure she passed satisfactorily, no marks were ever high enough to please her brother.

As if mocking Catie's apprehension, the room was alight with a comforting chandelier glow. "Hello," she opened with great enthusiasm, hoping to make light of the hour. She was happy to see they were still on the first course. Not *too* late, she reassured herself. She received equally cheerful responses from all but Ben, who remained grimly silent. *Yes, they most definitely had come.* She took a cautious peek at him as a chilled summer butternut squash soup was placed before her, making her stomach rumble with gratitude.

With everyone now in place and served, Ben sent the servant from the room with a slight nod of his head and waited until the pocket doors were pulled securely together before sharply questioning his sister. "Where have you been all afternoon, Catherine?"

She turned to him and her gut tightened. Her brother looked like he had been stewing for hours. Their relationship was a close and affectionate one, but on occasion she would unknowingly wade into the treacherous waters of his temper. "Why?" she asked cautiously as his knitted brow had more written on it than a few grades that didn't meet his expectations.

"Why? I'll tell you *why*! Because your riding lessons were to start today, and the instructor rang up from the stables and said that you never came round this afternoon. That's *why*!"

Shutting her eyes tight with a wince of clarity, Catie's memory was restored. "Oh," she uttered stupidly.

"*Oh?*" he questioned, sitting back in annoyance. "Is that *oh*, I daydreamed my afternoon away and forgot or maybe *oh*, I was elbow deep in one of those *rubbish* romance novels and couldn't tear myself away long enough for my lesson?"

Desperate, Catie cast a subtle but pleading look to Sarah, who took up the cause with the skillful diplomacy only a wife could possess.

"Bennet, could you not settle this matter later?" she put in smoothly. "The twins are eating, and I'm afraid all of this commotion is upsetting their digestion."

Ben looked over at his young sons and, as if on cue, the two, round faces stared back at him with wide, grayish-blue eyes that matched his own.

Having his father's attention, Geoffrey decided to speak up in support of his mother. "Yes, Daddy, we are eating and all this com…commo… What was it, Mummy?"

"Never mind, Geoffrey, your mother's right," Ben said quietly, giving his wife's scolding eye an apologetic glance. He turned to his sister and stated with a somewhat humbled authority, "I'll speak with you afterwards, Catherine."

Catie nodded unenthusiastically at him and then gave Sarah a grateful glance. She hadn't managed a pardon but the temporary reprieve was appreciated.

The rest of the meal went on without incident as Catie remained quiet in her own thoughts. Instead of eating, she moved food around her plate, having lost her appetite from the twinge of dread now lodged in her stomach. She was in for a sermon — a long one no doubt. Ben was determined that, when Catie finished Davenport, she attend Newnham, the all-female college of Cambridge University from which their mother had graduated. He would never neglect a ripe opportunity to lecture his sister on any defect of character that might keep her from being admitted. If only she had remembered that *stupid* riding lesson.

Lessons had been the bane of Catie Darcy's existence for as long as she could remember. Piano lessons, flute lessons, tennis lessons, French lessons — the list was endless and demanding and kept her confined to the country each summer, which was just how her brother liked it. Losing both parents before his twenty-fourth birthday, Ben was overly cautious with his loved ones. Nervous Nelly, Sarah had often called him, but Ben's grief had made him a wary man.

Catie Darcy may have been wealthy beyond comprehension, but her world was a sheltered one. The death of her beloved father in many ways had closed the green, rolling hills of Pemberley Estate around her like a grassy sea of solitude, and she, the lone survivor of a sunken ship. Nothing she had come from still existed.

On the way to Ben's study, the same study used by generations of Darcy men, Catie strolled leisurely down the long, wide gallery of Pemberley. No need to hurry; the longer Ben cooled the better. The ornate hall housed the portraits of their ancestors, each one with a story of their own. Some were noble while others... well, others were quite romantic. Catie stopped in front of Fitzwilliam and Elizabeth Darcy, hanging prominently side-by-side at the end of the gallery. Fitzwilliam's gaze was ardent and looked left towards his life's love, while hers, affectionately warm, flickered softly rightward in return. Their love was a legacy that had been passed down through the generations, a favorite story of the young descendant who stood before them.

Looking solemnly up at the couple, Catie sighed. "Romance wasn't always rubbish, at least not two hundred years ago when you two met and fell in love, eh?" Their descendant found her answer in their loving expressions, forever locked in a devoted gaze. She sighed again and left them to each other.

When she reached the study door, which was slightly ajar, her brother appeared to be working, so she spoke to gain his attention. "Bennet," she said softly, using her little sister voice. If Catie Darcy was the lone survivor of a sunken ship, her big brother Ben was her life raft. Fourteen years her senior, he was all she had left in the world. She hated disappointing him.

He looked up just long enough to wave her in and then returned his attention to whatever he was reading. She made herself comfortable in the chair in front of his desk and waited. He often made her wait, or squirm rather. Catie likened this tactic to when a predator lames its prey and then tauntingly circles the helpless victim for some time before finishing the kill.

He finally began, reading from the paper in front of him. "'Miss Darcy is an unmotivated student, she daydreams, lacks focus in her studies...' need I continue?"

They had come. "Was all that written on my report?" she asked, craning to see the paper in front of him.

"No. That is what Miss Spencer relayed to me when I called Davenport this afternoon to inquire why the devil I am paying such premium tuition for these grades."

"I may lack focus at times, but my grades aren't that bad." She met his eyes with a challenging look.

"Cambridge is a competitive university, Catherine, and *not that bad* isn't going to suffice. I'm sure that I need not tell you that I am sorely regretting not lining up tutors for the summer. It's important that you — "

"I needed the break, Ben," she interrupted. "I've had governesses and tutors every summer since…" *Every summer since Daddy died.* They didn't talk about Father, so the words remained at the back of her throat. Her eyes betrayed her though as they rested on the picture frame sitting on Ben's desk, her father smiling with his arm affectionately over Ben's shoulder. "I'll knuckle down next term, I promise," she said softly, lowering her eyes to her hands. The man had been dead for eight years, and yet his presence — or absence — beat between them like a living heart.

"Catie," Ben started. He had looked at the picture as well. This was never easy. He was Catie's guardian but not her father. He got up and came around the desk to be closer to her. "All right." He rubbed the back of his neck, his voice softer now. "Next term you'll knuckle down, but in the meantime, please take your riding more seriously. Both Mother and Father were avid riders, and I know they would have wanted you to be as well."

Ben had a passion for horses: a trait passed down to him much like the desk on which he leaned. For generations their family history was filled with champion horsemen and horsewomen. But unlike her parents, her brother, and her long dead ancestors, Catie Darcy was not a skilled equestrian. In fact, she didn't even like riding — feared it really. Having been thrown from a horse shortly after her father's death, she hated any real speed on horseback.

When she was eight years old, Catie had ventured out alone on her pony, which was no small infraction of the rules. Inexperienced, she lost control of her mount, and the panicked animal tossed its tiny rider like a weightless rag doll. But since she wasn't too badly hurt, no one ever discovered her little misadventure.

Negotiation, it seemed, was her best course now. "All right, for two weeks," she declared. It was bold of her she knew, but Ben and Sarah had promised her a summer free of tutors and lessons and hired the riding instructor at the last minute. "And then if I've made no real progress, I want to be allowed to quit."

"Two weeks!" Ben's face reddened. "I have already paid for six, Catherine!" He breathed deeply to calm his annoyance and, looking at her, contemplated for a moment. He shouldn't let her off so easy on her grades; she was certainly capable of higher marks. And furthermore, she deserved a sound talking-to for missing her riding lesson, but he didn't want to start the summer on a bad note.

"Fine, two weeks of *strong* effort," he said. Darcys were known for their negotiating skills, and he certainly wasn't going to come away empty-handed. "And then... well, we'll talk about it."

"Thanks, Ben." Satisfied with her success, Catie sprang up and gave him a sisterly kiss on his cheek. "Sleep well, Brother." Assuming herself the victor in their little agreement, she patted his shoulder consolingly and turned to leave.

"Catie." Ben grabbed hold of his sister's wrist before she was out of reach. "*Strong* effort!"

"Yes, Ben." She nodded to further her compliance and repeated, "*Strong* effort."

"And, Catie," he said, tilting his head. "Please come to supper on time from now on, eh, dear?"

"Oh, yes... of course, Ben, I apologize about that."

"And one more thing, dearest," he continued, still holding her. "In the future, do me the favor of bathing first?"

"Oh, right." She blushed, remembering the sweatiness from her ride and her muddy feet in the kitchen. "Sorry about that too."

As soon as the house was fully quiet and she was sure no one would notice her absence, Catie tip-toed down the service steps and left through a side door. With only the glow of her torch to guide her, she padded her way through the dimly lit, walled garden to the path beyond. Moving downhill, the terrain seemed to urge her forward as her bare legs brushed against the profuse, damp flora, leaving wet streaks that tickled her skin. An unusual but welcomed wave of heat had settled in the valley, ushering in a humid night after the warm afternoon, and she greatly desired a swim. When she arrived at the black, still water of the pond, she stepped out onto a small dock and began removing her clothes.

Catie slid out of each article of clothing and dropped them lazily to the wooden planks. Once finished, she stood fully naked and allowed the warm night to caress her skin. Stretching her body long and taut, she reached to the heavens as if sacrificing herself to the full moon that reflected on the water at her feet. Then, without further hesitation, she jumped in, instantly feeling the muck underfoot. She turned onto her back and drifted out toward the middle as the cold, relaxing water streamed smoothly over her bare limbs. Not quite to the deep center where she liked to float, she was startled by a man's voice.

"Who's there?" it called from somewhere in the darkness.

Shocked, Catie shot up out of the water and called back, "Who is *there*?"

"My name is Kelly, Sean Kelly."

"Sir, can you please turn away so I can climb out and dress?"

"Sure, miss," he answered with the faint undertones of a chuckle.

As Catie swam to the ladder to pull herself out of the water, she kept a watchful eye in the direction of the man's voice, hoping he was honoring her request. She hesitated momentarily but then scurried up the ladder and began hastily dressing, while she firmly informed the stranger that he was trespassing on private property. She heard the rustle of his footsteps and could tell he was moving towards her, making her quickly fasten her shorts and tuck in her wet tee-shirt to be as presentable as possible.

Finished, she nervously grabbed her torch, clicked it on, and pointed it directly in his face as he stepped out of the darkness and onto the dock, raising a hand to protect his eyes from the beam. He was young, attractive, and smiling at her. Catie took a sharp breath.

"I didn't mean to frighten you. I was just out enjoying the warm evening." He laughed lightly as he turned and gestured toward the direction she had just come from. "I'm a summer tenant of the small cottage on the other side of the drive."

His voice was solid and deep and accented with Irish, making Catie feel as if his words were sticking to her wet skin when he spoke. "Oh." She moved her torch away. "Sorry, I didn't mean to blind you. I just wasn't expecting anyone to be here."

"No worries." He smiled down at her now.

"From Ireland are you?" she asked.

The accent significantly thickened as he tucked his thumbs in his jeans, performed a little jig and responded, "Aye... what was it, lass, me name or me brogue that gave me away?" Catie grinned briefly. "Northern Ireland actually — ever been there?"

"No, I haven't. I'm Catie Darcy. I live at the manor."

"Yes, I know," he said.

"You know?" Her eyes narrowed with consideration. "I'm sorry. I don't believe we've met."

"We haven't. I know who you are because I've been hired as your riding instructor for the summer." He smiled again, wider this time.

Riding instructor? Stop staring at him! Audrey Tillman would have something extremely clever to say right now. "You..." she stammered, feeling suddenly awkward in her own skin. She wasn't expecting him to be young or good looking. Flustered, Catie knelt down and busied herself with tying her shoes. "You told my brother that I didn't come round for my lesson today." The words flew out of her mouth, hot and accusing.

Stunned, Sean looked down at her. He chuckled lightly. "Sorry. Was I mistaken? *Did* you come round for your lesson?"

She stopped and cut her eyes up at him as a rush of red raced up her neck and filled her face. "Listen...er...what did you say your name was again?"

"Mr. Kelly," Sean supplied formally. *Chew on that your majesty!*

Standing up, Catie's brows rose. "Did your parents bother giving you a Christian name, Mr. Kelly?" she asked so snappishly she surprised herself.

He chuckled again. "They did. I was properly christened Sean Donovan, but seeing as we are to have a student-teacher relationship — "

"*Mister?*" she interrupted him, her expression as incredulous as her voice. "Surely you don't expect — "

"I do," he cut her off as she had him.

"But that's ridiculous! Exactly which rock have you been under for the last century?" She mockingly glanced about as if she might see the offending boulder upturned somewhere.

Her hair had partially come loose from her ponytail during her swim and there were several wet ringlets plastered to the side of her face, distracting him. *All the more reason to keep all interactions with Catie Darcy as professional as possible.* Still, he had to admit he enjoyed ruffling her feathers. Clearly, the little miss wasn't used to being crossed. *And damned if she wasn't even more beautiful spitting mad.*

He answered coolly, "No rock. I just prefer proper boundaries if it's all the same to you."

Catie's mouth opened and closed. She reached down to gather the last of her belongings still scattered on the dock. "If it's proper boundaries you want,

Mr. Kelly, call me *Miss* Catie." She straightened again and met his eyes. "Just as the rest of the help does." It was a nasty remark she knew, but like Ben, her temper could get the best of her. Catie brushed by him and stormed off, sure she heard him laughing behind her.

She hadn't gone far when he called out, "Three o'clock tomorrow then, *Miss* Catie...sharp!"

Giving each step a portion of her fury, she made her way home along the dark pathways, knowing all the turns and steps. Reaching the sanctuary of her bedroom, Catie hurled her damp clothes on the floor, angrily changed into a pair of warm pajamas, and then fell on her bed. "*Mister*," she hissed hatefully. "He couldn't be more than three years older than me." As she seethed, her mind's eye drifted to his face. His sharp nose and firm chin were softened by his kind blue eyes that seemed to dance when he smiled. "*Mr. Kelly*," she hissed one more time before reaching up and turning off the light.

Chapter 3

A bird singing outside her window and the dull hum of a vacuum woke Catie from a deep sleep. Her eyes were having trouble adjusting to the light, reminding her that she had forgotten to close the drapes before going to bed. She sat up, only to let her body fall back to the mattress, and pulled the covers over her face. "Oh, why must they hoover so early in the morning?" she grumbled into the sheets. After a few minutes of trying to decide whether to get up or remain put, she picked up the receiver to ring down and have breakfast brought to her room.

Modern conveniences had been added slowly to the old stone manor for most of the twentieth century. Catie's own father, being a contemporary man and lover of technology, made his own prolific contributions to the seventeenth-century dwelling. From plumbing to electricity, security systems to controlled temperature zones, the house was eventually modernized with careful attention to maintain its historical integrity.

Unfortunately for Catie Darcy, however, no modern-day convenience could control who answered her call for breakfast. It was Rose's voice on the other end of the line. "Yes, Sleeping Beauty." Rose sounded antagonistic.

Catie grimaced but spoke cheerfully. "Good morning. Beautiful day, eh, Rose?"

"Morning?" Rose said. "Miss Catie, according to my watch, morning has been behind us for almost an hour now, child."

"Yes, Nan, so it has. Would there be any breakfast left?" Nan, short for nanny, was a loving endearment still used when Catie hoped to evoke favor or sympathy.

"A few bits about to be taken round to the hounds. If you hope to have them

23

for yourself, I'd recommend you dislodge yourself from your bed and come downstairs." Rose wasn't one to mince words, meaning any thoughts of a late morning breakfast in bed had vanished when she answered the phone.

Rose Todd was Pemberley's housekeeper, the highest position in any large house and a post she had earned. She had come to Pemberley when Ben was just a boy and raised the children and ran the house when the elder Mr. Darcy lost his wife in childbirth. Then, when tragedy dealt a second cruel blow to the Darcy siblings, it was Rose who stood next to Ben and Catie at their father's grave. She had in every sense become a surrogate for their deceased parents.

Catie laughed. "All right, Nan, I'll be right down. Don't feed the dogs just yet."

She saw him as soon as she entered the kitchen. There, sitting at the long trestle table with Rose, was the same face captured in the light of her torch last evening. Seeing him in the full light of day, she quickly noticed the darkness had not deceived her. He was as handsome as she remembered and wore a large smile as he shared a pot of tea with Rose. Catie's jaw tightened and her mouth twitched at the sight of him. *Sean Kelly*, she thought spitefully. "Good morning," she said quickly, wanting to be the first to speak.

"Good morning, Miss Catie," he responded with more delight than was necessary.

"Oh," Rose chirped, smiling. "Have you two met already?"

"Yes, Aunt, I met Miss Catie last evening."

"Aunt?" Catie looked up from the toast she was buttering. "What do you mean, *aunt*?"

"Rose is my mother's sister. You didn't know I was Rose's nephew, did you?" Sean gave Catie a conspiratorial wink.

Rose's nephew! Sean Kelly was Rose's nephew?

The old screen from the garden creaked open and Sarah stepped into the kitchen. Although Sarah Darcy was a striking woman, her ease and kindness was what drew people to her. Everything about her was unassuming and gentle, and made you feel glad you were alive just by looking at her. Her amber eyes were her most outstanding feature, flecked with gold and anchored below mahogany brows that arched into a triangle when she smiled. She was smiling when she entered the kitchen and greeted Sean warmly, praising him for getting George to mount his pony that morning.

Catie scarcely heard the pleasant exchange. She was staring at Sean Kelly, bitterness festering. Like everyone else, he knew all about her . . . or thought he knew. They all *thought* they knew, thought they understood. She hated the assumptions people made about her and despised their sympathy.

There was a sudden tiny spark in her chest, the kind of spark that abandons reason and usually meant trouble, either for her or someone else. But then again, reason never was any match for Catie Darcy's temper.

She interrupted their lively conversation. "It may be better for all concerned if Mr. Kelly were to resign his position as riding instructor." There was an instant hush, and they all looked at her, including Mr. Johnson, who stopped chopping carrots. "Well…" she hesitated. "It's just, he saw me naked last night and I'm afraid there might be an uncomfortable awkwardness between us."

"Sean!" Rose gasped wildly, grabbing her chest and turning to him. "What have you done?"

"Nothing! I…it was j-just a mistake…" he fumbled.

"What sort of mistake?" Sarah insisted.

"Nothing like *that*, Mrs. Darcy…" He paused and glanced past the questioning faces of the women in hopes of getting help from the one person who could clarify. It was only then that he realized the purposefulness in her act. Grinning smugly at him, Catie Darcy simply took a casual bite of her toast and shrugged her shoulders. Sean's mouth dropped open in surprise. He narrowed his eyes at her in disbelief and turned to his aunt to explain.

The eldest of five, what some might call rowdy boys, Sean had a talent for turning an angry mob. He had a natural wit and charm that had enabled him to talk the Kelly brothers out of many a scrape since they had left their mother's lap. He did his best to spin his chance encounter with Miss Darcy at the pond as humorously as possible, artfully speaking in his humble County Down brogue for effect. By the time he had finished, the room had become friendly again and a soft infectious laughter had started to spread. Victorious, Sean turned back to Catie with a checkmate smile he didn't bother to hide and pleasantly reassured her, "So you see, Miss Catie, you've no need to feel uncomfortable or awkward. It was too dark last night to see anything but shadows. You've a rather pretty silhouette though…if I might say." At this Mr. Johnson laughed out loud, and seeming eager to put the affair to rest, Rose and Sarah joined him, although a bit less heartily. Luckily for Sean Kelly, none of the three seemed to recall the previous evening's full moon or cloudless sky.

Mouth mashed into a thin, resentful line, Catie glanced around the room once more, primly folded her arms and left as the checkmate smile faded from Sean's face.

"ARE YOU BUSY?" SARAH KNOCKED and entered Ben's study at the same time. "Shall I come back?"

"You know better than that." He smiled up at her and motioned her to his lap. She released a small thankful breath. She was in need of his comfort and snuggled against his chest. "After the figures I've been looking at on that page, yours, Mrs. Darcy, is a welcomed one." His breath was warm on her neck followed by soft kissing lips.

Sarah rose up slightly to peek at the offending figures. "Something tells me if those figures had a few more zeros my figure wouldn't be nearly as appealing."

He chuckled quietly against her skin. "Probably not." Sarah tried to get up but he stopped her. "That was a joke."

"And a poor one," she admonished but settled back again without protest.

"You've something you wish to tell me," he said as if stating a fact.

"Do I?"

"Sarah."

"George laughed this morning." The words rushed out. Ben was right, she did want more than anything to tell him. She had been afraid that she was making more of it than there was but smiled now as she recalled the minor accomplishment. "His own laugh, not Geoffrey's."

"Didn't I tell you he was going to be fine?" Ben said. "He's a Darcy. We've a tendency to be a bit reserved. It's in our nature."

"Yes." She nodded, accepting his reassurance but by no means convinced. George was more than reserved. He never spoke unless he found the words of his brother worth repeating. He mimicked Geoffrey as if he had no real thoughts of his own.

"Geoffrey has a bold personality," he said as if reading her thoughts. "It's only natural for his younger brother to look up to him, wish to be like him."

"He is older by less than five minutes, Ben." Sarah made no attempt to hide her skepticism.

"What made him laugh?" he asked, redirecting her.

She smiled again, not fooled but willing to be led back to the promise of hope. "Sean Kelly. He even got our George to mount his pony. That young man certainly has a way with children. You'll remember I told you about his youngest brother. Rose says the boy — ”

"Sarah," he stopped her. "Young Kelly is a riding instructor, not some miracle worker. He couldn't put words in George's mouth any more than he could bring rain to a drought. The brother started speaking because he was ready, not because Kelly put him astride a horse."

"I know," she said quietly, studying her hands. "He is very good with them though. You must come watch one morning."

"Of course I will." He pulled her tightly against him. "So you're happy with Rose's nephew then?"

"Yes, although I'm afraid your sister is not so pleased. She and Mr. Kelly don't get on very well."

"Oh." He sat back, but Sarah didn't turn to him. Ben had a way of seeing past her words, and she had no intention of telling him how his sister went swimming *au naturel* last evening while nineteen-year-old Sean Kelly looked on. Shadows and silhouettes notwithstanding, Ben Darcy did not have the humor for any story that involved his sister unclothed within a mile of a teenage boy.

"It's no great matter," she said pointedly and gave him a look to match, hoping to hide what he needn't hear. "A condition we educators would describe as being too young and too full of themselves for their own good."

Sarah sighed through a brief smile. It wasn't often now that she thought of herself as the teacher she once was, but remembering always made her smile. She had only been teaching for two years when Ben proposed. It was her mother's profession, and she came to the calling naturally. He did not ask her to give up her work when fate handed him an eight-year-old girl to raise but she did. The decision was hers, and she looked up at him now without regret.

"Rose says Catie might have actually met someone who matches her own obstinacy."

He exhaled heavily. "I don't care whether they get on or not. I just want Catie to occupy her time with something other than taking off on her bicycle for hours at a time with nothing but a damn book as company. It's not normal, Sarah."

"Did you not just tell me that Darcys have a tendency to be reserved, that it's in their nature?"

"Reserved she can be all she wants," he said a bit more tersely than he intended. "But it's time she grew up and stopped romanticizing life. She's not a little girl any longer."

"You're right," Sarah agreed, not to pacify him but because it was true. Not only was Catie prone to melancholy, preferring her own company most of the time, but she was proving to be a rather late bloomer. "But, Bennet…" Sarah started to share these thoughts but was interrupted by a knock on his door. She moved to get up, but he held her in place. "Let go!" she hissed and giggled at the same time, squirming to free herself.

"Oh, let them have their gossip. The last good scandal was weeks ago when that dog ran up and down Kympton Way with old Granny Doyle's knickers over his head. Ashridge has been as dry as winter grass of late, and Mrs. Darcy all randy in the afternoon will provide well for them, don't you agree?"

"Bennet!" She swatted at him, but he reared back and she missed.

"Enter!" he called out, laughing low and roguishly in her ear, tightening his hold lest she leap out of his lap.

A maid entered. *Janice Kirby.* It was all Sarah could do not to visibly cringe. Unmarried and in her mid-thirties, Janice worked for the Darcys three mornings a week. Blushing, Janice ducked her head at the sight them, grinning despite herself. If Ben had hopes of creating gossip, Janice was by far the best vessel. Her father was the village grocer, and when she wasn't working for the Darcys, she minded his store.

"Yes, Janice?" Sarah spoke with such feigned dignity that she might have mistaken her own voice for some old dowager.

"The man Mr. Darcy asked me to watch for has arrived, madam." As Janice spoke, Sarah felt Ben grow tense.

"Thank you," he said as Janice bobbed her head and disappeared through the door.

"What man?" Sarah turned to him, suddenly unconcerned with being rumored as a wanton wife.

"A Mr. Sams. Charles Worthington hired him. All's well, Sarah, but I must go and speak with him."

She stood and watched him shrug into his jacket. "Has this to do with that Wesley Howell person?"

"It does," he answered, tugging at his sleeves. "And hopefully Mr. Sams has some promising news."

"What sort of man is this Mr. Sams?"

Ben stopped at the door and turned back to her. "The kind I'd prefer to speak with in the drive rather than invite inside the house."

"Bennet." Sarah's brows drew together with concern. "That sounds serious."

"Don't worry yourself, darling; he shan't be here long."

FROM HER WINDOW SEAT, CATIE Darcy had a lovely view of the front avenue, the lily pond, and the courtyard. The sun rose on the front side of the house, making her room cheery in the mornings and a tranquil refuge in the afternoons — the very reason the room had been chosen for her and many a young woman before her. And she, like so many of them, spent much of her time in the window seat. Centuries of afternoons had been passed there, dreaming of marriage or waiting for a social call from a lover. Today however, Pemberley's young Miss Darcy listened to music louder than was appreciated and flipped through an American teen magazine that her brother would call "rubbish."

A car pulled onto the gravel court, and she lifted her head. It was no one familiar, but this wasn't unusual. Ben often conducted business from the house. She watched as a man got out of the car, but oddly, he didn't approach. Instead, he looked around as if he was expecting someone and then leaned against the bonnet and lit a cigarette.

Several minutes passed before Ben finally descended the front steps, crossed the drive, and joined the man. Catie quickly reached over and turned off her music, but even with her window pushed fully open, she could hear nothing but muffled voices. So she resumed flipping through her magazine, content to glance down at the men in between pages. Like a watchful owl perched on a high limb, she liked to observe unseen and unnoticed.

The stranger lit one cigarette after another as Ben listened, calmly at first. Then he began to pace. Curious, Catie put the magazine aside and watched more closely. Although the man was still leaning against the car, casually smoking, Ben was now flailing his arms as he spoke. Filled with that strange sense of safeguard that exists between siblings, she jumped down from the window seat and hurriedly made her way downstairs.

A bank of windows stood fully open in the small parlor off of the hall, and she went to them. Sister or not, she couldn't very well race out to Ben's side, but she could listen and be there if he needed her.

When Catie reached the windows, she smacked her lips with regret. It was over. Ben was already heading back to the house, bringing a look of sheer rage with him that made her gut tighten. She started to go and meet him, but he stopped and turned back. Then, with a voice more livid than his sister had ever heard, he shouted, "Take care of this, Sams! I don't give a damn about the money, but I refuse to allow my family's good name to be tarnished. And furthermore, I'll be bloody well damned to the devil before I let Pemberley fall into the wrong hands again."

"*Again?*" Catie echoed in a whisper.

She was at the parlor door when he came inside the house and her presence surprised him. "Catie! What are you doing there?" Ben's expression was as hard as his tone.

"I heard shouting. Is everything all right?"

"What did you hear?" he asked, softer but still firm.

"Just shouting," she said, swallowing the truth. "Who was that man?"

His eyes flicked over her head and into the parlor. "A business associate, no one for you to concern yourself with. Now run along and stop eavesdropping at open windows."

"I wasn't," she said, not caring how insulted she sounded. *God, I hate when he treats me like a child.* "I heard shouting and thought you might need help."

Ben studied his sister momentarily. The top of her head had yet to fully reach his shoulder and he easily outweighed her by five stone. "Thank you, Sis," he said contrite and somewhat amused. "But as you can see, I am quite capable of taking care of myself." He raised his wrist and looked at his watch. "Now shouldn't you be heading off for the stables? I don't really care to make another round of apologies to young Kelly."

Staring up at him, Catie made no attempt to move. Annoyed, Ben breathed deep and then released a rush of frustrated air while thoughtfully rubbing the back of his neck, as if he might find there beneath his hairline some better way of dealing with his sister. "Catie, sometimes business and money matters get heated, that is all. Now please do as I say and stop fretting over a few harsh words between men, all right?"

He might as well have given her a lollypop or a pat on the head for all that explanation was worth. But it was all she was going to get, and she knew it. "All right," she repeated quietly.

"Good. I'll see you at supper then." Smiling now, Ben gave her one of his brotherly winks that felt more patronizing than usual, and then he was gone.

Chapter 4

Sean heaved the last two buckets of water over the stall doors with a grunt. By the twelfth trip, the buckets had grown heavy and his arms tired. "Don't be a glutton now, *buachaill*," he warned the aging gelding behind the door. He removed his flat cap to swab a handkerchief over his brow and the back of his neck as the horse whinnied loudly and snorted in response. Sean chuckled and patted an offered nose. "Aye, you like the Gaelic, eh, *mo buachaill*," he crooned to the horse. "Perhaps your ancestor was the steed of a great Celtic warrior then? Cùchulainn's Liath Macha maybe; he was a fine Ulster lad, eh?"

"That the last of it, Kelly?" Clancy asked brusquely. He was a tiny man, a former jockey according to Aunt Rose, but he had a deep and ragged voice, much like Sean's larger, barrel-chested father.

"Yeah, that's it." Sean smiled down at Pemberley's stable master. Tiny or not, the sixtyish man ran a tight ship — or stable rather. Nothing was out of place, and the cobblestone floor was as clean as the kitchen's. "Need anything else?" he asked. Clancy was without a groom today, so Sean had graciously filled in. He wasn't hired to water horses or muck stalls, but the work was familiar to him, and he liked the routine.

"No, I thank you for the hand though. Me brother-in-law will be back tomorrow, or he'll be out on 'is ear. I'll see to it that you get 'is wages for the day."

"There's no need. I was glad to help." As he spoke, Sean knocked the stable dust off of his cap and pulled it back on his head, smiling good-humoredly down at Clancy.

If only slightly, Clancy reflected the smile. *A rare thing for the old curmudgeon*, Sean thought.

"You did the work… you get the pay," Clancy stated in a manner that would brook no argument, and he walked away, grumbling under his breath about his useless brother-in-law.

Shaking his head, Sean laughed and leaned over the stall to put out his hand again to the horse. The animal came to him, and he briskly scratched the long neck, cooing softly in Gaelic. Before long, Catie Darcy was standing behind him. As tiny as Clancy but lighter of foot, she had padded silently into the stable, but he knew she was there. He could feel her presence as readily as he could feel the mass of horse under his hand. He turned to her but only caught the glimpse of a buttercup yellow shirt as she disappeared into the tack room, leaving behind a whiff of her scent, flowery and fresh against the raw stable air.

There was more to Catie Darcy than that haughty, rich-kid mask behind which she hid. Having been around horses all of his life, he understood that what a creature appeared to be outwardly wasn't necessarily a peek at the soul. His father had taught him this. Since he was old enough to pull up to a fence rail, Sean had watched the man break horses, and whether it was an aggressive stallion or an overly shy mare, Seamus Kelly could reach into their core and drive to the surface the noble animal within. "Horses are no different than people, Seany," his father said often. "They all have a story to tell if only someone will take the time to listen properly."

But Sean hadn't come to Pemberley to figure out what lay within Catie Darcy. She wasn't his problem. She had family enough, and Aunt Rose certainly had a strong affection for the girl. All he had to do was teach her to trot and canter, collect his university tuition, and catch a ferry back to Ireland in six weeks. He gave the aging gelding a parting pat and went to saddle his horse.

When Catie arrived at the stable, Sean Kelly was affectionately rubbing her father's beloved Abastor, a horse in his last few seasons of life, but still a fine-looking animal. Abastor was thoroughly enjoying the extra attention and Sean Kelly's gentle voice, but his words were unfamiliar to Catie. She had studied French and Latin; this was neither. Gaelic, she thought, the Irish language once forbidden by the government in order to create British subjects amongst the Irish population. Like the Darcys' antiques, jewels, and silver, the language had obviously been carefully preserved and protected and, even in the face of adversity, passed down through generations of Kellys. Although the words were not familiar they felt calming, like the easy flow of a fairy tale or lullaby. She opened her mouth to ask him their meaning but stopped short, deciding instead to fetch her riding hat, crop, and gloves. Why was it, she thought a little bitterly as she stepped into the warm, musty smelling tack room, that every bit of oppression suffered in the last few centuries had been at the hands of her bloody English ancestors?

When she returned, he was standing there with a large smile on his face. "Hello, Miss Catie." He spoke in a pleasant tone that matched the smile. "Are you ready to begin?"

"Sure." She nodded, glad to see he wasn't one to hold grudges. She hadn't been sure what her reception might be after that morning.

"Right, which horse is yours, then?" He raised one questioning eyebrow and looked down at her.

Catie gazed up into his face, but before she could answer, she found herself struck by a set of blue eyes that seemed to glow below his thatch of onyx hair. Really staring into them for the first time, she saw they were different from the steel blue color of Ben's, which gave you an instant awareness of his charge. No, the cerulean orbs of Sean Kelly were feral-like and sparkled with a free spirit...

"Miss Catie?" His voice interrupted her thoughts. "Catie!"

"C-Chloe, the grey mare," she said, the words tumbling awkwardly out of her mouth. She knew she had been staring at him, and her cheeks grew hot. Not daring to meet his eyes again, she turned to Clancy and asked sharply, "Why has Chloe not been saddled yet?"

"Been a bit short-handed today, miss, but she'll be ready at once."

"Yes, see that she is." The flash of humiliation had faded, but her voice held its purpose.

"Yes, miss," Clancy replied, casting Sean an apprising glance.

Catie busied herself with her hat straps to keep from looking at Sean Kelly again, and didn't see the meaningful look he gave her.

Once Clancy brought Chloe around to the mounting block, Sean stood in front of her before she mounted. "You'll have no need for this." He pulled her crop out from where it was wedged between her arm and torso.

Catie watched nervously as he tucked it out of sight behind his back. She had never ridden without her crop before and didn't like the idea, but she didn't protest.

"Mount up!" He took the reins from Clancy to hold the horse steady so the man could get back to his work. "You'll take the lead. I like to observe the skills of a new student. Just follow my instructions. I'll mostly be watching today."

Wishing she were anywhere else in the world right now, Catie nodded.

"All right then, we'll walk for a bit then move into a working trot," he instructed as he hoisted himself into his saddle. "Away off now."

The day was hot for England's Midlands, making the afternoon crawl slowly along. By the time they reached the flat grassy fields that ran along the riverbank, Catie had grown hot and thirsty.

"Halt," Sean called out, and she gratefully pulled Chloe to a stop. He rode slightly past her and pointed down the long low lands by the river. "See the end of the field there?" He waited for her acknowledgement. She nodded. "You'll wait for me to reach it, and when you see my hand drop, gallop hard in my direction."

"Gallop?" she repeated. Of course she knew this was coming but wasn't expecting it the first day.

"Yes, gallop... is there a problem?"

Having no desire to share her fears with him, Catie argued back, "I have no crop. You took it from me, remember?"

"You have no need for a crop. Your legs and position will tell your horse what you expect of her."

"But that's not how I've learned."

"Then you will," he said resolutely.

Catie's mind raced back to that day eight years ago when she was thrown from her pony. She remembered lying alone in the grass. She remembered being afraid. Afraid she was hurt, afraid that Ben would find out and be cross with her. She remembered the pain from the fall, the loneliness of her father's recent death, and the agony of Ben's grief. She remembered the stinging tears that had finally come. She never wanted to sit astride a speeding horse again, but she couldn't tell this man why.

"It cannot be a fear of speed," he declared impatiently, growing tired of her dithering. "I've certainly seen you race by the cottage on your bicycle fast enough."

"You have seen me on my bicycle?" she asked, happy to draw out the conversation.

"Well, yes." He leaned forward in the saddle and gave her a *stating the obvious* expression. "We *have* occupied the same grounds for more than three days now."

"But I...haven't...seen you," she stammered, uncomfortable with his close proximity.

He released a cynical sounding grunt. "That doesn't surprise me."

"And what is that supposed to mean?" she asked, detecting the sarcasm in his voice.

"It means nothing." He waved off the question and started off.

"Wait!" Catie quickly caught up to him. "If you have something to say to me, Mr. Kelly, say it!"

Straightening in his saddle as if he were heading into battle, Sean stared at her. "It's not my place to correct your manners, Miss Catie. Now, if you'll please gallop hard in my direction when I reach the end of the field there, I'd appreciate it. I need to check your balance and position."

"And do you think my manners need correcting?"

"Maybe you should ask Clancy that question."

"Clancy!" she repeated incredulously, but then remembered snapping at him for not having her horse saddled. Still, who was Sean Kelly to reprimand her? And furthermore, it wasn't Clancy's opinion she wanted. Narrowing her eyes, she raised her chin in challenge and stated boldly, "I asked you."

Sean Kelly's mother may have been English but he was an Irishman from his flat cap to his boots, meaning he had been blessed with a fire in his temperament that would only be harnessed for so long. Be damned the job and be damned his tuition; all he wanted to do was to drag Miss Catie Darcy off that bloody horse of hers and send her walking back to the stables…her pedestal in hand.

He took a deep, purposeful breath, but it did him no good. So he again pulled his horse alongside hers and said, "What I think, Miss Catie, is that despite the efforts of my good aunt and your guardians, you have turned out spoiled, insolent, and selfish, with a complete disregard for the feelings of others. And I also *think*, since you asked, that it would serve you greatly to take a good long turn over the knee!" Sean pulled his horse about, kicked the animal into a quick gallop, and headed down field.

Shocked, Catie remained still. Unable to do anything else, she just sat there and watched him ride off. In less than a minute he reached the end of the field and turned back in her direction. He raised his arm and lowered it. Catie reached back to thwack Chloe's rump but realized she held no crop. Exhaling her frustration in a loud garbled unladylike spew, she pulled back her hand and slapped the beast on its hindquarters with all of her might.

Although it wasn't a fast or graceful gallop, she quickly arrived at the other end of the field. Catie stared at him hard but remained silent. He, however, spoke as if nothing had taken place.

"You are not adopting a forward seat," he said in his sternest voice.

"Excuse me?"

"A forward seat, it's why you feel awkward and uncomfortable with the gallop. Next time I want you start slow then spring forward and hover over your saddle as if you were going to make a jump."

"Mr. Kelly —"

"That's enough for today," he interrupted her then stated matter-of-factly, "We'll resume tomorrow at three." Sean turned his horse around and cantered off in the opposite direction of the stables.

"Where are you going?" she called out after him.

"My work day is finished, Miss Catie, if that's what you are worried about," he called out, not looking back at her.

"But…I'm not allowed to ride alone." Catie hated how childish her voice sounded, but she didn't want to be left alone with a horse, even if it was good-natured Chloe.

He stopped now and turned his horse to face her. "We are less than a half mile from the stables, and I have watched you for well over an hour now. Your skills in riding, Miss Catie, are better than you think." *It's your skills with people that need work.* The latter he wisely kept to himself. "I wouldn't send you back alone otherwise." Sean mockingly tipped his cap to her and took off once again.

Catie watched the departing horse and rider until they were completely out of sight. Chloe became restless and pranced gently under her. "Shhh, girl." She patted the horse and to her relief, Chloe calmed. Catie looked once more in the direction Sean Kelly had gone and then carefully slid from her saddle to the ground.

Sean reined in his horse and looked back over his shoulder. He had ridden a good distance, far enough that Catie Darcy had disappeared into the landscape as if the ground had simply opened up and swallowed her. "Bloody hell! Bloody hell!" He cursed himself for caring, cursed Catie Darcy for those damn eyes of hers, and then turned his horse back to make sure she arrived safely at the stables.

When she came into sight again he drew up and stared at her in disbelief. "Why is she walking?" he asked out loud as if hearing the words might make better sense of why Catie Darcy was leading her horse on foot. Now heading in the direction of home, his mount was growing anxious to be back at the stable and snorted loudly in protest of stopping. "No oats for you yet, mate," he scolded the animal and steered him up into a dense patch of Scots pine.

Taking the steep rougher terrain, he was quickly ahead of her and watched from a rocky outcrop as she came up the horse path to the stables. Sean put a hand to the horse's nose to discourage any further snorts that might expose him. As she grew nearer, he heard sniffing and faint sobs. Then she stopped and he held his breath, fearing she had seen him. Sean swallowed hard as he watched her raise her hand and wipe her cheeks. He closed his eyes and then looked once more, but his eyes had not deceived him. Her face was blotchy and her eyes were rimmed red. "You're an arse, Seany," he whispered to himself and then for good measure added, "a real arse."

As SHE SOAKED IN THE tub with a wet cloth over her face, Catie slowly drifted to the edge of consciousness. Her tears were gone but the emotion that had been her undoing still hung heavy in her chest.

"Miss Catie," Annie called from the other side of the door, startling her back to reality. "You left your dressing gown on your bed. May I come in?"

"Yes, Annie...I'm finished."

The door opened and Annie stepped in. As Catie had long since grown too old for a nanny, Annie had, for several years now, attended to her needs when she was home from school. Annie had recently married a groundskeeper by the name of Mark Philips and now lived in one of the estate's tied cottages. The Darcys had even hosted their wedding reception at Pemberley last summer. This wasn't unusual; times had changed dramatically since the old manor was first built. And since Pemberley no longer required the army of workers it once did, Ben and Sarah Darcy were much more intimate with their small devoted staff

Annie hung the dressing gown within reach and asked, "Will there be anything else this evening, Miss Catie?"

"No," came from behind the wet cloth.

Annie couldn't help but smile at the bubble-covered young woman whom she had watched transform from a child over the last couple of years. "I will leave you then. Oh, Mr. Darcy wanted me to tell you that supper is going to be upstairs tonight."

A corner of the cloth was lifted. "Is he to be out?"

"No, Miss Catie, he's in," Annie replied and shut the door behind her.

It wasn't like Ben to have dinner upstairs, and curiosity urged Catie to dry off and dress quickly. She gathered her damp heavy tresses into a ponytail and, grabbing the book she had been reading, hurried to the sitting room.

Attached to the family wing, the large but cozy lounge had been a favorite gathering place for private family evenings well before Ben and Catie Darcy were born. Although the room was slightly less grand than the formal public rooms, it was still rich in architecture with large mullioned windows that faced the lake and intricate moldings that crowned a high ceiling. But this was a place for children. Large comfortable chairs and a floral print sofa tossed with pillows sat under the spread of lamplight, and a television sat on a chest in the corner.

Catie could hear squealing and laughter as she approached the door and pushed it open to find Ben on his hands and knees, with two spirited riders atop his back. The twins jumped off their father and scampered wildly over to her.

"Daddy is a horsey, Auntie!" Geoffrey said boisterously, and George followed, mimicking his brother's every word.

"I can see that," said Catie, giving Ben a quelling look. She knew Sarah wouldn't be pleased to see them so rowdy that close to bedtime.

"Right," Ben answered her unspoken warning and told the boys to turn on the television.

Looking at her brother, Catie had a sudden desire to rush crying into his arms and seek his comfort. But she wasn't a little girl any longer, too big now to climb up into his lap and be coddled like a child.

"You all right, Sis?" he asked curiously.

"Yeah," she breathed softly as she fell into her usual spot on the sofa and opened her book.

"How did it go?" Ben sat down at her feet and snatched the book from her hands to have her full attention.

"Where is Sarah, and why are we eating in here?" replied his sister, avoiding his question.

"She had some errands in the village and is bringing supper home."

"But why are we eating — "

"Catherine Elizabeth," he interrupted her. "*How* did your riding lesson go?"

"Oh." Catie looked at him and considered. It would be easy to tell him the truth about her afternoon — how Sean Kelly had spoken to her. Ben might even go have a word with him. But then again, what had the man said that wasn't true? It was that realization that had brought her to tears in the first place. It wasn't that she hadn't heard similar accusations before. Remarks about her behavior had often been whispered behind the gossiping hands of maids or grumbled under a nanny's breath. But Sean Kelly was the first ever to say such things to her face. "Good, Ben…jolly good," she assured her brother as convincingly as possible, determined to handle the young Irishman herself.

"I'm glad to hear it." He smiled. "I was worried. Sarah said you weren't getting on with Rose's nephew very well."

A smile curled up one side of her mouth as she teased her way out of the conversation. "He's just…you know…bossy like the rest of your lot."

"Oh, is that so!" He laughed.

"Yes, it is." Grinning, she reached over and snatched her book back. Catie loved when they could be brother and sister like this. They so often now forgot to be the siblings they once were.

Ben stared at her for a moment. "You know, Catie. I'd love it if you would take a ride with me next Monday. I haven't been 'round to see all the crops yet, and there are several tenants I haven't called on in over a month. Plus," he added, tapping her knee affectionately, "it would be nice if you and I were to spend some time together."

"I'd like that." Catie smiled at him as Sarah came through the door, arms loaded and smelling of chicken curry.

"Ah, here's our supper!" Ben jumped up to help her, and the commotion of dinner quickly commenced.

An hour later, the calm of evening had settled over the room, and everyone was busy with their individual diversions. Catie was again on the sofa with her book. Sarah was in the large chair by the window with a child on each knee reading a bedtime story, while Ben, seated at the opposite end of the sofa, had his head buried in the newspaper. Catie admired him momentarily. Bennet Darcy was her first love. So young, dashing, and handsome, she had resolutely planned on marrying him until about the age of six when she grew old enough to realize the impossibility of it.

The question is: Why would she want to marry him? Ben was always serious and deliberate, nothing like their spirited, adventurous father. Ben made her behave as a child when their father didn't. He was much stricter and harder to please. But that was probably the root of Catie's infatuation with her brother. Most women prefer a man who challenges them. Even little women, who can't tie their shoes yet, enjoy a rambunctious clash of wills. Catie forever strived to earn his praise or gain his attention, but sometimes, like now, she just preferred to sit and study him. She often wondered if he was more like their mother in personality, and if so, what sort of relationship would she have had with her?

Seemingly bored with the news, Ben laid the paper on his lap and studied his hands for a moment while twisting his wedding band. Catie had seen him do that before. When he was worried or bothered he would unconsciously turn the golden ring. It was as if he found comfort simply by touching the object. He sighed heavily, restlessly even, and then turned toward the window, propping his chin on his knuckles.

A few minutes later Geoffrey and George scrambled over to say good night and temporarily broke their father's meditation. But as soon as they were gone, Ben again turned his thoughts to the now dark windowpanes.

He's troubled, Catie thought, suddenly ashamed. She had been so caught up in her own childish problems that she had completely forgotten about Ben's encounter in front of the house that afternoon with the man named Sams. It must be some serious matter, certainly more serious than her not 'getting on' well with Rose's nephew. "Selfish," Sean Kelly had accused her of being. She frowned at the thought and called out to her brother, "Bennet!"

With a visible start, Ben turned from the window and looked at her. "Yes, Catie?"

"Is something the matter?"

"No, dearest, nothing's the matter," he said as he folded the newspaper and set it aside. He crossed the room to Sarah, kissed her and whispered, "I'll be in my study if you should need me. It may be late before I come to bed. Good night, Sis," he added on his way out.

Catie, however, wasn't so willing to drop the subject. "If nothing is the matter, then why are you going to your study at this late hour?" Her question stopped him at the door, and he turned and gave her a look that made Catie realize a little too late that she had tread too heavily on her brother's steadfast reserve.

"You're right, Catherine, the hour is late, so say good night to Sarah and be off to your bed."

Blushing and feeling half her age, Catie didn't argue. She closed her book and quietly told Sarah good night before hastening out of the room, purposefully not meeting her brother's eye as she passed him.

"Bennet, was that necessary?" Sarah asked in a reproachful tone once Catie was out of earshot.

"Yes, I believe it was." He stepped back into the room and shut the door for

40

privacy. "She was listening to my conversation with Mr. Sams this afternoon or eavesdropping would be the more proper term, and I do not wish to condone such behavior."

"Your sister watches you more intently than you appreciate." Sarah sat up in her chair. "What you take for prying I see as concern. A father should not be so quick to reprimand his children. He must be assured that they are truly deserving of his rebuke or it will become commonplace and lose its power."

He grimaced ruefully and nodded. "You're right. I could have handled that better, but I don't want Catie to know of this Wesley Howell business. Explaining Wesley Howell to her will mean going into Cousin Mary's whole sordid history. Mary Darcy Howell was a fine woman, Sarah, and I loved her very much, but she made some dreadful mistakes when she was Catie's age." Ben looked at Sarah very seriously now. "I need not tell you how impressionable my sister is. She would glorify the whole affair as some romantic tragedy — *Romeo and Juliet* or the like."

"You can't shelter her from the world forever, Bennet Darcy." Sarah returned the serious look but then smiled despite her frustration, for how could she admonish a man for caring too much?

He smiled back. "I can for a few more years yet, my love, so you will just have to indulge me."

She raised a brow in question. "And will our sons be subjected to such careful guarding?" He hesitated in his response so she took the liberty to answer her own question. "That is a double standard, Mr. Darcy, and rather sexist I might add."

"I disagree," he argued. "A sexist thinks a woman his inferior. I, on the other hand, believe that the female is to be valued above all things and should therefore be protected. It is not sexist, it's male instinct. Like this conversation for example. My male instinct tells me I cannot win, and if I hope to hear my wife return my greeting at the breakfast table in the morning, I should go to my study before I say more than will be good for me." She laughed, and he noted a twinkle in her eye. "Can I take your good humor to mean that you will be awake when I come to our bed, Mrs. Darcy?"

She grinned at him. "You can take my good humor to mean that I will return your greeting at the breakfast table in the morning. As for the reception you will receive in our bed…" Her eyebrows arched again, only this time it was most definitely mischievous. "That, sir, is a question you will have to mull

41

over as you finish your work."

"I shan't be more than half an hour," he replied, sounding more the schoolboy than the master of Pemberley House.

Chapter 5

In the dark, Catie sat in her window seat thinking about the day until her eyelids grew so heavy that she was forced to give in to sleep. Yawning and rubbing her eyes, she moved to get down and clumsily banged her foot into one of the decorative panels that ran the length of the window casement, feeling it give way. "Bloody clod," she berated herself as she turned on a lamp to investigate the damage.

She pushed the heavy curtain fully out of the way and saw a void. The panel wasn't broken at all and slid off easily. Catie grabbed her torch and shone the beam inside the hole, and gasped. There was a book, bound in leather and very worn. She brushed away years of dust and thumbed through the pages. Several dried flowers and bird feathers floated out, freed after a long captivity. Then a picture dropped, which Catie caught up and rushed over to examine under her lamp. A handsome man and a pretty young woman were smiling back at her, frozen forever in the sepia toned snapshot. She turned the picture over and read: *Mr. Arthur Howell and Miss Mary Darcy, August 1919.* Below this was the word: *Lovers*, written in a flourished hand.

"Lovers," she read aloud. Then she set the picture aside and opened the book to the first page.

The Personal Diary of Mary Elizabeth Darcy

15th of July 1918
Home, finally, the Season was a great bore according to Mother, and she fears for my prospects next year when I am presented. Everything it seems

has changed since the start of this dreadful war! I spent the day walking the grounds, taking in the early blooms of summer. Father hasn't arrived yet, but Mother is well and happy to be home.

For several pages the entries were similar, so Catie flipped forward until she found a passage that interested her.

Dinner Party at Pemberley 24th of July, 1918
My excitement can hardly be contained. Tonight I met a most handsome man by the name of Maj. Arthur Howell. He is almost ten years my senior and delighted me with lively conversation all evening whilst other men chose each other's company to debate the best way to end the Great War. He is in Derbyshire for at least a month and is a guest of the Thompson family, whose respectably sized farm joins our land on the south side. He made several points to assure me he takes his strolls by the river just before dinner each evening. I will oblige his assurances with a chance encounter within the next couple of days.

I do, however, have an obstacle… Cousin Geoffrey, who follows me everywhere. His visit from Rosings Park will most assuredly last into next week. I must find a deterrent that will preoccupy a 13-year-old lad from the joys of vexing his 16-year-old cousin.

Confused, Catie reread the last two sentences three or four times. The only Geoffrey she knew from that era was her grandfather. But why would he be *visiting* Pemberley?

"*Visiting*, humph," she uttered absently.

Rosings Park. She closed her eyes and tried to remember. Catie was sure she had heard it mentioned before. Heavy-eyed as she was, however, Rosings Park and Mary Darcy's diary would have to wait until tomorrow. Yawning, she reached over and turned off her bedside lamp and snuggled cozily under the covers.

Wearing my blue frock I walk to the library beside Grace, the tallest nanny I've ever had. The blue frock is my daddy's favorite. He's leaving today, and I wore it for him. She knocks, but I open the door and propel myself across the room to

Daddy. I can see him putting his book and glasses aside to catch me. "Catherine!" I hear Grace scold from the doorway, but I am already on my daddy's lap. Safe.

"I'll bring her to you before I leave, Grace," Daddy says. Lying against him, I can feel the words as well as hear them.

"Yes, sir," she answers, and the door closes.

"Grace thinks you're handsome, Daddy!" I sit up and announce.

He laughs. "Is that so?"

"Mm-hmm." I nod. "But Nanny Rose is in love with you. Will you ask her to marry you, Daddy?"

"Have you been planning my happiness in romance for long, my child?" He bounces his knee, and I giggle.

"Don't leave, Daddy." I lean my head on his shoulder.

"I shan't be gone for long, Catie Bug." He pats me and I snuggle even closer. "Tell you what. I'll escort you to church on Sunday…fair enough?"

I shake my head, and he laughs again. "A woman who can't be pleased. I see I've cut out the work for some young man one day, eh?"

"Who will tell me a bedtime story?" My voice is pouty. He's never coming back home again. There is a knot in my tummy that tells me so, but I shan't listen to that knot.

"What if I tell you a special story now? Will that do, dearest?" He softly pats me again.

"Tell me about Fitzwilliam and Elizabeth."

He smiles. "If you like, but it is such a pretty day I thought you might like a walk in the garden."

I shake my head again. "Story."

"All right, all right." He chuckles. "A true romantic you are, my child, maybe the last of your lot. Let's see, then. A long time ago at Pemberley House there lived a young master by the name of Fitzwilliam Darcy. He was betrothed to his cousin, Anne de Bourgh. Anne was the daughter of Lady Catherine de Bourgh, Mistress of Rosings Park and the young master's aunt.

"But he didn't love Cousin Anne did he, Daddy?"

He shakes his head. "No, Catie, he didn't. Anne was a sickly, homely child who rarely left the house. Not a good match for our noble Fitzwilliam, for he was a hale and hearty lad. But it was a time when few people married for love…"

"Will I marry for love?" I ask.

"I shall personally see to it, Catie."

"Who do you think I will marry?"

"I don't know his name but I say fervent prayers for him every night."

"Daddy!"

"Right, where was I? Oh, yes… Once on a visit to a close friend in the county of Hertfordshire, our handsome Fitzwilliam met Elizabeth Bennet. She was the most beautiful creature the young Darcy had ever seen, but he ardently fought any feelings for her."

"But why?"

"Listen, Catie Bug, and I'll tell you." He settles me with a soft stroke over my head and continues. "Elizabeth was a kind, gentle, respectable woman, but unfortunately had few connections and no money to speak of. It may be hard to understand today but our Fitzwilliam was bound by tradition and society to marry within his set."

"But he loved her, didn't he?"

"Yes, Catie, he loved her very much. His affection for Miss Elizabeth was strong and his heart was hers."

"So he disobeyed his aunt and married Miss Elizabeth. Right, Daddy?"

"That he did. To the great shock of Lady Catherine, Fitzwilliam went against her. He refused to marry Anne and instead made Elizabeth Bennet the mistress of Pemberley."

"And they lived happily ever after!" I add enthusiastically.

"Mm-hmm, the couple was very happy. They lived out a long life here in this very house and were blessed with two strapping sons, William and Geoffrey. Geoffrey was your great-grandfather many times over."

I smile up at him, but Daddy is gone and suddenly I'm in the chair alone. "Daddy!" I cry out, looking all over the library. "Daddy, where are you?" I run to the library door but I can't reach the handle and start banging my fists against the door. "Daddy, come back, come back!"

Catie opened her eyes. "Daddy, come back," she whispered and shut her eyes again against stinging tears, trying to keep him in her memory for a few seconds longer. But he was gone. Sniffing, she rolled onto her back and stared up at the ceiling. "*Rosings Park*…Lady Catherine de Bourgh of Rosings Park. Now I remember." She pushed back the covers to go wash her face.

The sun came in brightly through the break in the curtains and cast a warm streak of light across her floor which she stepped over on her way to the bathroom. Catie turned on the hot water, checking its temperature every few seconds with the tips of her fingers. "Good Lord, a person could grow old waiting for hot water in this house," she grumbled. When the water began to grow warmer, she wet a washcloth under the tap and brought it to her face. Looking at her image in the mirror, she began to wash, slowly at first, but then she started to scrub. She scrubbed harder and harder until her skin began to burn.

"Catherine, stop that!" Rose said as she took the cloth from Catie's hands. "For heaven's sake, child, what are you doing?"

"I don't know." Catie looked down and shook her head.

"Come and sit." Rose put an arm around her and led her from the bathroom. Catie sat down on the edge of the bed as directed while Rose pressed her cheek to her forehead.

"I'm not sick, Nan," Catie protested, her skin still a bit rosy from the assault.

"Then why, dear, were you trying to scrub your face off?" Rose asked.

Catie shrugged. "No reason."

Frowning suspiciously, Rose straightened and announced, "I'll go and fetch the castor oil then. There's no better cure for constipation."

"Rose!" Catie jolted up, looking appalled. "I'm not constipated!"

"Then tell me what is ailing you." She took Catie's face in her hands.

Catie stared into Rose's narrow grey eyes. Still youthful, they sat above glowing high cheekbones. Rose Todd had a face that could look kind or ferocious, depending upon her mood. At the moment she was somewhere in between. "I dreamed about Daddy." A tear slipped down Catie's cheek.

"The one you've had before about the plane crash?" Rose sat next to her now and pulled Catie tightly against her chest.

"No," she replied softly. "I dreamed about the day he died, when we were in the library just before he left. He was there and then he was gone, and I couldn't find him."

"Oh, Catie, why didn't you ring for me?" Rose tightened her hold in a motherly fashion, trying to squeeze the pain away and absorb it herself.

"I had it just before I woke up. I guess he's been on my mind more than usual." Catie sniffed, and Rose took a handkerchief out of her pocket.

"Here, love, calm yourself whilst I have a tray brought up. Sweet tea will settle your nerves."

As Rose stepped out of the room, Catie walked over to her window and saw Ben's black sports car pulling away from the house. She pushed opened the heavy mullioned sash and leaned out, forcing herself not to call out to him.

"Catherine Elizabeth Darcy! Are you trying to kill yourself?!" Rose screeched, and Catie scrambled back inside, bumping her head in the process.

"Don't be ridiculous, Nan!" She pulled the window closed and rubbed her head gingerly. "And if I did die, it would be because you frightened me so that I tumbled out!"

"Well come away from that window or it will be *my* nerves that need settling."

As they waited, Rose began straightening the bedcovers. Never one to sit idle, she was a woman who needed to be doing something, although never without a fuss. At the moment it was Catie's cleanliness or lack thereof that had Rose carping under her breath.

"I can go downstairs and have tea in the kitchen, Nan. I'm feeling fine now." Catie rescued a pile of magazines before Rose swept them into the waste bin.

"You'll do no such thing…" Rose started but a light knock on the door interrupted her. "Ah, there's the tray now."

Catie obediently sipped the tea and ate toast. "Where did Ben go?" she asked.

"London. That's what I had come to tell you when I found you in the bathroom."

"Why?"

"Because he asked me to," Rose said as she came over and eyed the tea and toast. "There's a good girl. You don't eat enough which is probably why you're having bad dreams." According to Rose, most every illness was brought about from a lack of nourishment, and practically everything could be cured with a healthy dose of castor oil.

"No, why is he going to London?" Catie clarified.

"Business, I assume, Catherine. Isn't that normally why?"

"I suppose." Catie sat quietly for a minute. She had hoped to ask Ben about Rosings Park, but Rose was almost as knowledgeable of her family history as her brother was. "Nan, do you remember the story Daddy used to tell me about Fitzwilliam and Elizabeth Darcy?"

"I think I remember it. Why?"

"Whatever happened to Lady Catherine, the aunt who lived at Rosings Park?"

Rose gave her a sidelong look as she pulled the curtains fully back, letting a rush of brilliant light pour into the room. Catie had fixed the panel on the window casement where she found Mary's diary as best she could, but with Rose's keen eye, she held her breath to see if the woman noticed. Rose, however, seemed more interested in changing the subject. "I can't say as I know for sure, Catie. You will have to ask your brother."

Catie sighed. It was the answer she had expected. "Rose." She hid a grin behind her teacup, suddenly remembering another curious piece from her dream. "Were you in love with my daddy?"

Since Ben wasn't to return home until the weekend, Catie would have to wait to discover the meaning behind Mary Darcy's entry. Rose had rolled her eyes and threw her hands up in exasperation at Catie's last question. Still, she had to wonder whether her youthful insight hadn't been somewhat correct.

It was approaching three, and Catie was changing into her riding breeches when her telephone rang. Glancing at her clock, she considered not answering it, but thinking it was most likely Audrey Tillman, she decided to make it quick. "Hello."

"Catie?" said an unfamiliar male voice. "Is this Catie Darcy?"

"Yes, it is."

"This is Aiden…Aiden Hirst. Remember me?" Catie hesitated. "London, last spring, you came to a party at my house in Holland Park."

"Oh, yes!" She remembered now. The party in Holland Park; the party she had attended after telling Ben she was going to the cinema with Jenna Makepeace. Catie hadn't deliberately planned the deception. She had honestly believed they were going to the pictures, but Jenna had gotten word of the party and begged Catie to go with her.

Sounding pleased, Aiden continued, "I was ringing to see when you were coming to London this summer. I thought we might see each other."

"I don't know if I am, Aiden." Catie twisted the cord around her fingers. "I…I thought you and Jenna Makepeace were…you know…"

"Oh, that's ancient history. Where have you been?" He laughed.

"Derbyshire…where else?" she replied glumly. *Yes, where else for sure.*

"Well, maybe I'll just come out to the country. My uncle and aunt live in Matlock. Can I…" he paused, a hint of nervousness in his voice. "Can I pop 'round to Pemberley if I do? I'd like to see you."

Catie grimaced, feeling her cheeks color even though she was alone, but she might as well be honest. "Aiden, I couldn't say." This was true. She'd never had a boy ask if he could "pop 'round" before. But she knew Bennet Darcy all too well. "My…it's just, my brother. He's…well, he's sort of a traditionalist.

I think you would need to speak to him first. I'm sorry, I know it's archaic. Please don't laugh."

"Not a chuckle," he said. "My dad grew up in Derbyshire, and I happen to appreciate old-fashioned country manners. If I had a sister, I would be the same way."

"Really?"

"Really," he repeated.

"Thanks for saying that."

"I meant it," he said sincerely, and she heard his smile.

"Well, I must be off." She glanced at her clock once more. "I'm late for my riding lesson. Cheers, Aiden."

"Bye now," he said and hung up.

"Aiden Hirst," she whispered to herself, biting the corner of a smiling lip as she returned the receiver. "Hmm."

Chapter 6

Percival was not a name that fit Clancy's brother-in-law. The man was taller than Sean and at least six stones heavier. He was a nice enough fellow, just big and a bit simple-minded, according to Clancy. *Percival* was just not a proper name for the man, Sean mused as he came towards him, carrying Sean's saddle.

"It's all right, Percival." Sean met him midway. "I'll saddle me own horse."

"Clancy did say as I was to saddle the horses for you and Miss Darcy." Percival said this as if no other alternative existed.

"Thank you, Percival, but Miss Darcy and I will saddle our own horses."

"*Miss* Darcy, saddling her own horse?" Percival repeated incredulously, looking at Sean as if he had just requested the honor to dig his own grave.

"Yes, *Miss* Darcy is going to learn to saddle a horse. Caring for your mount is the only way to become well acquainted with it. And the more acquainted she is, the more comfortable she'll feel." Sean tried to take the saddle from Percival, but Percival wasn't letting go.

"Clancy did say…"

"Aye, Percival." Sean stopped him from repeating himself again and assured, "I understand what Clancy said, and I'll explain it to him meself."

"Your hide, mate." Percival shrugged, let go of the saddle, and walked away.

"Say, Percival," Sean called.

"Eh?"

"How long have you been working for the Darcys?"

Percival smiled proudly. "'Bout thirty years now; three generations of Darcys I've been saddlin' for, yes sir. Mr. Geoffrey Darcy, Mr. William Darcy, sad thing that, Mr. William was a good man, a finer man you'll not meet from 'ere to London, an' now 'is boy, Mr. Ben Darcy. I put lit'l Master Ben on 'is first pony. Lit'l scamp, he was, wouldn't be led around like a baby, no sir. All afternoon that pony tossed the lad in the dirt, but he just kept gettin' back up." Percival laughed. "His daddy and me watched all afternoon whilst boy and horse reached an agreement."

Sean chuckled reflexively. "Sounds about how me da taught me."

Percival nodded. "Aye, hard knocks is what makes the man, eh?"

"To hear me da tell it," Sean agreed. "So you've known Miss Catie all her life then?"

"Of course. A favorite of 'er daddy's that one was. Mr. Darcy would put the lit'l missy in from of 'im on ol' Abastor and ride all round the estate, and she'd sit tall and dignified like a queen on parade. The spit of 'er ma, she is, and a prettier child you'll not meet from 'ere to London — a bit of a temper though." Percival winked and nudged Sean. "What we chaps will put up with for a pretty face, eh, Kelly? Me Connie was a fetching bird in her youth, no doubt, but she's got a tongue on 'er that would slice cheese."

Sean's eyebrows rose. He couldn't imagine any sister of Clancy's being attractive. At the moment, however, he was more interested in Catie Darcy's equine history. "Has Miss Darcy ever been hurt while riding? You know, fallen or been thrown?"

"No." Shaking his head, Percival lifted his hat and wiped his sweaty brow with his sleeve. "Mind though, she's only ridden with her brother, so I'd ask him to be sure."

"Thanks, Percival." Sean clapped the man's beefy shoulder warmly and went to saddle his horse. "I will."

Although she rushed as fast as she could, it was a quarter after three before Catie made it to the stables. When she came in, Sean Kelly had his back to her, checking his saddle straps. "You're late, Miss Catie," he stated in his deep heavy brogue without turning around.

To his back she scowled but answered pleasantly enough, "Yes, sorry. I'll hurry and fetch my riding hat." Two weeks, she reminded herself, two short weeks and her commitment to Ben was satisfied. And in the meantime, she also reminded herself, she had resolved to be only as civil as necessary, and under no bloody circumstance was she going to stare at him like a moon-eyed, immature, fourth former again. *God, being sixteen must be purgatory.*

On her return she found him standing beside Chloe, holding her saddle and smiling his big, stupid smile. "Percival is happy to saddle my horse for you, Mr. Kelly," she told him as she finished working her fingers into her gloves.

"Oh, I'm not saddling your horse, Miss Catie." He held the saddle out. "You are."

Catie felt a quick swell of indignation but stamped it down like a minor brush fire. "And why would I do that when Percival can do it for me?" she asked nicely.

His stupid smile grew larger. "Because I told you to. What good is it to improve your riding skills if you can't even saddle a horse?"

"Ah, then let me assure you: I *can* saddle a horse."

"Kelly!" Clancy called out brusquely, bringing their debate to a halt. He came quickly towards them with a determined gait that told of his former occupation. "I'll not have the miss saddlin' 'er own horse. If it's not done properly, and she was to get hurt, it'll be me answering to Mr. Darcy."

Still holding Catie's saddle, Sean gave Clancy a shrug. "Watch her then, mate, and inspect the job when she's finished."

Sean's suggestion played quickly over Clancy's features as he gave a single nod of approval and said, "All right then." Both men turned to Catie, who stood before them with her arms folded.

Determined to keep the upper hand, she marched forward and snatched the saddle from Sean Kelly's hands. Eyeing each of them daringly, she stepped over to Chloe and started to work. "Oh, yes, Clancy, *please* supervise me, for that will surely heighten my consequence for Mr. Kelly." Catie gave the young instructor a fierce glare over her shoulder, sure that his true purpose was to humiliate or punish her for being rude to Clancy yesterday.

"Miss?" Clancy looked as confused as he sounded.

Catie finished fastening the girth and spun around. "To make it simple, Clancy, Mr. Kelly has abandoned his post of riding instructor and has started a new career." She paused and boldly cast her eyes over to meet Sean's. "He's now teaching lessons in etiquette."

Although he was no longer smiling, Sean Kelly's eyes seemed to light up in the face of confrontation. "I say, Clancy." He tried to sound serious, but Catie noted a tinge of amusement in his voice. "Have you ever heard a *girl* blether on as much as this one? I'd wager the instructors at that fine boarding school of hers must have to paste her lips together in order for her to learn anything."

He was very proud of his last comment. Catie knew it because he stood looking down at her like a gloating peacock. Irish farm lad or not, Sean Kelly did have a rather noble appearance with his aristocratic nose. But it was his gypsy black hair, which lent him a slight air of wickedness, that truly stirred the blood. Clearly he was challenging her, but Catie wasn't taking the bait. Ignoring him, she finished her task and then stood back for inspection.

When both men were satisfied, Clancy left them without a word, and Sean had no choice but to state the obvious.

"I'm impressed. Where did you learn to saddle a horse?"

"Oh." She smiled and batted her eyes innocently as she spoke with a distinct and well-bred shire accent. "At my fine boarding school. I believe the course fell between *How to marry a rich husband* and *Hosting a grand dinner party*."

He smiled at her quick wit and gestured to her horse with his chin. "Mount your horse, Miss Catie. We have a long afternoon ahead of us."

Other than a small remark about the unusual heat, he rode quietly beside her. Catie knew they were heading back to the open grassland by the river, and her stomach tightened at the thought of a long afternoon spent trying to gallop. She was busy rationalizing the need to overcome her fears when he abruptly pulled his horse to a stop and, by natural reaction, Catie did the same.

"Miss Catie, I just want to clarify something. I didn't ask you to saddle your horse for any reason other than to improve your skills."

"Oh," she said, wondering if this was his idea of an apology.

"But truly," he questioned, "where did you learn to saddle a horse?"

"We must tack up our own mounts at school. But my dad," — Catie paused and swallowed — "he wouldn't allow me to ride until I learned."

"Really?" He seemed surprised. "I respect him for that."

"He also would have given me a good wigging for being cheeky with Clancy yesterday." She didn't know why she said this, but for some strange reason, she wanted him to know.

"Then I respect him even more."

She stared at him momentarily and then looked away. There was silence until a slight breeze went soughing though the trees overhead and sent a few birds loudly off in flight.

"Why?" His voice startled her, and she jerked her head back to meet his eyes again.

"Why?" she repeated.

"Yes." He smiled now. "Why then did you snap Clancy's head off yesterday if you were taught better?"

Catie shrugged. "I guess when you have been told all of your life that you have a temper, you start to believe it."

He watched her for a moment with a rather solemn look on his face then a grin started to tug at the corners of his mouth.

"Is something funny to you, Mr. Kelly?"

"Well, yeah." The grin grew larger. "I was just thinking how much easier my work would have been this summer if you had been told that you were an expert horsewoman." The grin broke free and spread over his face, soft and good-humored. It was a nice expression — one with which Catie surmised those closest to him would have been familiar.

Fighting the urge to grin back at him, she straightened in her saddle to her full height and declared, "You're an ass, Mr. Kelly — a complete and insufferable ass!"

Not being able to help himself, Sean burst out laughing at her insult, and Catie narrowed her eyes at him, affecting to look insulted.

"Humph," she grunted and trotted off rather tall and dignified, just as Percival had described her.

Still laughing, Sean shook his head and murmured, "Like a queen on parade."

After a long hour spent practicing the gallop in the dappled shade of the river's tall white willows, Sean saw that Chloe's willingness to continue being a good sport to her mistress was beginning to wane.

"That'll be enough for today then," he called out as she cantered back towards him, hands fiercely gripping the reins, he noticed.

To cool their mounts they walked slowly and quietly side by side back to the stables. As they climbed the gentle incline away from the river, a much welcomed breeze slightly picked up, rustling the grass and brush. Hot, Catie lifted her head and closed her eyes to let the light wind blow over her. He was watching her. Her eyes were closed, but she could feel his eyes roaming over her slender, extended neck and for the first time ever felt the surge of power that her feminine body possessed. She peeked at him through a slit in one eye, and he turned abruptly away, his ears pink at the tips.

"You need to give your horse more head," he stated with an exaggerated authority, refusing to look at her again "You must relax but keep your position.

Try and become one with her stride."

She bit back a grin. "I'll try harder tomorrow."

"Good." Hazarding a glance her way once more, he gave her a teacherly nod that seemed older than his years and then kept his eyes trained forward the rest of the way.

Percival was standing in the stable yard when they rode back in and threw up a hand in greeting as he approached the horses. "Afternoon, Percival," Sean said warmly as he drew his horse to a stop and swung out of the saddle.

"Afternoon!" Percival returned. "Can I take your horse?"

"Thanks, mate." Sean passed his reins over to Percival's big, calloused hand and then turned to Catie, who was just dismounting. "Give Chloe a good brush down and a warm wash after you remove her saddle, aye."

She spun around to face him and opened her mouth to object, but he stopped her.

"And mind that you do a good job of it because I'll be checking behind you." Ignoring her flabbergasted expression, he made a friendly parting comment to Percival and started off.

"Where are you going?" she demanded.

Sean stopped and turned around. "It's a hot afternoon, Miss Catie, and I fancy me a pint at the Green Man. Is something amiss, miss?" He grinned at his own cleverness.

Still flushed from her ride, Catie's face went almost scarlet. "Yes, something's amiss! Why is it that Percival can see to your horse but not mine?"

He held his arms out to his side and gave his shoulders an apologetic shrug. "Sorry, but I have long since mastered the gallop."

"And what does that have to do with it?" Now thoroughly enraged, Catie folded her arms tightly over her chest and glowered at him.

"As I said earlier, to improve your skills," he said then gallantly bowed. "Till tomorrow, m'lady."

2 AUGUST, 1918

He was waiting by the river again today. He smiled when he saw me. My heart is Arthur's. Taking my hand, he led me into the woods and kissed me tenderly, then harder. I thought I might fall through a hole in the earth or float over the forest canopy. He brushed my cheek and brought his lips to mine again. The sound of a carriage startled us. He grasped my elbow and together we ran farther into the woodlands. I would have run all the way to Scotland had he asked me.

"All the way to Scotland... how romantic." Catie rolled onto her back and looked dreamily at the vast blue sky overhead. In the next few pages, Arthur and Mary's romance heated up rather quickly, and the clandestine nature of the affair only added to its intrigue. Biting her lip in constant apprehension of the lovers being discovered, she read breathlessly until she heard the hum of Ben's car speeding up the approach road. "Finally!" she said, slamming the diary closed.

"Good Heavens, child, you smell like a barn," Rose fussed and stirred the air with a tea cloth when Catie entered the kitchen.

Catie sniffed, wrinkled her nose, and headed straight for the sink. "Thank your nephew. He has had me doing everything but mucking stalls these last few days."

Rose nodded with understanding. "Oh, he is a hard one, that boy, just like his father. Not a day goes by that my dear sister doesn't have to work just to keep on equal ground with that man."

"Is he cruel to her, Nan?" Catie asked as she turned off the tap and accepted the towel Rose offered.

"Oh, no." Rose shook her head. "As a matter of fact, Seamus and Emma Kelly have a passionate love that you will rarely find these days, Catherine."

"Really?" Catie's eyes widened. Sean Kelly had only mentioned his father a couple of times, but from his reports, Seamus Kelly didn't sound very romantic.

"Mm-hmm." Rose nodded. "But the man can be impossible. I have known my poor sister to be driven to take a drink well before lunch time. It will most certainly take a strong woman to stand beside my nephew in life. Kelly men are a fiery, Irish lot and notorious for being difficult to live with."

Strong, Catie thought sarcastically. She'd more likely have to be stupid to want to marry Sean Kelly. But she wisely held her tongue on the matter.

"Now, get out of those filthy clothes and dress for dinner. Your brother's back and he'll be in no mood to dine with a mule!" Rose shooed Catie out of the kitchen and up the stairs.

Bennet Darcy's trip to London had not been a successful one. He was tense, and his family went about the business of eating quietly. Even Geoffrey and George were subdued. All but slumped in disappointment, Catie felt rather subdued herself. It had been her hope to question Ben immediately on Rosings Park but, seeing the grim expression on her brother's face, she prudently decided to wait.

"By the way," Ben said to Sarah, breaking the droning rhythm of clanging glass and scraping forks. "I purchased that rescued thoroughbred I was telling you about. His health has substantially improved from the abuse and malnutrition he suffered, and he's ready to be trained. If all goes well, he should make a good horse for Geoffrey in a few more years." He glanced over at his son while speaking and frowned at the trail of peas the child had made neatly round his potatoes. "Geoffrey, stop playing with your food!" The boy, startled at his father's voice, quickly disassembled his artistic endeavor.

"With everything that is going on, do you really need the obligation of training an abused horse?" Sarah replied, a hint of annoyance in her tone.

"I could use the diversion. And besides, that young nephew of Rose's is supposed to be some sort of expert with horses. So I thought I would take advantage of his being here. Geoffrey! Stop chasing the peas round your plate, lad. Smash your peas on the back of your fork and then eat them, Son."

A look passed between husband and wife, and Catie saw it. Sarah then looked pointedly at her and asked, "Catie, will you be a dear and take the boys up to Mrs. Newell and help her ready them for bed?"

Catie didn't appreciate being sent away with a couple of five-year-olds, and furthermore, there was more going on between Ben and Sarah than whether or not he should have bought a horse. She considered arguing the point but, after another glance at Ben, thought better of it.

"But we haven't had our dessert, Mummy!" Geoffrey quickly protested and George echoed his brother's sentiment, "We haven't had our dessert, Mummy!"

"I shall have your dessert sent up to you," Sarah assured them, kind but firm, and gave Catie a dismissive nod that was meant to be obeyed.

"Yes, Sarah," she assented softly. "Come then, lads. I'll tell you a story."

Geoffrey and George jumped down happily from their seats and followed their aunt from the room. Once they cleared the door, Catie grabbed the two boys by the collar and pulled them out of sight. "Make a peep and I'll box your ears!" she hissed menacingly.

Wide-eyed, Geoffrey clamped a hand over his mouth lest he slip up. George did the same.

"Forgive me, Bennet." Catie turned back just in time to hear Sarah speak.

"I know you are terribly distressed with this Wesley Howell situation, but you mustn't take it out on the children."

"*Howell*?" Catie repeated softly as Ben pushed away from the table, crossed the room and closed the door.

"I'm sorry, Sarah," he said, turning back to her. "I'll pop in and speak with the boys before they go to bed."

"Do you wish to talk about it?" she asked.

Shaking his head, he sat back down. "Not tonight, Sarah. There is nothing more to do with Wesley Howell at the moment but wait. Tell me instead what has been going on around here. How are Catie and that Kelly lad getting on?"

"Well, I have heard her refer to him with a few names that would make you blush. How's that for getting on?"

"Do you think I should intervene?"

"Not unless you can somehow change his appearance."

"His appearance?" he questioned.

"Yes, Ben, certainly you have noticed that he is a rather handsome, young chap."

"I'm sorry, Sarah, but I'm rather ill-equipped to judge a handsome chap from one that is not. And forgive me if I'm daft, but what the devil does that have to do with it?"

"I don't know. It's possible that Catie might be developing a slight schoolgirl crush on our Mr. Kelly."

"A crush!" he exclaimed. "But she's...she's..."

"She's sixteen, Bennet!" Sarah filled in for him. "And whether she's developing a crush or not, no girl that age wants a nice-looking chap for an instructor."

Ben rubbed tiredly at his face, murmuring, "I should have insisted on that French tutor instead. The man was seventy-five if he was a day."

"Or...she could have actually toured France," Sarah said, as a wary look came over her husband's face.

"Toured France?" he repeated.

"Yes, Ben, Diana Harold telephoned while you were in London. She was most disappointed that Catie wasn't allowed to join her and Horace on their holiday in the French countryside." Sarah met his eyes testily. "And I was most disappointed that it was the first I had heard of their invitation."

"Do you not remember when they took her to Scotland? Catie became sick with pneumonia, and I had to travel to Edinburgh. God, Sarah, she was in hospital for three days. France is too far away if something were to go wrong. I know I should have told you, but… I didn't want a big to-do over it. I made the decision that she wasn't going, and that's that! I shan't excuse my behavior further."

Sarah exhaled a frustrated sigh. "Good Lord, Bennet, Catie could very well become ill right here at Pemberley. You must stop governing her so vigilantly. Now Diana thinks you are keeping Catie from them because of your row with Horace. I told her you would never do such a thing. I hope I'm correct. Catie *is* their goddaughter."

"Horace and I did not have a *row*; we have only parted in business. He was not only my father's solicitor but his best friend as well. Our personal lives are still intertwined and always will be."

It occurred to Sarah to suggest he ask Horace Harold to look into Wesley Howell's background, but she pushed the idea out of her mind for now. Horace Harold had known Ben since the day he was born, which unfortunately had been the root of their undoing. Horace still thought of Ben as his father's son and treated him as such. Ben, on the other hand, wanted — needed really — to step out of his father's shadow and run Pemberley and his financial investments his own way.

Not tonight. He was home again and she was glad for it. She smiled at him across the table and asked, "Shall I have our dessert sent up as well, Mr. Darcy?"

Ben's shoulders seemed to relax instantly at the invitation, and he lifted his wine glass in acceptance. "That, madam, would be wonderful."

Chapter 7

Sunday morning Bennet Darcy followed his usual routine of shaking hands and exchanging small talk with his fellow parishioners at Ashridge's Church of the Holy Trinity. Like his forefathers, he was the village's wealthiest resident and much admired by its citizens. Today, however, that admiration was compounded by the announcement that the proceeds from Pemberley's Annual Garden Party, a yearly charitable event to raise money for local causes, would provide a much needed new roof on the parish school.

After he and Sarah made their way through the throng of well-wishers, the family sat together in their usual pew at the head of the nave. Attached to the end of the pew box was a brass nameplate engraved *Darcys of Pemberley*, placed there in the eighteenth century. Reserved pews were no longer a practice of the Church of England, but no one in Ashridge would feel comfortable sitting where the Darcys had sat since the church was built in 1764. Being a rural community, Ashridge's populace still preferred many of the old English standards and was proud of their little hamlet's history.

Once seated, Catie began scanning the church for Audrey Tillman. Since Audrey evenly split her school holidays between divorced parents, she only lived in Ashridge part-time. And when she wasn't in Ashridge, Audrey might be traveling anywhere in the world with her professional violinist mother. Not only had Audrey seen most of the Continent, she also had visited America and Canada. Catie, who was extremely lacking in adventure of any sort, envied her friend tremendously. Though she did not find Audrey, Catie's search did bring her attention to Rose and the person sitting beside her — her nephew. Their eyes met, and his face lit with that big stupid smile that he seemed to reserve especially for her. She faintly reflected the sentiment then promptly turned away, feeling the smile grow larger behind her.

Before the service started, a loud whisper echoed from the back of the church. "*Catie, Catie Darcy!*" Catie turned to find Audrey sitting two rows behind Rose, and beckoning her impatiently. Sarah softly nodded her approval to Catie's request to change seats, so she stood and walked back through the church, purposefully not meeting Sean Kelly's eyes again.

Audrey was in a tizzy to learn the identity of the young man sitting next to Rose, for handsome young lads were a scarce commodity in Ashridge.

"The chap, beside Rose?" she whispered eagerly, as Catie sat down. "He was the dreamboat at the Green Man last week. You remember — the one looking at you."

"Sorry to disappoint, Aud," Catie whispered back as the two girls leaned close so they could talk without drawing attention. "But he's only Rose's nephew, here for the summer to give riding lessons to the twins and me."

"Lucky you!" The girl carefully inspected the back of Sean Kelly's head as she spoke.

"Not really," Catie whispered, even lower now. "He can be a real... pain." It wasn't the nastiest insult she could think of, but she *was* in church.

"Maybe I'll ask my father for riding lessons then. I could easily put up with a little *pain* from a man with those good looks," Audrey said, clearly unconcerned with where she was.

Not being able to control themselves, the girls giggled a little louder than they should have and received a chiding look from Ben. Among her brother's many community titles, churchwarden was one he took most seriously. Seeing her brother's expression, Catie shushed Audrey and opened her prayer book.

The sermon was long and the children who weren't squirming had fallen asleep, heavy and limp in their parents' arms. To close the service, the vicar announced that a special visiting soloist would sing the last hymn and asked Sean Kelly to come forward. Shocked, Audrey looked at Catie and mouthed, "He can sing?" Catie shrugged.

Necks craned like a herd of curious giraffes as Sean made his way to the front, for visitors to the small parish church were as scarce as handsome young lads. He stood beside the piano and with a slight lead from the pianist, began singing. As his voice lifted and filled the ancient stone church with the old Irish hymn, "Be Thou My Vision," the squirming children sat still and the congregation listened, mesmerized. Catie Darcy included.

Afterwards a crowd gathered around Rose's nephew to comment on his talent, and Catie watched intently as he graciously accepted their praises. Even among strangers, he was completely at ease — so opposite to her cool demeanor.

"Catie, dear." Donald Tillman, Audrey's father, broke her reverie, making Catie wonder whether he had noticed her staring at the young Irishman.

"Yes?" she answered, turning around. Each year Mr. Tillman's thinning hair turned grayer and his smile showed a few more wrinkles around his gentle, green eyes. Catie wondered how her own father would have aged.

"It's such a nice day. Would you like to join us for a picnic to the Peak District this afternoon?"

"Oh, yes, thank you, Mr. Tillman. I'd love to come," she said as she waved Ben and Sarah over. A day away from the house was just what she needed.

The Darcys used Catie's summons to politely leave the Bells, a chatty, elderly couple who had farmed for Ben's grandfather. Inevitably, the Bells would corner Ben and Sarah most Sundays with stories from the "simpler days," as they called them.

"Thank God we got away from them," Ben whispered furtively, clapping Mr. Tillman's shoulder in welcome. Donald Tillman had been a good friend of the late Mr. Darcy and remained close to Ben and Catie after his death. "I do believe Mr. and Mrs. Bell were going to tell us about the winter of forty-eight again."

"The long version," Sarah added ruefully, waving sweetly back at the elderly couple as they left the church.

"The Bells could talk the hind legs off a donkey." Donald Tillman chuckled and shook his head. "The old dears caught me outside the butcher's the other day, and I thought my sausages would spoil before they'd shut up."

Looking past Mr. Tillman, Catie noticed Sean Kelly walking in her direction. Audrey noticed him as well and nudged Catie for an introduction as he drew closer.

"Good mornin', Miss Catie," he said when he reached her, the tune of Ireland heavy in his speech. Having an English mother, Sean Kelly had the ability to soften his accent when he wanted, but Catie had come to prefer his thick, Irish brogue.

"Good morning," she replied. "This is my friend, Audrey Tillman; Audrey, Sean Kelly."

"It's a pleasure to meet you, Sean," Audrey purred daintily, offering her hand to him with a coy smile that fooled no one. "You have a lovely voice."

"Thank you, pleasure meeting you also." Sean held the proffered hand only briefly before releasing it and turning back to Catie. "How about you, Miss Catie, did you enjoy the hymn?"

"Oh, yes of course," Catie said, slightly regretful for not having already complimented him. "I don't see how anyone could not have enjoyed it."

"I'm glad," he answered softly as his eyes caught hers and held them in an unwavering gaze that was thankfully broken by Audrey's shrill, excited voice.

"Oh, Dad, I have a lovely idea! Can Sean join our picnic this afternoon?"

"Yes, Sean, why don't you join us?" Mr. Tillman readily satisfied his daughter. "Have you seen our Peak District?"

"Only in parts, sir, but I haven't had the chance to do any proper exploring. I'd love to come."

Catie's stomach lurched when Sean accepted. *All afternoon with him?*

"Wonderful! We'll be glad to have you," Mr. Tillman said. Councilman Tillman was the authority on tourism in Derbyshire and loved showing newcomers the sights. "Though I'm afraid we'll need another vehicle, what with Mother and the dog coming along."

"No worries, sir," Sean said. "I brought my old Land Rover over on the ferry, and once I'm in more suitable clothes for a picnic, I can collect Miss Catie and meet you." He quickly looked to his employer lest he overstep his bounds. "That is, if Mr. Darcy has no objections?"

Ben hesitated, glancing from Sean to his sister as Sarah's talk of schoolgirl crushes and handsome young chaps echoed loudly in his head.

"I believe that would be fine, Sean," Sarah broke in. "Bennet, you see no reason why Sean shouldn't drive Catie to meet the Tillmans?"

"No, of course not; just please be careful," Ben conceded as he placed his hands protectively on Catie's shoulders. "In fact, I'm glad you're going along. The Peak District can be a dangerous place, and my little sister has a tendency to be a bit risky in her behavior. Understandably, Mr. Tillman may be distracted with his mother, and it will put my mind at ease to know there is another set of eyes on her."

As Ben spoke, Catie's cheeks glowed bright with embarrassment, but she didn't dare say a word. She detested his mother hen-like nervousness, but refused to give him reason to keep her home. She couldn't bear the idea of Audrey Tillman and Sean Kelly enjoying an afternoon exploring the Peak

District while she sat at Pemberley.

"Sure, Mr. Darcy," Sean agreed, astonished by the girl's sudden meekness. Evidently, he surmised, the cheeky Miss Darcy was not so bold in the presence of her guardian.

CATIE WAS DONNING THE JUMPER that Rose insisted she wear when she saw Sean Kelly pull onto the gravel court. "I'm off!" she called up the grand staircase and left the house.

He got out and helped her load the picnic hamper then rushed past her to open the door. "Thanks," Catie said quietly and slid into the car.

The Rover had seen better days. A crack ran across the windscreen and the radio hung precariously from a few exposed wires. "Sorry." Sean caught her inspection and tried to right the radio as best he could. "Me brother fixed it."

"*Fixed* it?" she questioned.

"Well, at least it plays now." He smiled self-consciously as he glanced around the tattered interior. "Bit of a rattletrap, eh? But she gets me from here to there well enough. Ready?"

Catie bobbed her head and he put the car in gear and pulled off.

"Your hair looks nice down. I've only seen it pulled back," he said, trying to make conversation.

"Thanks." She ventured a sidelong glance at him. "Sarah likes me to wear it down to church."

"You're lucky to have her." He paused. "I mean...with your parents...er, well, it's good you have her...and your brother as well."

Catie shrugged. "I suppose."

"You are quite the little mouse around him, I noticed." Sean shifted gears and then looked over at her. "Is he very strict?"

Annoyed with his forwardness, she turned to him with an expression to match. "No, he is not *very* strict! He is standing in place of my father and respect for him is expected. Are you disrespectful to your father?"

"Oh, no." He chuckled and shook his head. "A lesson I had to learn the hard way. But learn it I did. You may not have noticed, but I'm a wee bit pigheaded at times."

"Not at all," she said mockingly, cutting her eyes sideways at him once more. "So, what's the *hard* way?"

"At the end of a strap, how else?"

"Oh." She turned away to mask her alarm.

"So, was it difficult for you and your brother when he had to switch roles? You know…become your custodian, your parent practically?" Sean couldn't help but ask. The orphan of Pemberley had long been his aunt's charge, and often discussed with his mother. Never did he think he would actually meet the child, or rather, young woman, he corrected himself.

"My brother is fourteen years older than me, so he's always bossed me around." Catie looked out the window and sighed. "I don't think it was too difficult, no."

It occurred to Sean that he had probably hit a sensitive subject, and he quickly shifted the conversation. "So, the Peak District — Britain's first national park, am I right?"

Bearing a faint but grateful smile, she turned back to him and nodded.

AFTER A NICE BASKET LUNCH, Sean, Catie, and Audrey took off exploring. They followed a well-worn footpath and hiked almost a mile from the picnic area, stopping now and then to see how high they were getting. "I've climbed to that outcrop before," Audrey announced, pointing. "It's not too difficult."

Sean cupped a hand over his eyes. "All right, I'm game."

Catie was quickly far ahead of them, tackling the first few boulders with ease. Her small and solid stature made her ascent so effortless that even Sean couldn't keep up with her. Several times he called out for her to slow down, but she ignored him and kept her pace.

Reaching the ledge, she stood and took in the outstanding views of the valley floor while waiting for the others. Behind her she could hear Sean having to help Audrey along and rolled her eyes, knowing it was a ploy on Audrey's part to keep his attention. Hearing them close, Catie looked down and teased, "Climbed here before, eh, Tillman? Come on you two, it isn't Everest!"

When Sean saw Catie, he left Audrey behind and scrambled to the top. "I told you to wait!" he barked angrily as he reached out and grabbed hold of her hand. "Do you listen to no one?"

"Let go of me!" She gave a swift but unsuccessful jerk to free herself. "I don't need you to hold my hand!"

"Stop being so stubborn! We are very high up, and I promised to look after you. Remember?"

"I can look after myself!"

Sean pulled her close, so close she gasped. "I'm not going to return to that brother of yours empty-handed!"

"Insufferable…"

"Ass!" he finished for her, panting and hot from his climb.

His breath was warm on her face, and his taunting grin tempted her like she had never been tempted before. Moved by some primordial instinct, Catie closed her eyes and raised her mouth to offer him her lips, but was snapped from the moment when he pulled her along to help Audrey.

"I don't mind holding your hand, Sean," Audrey said in a demure voice as Sean pulled her onto the ledge.

Ridiculous flirt, Catie thought spitefully, praying Sean Kelly didn't realize that she had wanted to kiss him.

The sky was a crisp blue, deepening the emerald green of the dales below them. Audrey, acting expert in place of her father, pointed out locations to Sean — the direction of the old mill and sixteenth century yeoman's house they had passed on their way up, the river and its part in the Industrial Revolution — until Catie could take no more.

"Spare us the history lesson, Tillman!" she interrupted her friend. "We're on holiday, remember."

"Humph," Audrey grunted but fell silent nonetheless.

The three stood still as a sweet-smelling breeze swept up from the valley. Eyes closed, Sean inhaled deeply and relaxed his hold on Catie's hand. She was then able to feel a few small calluses from his work, the length of his fingers, and a tiny raised scar just below his thumb. The hand was strong and masculine and gave her an odd sense of security. She felt a soft squeeze and turned to the silent summons. Using only his eyes, Sean drew her attention to a magnificent Peregrine falcon riding the thermals above them. Catie looked up, watched the bird for a moment and then turned back to him. He smiled at her, and she smiled back, wanting to kiss him more now than she wanted to take her next breath.

It was getting late when they returned to Mr. Tillman and his mother, so Sean and Catie quickly said their goodbyes. They loaded the picnic hamper and began their short journey back to Pemberley Estate.

The sun had lowered and was blazing hot on the windscreen, forcing them to roll down the windows to get relief. As she directed him home, Catie took the opportunity to study Sean as he navigated the unfamiliar roundabouts. Although she hadn't readily recognized him, she had always known Sean Kelly.

He was one of "the nephews" as they had been duly dubbed — five handsome boys, each black headed and smiling back at Catie from an annually changed photograph Rose kept on her bedside table. For a lifetime Catie had despised those spirited looking lads, for they took her Nan from her at least twice a year and never for less than a fortnight. Her interest however was not in Sean's brothers, but rather the comment Ben made at supper on Friday night.

"So, I hear you're an expert with horses?"

He smiled. "I reckon I should be since I have been around them the whole of my life. I grew up at Kells Down, my family's equestrian farm. We train horses, give riding lessons, offer livery services, you know … the whole lot. I've been giving riding lessons since I was your age."

"How did you end up at Pemberley for the summer?"

Sean shrugged. "My best guess is that me mam grew tired of watching my old man and me lock horns."

"Lock horns?" Catie questioned warily.

He smiled again. "Aye, but don't look so concerned. That old story has been lived and relived ever since time began."

"I don't understand."

"Fathers and sons," Sean clarified. "One never lives up to the other's expectations. Fathers are never the men their sons idolized as lads. Not surprising. Most boys think of their old man as Superman or something."

"And the sons?"

"The sons," he repeated with a rueful chuckle. "Now here's where it gets complicated. You see, Catie, fathers put all their hopes and dreams into their sons — everything they weren't able to be."

"Why shouldn't they?"

Glancing from the windscreen over to her, Sean gave another shrug. "Not all sons want to fulfill their old man's dreams. Sometimes sons have dreams of their own."

"So which was it? Did you discover your dad wasn't Superman or…" Catie leaned eagerly towards him. "*Or*, do you have a dream of your own?"

"I needed the quid," he replied flatly.

Dissatisfied, Catie slumped back in her seat. "Then what was all that rubbish about locking horns?"

"The rubbish is complicated. I've just finished my first year at Queen's in Belfast, and university tuition is expensive. Plus…" he hesitated.

"Plus what?" she insisted. Interest once again sparked.

"Well, I don't know what Mrs. Darcy has told you, but at one time my youngest brother Joseph was a lot like George. Only he stopped speaking all together around the age of six. Still, me da was determined he would learn to ride a horse and gave me the responsibility of teaching him. So I did." He turned to her and cocked a single eyebrow. "You *can* communicate with horses without hitting and yelling, you know."

"I know," she replied irritably and colored. Sean had just lectured her on Friday for giving Chloe's rump several swats and yelling at the animal for not obeying her command. "The very reason you aren't allowed a crop!" he had criticized sternly. "They are never to be used as an instrument for punishment." Sean even went so far as to apologize to the beast for her mistress's "wretched manners," as he called them.

"Well," he continued, "it wasn't long before he was riding with confidence, and then — "

"Let me guess; he started talking again."

"Aye, a miracle according to me mam, but I think it was the riding that brought Joseph back to us."

"So you're saying riding a horse cured your brother's muteness?" she stated with unmistakable cynicism.

"The horse has assisted man throughout history, Catie. So why not?"

"Do you think George will start speaking? On his own, I mean?"

"I don't know, but I have already seen some improvement in his independence from Geoffrey. And as long as he is enjoying himself, how can it hurt?"

"True." With that at least, she had to agree.

Tired from the day, their conversation fell into a light, friendly chatter the rest of the way home. When finally Sean pulled to a stop in front of the house, Catie thanked him and got out of the car. To her surprise, he turned off the engine and joined her at the bottom of the steps.

"Would…you…like to come inside the house?" she questioned hesitantly.

"Yes. When you return a young lady home it is proper to address the family." Catie laughed.

"What's funny?" he asked.

"That's rather old-fashioned. Don't you think?"

"I was taught better than to leave a girl on the doorstep, miss." His expression was a serious one, and Catie wished she hadn't teased him.

"Sorry." She gestured to the steps. "Please."

Once in the hall, Sean was somewhat overwhelmed by Pemberley's interior. Though he had been in the kitchen almost daily and twice in Mr. Darcy's study, he hadn't yet seen the grander parts of the home. Due to the season, the doors to the formal rooms were wide open to allow air circulation, and there wasn't a place he could have rested his eyes that didn't hold the sight of grandeur. Tapestries and art hung on walls painted in bright pastels, balancing the abundance of dark wooden antiques and upholstered furniture. In the grand dining room three crystal chandeliers were suspended from high coffered ceilings over a table that could seat twenty or more. "You *live* here?" he asked, unable to comprehend the reality of it.

"Yes," she replied simply, "though these rooms are rarely used nowadays. At one time Pemberley was open to tours a couple of days a week, but my brother closed the house to visitors after my father died."

A painting of a horse caught Sean's attention and he asked excitedly, "Is that a Stubbs?"

"Are you an admirer of Stubbs, Kelly?" a deep voice asked behind them, and Sean and Catie turned from the painting to see Mr. and Mrs. Darcy descending the grand staircase.

"Yes, sir," Sean answered, "me dad as well. He has several prints in his farm office."

"My great-great grandfather won that painting from a duke in a high stakes card game," Ben said as he and Sarah joined them in front of the painting.

"If you don't mind my asking, sir," Sean said, "what was your grandfather's wager?"

Ben grinned. "It is legend that the hand of his eldest daughter was on the table. But since we Darcys have always been better storytellers than gamblers, I'd say it was just that...a legend. He probably bought it at an estate auction on a rainy Saturday afternoon."

Sean laughed softly.

"Is Stubbs your only interest?" Ben asked.

"No, sir — Munnings too," Sean said, smiling unevenly, "though my father argues that Stubbs was the greater genius."

Ben grinned again. "I have to agree with your father. Stubbs had no influence of photography. But still, Sir Alfred had his merits. Follow me to the billiards room, and I shall show you a piece of his work."

"Very nice, sir," Sean said after they had studied and commented on the stately horse and rider for several minutes. "Thank you for showing it to me. My father will be quite jealous."

"Trust me, Sean, the pleasure was all his." Sarah smiled at her husband with a teasing eye.

"Well, I'm sorry to have disturbed you on a Sunday afternoon," Sean said politely. "I only wanted to see Miss Catie safely home. I'll not keep you any longer."

"Actually, Sean, I was hoping to see you." Ben stopped him. "I had a delivery at the stable a few hours ago that I believe *might* interest you. Can you come with me now?"

"Yes, of course, Mr. Darcy."

"I'd like to see, may I come?" Catie asked eagerly.

"Really?" said her brother with one eyebrow arched in suspicion. "And since when were you interested in horses, Catherine?"

Catie's cheeks flushed a bright pink.

"We'll both join you," Sarah sympathetically interjected. "I could use a little exercise before supper."

"As you wish, madam." Ben gave her a perceptive smile and stood aside to allow his wife and sister to pass. "Are you as knowledgeable in literature, Kelly, as you are in art?"

"Somewhat knowledgeable, Mr. Darcy."

"Do you know who wrote, 'Women are meant to be loved, not to be understood.'?"

"I believe that was Oscar Wilde, sir. *The Sphinx without a Secret.*"

"I believe you are right!" Ben said with unnecessary exuberance.

"I believe that will be quite enough from you, Mr. Darcy," Sarah admonished playfully without turning around.

The thoroughbred Ben had purchased was a handsome dark chestnut, solid except for a small patch of white between his eyes and around his mouth. His temperament, however, was less appealing. Unlike the regal and stoic animals in Ben's paintings, the gelding anxiously pranced about inside the paddock with a wild distrust in his eyes.

"What do you think?" Ben asked after he had given Sean a rundown of the animal's unfortunate history. "Fancy a go at him? I shall compensate you for the extra work of course."

"Yeah." Sean nodded gamely and climbed over the fence.

Surprised, Ben said, "What — *now*?"

"Aye, sir, I intend to introduce myself and welcome our friend properly." Sean approached the animal, cooing softly in Gaelic.

With raised brows, Ben glanced at Sarah. "Now," he repeated and joined Sean in the paddock.

Catie watched in disbelief as the animal responded almost magically to Sean's voice. The horse even whinnied and lifted its head with a coltish snort, demanding more attention. Once the gelding's anxiety began to ease, Sean disappeared into the stable and came back with a bridle. Thrilled, Catie climbed upon the fence and sat on the top rail to gain a better vantage.

"Get down, Sis!" Ben hissed at her under his breath. "Can you not see how unpredictable the animal is?"

Catie obeyed but grumbled, "Must he always speak to me as if I'm seven years old?"

Sarah laughed shortly. "He will not always be so blind, my dear sister. But until he sees better you must do what women have always done."

"What's that?" Catie asked, glowering at her brother.

"Endure."

Neighing contemptuously, the horse wasn't so keen on the bridle, repeatedly rejecting it. Sean coaxed gently but firmly until the gelding submitted and allowed the bridle to be hung loosely over his ears. Caught up in the moment, Catie jumped carelessly upon the fence again and cried out, "He did it!"

The sudden movement spooked the horse, and the feral shadow fell back over him in an instant. Wild-eyed, the powerful thoroughbred reared back and charged aggressively towards Catie. She hit the ground hard as the thud of hooves crashed down around her like the rain of a sudden and violent storm. Terrified, she coiled into a protective ball, expecting the heavy blow of a hoof, but the clopping grew faint. The horse had galloped off, leaving her filthy but unharmed. Excited voices came from all around but all she could hear was the thumping of her rapidly beating heart.

"Don't move, Catie," Sarah, who was first to her side, cautioned frantically. "Is anything broken?"

"No," Catie replied, rolling onto her back and wiping dirt from her face.

"My God, Sis, did he come down on you?" Ben stooped, checking her carefully from head to toe. "Are you hurt anywhere?"

"No." Catie shook her head. "He didn't land on me."

"Are you sure?"

"I'm fine, Brother — just dirty."

"Help her up, Ben," Sarah instructed, and he carefully lifted his sister to her feet.

Catie looked down at her hands, which stung badly, and saw that she had scraped off a good deal of skin in trying to brace her fall. "Bloody horse!" she uttered spitefully.

"Bloody *horse!*" Ben gave her shoulder a censorious shake. "You're lucky you weren't trampled!"

"I know." Catie didn't dare meet her brother's eyes. Even worse, Sean Kelly stood in the background listening as Ben scolded her like a child.

"Shall I go fetch the horse, Mr. Darcy?" Sean asked as if sensing Catie's discomfort.

"Yes," Ben answered in an aggravated tone. "Sarah, take Catie to the house while I go with Sean. The horse took out the top rail of the fence, and I'll need to be there if he's broken his leg."

Startled, Catie looked at Ben. "You won't shoot him, will you?"

"If he's hurt badly, Catherine, I'll have no choice."

After Sarah bandaged Catie's hands, Rose gave the girl two aspirin with a nip of brandy and marched her off to lie down until suppertime. With Catie safely upstairs, Sarah murmured a silent prayer for the horse and went to her sons, who were playing in the garden. She took a seat on a cushioned wicker lawn chair and was soon joined by her husband.

"Oh, Ben!" She sat up when she saw him. "How's the horse?"

"Just a bad scratch," he said, sitting down next her. "Sean's wrapping his leg now."

"Then you must go straight in and tell Catie. Her conscience is heavily burdened with that horse's fate."

Ben glanced at his watch. "It's less than an hour till supper. Let her conscience suffer a bit longer." Sarah gave him a disapproving look that made him chuckle and kiss her. "It'll do her good, my love. Now tell me, how is my foolhardy sister?"

"She'll recover. Though I doubt she'll be sitting comfortably for a few days."

"Oh?"

Sarah's triangular brows arched with amusement. "Rose and I discovered a rather large bruise on your sister's backside. When she fell she must have landed on a stone."

Ben laughed. "Lessons learned from that end up are lessons learned indeed."

"That's what Rose said!" Sarah looked at him in amazement.

"It was one of Dad's sayings." He smiled thoughtfully. "How would we have managed Catie all these years without Rose?"

"We would have failed … miserably."

Ben gave a soft grunt of agreement and fell silent as he watched Geoffrey and George chase each other around the lawn.

"What's on your mind, Bennet?" Sarah asked. "Catie? Don't worry so, darling, she still has girlish impulses."

"No, I was thinking of Dad." He released a burdensome sigh and added, "And Wesley Howell. I haven't yet told you about my trip to London."

She turned to give him her full attention. "Go on."

"I'm afraid this whole affair is going to cost us more than I had hoped, Sarah. Charles Worthington and I are meeting next week to try and work out some kind of a negotiation, but I don't see how we can avoid making the man some sort of an offer."

"So, Wesley Howell is who he says he is?"

"It appears so. Everything, documents and all, appear to be in order. My only hope now is to reach a settlement with the man quickly and privately, without London's tabloids getting hold of the story."

"What about Pemberley?" Sarah asked, the trepidation in her voice evident.

"Pemberley will not be a part of any settlement!" he said hotly. "I shall let this matter go public and before the courts first; I made that perfectly clear to Charles." Ben paused for a moment and then whispered, "God, Sarah, how I wish I could ask Father's advice."

Sarah affectionately took her husband's hand. "I know, darling, I know." They sat quietly until a few drops of rain forced them to gather the twins and head indoors.

Chapter 8

The few drops of rain turned into a steady downpour that lasted several days. Catie looked out of the rain-streaked windows in the drawing room and moaned. She hated more than anything to be closed up indoors, but there was more fueling her foul mood that morning. Audrey Tillman had unexpectedly flown off to meet her mother in Turkey and felt it essential to call her friend before leaving London to crow about her upcoming trip. Audrey was most likely walking on the white sands of the Aegean Coast at that very minute.

"I hope she gets sunburn!" Catie scowled at her reflection in the glass then opened Mary Darcy's diary, her only companion for the last dreary days.

Mary and Arthur's zealous summer romance was never discovered, and he left his friends at Thompson Farm at summer's end with a promise to write Mary every week. Mary Darcy fancied herself to be ardently in love with Arthur Howell and was in a desperate state after his departure from Derbyshire.

31st of August 1918
I must pull myself together. Both Mother and Father are eyeing me with
suspicion. It is just misery, pure and complete misery. I love Arthur so that I
feel my heart will explode right out of my chest. He has already written and
promises to return summer next. Oh how I shall suffer until then.
How indeed!

"Oh, Mary, you poor, poor dear," Catie whispered, shaking her head. After several more anguished outpourings, Mary's entries were scattered until

Christmastime, when she again wrote of Catie's Grandfather Geoffrey visiting Pemberley from Rosings Park for the Christmas season.

21st of December 1918

The house is most merry, adorned with greenery and holly. The Darcys of Rosings Park have arrived in their new shiny automobile. "Ostentatious," Father whispered in Mother's ear as we all waved them in, their horn blaring. However, I think Papa is still a bit miffed because Cousin Geoff made a fortune during the War. It is rumored that Rosings Park is now fully electric, even in the servant's quarters. Thankfully, Cousin Geoff and young Geoffrey took Papa automobiling, and the three returned in high spirits. Now it is Mamma who is miffed, as the men have spent the whole of the afternoon in the carriage house staring at the engine. Arthur continues to write weekly and is presently in the north with his regiment. His latest letter was addressed to My Dearest Mary . . . my dearest! Oh, I think he must love me . . . surely he must!

Catie closed the diary and sat up. "Wesley Howell — Arthur Howell — Rosings Park — what does it all mean?" she mulled over the mystery once more, as the large hall clock belled the hour. Mr. Johnson would be preparing Ben's lunch. She'd had every intention of broaching the subject of their grandfather being raised at Rosings Park with her brother, but the success of these types of conversations depended greatly on timing. She heaved a determined sigh. "I suppose now is as good a time as any."

Upon entering the kitchen under the pretense of getting a glass of milk, Miss Catie was not a welcomed sight. As grand and enchanting as Pemberley was, even it could grow small and grey when one found oneself imprisoned within its walls for too long. And with the Aegean Coast weighing heavily upon her temper, young Miss Darcy had become a most disagreeable inmate of her ancestral home, sulking about the house the last few days, as stormy as the weather and never opening her mouth except to complain. Confident she would find something to be unhappy about, Mr. Johnson went about his business and ignored her.

Soon enough, Catie justified the man's disregard by pouring her milk down the sink, claiming that it tasted a day or two old. Then, while advising Mr. Johnson to purchase from a different dairy next time, she emptied the rest of the container down the drain as well. Mr. Johnson grumbled under his breath as he filled a tray with Mr. Darcy's lunch. He had just bought the milk fresh.

"What'd you say, Mr. Johnson?" Catie stepped over to the man.

"Nothing, miss, just speaking to me dearly departed mum," Mr. Johnson replied as he forcefully brought down a sharp knife to halve the sandwich, making Catie flinch. He turned to call for a maid to deliver the meal.

"If that's for my brother, I'll take it." Catie rushed forward. "I must pass his door on my way. No need to disturb anyone."

Happy to see her with reason to leave, Mr. Johnson handed the tray over to Catie as he warned, "Careful now, missy. The soup is hot and the bowl's full."

"Enter." Catie heard Ben respond to her knock and opened the door to his study, clumsily trying to manage the heavy tray.

"I have your lunch, Brother," she announced pleasantly as she came in but drew up short at the sight in front of her. Aiden Hirst. Athletically built, eighteen years old and, like her brother, bearing a handsome, rectangular British face. Catie swallowed at the sight of him and glanced nervously at Ben.

"Allow me." Aiden came forward to take the tray from her hands.

"Thank you." Catie watched him edge it carefully onto Ben's desk and ventured another look at her brother. He didn't appear to be too nettled — no more than usual anyway. Ben stood and smiled, slightly easing her rapidly beating heart.

"Aiden, allow me to introduce my sister, Catherine; Catherine, Aiden Hirst."

"Pl-pleased to meet you, A-Aiden," Catie stammered and blushed when she noticed Ben grimace at her awkwardness.

"Likewise, Miss Darcy," Aiden said.

"Catherine, Aiden is the nephew of Lawrence Hirst of Ardsley Manor," Ben continued. "His uncle and our father go way back."

"Is that so?"

"Yes, it is." Aiden gave Catie a conniving wink. "Well, Mr. Darcy, I must be off. Thank you for seeing me, sir." He shook Ben's hand and turned back to Catie. "Miss Darcy, I hope we shall meet again soon."

"Yes, s-soon," Catie repeated anxiously, glad he was leaving.

"Please don't ring anyone, Mr. Darcy, I'll show myself out. I'm rather used to rambling old houses," Aiden said, waving back at them. "Cheers."

"Nice lad, that Aiden," Ben said as soon as the door closed.

"Is he?"

"He seems to be." Ben sat back down.

"Because Lawrence Hirst of Ardsley Manor is his uncle or because he's rather used to rambling old houses?" Catie asked as she flopped down on the chair in front of Ben's desk, legs dangling over the arm. "Really, Ben, don't be such a snob."

He looked at her with a mixture of impatience and sympathy. "You will soon be coming of an age, Catherine, that impressions will be important. You must start considering how you present yourself and how you speak to... you know... young men."

Catie sat up and said dramatically, "Have you offered Aiden Hirst my dowry, Brother? Is he to be my husband?"

"Must you always be smart?"

"Sorry." She surrendered, wanting to keep on his good side. "So, what did the nice lad want?"

"He came bearing a dinner invitation to Ardsley this evening."

"Did you accept?" she asked worriedly.

Ben's brow furrowed. "No, I had to decline. Sarah and I already have dinner plans for this evening. Why are you acting so concerned?"

"I'm not concerned," Catie replied as coolly as possible.

"Good, because I returned the invitation for this Friday night," he said. "And I would prefer, dear sister, that you leave the serving of young Aiden's dinner to the staff."

"Yes, Bennet," she acquiesced softly, obediently, so obedient in fact that her brother gave her a wry smile.

"What did you want, Catherine?"

"Want?"

"I assume you brought me my lunch for a reason. What is it?" he asked as he reached over and moved the tray in front of him.

"I'm just bored." She slumped back in the chair again. "Will this rain ever cease?"

Ben studied her for a moment. He was busy and considered sending his sister on her way. But he did have to eat and so decided to entertain her for a few minutes. "You could be practicing your instruments. I haven't heard you play at all this summer."

"I'm not *that* bored!"

Ben pointed at her with his spoon. "That attitude is the reason I'm left with nothing to do but stand by and listen while Donald Tillman prattles on and on about Audrey and all her accomplishments on the violin."

Offended, Catie sat up again. "That's not fair, Bennet! Audrey's mother is a professional. Audrey was *born* with talent!"

"And your grandmother on Mother's side was a concert pianist! But that makes no difference. One does not inherit talent, Catherine. It is earned through diligent practice."

"The only thing Audrey Tillman practices is how to be a ridiculous flirt!" Catie argued, with instant regret. What her brother derived from her attack on Audrey Tillman she did not know because she wouldn't dare look at him. But from the lack of sound, she could tell that he had stopped eating. Catie only hoped he would not relate her criticism of Audrey in any way to Sean Kelly and thought it best to move the conversation in another direction.

"Speaking of inherit, do you remember the story Daddy would tell us about Fitzwilliam Darcy and Elizabeth Bennet?"

Ben had not caught up with the discussion, as Catie's offensive remark did give him pause. Then he said, "How could I possibly not remember? I must have suffered through Dad telling you that story a million times. What of it?"

"Rosings Park…from the story, I think I remember Daddy saying that Grandfather Geoffrey had been raised there?" That was of course a lie but an unavoidable one, she rationalized.

Ben looked at his sister briefly then stated with a frankness that surprised her. "Both Father and Grandfather were born to that manor, Catherine, not this one…not Pemberley."

"What?" She was both shocked and confused. "But…then, how did we end up here?"

Ben exhaled a long sigh while in his mind he tried to shorten an explanation that was many generations long. "After old Lady Catherine died, Fitzwilliam and Elizabeth Darcy renewed their relations with Fitzwilliam's cousin, Anne de Bourgh. By then the Darcys had two sons. Their youngest, Geoffrey, was a favorite of his mother's and quickly became a favorite of Anne de Bourgh's as well. Like his mother, Geoffrey Darcy had a kind heart and traveled to Rosings Park on several occasions to comfort Anne through her illnesses. In turn Anne became so attached to Geoffrey that when she died she willed her estate and holdings to him. She had no heirs of her own and — "

"And she knew he was a second son and would receive very little from his own father's estate," Catie said, comprehending. Although her parents had set aside a comfortable inheritance for their daughter, the bulk of her parent's wealth would stay with her brother for Pemberley's safekeeping.

"Yes," Ben replied softly. "She did."

"Then we, you and I, are the descendants of Geoffrey, Fitzwilliam and Elizabeth's second son?"

"Yes," Ben affirmed as his sister gazed around her surroundings as if seeing them for the first time. She met his eyes again with a questioning look that he answered immediately. "Grandfather inherited Pemberley after World War II, Catherine."

"Then what happened to Rosings Park?"

"He sold it."

"Why?" she asked but before Catie could get her answer, there was a small rap at the door.

"Enter," Ben called out.

The door opened and a maid took a couple of steps inside the study and announced, "Mr. Charles Worthington has arrived, sir."

"Thank you. Please inform Mrs. Darcy."

"Yes, sir," she replied and left, closing the door behind her.

"Come along, Catie, Charles hasn't seen you since Christmas, and I'm sure he'll want to say hello." Ben stood up and shrugged into the jacket that was hanging on the back of his chair.

Catie's mind raced with this new information as she walked alongside Ben to the drawing room. "Ben," she finally spoke, "I still don't understand."

"If you're truly interested in the Darcy family history, Catherine, there are volumes in the library that will assist you." Ben told his sister where she could find the records but warned, "However, some of the books are very old and must be handled with extreme care."

Catie nodded so gravely that Ben chuckled. "Relax, Sis, they're not the Dead Sea Scrolls." He put an affectionate hand on her shoulder and led her into the drawing room.

Sarah was already seated and talking to Mr. Worthington when Ben and Catie arrived. It was only in the last six months that Charles Worthington had replaced Horace Harold as Ben's chief legal advisor. Uncle Horace, as Catie called him, was her godfather and had been a great condolence to the Darcy siblings in the years since their father's death. Until recently that is. Catie knew that Ben had had a falling out with Uncle Horace. Tensions between the two men were obvious when the Darcys spent Easter with the Harolds. It may have been unfair of Catie, but she blamed Charles Worthington for the rift. Still, he was a guest and courtesy was expected, so she entered the drawing room wearing a pleasant smile.

Though not overly handsome, Charles Worthington was a nicely built man with a thick head of brownish-blond hair that curled in odd places. He dressed extremely well and always reeked heavily of cologne. "Ben Darcy!" He stood when he saw Ben and Catie. "Who is this young woman next to you? I don't believe I recognize her."

"It's me, Mr. Worthington... Catie," she replied, giggling sweetly at his joke, though she inwardly moaned. Many of her brother's friends and business associates liked to play silly games with her as if she were incapable of carrying on an intelligent conversation.

"Catie Darcy, it can't be; good Lord, how you've grown since I saw you last." Catie smiled but knew, as she was sure Mr. Worthington knew, she hadn't grown an inch since Christmas. "And such a pretty girl, I do believe you get prettier every time I see you!"

"Thank you, Mr. Worthington," she answered politely but unimpressed.

Charles Worthington smiled and patted her shoulder like a puppy that he no longer wanted to play with and turned his attentions back to Ben and Sarah.

Half an hour later Catie sat begrudgingly yet properly attentive to a conversation she had no part in. When able to do so unnoticed, she glanced out the window and smiled in delight as the clouds began to pull sluggishly away from each other. Blinding rays of sun began to pour in through the panes, and their bright warmth spilled across the oak floors and landed teasingly at Catie's feet. Wanting to be away, she inadvertently sighed so loud that Sarah gave her a subtle disapproving look.

A tray of refreshments was brought in but before there was any partaking, Mr. Worthington's mode of dialogue changed drastically from friendly and informal to more serious.

Legal words like "negotiation" and "proposal" would have normally fallen on deaf ears in regards to Catie Darcy, but when she heard the name Wesley Howell, she sat up.

"Who is Wesley Howell?" she asked.

"No one, dearest," Ben replied hastily. Then he smiled and with a more composed tone, said, "We'll not keep you any longer, Catherine. I'm sure you have more interesting things to do with your afternoon."

Catie nodded, disappointed, wishing she could stay and hear what Mr. Worthington had to say.

Charles Worthington came to his feet as Catie did, bearing a tinge of color due to his obvious lack of discretion. "It was nice to see you again, Catherine."

"Yes, cheers, and I shall show myself out. I'm rather used to rambling old houses."

"What was that about?" Sarah asked Ben quietly.

"Always true to form, my dear, my sister is being cheeky."

PEMBERLEY'S LIBRARY WAS FILLED WITH an accumulation of efforts from generations of Darcys. Every master and mistress of the house had made considerable contributions to the estate's collection over the last three hundred years. The room itself was predictable. Aside from an oversized fireplace and a set of French style doors that led to a small terrace, the walls were lined with shelves packed full of volumes old and new. A large fresco adorned the ceiling — fat cherubs holding lambs and chasing chickens — while loosely draped, full-bodied women smiled and looked on at their antics. Of the manor's many rooms, this was Catie's favorite. She found escape by a crackling fire here on cold winter days, snuggled in the large leather chair that her father loved. Even now, his reading glasses lay on the side table atop the last book he read. This was at Ben's insistence, and no one dared move them.

Her nostrils flared as she entered, attacked by the smell of old books and a pungent fresh application of lemon oil. She closed the large door to the hall.

"How'd I do?" Aiden Hirst asked, and Catie jumped. He laughed and took her by the shoulders. "I didn't mean to frighten you."

"Wh-what are you doing here?" She felt suddenly cold.

"Ingratiating myself in your brother's good will, what else?" A crafty grin creased his mouth, and Catie pulled from his grasp.

"You shouldn't be in here," she whispered, glancing apprehensively at the door.

"Now, now, don't play Miss Innocent, I know this isn't the first time you have deceived your brother. Poor chap had no idea his little sister had attended an unchaperoned party at my house last spring." Clicking his tongue, Aiden scooted casually upon a shiny library table.

Catie's stomach tightened and her eyes grew round. "Did you tell him?"

she cried.

"Give me a little credit, will ya?" He raked his fingers through his hair — a mop of loose, dirty blond curls that always returned to their rightful position each time he nervously ran his fingers through them, which was often, Catie noticed.

"What was your story?" he asked, grinning still. "No, let me guess…the *cinema*."

"How did you know?" She didn't like this interrogation.

He laughed again. "It's always the cinema. You're quite the little imp, Miss Darcy. I must admit…I'm impressed."

"Well, don't be." Catie was starting to get annoyed. "I didn't deceive Ben purposefully."

"Sure, Cate," he said slyly. "Whatever makes you feel better."

"It's Catie and I'm not trying to make myself feel better," she snippily corrected him. "It happens to be the truth. When I told my brother I was going to the cinema, I truly believed I was. I could never lie to him about something like that."

"Yet, you never told him the truth afterward." Aiden leaned close and whispered, "Touché."

Catie looked abashed. It was true. She hadn't confessed to Ben. It wasn't his punishment she feared but rather his disappointment. That she couldn't bear.

Aiden slid off the table and began looking around the library. He picked up and thumbed through a few odd books while she regarded the door with concern. She didn't know what Ben might say if they were caught alone. He didn't even know they knew each other. And truthfully they didn't. She had only met Aiden that one time. He reached for her father's book, and she tried to stop him. "No!"

"Some rare first edition?" he asked, knocking the glasses to the side and picking the book up.

"It was my father's." Catie took the book from him and placed it back on the table. "Please don't touch it."

"Sorry," he said, watching her put the glasses back. Shoving his hands in his pockets, Aiden took an uninterested look around the old room as if he were horribly bored with its quaintness. "Well, I suppose I'll leave you to your studies. What does the old fellow have you slaving over this summer anyway? Latin?"

"Uh…yes…Latin, and I best knuckle down or the old fellow will have my head."

Aiden laughed at this. "You shire girls do like to impress Daddy, eh?"

"Brother — and, yes, I do."

"Friday then," he said, stepping close and lifting her face with his fingertips. "Just don't slave too hard. I'll not be happy if I have a dull dinner companion."

"Cheerio, Aiden," Catie said shortly, uncomfortable with his closeness.

He tilted his head like he might kiss her, causing a sudden panic in Catie's midsection. Never having been kissed before, she had long dreamed of the moment, but this wasn't right; Aiden wasn't right. She turned away, and he chuckled but was not amused. The laugh sounded more like the cat that just lost the mouse but wouldn't give up his chase.

Instead of going out of the door that led to the hall, Aiden left by way of the terrace, hopping over the balustrade with youthful ease. Catie turned back to her father's book and glasses. She knew they had been moved many times over the years for dusting, but she hated that he had touched them.

There was no searching for the books; their location was precisely where Ben had directed. Catie took them to the leather chair and lounged comfortably to read. The centuries-old Darcy records were in excellent condition for their age, but eighteenth and nineteenth century Darcys were of little interest to Catie. It was the twentieth century Darcys, in particular one Mary Elizabeth Darcy, about whom she was most curious. Reading carefully through the pages, she unwittingly happened upon the entry of her father's death.

William Geoffrey Darcy b. 31 December 1929 s. of Geoffrey Fitzwilliam Darcy and Lucille Isaacs Darcy m. The Hon. Margaret Cecil Sumner 1 June 1951 daughter of Lord Byron Sumner c. one son Bennet Fitzwilliam Darcy b. 19 January 1956 one daughter Catherine Elizabeth Darcy b. 6 November 1970 d. 10 May 1979

She ran her fingers across his name several times and took a deep breath to calm the emotion swelling in her chest. Catie and her father had shared a very special bond. He had a partiality for her driven by both the loss of her mother, and Catie's uncanny resemblance to the woman. Catie had long ago accepted that she would never truly come to terms with his death. Her mother, however, held a different sort of grief as her love and attention were never known. She was a mystery to the girl, an unknown, and what Catie naturally sought next was the name of the woman she never knew.

The Hon. Margaret Sumner Darcy wife of William Geoffrey Darcy d. 6 November 1970, Complications of childbirth

Catherine Elizabeth Darcy b. 6 November 1970 daughter of William and Margaret Darcy

The entry was harder to absorb than Catie had anticipated. *Complications of childbirth.* Remorse overpowered her thoughts. The information was not new. But somehow, seeing it written down, forever registered alongside the date of her birth, caused a sharp spike to form in her chest. *Why had she survived?* She closed the book and rested her head against the back of the chair. Catie reached into her shirt and pulled out a locket hanging on a long chain. She hesitated for a second then released the clasp to view a picture of her mother. Margaret Darcy was standing to her side with a swollen belly; it was the only picture of mother and daughter together. She sighed deeply and moved on to Mary Darcy.

Mary Elizabeth Darcy b. 17 March 1902 daughter of William Corbin Darcy and Ester Doyle Darcy m. Arthur Thomas Howell 6 September 1919 c. one son Thomas Darcy Howell b. 15 April 1920 d. at Pemberley House 10 October 1968

Arthur Thomas Howell d. 15 February 1945

Thomas Darcy Howell d. 2 August 1945, Malaria

Mary Darcy did in fact marry Arthur Howell. They also had a son, Thomas Darcy Howell. But nowhere could Catie find the name Wesley Howell. Mary had outlived both her husband and son. Thomas died at the early age of twenty-five after contracting malaria while on a religious mission to Africa. According to the family's own records, Thomas had never married nor had any children. Interestingly, Mary Darcy Howell lived out her life at Pemberley after Catie's grandfather had taken proprietorship of the estate and sold Rosings Park.

Wesley Howell was not mentioned. His connection with the Darcys or the Howells of Pemberley, if any, was not to be found in the Darcy library. "Wesley

Howell," she whispered. "Who are you?"

Chapter 9

The Davenport School, established in the mid-nineteenth century by its founder Evelyn Davenport, was no ordinary school for girls. A small remote institute created for the daughters of Britain's aristocracy, admittance was for the selected few. Over the last hundred some odd years, very little had changed at Davenport, in effect, making Catherine Elizabeth Darcy of Pemberley Estate in Derbyshire one of those selected few. Her mother had attended Davenport and Catie's placement at the school was arranged well before her father died.

There was much public interest after her father's tragic accident, which caused Ben to close Pemberley House to visiting tourists. He also had Catie removed from the village school and privately tutored at home for the two years prior to her admittance into Davenport, making the initial separation difficult for Catie. She clung to him, wailed, and begged him not to leave her. Ben, however, was resolved and sternly scolded his sister for acting like a baby. In an embarrassing initial separation, he had to forcibly pry her arms from his waist before handing her over to the housemother, leaving his sister screaming after him. When Ben reached the car, he heard a noise and looked up to see her blotchy, tear-stained face staring down at him as she banged desperately on the window. It took everything Bennet Darcy had in him to put his little black sports car into gear and pull away from the school that day.

During the rainy drive back to Pemberley, Ben fought back his own emotions and reminded himself that this was what his mother and father would have wanted. She was a Darcy; she must stand strong. A family riddled with tragedies notwithstanding, Catie would have a proper English education.

Although his convictions were solid, they didn't ease the throbbing ache in his heart. The memory of his little sister in that window haunted Ben and made him sick with worry. To ease his conscience, he called the headmistress's office twice a day for the next two weeks to check on her. He never knew it, but Ben Darcy had been dubbed the fussiest mother hen Davenport's administrators had ever encountered.

Catie remained at Davenport and soon made friends, many friends in fact, a pleasant and welcomed change from the isolation of Pemberley. By the beginning of Catie's second term, her brother barely received a kiss before she hurried off to join her schoolmates, and, like a father, he suffered a slight pang of regret that she no longer cried for him.

Davenport was noted for its excellence in academics, its dedication to the arts, and the development of proper moral character through the teachings of scripture. But within the circle of the privileged, it was also well known that Davenport prided itself on a record of virtue, in particular the virtue of the eleven- to eighteen-year-old girls in its charge.

Socialization with boys was strictly supervised and dating completely forbidden. On the rare occasion when there was a social gathering with a neighboring boy's school, the watchful eyes were so keenly observant, hardly any of the adolescents even ventured conversation. As minimal as this was, it was all the experience Catie Darcy had with the opposite sex thus far.

She might have been a tad unsophisticated but Catie knew her own heart. She was flattered by Aiden Hirst's sudden attention, but it was Sean Kelly who had begun to occupy her thoughts. He stirred her emotions — all of them. He challenged her until her insides boiled. He humbled her, brought her to tears, and yet he made her feel — really feel. He also made her giggle like the little girl she remembered. He didn't pity her. He was like no one she had ever met before.

When the rain finally ended, so had Catie's tolerance for being indoors any longer. Wearing her hair down due to Sean's compliment, she set out for the stables.

Finding him with the chestnut thoroughbred, she slowly approached but didn't dare touch the fence. The horse was not only bridled but saddled as well, and his demeanor was much more relaxed. At the sight of someone unfamiliar however, he neighed anxiously and thrashed his head. Taking a step back Catie said, "I don't think he likes me."

Sean couldn't help but smile at her cautiousness. "It has naught to do with like, Catie. Our friend Thunder here has an issue with trust."

"Thunder?"

"Aye, Geoffrey named him that because it was thundering when Mr. Darcy brought him and George down here to see the horse yesterday." Sean rubbed Thunder's nose then came out of the paddock and leaned against the gate, his arms crossed. "Which reminds me: you and I need to have a talk."

Catie's brows knitted. "About?"

"You never told me that you've had a bad experience on a horse. How am I to teach you if you're not honest with me?"

Catie felt more than a little disbelief. She had never told anyone about getting thrown from that pony when she was younger, and no one had seen her. Hoping her expression wasn't betraying her, she replied, "I have no idea what you're talking about."

"Come now, Catie, I saw your face Sunday when that horse spooked. You were terrified."

"Yes, I was! He charged at me. Who wouldn't have been terrified?"

"Then what about your gallop? As soon as Chloe picks up a good speed, you pull out of position to slow her down. And..." he wavered.

"*And?*"

"And I saw you...walking back to the stable that first day." Sean stopped short of telling her he also saw her crying.

"You were watching me?"

"I doubled back to make sure you got back to the stables safely."

Catie stared at him. She didn't want to talk about it. It was in the past, over and gone like her father. "As I said, I have no idea what you're talking about."

"You're lying."

Catie's mouth fell open. "How dare you say such — "

"I may not know everything, Catie Darcy," he interrupted her, his accent growing suddenly heavy. "But I know horses and I know people around horses. I also know fear and reluctance when I see it. Problem is...I don't know whether you are afraid or holding back for some other reason. Only you can answer that."

She glared at him. "This may come as a shock to you being a *wee* bit pigheaded and all, but you're wrong. I'm holding nothing back, and I am certainly not afraid!"

"*Pig*headed?"

"You said it, not me!"

They stared at each other for a moment, he looking down at her with folded arms, and she with her mouth pursed. Finally Sean walked away, cutting his eyes at her as he did.

"Saddle your horse and meet me in the schooling ring, lass," he said over his shoulder.

A bit befuddled, she watched him strut away. She hadn't expected to meet with the same bossy and unbearable riding instructor after their trip to the Peak District. *Hadn't they shared a moment?* "Insufferable ass," she uttered spitefully under her breath and went to saddle her horse.

An afternoon of trotting for a girl whose concentration was most assuredly not on the task at hand proved to be long and frustrating. Catie's posting rhythm was so off that Sean had resorted to calling out her rise and fall, which only distracted her more.

Afterwards, Catie was in the stable with Chloe. She removed the bridle and turned to get Chloe's halter only to find it dangling from Sean's fingers.

"Thank you," she said softly.

"Well?" He raised an inquiring eyebrow.

"Well what?"

"Are you going to tell me or not?"

Catie Darcy may have been the perfect image of her mother, but she definitely had her father's blood running through her veins — blood that at times ran hot, even when she didn't particularly want it to.

"I am not!" she sharply replied and, taking the saddle, walked off to put it away. When she returned, he was gone. Catie looked down the long cobblestone floor to the large stable doorway but he was nowhere in sight. She would have liked to think herself happy she had sent him away. But in truth, his leaving tugged at her in a way she had not felt before. "Insufferable ass," she whispered again.

GUESTS FOR DINNER MEANT THE house was brightly lit. The hall and dining room glowed with anticipation as it had when the house was first opened to visitors so many centuries ago. Day maids stayed on past their shift to help and bustled to and fro at Rose's direction, dodging Catie who remained underfoot.

"Catherine Darcy, can you not see we're busy?" Rose fussed for the fourth or fifth time. "Run along, child, and get ready before your guests arrive."

Although Catie did try and stay out of the way, she didn't leave. She wanted to be close to Rose, even if the woman was a bit ill-tempered that evening. It was stupid, she knew, but Catie was a little nervous and being near her Nan always made her feel better. Though Ben and Sarah weren't aware of Aiden's true intentions, Catie fully understood his purpose. She didn't necessarily dislike Aiden, but neither was she completely sure that she wanted him ingratiating himself with her brother.

When Rose noticed her scolding fell on deaf ears, her keen motherly senses brought her to Catie's side. She gave a few last directives then put an affectionate arm over Catie's shoulder. "Come, dear, I'll help you dress."

A half hour later, Rose had her charge in a proper frock and sat resting as she watched Catie tug at her tights. "Careful not to run those," she said.

"Yes, Nan," Catie answered, grinning gratefully. "What are you having for dinner tonight?"

"Oh, Sean and I will probably go down to the village for a pizza."

Catie stopped tugging and looked up. "I wish I could go with you. I hate boring dinner parties."

"Well, you can't." Rose gave her a hurried wave. "Keep tugging."

"I don't see why not. I used to eat with you when Ben and Sarah had dinner parties."

"You're not a child anymore. Aren't you the one constantly reminding me of that?" Rose asked, and Catie nodded begrudgingly. "Yes, I thought so. Now, which shoes are you going to wear?"

LAWRENCE AND ELEANOR HIRST WERE a childless couple who doted excessively on their nephew. They had seen him through the best schools and relished greatly in his accomplishments, the latest being his upcoming admittance to Cambridge University. "…Aiden won the mathematics prize for three years. I say Trinity will be fortunate to have him." Eleanor Hirst winked at her nephew after a long praising speech. Catie wondered if she should applaud.

"I'm a Trinity man myself, Aiden," Ben put in, "but contrarily I was fortunate they'd have me."

"As am I, sir." Aiden spoke humbly, smiling affectionately at his aunt. "My aunt believes in my genius because she never sees the long hours of studying I must apply myself to."

"That's nonsense!" Eleanor Hirst contradicted vehemently and went into another bombastic rave. "That boy was multiplying before…"

Catie watched Ben and Sarah vigilantly. If Sarah relaxed her formal posture and dropped her proper hostess air, she liked her guests — felt comfortable around them. With Ben it was a bit more complicated. His constant reserve made his true feelings only known to the astute eye. He appeared pleasantly engaged with the Hirsts, but then Catie caught the twitch. It was small, but a tiny twitch at the corner of Ben's mouth told more than he would ever care to disclose.

By dessert she had caught the twitch several more times, and Sarah was still playing mistress of the manor like a bad BBC sitcom.

In truth, the Hirsts weren't bad company, but they were clearly "putting on airs" for Ben and Sarah. It wasn't the first evening the Darcys had suffered through such charades, but it always made for a tedious affair. Even Aiden was all manners and dignity. He showed little interest in Catie, choosing instead to hang on her brother's every word, even laughing at Ben's quirky jokes.

When the evening was finally over, the party gathered in the hall for their adieus. It was only then that Aiden caught Catie's eye and gave a slight raise of an eyebrow. Catie knew he was asking her to gauge his performance and returned an equally slight nod. Aiden smiled, and Catie smiled back. She couldn't help it really; Aiden Hirst *was* a handsome lad.

"I have never been so grateful for ten o'clock in all of my life," Catie heard Ben say as she closed the door. She turned to see him sliding out of his dinner jacket as Sarah leaned clumsily against him and removed her heels.

Always the diplomat, Sarah gave him a reproving eye and amended, "Yes, it was rather a long evening but pleasant enough. I for one enjoy the occasional dinner party."

Ben responded to this statement with an incredulous look, and Sarah tilted her head meaningfully.

Though fairly well schooled in his wife's nonverbal discourse, it still took several seconds for Ben to make sense of her remark and to confirm the meaning behind the look she was giving him. "*Ohh*, right!" he said, then turned to his sister. "Good night, Catie."

Passing a petulant look over her guardians, Catie folded her arms and sighed huffily before walking away.

"Now what's wrong with her?" he asked his wife, watching the rigid, offended form mount the stairway.

"My guess would be your inability to be subtle," Sarah said and stepped back into the drawing room to be near the hearth where a small summer fire had been laid.

"*My* inability to be subtle?" he questioned, following her. "What about that *watch what you're saying the kid's still in the room* look on your face? That wasn't exactly discreet, my dear."

"Took *you* long enough to figure it out."

"I've had a long tiresome evening and several Scotches. Please forgive me if my skills in mind reading are a bit wanting at present."

"Oh, pour yourself another; maybe it will improve your temper." Sarah waved him towards the sideboard and seated herself near the heat. "What do you make of the Hirsts' sudden interest?" she asked, turning from the flickering flame to her husband.

Ben held up the decanter but she declined the offer with a small shake of her head. "Lawrence and my father were friends, I told you that."

"You don't think…" Sarah stopped.

"I don't think what?" He sat down and pulled her feet into his lap.

"Catie," Sarah said. "You don't think Aiden Hirst is interested in Catie, do you?"

"I most certainly do not!" he said, looking scandalized. "The two had never even met before I introduced them. And in any case, Catie is far too young yet to have boys calling. I'm sure it's nothing more than Lawrence Hirst being a busybody. He probably heard I was re-opening Pemberley to tourists and wanted the details. You know how tongues begin to wag with the slightest piece of gossip."

"Your sister's almost seventeen, Bennet," Sarah said in an almost consolatory tone.

"So you keep reminding me." He swallowed the remainder of his Scotch and turned to the fire. He stared at the flames for a moment, then turned back to her and said in a hoarse whisper, "She was as awkward as a newborn foal around Aiden in my study the other day. She's not ready, Sarah, but when she is…I'll be ready too. I promise."

"See that you are, darling." Sarah smiled and nestled against him. "See that you are."

Chapter 10

Bennet Darcy's Monday morning rides out over his estate were not of a business nature but rather a personal one. He was visiting not collecting, offering advice not orders, and making himself accessible to those who lived and worked on Pemberley land. These visits were a long-standing Pemberley ritual, like the fox hunt on Boxing Day and the annual garden party. The farmers and their families looked forward to having Mr. Darcy call and usually had a meat pie or fresh baked buttered crumpets for his visits.

On Monday morning, Ben stalked heavily down the long corridor of the family wing. So far, the morning was not going as planned, and he was rather disjointed. George had a fever and the sniffles, Sarah was nauseous, and Catie, who was to join him on his ride, had yet to stir from her bed. Fortunately, Rose arrived on the scene and relieved Ben from any further running back and forth from his and Sarah's room to the nursery, delivering instructions to Mrs. Newell on George's behalf. Now that Rose had taken over, all that was left to do was to take Geoffrey to breakfast and rouse his sister.

"Catherine," he said loudly as he opened her door, his soft morning voice having faded over an hour ago. "Be down to breakfast in fifteen minutes!"

Catie pulled the covers over her head. "All right," she grumbled with an obvious lack of enthusiasm. She did want to go. As a matter of fact she looked forward to spending some time alone with Ben and was rather disappointed when they had to cancel the outing last Monday due to the weather. But Catie loathed rising before eight when on holiday from school.

Fifteen minutes came and went, and it was pushing hard on half an hour by the time she made it to the breakfast room. There was only Ben, stashed behind a newspaper, and Geoffrey eating a bowl of porridge.

"Where are Sarah and George?" she asked as she sat down and unfolded her napkin.

"George has a cold, and Sarah will be down shortly," said the newspaper, adding accusingly, "You're late."

"Sorry." She rolled her eyes. She would have argued that a woman needs more than fifteen minutes to ready for such an outing, but she wasn't awake enough yet to state a proper case. And, since they were in for a very long morning together, Catie much preferred her companion be friend rather than foe.

With her usual grandmotherly smile, Mrs. Graham came forward with freshly squeezed orange juice. She was an elderly servant who had come to Pemberley a young woman forty years ago. Her late husband had been Pemberley's last butler, an extravagance Ben believed the family could live without nowadays. The widow was up in years, but adamantly refused to retire. The Darcys and Rose knew Mrs. Graham had no family to care for her, so she continued living in the butler's apartment and served the family their breakfast every morning to be useful.

"No, thank you, Mrs. Graham." Catie waved off the juice. "I'll have coffee."

"She'll have the juice." Her brother's voice emanated once again from behind the paper. "Juice benefits the body; coffee does not."

Looking over at Ben's half empty coffee cup nettled Catie greatly. Foe or not, she would have her coffee. "How's that, Bennet?" she asked peevishly.

Ben lowered one corner of the paper and looked at her. "Did you not hear me say George has the sniffles? The juice will keep you from catching them."

"The sniffles will be the least of my worries if I fall asleep in my saddle and tumble to my death because I wasn't allowed my coffee."

Ben heaved an annoyed sigh. "Must life be so melodramatic, Catherine?"

"Only until I've had some caffeine, Brother. After that life becomes rather dull."

"Then please, Mrs. Graham, pour my sister some coffee so she can spare us any further theatrics," Ben said and snapped the newspaper back to its former position.

Breakfast was served, and Catie's eyes went wide with astonishment. On her plate were three fried eggs, sausage, bacon, fried tomatoes and mushrooms, beans, and toast. "What's all this?" she asked, waving her hand over the steaming meal.

"*That*, my dear sister, is a proper English fry up." Ben casually turned a page as he spoke.

"Yes, I can see that, but I didn't ask for a fry up. Did I?"

"As I said, you were late to breakfast. So I took the liberty of ordering for you the same breakfast as I did for myself." This made perfect sense to him as they were both in for a long ride that morning.

Looking at the back of the paper in disbelief, Catie figured that the coffee was victory enough for one morning and decided to eat as much she could. That was going to be easier said than done however, for the eggs were not cooked as well-done as she liked, and the show of disgust on her face when she speared the barely cooked yolk made Geoffrey giggle.

Catie smiled mischievously at her nephew. Teasing Geoffrey would be much better sport than choking down the large plate of food, and so another yolk suffered a violent attack at the end of her fork. Geoffrey's giggle erupted into an all-out guffaw, and his father folded the paper in defeat.

With his cup, Ben gestured for more coffee as he jokingly scolded the two. "Mrs. Graham, is it not a sad state of affairs when the master of Pemberley is unable to read his morning news because of so much commotion at the breakfast table?"

"Oh, yes, Mr. Darcy, a sad state of affairs indeed." She winked at Ben and clicked her tongue disapprovingly.

Sarah entered, looking a bit pale but bearing her usual soft smile. She refused her tea, requesting ginger ale with a slice of dry toast instead. "Catie," she looked over at her and remarked. "It's nice to have you at breakfast for a change, dear." Catie smiled in response as Sarah gazed at the other end of the table. "And Mr. Darcy too... my, Geoffrey, we *are* honored this morning."

Looking puzzled, Ben rebutted, "I beg your pardon, madam; Mr. Darcy is at this table *every* morning."

"I'm sorry, Bennet, but how could I know? Normally there is a newspaper staring back at me from that end of the table," replied his wife stiffly. Sarah obviously wasn't herself.

Like spectators at a tennis match, Catie and Geoffrey's heads snapped to the opposite end of the table to see the return. Ben said, "Regrettably, I had to abandon the newspaper this morning as these two woke up quite full of themselves and made reading rather impossible." He gestured to the miscreants.

"It was a sad state of affairs, Mummy, because Daddy is a master!" Geoffrey said and grinned, happy to have something to add to the conversation.

Sarah smiled sweetly at her son. "Geoffrey, darling, please don't encourage your father's pretentious manners."

The joke was lost on Geoffrey, but Catie fully understood Sarah's humor and snickered.

The snicker brought Sarah's attention to Catie and in turn to Catie's plate. Shocked at the amount of food, Sarah gasped. "Good heavens, Catie!" She would have said more, but the runny eggs made her stop.

Catie watched as a strange shade of green washed over Sarah's face. Then, cupping her mouth, she pushed urgently away from the table and ran from the room, Ben fast on her heels.

SITTING ON THE FRONT STEPS, blinded by the sun that was now warming the large façade of the house, Catie rested her face on folded arms. Then she untied and retied her boots and made small talk with Clancy, who had brought the horses up from the stables. Geronimo, Ben's horse, was an impressive animal, solid black and a good two hands taller than Chloe. Being a lover of all things equine, the American Wild West fascinated Bennet Darcy as a boy and was reflected in the names of every horse he had owned.

When Ben finally exited the house he bid Catie to her feet with a simple, "Mount up!"

"How's Sarah?" she asked, double-stepping to keep up with him. "Maybe we shouldn't leave her."

"Rose is with her, and I was shooed from the room." Ben settled Catie in her saddle and smiled at the worried look on her face. "She's fine, Sis, and you and I've work to do." He patted her leg and then mounted Geronimo.

The first order of the day was to observe Catie's improved riding skills. Ben was pleased with her post, but when she moved easily between her trots and canters, all while keeping her posting rhythm, he beamed. Quite pleased with herself, Catie pulled Chloe to a halt alongside Geronimo.

"Pretty good, eh, Brother?" she said proudly.

"Jolly good, Catherine! That Kelly lad is quite the riding instructor."

A cross look spread over her face. "I beg your pardon, Ben. These are my accomplishments, not Sean Kelly's!"

"And so they are!" He grinned. "Either way you've made significant progress.

And you, my dear sister, will finish the full six weeks of riding lessons as we agreed."

"But…I thought you said we would talk about it." Of course Catie no longer had a desire to quit her riding lessons but would've preferred making the decision for herself.

"I believe we just did," he replied as he took off, calling back over his shoulder for her to hurry along.

Rolling her eyes for the second time that morning, Catie pressed Chloe into a canter and followed her brother.

As the Darcy siblings trotted between growing crops of corn, wheat, and barley, Ben pointed out to Catie which fields were leased and the few that were still maintained by Pemberley. Throughout history the estate had always been a fully working farm, but now there was more profit to be made by leasing the land to dairies and food companies. Pemberley's acreage had grown significantly in the nineteenth century, but was reduced just as significantly during the early part of the twentieth century. Currently the estate was just over four thousand acres of grazing fields and rich, arable farmland.

While Ben talked, Catie glanced down the valley and over sheep grazing between the hedgerows to Lambton, the ruins of a little hamlet that sat at the base of a knoll. At one time the village had been essential to the success of an estate the size of Pemberley, but now the ancient structures were crumbling, and scraggly trees and brush grew between walls where life once existed.

"When did Lambton burn down, Ben?" she asked over his talk of farming.

Ben smiled. As usual his sister was more interested in Pemberley's romantic past than its agricultural accomplishments. "Over a hundred years ago. The fields on that side of the river caught fire and winds swept the blaze into the village. There was no reason to rebuild. Most folks had left to work in factories or on the railroad by then."

As he watched his sister stare wistfully down at the remains, a whiff of burning came to Ben like a ghost. He turned to see a billowing cloud of smoke rising from an overseer's cottage. "Blast," he said under his breath.

"What?" Catie asked, snapped from her reverie.

"It is far too dry and windy to be burning rubbish today. Come, Sis, we must call on the Ledfords first."

Ben steered Geronimo up a narrow dirt road with Catie following close behind. Of the hundred or so cottages that once dotted the estate's property in the years when sowing was done by horse and plow, and reaping by scythes and strong backs, less than a dozen remained. Of these, most were occupied by employees of the companies that leased Pemberley's fertile low lands.

Once the cottage was in sight, Catie could see a man tending a small fire set away from the house and a woman hanging laundry on a wash line. The man stopped poking at the hot embers and approached the riders.

Ben dismounted, and Catie was promptly at his side. "Good day, Mr. Ledford." He offered his hand.

As the men exchanged greetings Catie glanced at the woman putting out the wash. She stayed at her task and made no acknowledgement of her visitors. Standing at the door was a small, dirty faced girl who stared intently at Catie. She gave the little girl a friendly wave, but the child didn't return the gesture.

"….increasing winds are forecasted," she heard Ben say as she came back to the conversation. "I'm sorry, but you'll need to douse the fire."

"Aye, Mr. Darcy, it's naught but a bit of kitchen rubbish that I can see to later," the man amiably agreed.

"Thank you, Mr. Ledford, one cannot be too careful," Ben replied, and then called out to Mrs. Ledford. She clearly wasn't the talkative sort but stopped her work in order to respond to his polite queries about herself and the children.

As they spoke, Catie looked back at Mr. Ledford and the small hairs on her neck rose. Taking advantage of Ben's turned back, the man stared freely at the young budding flower before him. Dragging his tongue across his parched lips, Mr. Ledford let his eyes travel deliberately and slowly down her form.

Catie felt uncomfortable, violated. Mr. Ledford smiled at her in a way that caused gooseflesh to stipple on her arms. She nervously touched her brother's elbow.

Ben turned abruptly, and, although Catie was unaware of it, he caught the leer. Leaning down, Ben spoke in a low angry voice that caused a spike of fear to fill her stomach. "Mount your horse and ride out."

Catie immediately obeyed him, but curiosity would not keep her from looking back over her shoulder. Ben moved close to Mr. Ledford and words were exchanged. Their voices were low but heated. She saw Mr. Ledford wave his hands in an, "I don't want any trouble" fashion. The conversation was brief. Ben left quietly, but the look in his eyes could have set Lambton ablaze again.

Catie hurriedly moved Chloe down the path and waited at the bottom of the drive. When Ben caught up, he didn't look at her. She privately counseled herself on whether or not she should ask what had happened, but the fear in her stomach won the internal debate and curiosity was defeated. She remained silent.

They had not gone far when Ben stopped his horse and called his sister over to him. Pointing to the ground he asked her, "What is this?"

Catie looked where he was pointing but saw nothing.

"Are these tracks from your bicycle, Catherine?"

Catie looked again and saw her tire treads from a muddier day. "They are," she said cautiously.

"You have been this far down the river on your bicycle?"

"I have," she confirmed, cautious still.

Ben drew in and released a deep breath as he turned and glanced back in the direction of Ledford's cottage. She waited for him to say more, but he only motioned for her to move on. His anger was not for his sister but rather himself. Sarah had tried to tell him, but Ben had preferred to turn a blind eye to his sister's maturity, leaving her in possession of a woman's body but uneducated on the evils of man. *How could he have let her stray so far from the house?* He shuddered when he thought of what might have happened had Catie come upon Ledford alone.

In silent contemplation over the next half hour, Ben decided that there was no help for it, Mr. Ledford must be evicted. Regret for the family was a small price to pay for the safety of others. *How dare that man look at his little sister like that?*

Having matters settled in his mind, Ben became slightly better company, and Catie was glad for the return of conversation. Now in the far outskirts of their estate, where she had seldom visited, Catie watched as her brother stopped and spoke to everyone who crossed their paths. Bennet Darcy was not just at ease with the rural farmers and country people, he was at home. He even rolled up his sleeves and spent the better part of an hour helping to restart a tractor that had seen better days.

"Not a piece of Pemberley machinery," he was quick to inform her upon remounting his horse.

Catie smiled up at him. This was the Bennet Darcy she had fallen in love with as a child: strong, handsome, and good to those who depended on him.

The morning waned and the wind picked up as Ben had forecast. Finished with their business, they headed back home. Catie was dusty and exhausted. For several hours she had suffered talk relating to fishing, hunting, crops, and the weather. She was even offered a bowl of rabbit stew with the assurance that every ingredient had come from Pemberley soil, including the rabbit. Catie politely declined and watched her brother finish off his stew by mopping the bowl clean with the accompanying brown bread. She laughed softly to herself, thinking how Sarah would have scolded his manners.

The return trip moved along faster, as most work had stopped for the midday meal. A narrow drive they had passed earlier now echoed with the strums of a guitar, and the music persuaded Ben down the lane with a tired and hungry sister in tow.

"Maybe you shouldn't have refused the rabbit stew, Sis," was the reply she received for her complaints.

"I don't eat cute furry animals, Bennet!"

They approached a small cottage surrounded by a stone fence, and Catie saw that a man in a wheelchair was playing the smooth, folk-like tunes. Seeing Ben and Geronimo, the man stopped strumming and put down the instrument. Smiling broadly, he threw up his hand and yelled, "Bennet Darcy! Halloo, lad."

Once on the ground Ben motioned for Catie to join him, which she did though she hated the thought of another mount. Chloe seemed to get taller and taller as the morning wore on. They entered through a flimsy whitewashed gate and joined the man in the front garden.

Ben put a proud hand on her shoulder. "Mr. Reid, do you remember Catie?"

"Do I? But...she was only a wee lassie when I last saw her! Come close and let me see you, child." Mr. Reid reached for the glasses hanging from a chain around his neck.

His hand still on Catie's shoulder, Ben urged her forward as if to reassure her it was okay. Catie moved a few steps closer and saw Mr. Reid's eyes widen. He turned to Ben and said, "Great God, It's astonishing!"

Ben smiled. "I know; she looks more like Mother every day."

Upon closer inspection Catie could see the man had no legs. Whatever had befallen Mr. Reid had left him with only one stump of a knee. The other leg was missing altogether.

Overly delighted to have the company, Mr. Reid briefly chatted with Ben about local happenings and then, for Catie's sake, went into a long detailed story of how their mother, Mrs. Darcy, had delivered Mr. Reid's eldest daughter.

Margaret Darcy had stopped by to bring supper to his bedridden wife, when the poor woman went into labor. "The midwife was called, but that girl o'mine wasn't waitin' on no midwife. No, Mrs. Darcy herself had to catch the bundle!"

With obvious skepticism Catie looked at Ben, who was now relaxed against the stone wall. "It's all true!" he said.

They reminisced a while longer as the sun reached as high as it was going to get that day. Noticing the hour, Ben declared that the two had better head home before a search party was sent out on their behalf. Shaking Mr. Reid's hand, he asked if there was anything the family needed.

"To be honest, lad, me girl could use work. The missus can't keep up the hours. Her health is not what it used to be. Maggie tried waitin' tables at the local, but…" Mr. Reid stopped and glanced at Catie. "To put it simple, Benny, it weren't a proper place for the lass. The girl can make a tight bed though."

The words had barely left the man's lips when Ben said, "Mr. Reid, that's not necessary. As you know Father left me with strict instructions to care for you and your family."

Mr. Reid sat back as his friendly expression washed suddenly with offence. "Your father blamed himself for my stupidity! Me and mine won't be beholden to no one. The only thing a Reid is going to take from the Darcys is pay for an honest day's work."

Ben glanced down at his boots like a scolded boy. "Yes, sir," he responded quietly.

Catie was stunned. She had never seen anyone speak to Ben that way.

With a slight turn of his chair, Mr. Reid banged on the large plate glass window and called his daughter's name. While they waited for the girl, he told Catie that Maggie was named for the fine lady who brought her into the world.

When the girl appeared at the door she seemed apprehensive, but her father's insistence persuaded her out. Keeping her eyes low, she moved to his side. Mr. Reid told the girls they might remember playing together as children, as Catie's father would often bring her on his visits. Catie searched her brain but couldn't recall the girl. In truth, even her father's face was no longer easily remembered. She knew that if it wasn't for Ben's strong resemblance and pictures, her father would've already been lost to her forever. Recall the girl or not, an urging look from Ben told Catie to acknowledge her. She smiled pleasantly. "Hello, Maggie."

Finally looking up, the girl replied, "G'day, Miss Darcy."

She was taller than Catie and very slender. Her face was pretty, but clearly the two girls had traveled very different roads since the days of playing together on the small lawn. Her tight jeans were worn and the words on her t-shirt had

102

faded. Catie glanced down to keep from staring and noticed that Maggie's frayed shoe laces only filled the eyelets half way up. For the first time in her life, Catie Darcy felt uncomfortable in her expensive clothes, and she couldn't help but think what a sight she and her brother must be in their fine breeches and shiny boots.

"How old are you, Maggie?" Ben asked.

"A month from eighteen, sir," she answered softly.

Ben looked back to Mr. Reid. "I will speak to my wife. Management of the house is her jurisdiction. A married man yourself, I need not tell you what risk a man takes trespassing on a woman's domain. But I'll see what I can do."

"Aye, Benny, that's much appreciated, lad."

Ben smiled at the man. "Cheers, Mr. Reid...Maggie." He motioned for Catie to take the lead out of the narrow gate.

After Ben hoisted her into her saddle, Catie stole another long glance at Maggie Reid while waiting for him to mount Geronimo.

"What happened to Mr. Reid?" she asked as soon as they had started down the lane, away from the house.

"Farming accident."

"Did he work for Daddy?"

"He did. For about ten years Mr. Reid ran this estate. He answered to Dad, everyone else answered to him. He was Dad's steward, his right hand man until he was injured." Ben smiled as he remembered. "I used to ride alongside him on my pony from the time I was about the twins' age."

"You did?"

"Mm-hmm, Mr. Reid taught me almost everything I know about farming." Ben chuckled. "He also gave me more hidings than I'd care to own up to."

Catie was surprised. "You? What for?"

"Oh, many things really, I was a boy once, Sis, and not always a well behaved one, I'm ashamed to admit. One time..." He stopped and glanced apprehensively over at her. "Never mind."

"Oh, tell me, please, Ben. I must hear it."

He laughed. "Well, all right then, but I'll deny it if you ever tell anyone." She nodded, so he continued, "Once a mate and I, bored I guess, let the cows out of the pasture to block traffic on the highroad. Then we entertained ourselves by throwing cowpats at the stopped vehicles. That is until Mr. Reid came along on his tractor and chased us into the field and up a tree."

"Did he come up the tree after you?" she asked, her eyes wide with disbelief.

"No." Ben shook his head. "He just waited for us to climb down."

"And he thrashed you...both of you?"

Shifting in his saddle, Ben seemed to wince at the memory. "Soundly, Catie, quite soundly."

She laughed out loud. "What did Dad say?"

"If I remember correctly, I believe he slapped Mr. Reid on the back and said, 'Good man, Reid,' and sent me to bed without my supper."

Catie's laugh intensified, and after a mocking glare at the enjoyment she was having at his misfortune, Ben joined her.

"Why do you not have a steward?" she finally asked.

"I just prefer to handle my affairs myself," he answered quietly, as they both fell into a tired silence, with only the music of the wind soughing through the trees and the clopping of the horses to see them home.

Within half an hour they were back by the river. Ben pulled Geronimo to a stop. "I'll be back directly," he said as he jumped to the ground. "I must stretch my legs a bit."

Catie giggled and shook her head. Strangely, 'stretching his legs' always involved him disappearing into the woods for a few minutes, and she couldn't help but be amused by her brother's unyielding discretion.

Tired, her mouth stretched into a full yawn, which she made no attempt to cover for propriety's sake. She removed her riding hat to let the wind cool her head and, lifting her face to the sun, closed her eyes. The sounds of the river had all but entranced her when a strange noise snapped her head back to attention. Now with acute eyes and ears, she listened and almost instantly heard the sound again. Initially, Catie thought it an animal but, by the third cry, she was convinced it was the screams of a woman.

She called for Ben several times, but he didn't answer or reappear. Another scream, coming distinctly from ahead of her, and she urged Chloe into a quick canter. "Go now, off girl."

Around the bend was the small dirt lane that led to the Ledfords' cottage. She could hear voices, angry and loud. Catie hesitated. But what if someone was hurt? She glanced back once more, still no sign of Ben, so she started up the road.

Stepping out of the woods, Ben was surprised not to see his sister waiting for him. Being so close to the rushing water, he had not heard her call for him.

Her riding hat lay on the ground, and he stooped to pick it up. He glanced up the path and soon heard the same cries and screams. "My God!" he exclaimed, tossing the hat down and hastily mounting his horse. He and Geronimo were fast around the bend where the sight he came upon brought him to an abrupt stop, possibly in the hopes that his eyes were deceiving him. Catie was more than halfway up the lane to the Ledfords' and clearly the commotion, whatever it was, lay ahead of her.

"Damn it, Catie!" Ben cursed her foolishness and kicked the horse back into a fast, hard gallop.

Reaching the edge of the garden, Catie froze in fear. Before her was a very different scene than the domestic serenity from earlier. The laundry, which had been so neatly hung, now lay scattered over the lawn and several pots and dishes lay amongst the clutter. Amidst this disarray were the Ledfords, having a rather heated row.

Yelling angrily, Mr. Ledford grabbed his wife by the neck of her housedress. The woman screamed, and Catie noticed there was blood in the corner of her mouth and one eye was beginning to swell. Mr. Ledford drew back his hand, and Catie gasped as he struck his wife so hard she lost her feet.

Once she was on the ground, he slowly and deliberately unbuckled his belt from his trousers and pulled it off with one swift jerk. The sliding, hissing sound of the belt seemed to slice into Catie's gut. She opened her mouth to scream, but the sound of Geronimo's hooves forced her attention back to the road. Ben was off of his horse almost before the steed came to a complete stop.

"Ride off! Now!" he shouted.

"But, Ben!" Catie cried back, frightened.

He half-turned back in her direction. "You will do as I say! Now be gone!" he shouted again, pointing a finger at her as if to stress his threat.

Catie tried to leave, but it wasn't an easy scene to turn away from. Paying no heed to his audience, Mr. Ledford had begun to violently whip his wife.

"Stop!" Ben demanded several times, but Ledford was white with rage and ignored him.

Ben tried wresting the belt from Mr. Ledford's hand and in the scuffle the strap wrapped around Ben's neck with a loud smack. Ben flinched, but it was the advantage he needed. With a quick snatch, he jerked the belt from Mr. Ledford's grip.

Knowing he stood no chance against the taller, more solid Ben Darcy, Mr.

Ledford took a cautious step back.

"Bloody coward!" Ben roared and flung the strap across the yard. "You'll not fight a man?"

Not liking the commotion, Chloe pranced nervously underneath Catie. "Steady on, girl." She patted the horse as a tiny whimper caught her attention. She turned and looked down. There was the little dirty-faced girl, standing near the extinguished rubbish fire and holding a squirming fussy infant with great difficulty. Fearing the child might drop the baby, Catie slid off of her horse and took the infant from the child.

Now holding the Ledfords' baby, with their little girl crying and clinging to her leg, Catie looked on as Ben repeatedly ordered Mr. Ledford off the property, but the man adamantly refused to leave without his wife and children.

As they quarreled, Mr. Ledford paced about like a cornered animal that might attack at any second. Catie's mind raced. Should she go for help? But what might happen if she left Ben? At last, Mrs. Ledford made it to her feet and pleaded with her husband not to make any more trouble, promising to join him as soon as she could collect their things.

His wife's words seemed to calm him. "I'll just be fetching me keys then," he said flatly and disappeared into the house.

Ben rushed over to Mrs. Ledford to check her injuries. She had taken quite a beating and stumbled several times as he tried to help her to a garden bench. Neither noticed Mr. Ledford exiting the house.

"Ben, he has a gun!" screamed Catie, eyes round with fright.

At the sound of his sister's voice, Ben turned to her.

"Bennet, he has a gun!" she cried again, pointing frantically.

As Catie's words rang clearer that time, Ben's attention snapped to Ledford and to a rusty rook rifle that appeared to be older than Mr. Ledford himself. Poor condition or no, Ben knew better than to take chances on whether or not it would still fire.

"Take your hands off me wife, Darcy! You don't own everythin'!"

"Get hold of yourself, man!" Ben shouted back as he began to position himself between the weapon and Catie. "You're going to hurt someone!"

Ledford smiled a cruel smile that contained only a few rotting teeth then turned and aimed the weapon at Catie. "How's it feel, Darcy? Eh? You like havin' yours threatened?"

With the gun pointing directly at her, the alarm in Catie's face visibly heightened. In what seemed to Ben like slow motion, she glanced over at him and then down at the baby in her arms. Then, she shut her eyes tightly and turned away from the gun.

Chapter 11

When the shot fired, a bolt of terror flashed through Catie. She expected to feel a burn, a sting, but she felt nothing. After the initial blast, a loud crack felt as if it split the fine hairs on her left ear and echoed deep in her stomach, causing her knees to buckle and give way. Without warning her legs folded in half and she fell to the earth, all the while keeping the infant in a tight hold.

The two children were wailing, but their cries sounded far off as if they were in a tunnel. There was scuffling and loud voices behind her, but shock had an iron cage over her senses. She could focus only on the ringing in her ears.

By the time it became clear that she hadn't been shot and could make her legs work well enough to stand, Catie turned around to find Ben holding the butt of the rifle over Mr. Ledford's bloody face. His steely eyes were fierce with a look determined to crack the man's skull with the next blow. From beneath him, Mr. Ledford raised a trembling hand in defense.

"No, Bennet!" she cried out. "Don't!"

Hair pasted to his head with sweat, Ben's breath was short and ragged as he looked over at his sister. "Don't, Brother," she said softly. "Don't hurt him."

Straightening himself up, he angrily flung the gun across the yard and stumbled back a few steps. "Leave my property, Ledford!" Ben spoke the words so low and raspy they seemed to grate through his teeth. "Leave now, damn you!"

Never reaching a full upright stance, Mr. Ledford scurried to a rusting truck, which took several attempts to start, and sped off, leaving behind his wife, his crying children, and a billowing cloud of dust.

Mrs. Ledford rushed to her infant and murmured, "Bless you child," to

Catie. She took the squalling, heavy burden from Catie's arms and, clutching her daughter's hand, disappeared inside the house with her children.

Now alone with Ben, Catie stared at her brother. Strangely, she didn't cry. She couldn't. Her eyes were too dry for tears. Ben walked over and pulled her to his chest. His heart was racing, she could hear it. Taking her face in his hands, he looked upon it for some time and without a word, brought her back to his chest. So tight was his hold, her hair became damp from the perspiration seeping through his shirt. Catie heard, "*Christ*," faintly escape the back of his throat.

Refusing medical care, the only aid Mrs. Ledford agreed to accept was transportation to her sister's house a little over an hour away. Ben repeatedly assured her she could stay as long as she needed, but the woman politely refused, stating she would feel safer at her sister's. That hadn't been the first time her husband had "knocked her about," as she called it.

Ben rang up to the house for Clark to bring a car. Clark Ferrell, Pemberley's jack-of-all-trades, mended everything from fences to doors but also kept a clean white shirt in the kitchen in case a driver was needed. While they waited, Catie helped Mrs. Ledford gather the things that still lay scattered in the yard. It seemed odd to be folding laundry after what had just passed.

When they had finished, Mrs. Ledford took the basket of laundry inside while Catie sat on the steps with the Ledfords' little girl perched on her knees as she introduced Catie to her favorite dolly. The car arrived and Ben came out of the cottage, stopping on his way down the steps to lift the child from his sister's lap. "Go help your mummy," he said tenderly as he stood her facing up the stairs. Then, with a firm grip under her arm, he brought Catie to her feet and said, "Mount up, Catherine."

The grip and words seemed to have meaning behind them, making Catie glance cautiously at his face as she nodded.

Lowering the stirrups, she hoisted herself into the saddle. She watched Ben speak with Clark Ferrell and walk across the lawn to pick up the rifle. She watched him mount Geronimo. She watched until he looked over at her. Then she looked down and fiddled with Chloe's reins.

"Come along, Catie," he finally said, steering his horse to home.

She followed.

Sixteen years of being Ben Darcy's sister had given Catie an understanding of his moods…especially the silent ones. He was quiet now, and she rode slightly behind to give him the space he needed, never taking her eyes off the gun resting on his leg. Guns themselves were a part of life at Pemberley. Both Ben and her father had enjoyed hunting on their land and often a party was made out of the affair. But the weapons locked in the gun room at Pemberley had never been pointed at Catie Darcy. She had been taught respect for weapons but never feared them…before now.

Urging Chloe forward a little, Catie glanced over at Ben's hand. His knuckles were swollen and red, two of them missing the top layer of skin all together. Ben had never struck Mr. Ledford with the rifle as she had initially thought…he had pummeled him with his bare hands.

Casting her eyes from Ben's hand to his face, Catie couldn't help but think there was no braver man than her brother, a hero who had fought for her life much like in a novel.

Her thoughts had filled her with exuberance by the time they reached the stable yard. Dismounting in a jump, she skirted Geronimo's hindquarters and was standing at Clancy's side by the time Ben handed the rifle down to him.

As he took the weapon, Clancy saw the injuries to Mr. Darcy's hand and noticed his clothes were dirty and disheveled. "Did you run into trouble, Mr. Darcy?"

Catie blurted out, "Oh, yes, Clancy, we did! But my brother — "

"Catherine!" Ben's tone was so sharp she felt it pool inside her stomach, like the rifle shot less than an hour ago. His eyes glued on her, he dismounted and approached his sister. His furrowed brow of disapproval caused her to swallow, but all she managed down her throat was a scratchy pocket of air.

"Go to your room," he ordered with a pointed finger.

"My room?" she repeated.

Ben took a step closer to her, his eyes intent. "Was I not clear?" he asked firmly.

She glanced at Clancy, who was a front row spectator, then back to Ben as a crimson shade crept up her neck and filled her face. There was a catch in her voice when she tried to answer, and she knew she was about to cry. Humiliated, she turned and walked quickly away.

Pending fatherhood was one of many heavy weights burdening Ben Darcy as he walked to the house with Mr. Ledford's rifle in his hand. Sarah had not yet shared her condition with him, but of course he knew. A first term miscarriage the previous year was the reason for her secrecy. Sarah's concealment was to shelter him from another loss. That irritated Ben, but he allowed her privacy, reasoning that, without the fear of disappointing him, her stress

110

would be lessened.

Although upsetting Sarah worried him, he knew once the grapevine of gossip got hold of what happened at the Ledfords' it would only be a matter of time before she heard. The news that Catie had almost been killed had to come from him.

When Ben reached the house he inwardly cringed. Rose was awaiting him in the hall; clearly, the grapevine had already been humming.

Seeing the weapon and his condition, Rose gasped. "Good Lord, what has happened?"

Not wanting to incite a big to-do before he had spoken with Sarah, Ben was business as usual. "Catie and I ran into some trouble with one of the tenants." He handed the rifle over to her. "Lock this up, will you, and call the authorities. They'll need to come by so I can give them a statement."

Rose took the gun from him. "But you're a magistrate. You have no need to explain your actions on your own property, do you?"

"There should be a record in case anything comes of it, Rose," he vaguely replied, making her head tilt admonishingly. "Yes, yes there's more to it," he admitted. "I'll give you all the details after I get out of these clothes and check on Sarah... all right?"

"All right," Rose said reluctantly. Ben started up the steps, but she stopped him. "Why did Catie come home crying and run to her room?"

Suddenly frozen in place, Ben looked back at her and then down to the steps. He was legally his sister's guardian, but Rose was her Nan, the woman who had mothered Catie in their own mother's absence. Feeling his chest suddenly go tight, he answered in a hushed voice, "She was almost killed this afternoon, Rose."

"My God," Rose exclaimed, touching her heart. *"Killed?"*

Ben looked directly at her now. "It happened so fast. I told her to leave and then... then she was there. God, I've spent the last hour trying to decide which I'd rather do... hug her and thank God she is still alive, or take her by the shoulders and shake some damn bloody sense into that head of hers."

Rose reached up and placed her hand atop his. "You are your father's son, Ben Darcy. You will do what's right; you always have."

Sighing, he nodded. "Thanks, Rose."

"And remember," Rose continued, "that sister of yours has her head in the clouds more than on her neck where it should be."

"That she does."

At the top of the landing, Ben stopped. He appreciated Rose's confidence in him, but truthfully he was at a loss. All he knew was that, if he spoke to Sarah before dealing with Catie, there was going to be a lot more hugging and a lot less shaking. And he needed his sister to understand the seriousness of her poor judgment. So it was to Catie's room he headed first.

Boots on the stairs grabbed Catie's attention from her perch in the window. With folded hands and crossed fingers for good luck, she prayed her brother would seek Sarah's advice first, but the sound of boots grew closer and stopped outside her door.

With puffy yet tearless eyes, Catie stood up as he came in. After closing the door behind him, Ben went to the unoccupied window, where he gazed out over the expansive lawn that had recently been mown into a diagonal crisscross pattern. He inhaled deeply and then slowly released the air.

Catie anxiously awaited, heart pounding in her ears, and wished he would shout rather than stare out the window.

It wasn't that she didn't understand his anger. He told her to leave, and she didn't. Couldn't, she corrected herself. She had hoped that since she still stood breathing, he would overlook that fact, but even Clancy could vouch for the naiveté in that assumption. Whatever his intentions were, the silence she could take no longer. At the very least she could apologize.

"Bennet, I — " she started but was instantly silenced by a slight wave of her brother's hand.

A few more torturous minutes passed before Ben finally turned from the window. "Do you even comprehend that you were nearly killed today?"

"Yes," she replied quietly and then added what she was planning to say before he silenced her. "And I'm sorry."

He crossed his arms and asked, "Exactly which behavior are you apologizing for, your foolishness or your defiance?"

Defiance she understood, but foolishness? "Foolishness?"

"Foolishness indeed!" he countered sharply. "Whatever would possess you to return to that house after the trouble we had there this morning?"

"There was screaming. I thought someone was hurt."

"Damn it, Catie, this is real life, not a bloody fairytale! That was a real gun that man pointed at you. Why didn't you leave when I told you to?"

I couldn't leave you there, can't you see that? She willed the words out of her mouth but instead lowered her head and whispered, "I just...just...thought I could help."

"*Help*?" he repeated so incredulously that she kept her eyes pasted on the floor. "You could've been hurt or worse yet killed! Do you not understand?" Still not looking at him, she nodded because she knew he wanted her to. Ben sighed heavily. "I think it would be best for you to stay in your room the rest of the day."

"What?" Stunned, she looked up and met his eyes. "You're punishing me?"

"I am," he replied resolutely. "I'm sorry, Catherine, but I feel I must."

"You can't be serious." It was her turn to look and sound incredulous.

"Catie, I *told* you to leave. It was very dangerous for you to disobey me."

"And I said I was sorry!" she argued.

Unmoved and determined, Ben went to the door and then turned back to her. "I'll speak with you in the morning. I'd advise you to use this time to think upon your actions."

Tearing up again, she pleaded with him, "Ben, please don't."

"Damn it, Catie, enough with the drama!" he shouted, slapping his hand hard against the door frame. "I can't protect you if you won't do as I say. Now for once in your life behave prudently!"

"You're not my father!" She squared her shoulders, intending to strike a nerve. It appeared she succeeded, for Ben stared hard at her a moment, his mouth pressed into a thin line.

He replied evenly, "No. No I'm not, but I'm all the father you've got."

"I hate you, Bennet." The words surprised her as much as they did him, but she was hurt and wanted him to feel hurt as well.

Without looking at her again, he said, "Taking care of you is my responsibility, Catherine. If you hate me for it, well, then I reckon I shall bear that burden along with the rest of the lot." He opened the door and left, slamming it hard behind him.

"Ben!" she cried after him, but he was gone. Tears streaming down her cheeks, Catie fell on the bed and wept.

In the hall, Ben listened with closed eyes to the cries of a heartbroken sister. He'd lost his temper, he hadn't meant to.

His spontaneous decision to rush Ledford had nearly cost Catie her life, but then again, quite possibly saved it. Did the gun go off when he made contact? He tried to remember. Did Ledford just want to scare him or...? God, he'd never know what that crazed man's intentions truly were. What he did know though, what had blared in his brain for the last hour was that less than six inches to the right and the bullet would have been fatally lodged into the back of his sister's head. "Damn it, Catie," he whispered. "Damn it to bloody hell."

Entering through their sitting room gave Ben the opportunity to have a much needed swallow of Scotch, in preparation for the next item on what had become a very unpleasant Monday agenda.

Against Rose's orders, Sarah had left her bed and started dressing when she heard Ben in the adjoining room. He was finishing a much needed second swallow when she came up behind him. "Why are you drinking in the middle of the day?"

Ben gave a slight start at her voice, the Scotch having not yet calmed his nerves. "Sarah, love, why are you out of bed? You aren't well."

"I'm feeling better." Coming close to embrace him, she noticed the large raised welt on the back of his neck that was already beginning to bruise. Her expression bore a similar aspect to that of Rose's, and her first words had a familiar ring. "Bennet, what happened?"

Persuading Sarah to the sofa, Ben relaxed in the closest chair and started relieving his feet of his boots. If Catie's flair for drama annoyed him, it paled in comparison to Sarah's abhorrence for her husband's tendency to downplay a situation. He methodically worked at his boots and then unbuttoned his shirt as he unemotionally recounted the morning, purposefully omitting the gun for now. Like pie, upsetting news was best served in pieces — especially to a pregnant wife.

Domestic violence and Ben's forced intervention itself were enough to heighten Sarah's anxiety and concern.

"Did Catie see all of this?" she questioned apprehensively.

"Unfortunately," he said, nodding. "I told her to leave but she didn't."

With a clear look of worry, Sarah asked, "Is she all right?"

"She's fine, performing a rather theatrical cry when I left her."

Sarah's expression changed from worried to puzzled, as Ben, now removing his socks, mumbled more to himself than to her. "A complete waste of talent if you ask me. Had she been born of less fortune, she could have earned a handsome living acting."

"What have you done?" She was not at all amused by his comment.

"I've confined her to her room for some much needed time to reflect upon her actions." Ben stiffened in defense of his decision.

"Instead of talking to her, reasoning with her?" Sarah asked. "Is punishment your *only* recourse?"

"And you would see to it she has no consequences at all?" he snapped back, and instantly regretted having done so. He didn't want to quarrel. Ben plastered on a credible, reassuring expression, which wasn't easy after the morning he had had, and gave her an equally reassuring kiss. "I promise you that she'll be none the worse after one afternoon pondering the costs of disobeying her brother."

"I just wish the two of you could learn to talk out your differences."

"We're Darcys, Sarah. Our tempers get the best of us, I'll admit but..."

"She's growing up, Ben," she cut him off, a severe look on her face. "You can't very well send her to her room every time she disagrees with you."

"Catie didn't disagree with me, she disobeyed me. Growing up or not, she's going to do as I say, especially where her welfare is concerned."

"But certainly a sound wigging would've sufficed."

Ben heaved out a heavy breath. Sarah was probably right, but then again, he hadn't been totally honest with her. However, the piece of pie that told of Catie's near demise at the end of Ledford's rifle was best not served at present.

Cocking a teasing brow, he attempted wit to lighten the air. "Sarah, my love, some men teach lessons and some men preach lessons. This is the reason you see your husband sitting *in* the pews on Sunday, rather than standing in front of them...I'm no preacher."

"This isn't a joke!" was her flat response.

"I never said it was. Let's drop the matter, eh? It's done." She sighed, flustered but resigned, and he disappeared into the bathroom.

WADE RADCLIFF WAS OFFERED THE position as personal assistant to Bennet Darcy following the death of Ben's father. Wade had been the late Mr. Darcy's assistant, so it seemed the natural course of things. Furthermore, he and the younger Mr. Darcy found the relationship worked on many levels. For Ben, the fact that Wade wasn't inclined to marry and favored the lifestyle of a single man was most appealing. Ben preferred an assistant without familial obligations, as his needs demanded Wade Radcliff be at his disposal.

As for Wade Radcliff, Bennet Darcy was as generous an employer as his father had been, so he had no desire to relinquish the comfortable, well-paid position. As he had done for the elder Mr. Darcy, Wade resided at and managed the Darcys' London townhouse. The Mayfair residence did double duty, serving as both a family home and London office, meaning Ben needed someone in town full time when he was in Derbyshire.

The only real grumble Wade had with the younger Mr. Darcy was his fondness for the country. The late Mr. Darcy spent a large portion of his time at the family's house in London, while his son preferred Pemberley and the countryside of Derbyshire. Wade loathed the country and country people.

Wade had left London on the first train out that morning and was already at the house arranging documents that needed signing as he waited for an unusually tardy Mr. Darcy.

Trying, sickening, even horrific were but a few words that could describe the day so far for Ben, who finally entered his study well after lunch. His indifference with Wade was not understood, neither was it questioned. Like Catie, Wade was accustomed to the man's moods.

"Good morning, Mr. Darcy," Wade opened pleasantly.

"My morning was not good, Radcliff, and it's well past noon. I believe a good afternoon would serve better."

"Ah, yes, sir, of course...good afternoon."

Ben sat at his desk and looked at the man, mildly apologetic. "Sorry to have kept you waiting."

"No worries, sir," Wade replied.

"Right, well, I need you to ring the cereal company that leases the land from the river east. I've evicted their overseer."

"Yes, sir." Wade assumed this was the reason for Mr. Darcy's being late and in a foul mood. "Oh, before I forget, sir, Charles Worthington rang several times this morning. The message is on your desk. I realize it's brief, but he said you'd understand."

Ben picked up the small slip of paper in front of him.

10:45 am — Mr. Charles Worthington telephoned:

The settlement offer has been rejected. Will be at Pemberley this weekend to reconsider our options.

W. Radcliff

Yes, Ben understood perfectly. Defeated, he blew out through puffed cheeks and ruefully chuckled. Not that anything was funny, but prior to entering his study he had the foolish audacity to pose himself the question: What else could possibly go wrong today?

Leaning back in his desk chair, Ben suddenly had another question that longed for an answer. Just how much money *was* it going to cost him to atone for Mary Darcy Howell's sin of tossing out her bastard grandson like Monday morning's trash? "Damn it to bloody hell," he whispered.

Chapter 12

A cold meat sandwich, a carafe of Rose's lemonade, and assorted fruits and biscuits were brought to Catie's room. As to who delivered the tray of food and set it on her writing table, she could not say, for she never lifted her face from the pillow. Although her crying had stopped almost in unison with the fading sound of her brother's boots, the pouting and self-pity had yet to ease.

Ultimately, it was the lemonade that roused her from her bed of misery. A dry scratchy throat from the morning's commotion had turned sore after her quarrel with Ben. Filling the glass, she rebelliously picked up a biscuit rather than her sandwich and took up her favorite perch at the window.

The sky was blue without a speck of white to be found and worked in perfect harmony with the deep green lawn. It had not the appearance of a day that had gone so decidedly wrong.

Thinking upon her actions as she had been told, Catie relived the morning over and over. From the frightening events at the Ledfords up to her row with Ben, she rehashed it all and then...rehashed it again. Strangely though, only two parts continued to come forward in her mind: The damage to Ben's knuckles from his literal fight for her life, and the word he used just before leaving her in her room...burden. He said burden.

Not only had their mother died leaving Catie behind, but only eight years later her father had also passed away. The responsibility placed on her brother had never occurred to Catie until today. *I am and always have been a burden to my brother.*

Pressing her forehead against the windowpane, Catie came to the conclusion that today obviously wasn't the first time her brother had scuffed his knuckles (figuratively that is) on her behalf.

" … think upon your actions," Ben had said, but Catie couldn't think any longer. Her brother, the Ledfords, and even Maggie Reid had all but consumed her for over an hour, and she desperately needed a diversion.

Moving from the window, she noticed Mary Darcy's diary lying on her desk. "Looks like it's just you and me, Mary," she said as she topped off her glass with the last of the lemonade and picked up the book.

Wanting to be left alone, she set the tray outside to be collected and gazed down the vast corridor. She noticed a few dust motes floating in the sun-dappled hall. The house was quiet that afternoon as if her sentence of solitude had been imposed on Pemberley as well. Sighing, Catie stepped back into her room and shut the door.

By Mary's seventeenth summer Arthur Howell had secured himself another invitation to the Thompsons', and their romance picked up at a ferocious pace from where it had left off.

16 July 1919
Our walks are beginning to consist of little walking. His kisses are passionate and cause a burning inside me that is unexplainable. Tonight he touched my leg and slowly moved his hand up my thigh. I shuddered, he paused, smiled, and then continued until he reached my …

Catie slammed the book shut and looked about the room. No one was there; no one knew what she was reading. Why was she so jumpy? She even wondered whether continuing to read might violate Mary's privacy. But the woman *was* long dead, she rationalized. She read on.

18 July 1919
It pinched and stung, but I shut my eyes tight to the pain. I wanted it. I wanted him, Arthur. He finally entered me. Finally made love to me! His touch is like a spark on my tingling, begging skin. "You are mine!" he told me. His woman, his lover, his! My body trembles when he is near … I am no longer a virgin … I am a Lover!

20 July 1919

Again today, I was naked in Arthur's arms, his hands caressing me. His
hands have touched places no other hands have touched. His mouth has
explored me, and my body aches for him, arching to his bidding without
command from its master. We are sinners, but our love must be forgiven. It
is so sweet and pure. I tremble as I write of my Arthur, my lover…

Catie's breathing was thick and uneven. A virgin who had never even been
kissed, she was curious and captivated by Arthur and Mary's lovemaking. Biting her bottom lip, she closed her eyes. Suddenly, she was Mary and Sean was
Arthur. He touched her, and she trembled. They kissed as she ran her fingers
through his gypsy black hair. She could almost taste the salty sweat of his skin.

The passages of forbidden, youthful lovemaking were long and detailed,
and Catie read through them with the ardency of an eager apprentice hoping
to learn a life's trade.

She turned the page and inhaled a small gasp. What she and Mary had
feared the most finally happened…

23 July 1919

OH! A most dreadful thing has occurred. Young cousin Geoffrey happened
upon Arthur and me in the boathouse. He rushed Arthur and hit him.
"You blackguard!" he yelled. "Geoffrey!" I cried after him, but he ran to the
house and told Father.

Mamma is in hysterics. I am ashamed. So ashamed, I could hardly face
Papa. He was furious and sent me above stairs. As I write this passage in
my room, I weep. Papa is speaking with Arthur. Papa says I am ruined and
must be married now. Pray Arthur, marry me my darling!

Catie hurriedly turned the page but it was stuck, and she worked hastily to
free the corners. "Yes!" she exclaimed when the paper finally broke free and
peeled back.

24 July 1919

Arthur has agreed to be my husband. He and Papa have made the
arrangements. We will marry on 6 September. I wish I could be happy but I

have disappointed Papa and Mamma so. My heart is heavy with both love and regret…

Catie flipped to the next page and then thumbed quickly to the end, but only empty white pages remained. She was disappointed, but at least now she understood why Mary chose to hide her diary. It would never do in the family library alongside the memoirs of the more genteel Pemberley ladies.

The decision to return the book to Mary's secret hiding place was an easy one. Mary had been violated quite enough, in more ways than one. There was no need for anyone else to trespass on her privacy.

Carefully removing the panel, Catie replaced the book and felt around the narrow cavity. Dust and cobwebs was all that was to one side, but to the other there was something wedged quite tightly. With one good pull, Catie was in possession of a small stack of envelopes bound in a blue ribbon. Assuming her find was the correspondence of the lovers, her face expressed visible delight.

There came a faint rap on the door, and her delight was dashed. Annie had come to run her bath and put fresh linens on the bed. She hid the letters in her bedside table and called out, "Come in."

Still feeling a bit blistered, Catie felt the necessity to quarrel on the matter of the bath. Placing her hands on her hips, she stoutly declared, "I do *not* need a bath. I am *not* going downstairs for dinner tonight!" In truth, she just wanted to be left alone — alone to read Mary's letters and to forget about the morning.

Annie replied just as stoutly, "Sorry, Miss Catie, but Rose said you were to have a hot bath, and I'll not cross her path tonight. She's in one of her moods, she is."

Catie gave a small stamp of her foot, but it was all the protest she could muster. After the exhausting day, she didn't have the strength to argue.

"In with you now." Annie motioned Catie to the bathroom. "Or Rose will have both our heads!"

Fatigue quickly caught up to her, and the hot water was more relaxing than Catie had anticipated. She yawned several times while she listened to Annie bustling around her room, making the bed, gathering laundry and straightening up. A moment later, Annie deposited a fresh towel by the tub and hung Catie's dressing gown on the door.

"I'll return directly with your supper, Miss Catie."

"All right," Catie answered, staring at the ceiling.

"Anything else you need, a book from the library maybe?" Annie asked, feeling a bit sorry for her.

Giving Annie a wry look, Catie shook her head. "Not unless you want to be arrested for smuggling contraband."

Annie's brows furrowed in question.

"I've been sentenced to think, not read."

"Ah." Annie smiled faintly at her humor. "I see."

As Annie closed the door, Catie used her toe to pop up the drain stopper and then dried off and dressed. Slightly rejuvenated from her bath, she grabbed Mary's letters and settled down into the clean smell of line-dried sheets ironed with a hint of lavender.

Once the letters were untied and shuffled through, she quickly discovered they weren't Mary and Arthur's, but rather the correspondence between Mary and her son Thomas. From the postmarks, Catie surmised they were exchanged while Thomas was in Africa. Catie wondered whether they had been sent back to Mary after her son's death along with his body and belongings.

Although the letters were more than forty years old, their condition was excellent, likely the result of being preserved inside the window casing for so long.

For the most part, the content of the correspondence was pretty much what one would expect between mother and son. But then Catie chanced upon the reason for Ben's strange comment to the cigarette smoking man named Sams. "... I'll be bloody well damned to the devil before I let Pemberley fall into the wrong hands again!" The "again," at least, now made better sense.

Apparently after Mary's father died, Arthur Howell stood at the helm of Pemberley House. That is until he drank himself to death. Having the wealth of the Darcy empire at his fingertips but never having been taught restraint had led to a destructive outcome both for Arthur Howell and Pemberley Estate. His and Mary's marriage had seemingly not been a good one...

4 April 1945
Pemberley Estate, Derbyshire, England

My Dearest Son,

Other than the abundance of Victory Gardens planted throughout the estate grounds, Pemberley is all but destitute. The fields are barren, the house is understaffed, and your father has left us almost bankrupt. I met with the solicitor today, and I am grieved to inform you the inheritance your grandfather intended for you has been drank, gambled, and squandered away. I have contacted Cousin Geoffrey at Rosings Park, and he has promised to help save Pemberley from ruin.

My only solace is that your weak constitution has kept you out of this dreadful war. It seems Pemberley's weak constitution has kept her from being conscripted into service as well. Although some of the acreage has been used for training grounds, the house itself was not deemed usable. A dying master and disrepair has kept Pemberley from being of much use to her country. I do not know whether to be grateful or ashamed.

Your Loving Mum

Catie remembered studying the Second World War. The Blitz, rationing, Victory Gardens and yes…many country estates were converted during the war years for institutional use, barracks, schools and such. She couldn't help but think of the Pemberley she knew today in comparison to the one Mary described. Arthur Howell's hands were the *wrong* hands indeed. Catie now theorized why her grandfather had to sell Rosings Park. Possibly it was the only means to save Pemberley House from ruin brought at the hands of Arthur Howell.

"Poor Mary," Catie murmured, wondering how they went from summer lovers to near destitution. It was not the "happily ever after" she had dreamed of for Mary and Arthur.

If Bennet Darcy had hopes of educating his sister on the evils of man, his sister had, in one day, been inundated by just that…the evils of man. From the perverse and abusive Mr. Ledford to the pillaging of Mary Darcy's virginity and fortune by Arthur Howell, Catie's education had begun indeed.

BARGING WAS NOT IN SARAH Darcy's nature, but barge she did into her husband's study. "Why did you not tell me Mr. Ledford had a gun?"

Ben sighed heavily in disgust. Though part of his disgust was born from the fact that gossip had the tendency to spread like the plague, the rest was for himself. He should have told her already. "Try not to get upset, Sarah; I was going to tell you."

"When?" she demanded. "And is it *true*…did Catie shield the Ledfords' child from being shot?"

"What!" Ben came to his feet. "Where did you hear that?" Only he, Catie, and Mrs. Ledford knew the particular details.

"It seems Mrs. Ledford boasted to Clark Ferrell all the way to her sister's house how young Miss Darcy put the infant's life before her own. Is it true, Bennet? Did that madman fire at Catie?"

Clark Ferrell, Ben repeated irritably to himself, committing to memory that he needed to have a word with that man.

Sarah waited, but before she could get her answer, the Darcys were notified that the police had arrived and were waiting in the front parlor.

"I am coming along." Sarah glared at him insistently. "If you will not be forthcoming with me, at least I can be assured you will not perjure yourself with the authorities."

"Fine…fine," Ben said, daring to put an arm around her in comfort. "But do calm yourself, dear. Remember, Catie and I are both unharmed."

In the small parlor, Senior Officer Hardy, a fiftyish man of great girth, waited for Mr. Darcy with Officer Conner, lanky in his youth and new to the force. Connor fidgeted, uncomfortable with the fine surroundings, but stood tall and still when Hardy cleared his throat, warning his young protégé to the sound of approaching footsteps.

Greetings out of the way, Ben offered the officers a seat and settled across from them. Then, without preamble, he recounted all of his dealings with Mr. Ledford, including the earlier morning incident, which he assumed started the trouble between Ledford and his wife.

Sarah listened in complete shock alongside Rose, who had brought in Mr. Ledford's weapon so it could be turned over to the police.

All now seemed finalized in Ben Darcy's mind, but Officer Hardy, who was painstakingly thorough, wanted to speak to Mr. Darcy's sister. "…and your sister, Mr. Darcy," Hardy continued, as he flipped a page in his notes. "Is she available to give an account?"

"She is." Ben gave a single nod. "But I was hoping she could be spared from speaking with the police." He breathed deeply. "Officer Hardy, allow me to be direct. I have no interest in pursuing this matter with Mr. Ledford, and he will not be returning to my property, of that I can assure you."

Officer Hardy turned uneasily to the younger officer. Mr. Darcy was a local magistrate, a principal and affluent member of the community, but not speaking to all the witnesses was certainly against protocol. He was clearly hesitant but relented to Mr. Darcy's request. "Please understand, Mr. Darcy, if anything else arises in this case, it will be imperative that I speak to Miss Darcy."

"Yes, of course. I thank you for your understanding, Officer Hardy, my…" Ben paused, emotion had finally got the better of him, but he spoke deliberately through it. "My sister is at a very impressionable age, and the less that is made of this… well… the better it will be for her." Ben stood, stepped away, and found a trinket on the mantel that needed readjusting.

Always the keen observer, Rose hastily but politely, saw the officers out. Knowing Ben needed a few minutes of privacy with Sarah, she closed the doors to the parlor and left the two alone.

WAITING FOR HER SUPPER, CATIE read through Thomas and Mary's letters fairly rapidly, as there was only a handful. Thomas apparently was in Africa less than a year when he contracted and succumbed to malaria. Whatever "weak constitution" his mother was referring to must have made his recovery impossible.

In reading, she learned that a religious mission is what took Thomas to Africa. Catie discovered Thomas Howell was a man of strong faith. His untimely death was a shame — a waste of a life with true purpose. From his letters, she thought she would have liked to have known her distant cousin, the man who should have been the current master of Pemberley instead of her brother.

The last letter his mother sent to him was sent back to her unopened. Evidently it arrived too late. Catie held the unopened envelope up to the light as she considered and reconsidered whether to open it or not. Fate intervened, at least for now, for Annie had returned with food, and Catie was suddenly violently hungry. She tossed the unopened letter into a scatter of other distractions that had entertained her throughout the afternoon and sat at her writing table to eat.

Annie had strict instructions from Rose to make sure Miss Catie ate properly. The earlier sandwich had been picked at; only the biscuits had received proper attention. Catie rolled her eyes. "I swear that woman creates full time occupation for herself by monitoring what I eat!"

Annie smiled at the complaint and started out, but Catie stopped her. "Where are you going? Aren't you supposed to make sure I eat?

"I have a few other things to do before I leave tonight," Annie said. "I'll be back shortly."

"But…can't you stay for a few minutes?" Catie asked, not really wanting to eat alone. Annie hesitated, so she implored further, "Please stay, Annie. Was your father *never* impossible?"

Annie chuckled and took an empathetic step back into the room. "All men can be impossible, Miss Catie. Fathers, brothers, and, since I have been married for almost a year now, I can attest to you that husbands can also be quite impossible."

"Then I shall *never* marry!" Catie stated boldly and started to eat.

Annie laughed. "We are not such easy creatures ourselves, remember. The secret to a good marriage is the ability to tolerate each other's difficult ways. One day soon a young man will catch your eye, and no matter how *impossible* he may be, you'll be blind to his imperfections."

Annie's speech restored a smile to Catie's face, and Annie warmed to see it. The girl had actually grown on her over the last couple of years. There was a tender side to Catie Darcy with which few were acquainted.

Annie stayed and talked while Catie ate a hearty portion of creamed potatoes and roasted chicken. When she finished, Annie said her goodnights and left with the tray as Catie moved back to the bed.

The warm meal and hot bath were starting to have the effect Rose had predicted. Fighting heavy eyes, Catie found a cool place on her pillow and let her thoughts drift to Mary, Arthur, and Sean Kelly.

What was Sean doing right then? Did he know she had been sent to her room? Her eyes shut tight with embarrassment at the thought of it — most likely. She had missed her riding lesson; surely Rose would have told him why. She envisioned him alone at the gardener's cottage, his big smile and blue eyes the color of cornflowers. Finding peace in the vision of him, Catie soon drifted off to sleep.

BY THE TIME THE DARCYS reemerged from the front parlor, supper had been served to Catie and the twins. George's fever had faded, and he and Geoffrey were watching television. After looking in on their sons, Ben and Sarah crossed the landing to the family's bedrooms.

The sight they encountered on the other side of Catie's door made them shake their heads in unison. Every light in the room was on, and the floor and bed were scattered with papers, magazines, and crude sketches of horses. Sound asleep amidst it all was Catie. It looked as though she had been in the middle of some very important business and simply passed out.

Sarah took up the job of settling her into the bedcovers, while Ben loosely brought the scatter on the bed into an unorganized pile. Amongst Catie's clutter was Mary Darcy's unopened letter to her son, Thomas. It went unnoticed by Ben and was haphazardly stacked with the rest of the papers on Catie's bedside table.

Gazing upon Catie's sleeping face, Sarah frowned regretfully. "Oh, I hate she's fallen asleep already." Sarah had been raised in a home where you did not go to bed with matters unfinished and had convinced Ben to speak with his sister tonight.

"This is between brother and sister, Sarah; don't worry yourself. We'll iron out our winkles in the morning."

His wife nodded and smiled at the sleeping girl. "I do hope we have a daughter this time, Bennet."

"Sarah Darcy!" Ben feigned surprise. "Are you with child?"

Sarah raised a mischievous eyebrow. "For a man who claims to have knowledge of everything that goes on under the roof of Pemberley, surely you are mindful of your own transgressions, sir."

"Oh! A transgression you call it!" he said a little too loudly, which caused a cross look to spread over Sarah's face and a finger to be brought to her lips.

"Shhh, you'll wake her."

Ben stood tall, folded his arms, and narrowed his eyes. "You may have as many children as you wish, Mrs. Darcy, as long as you give me sons. No daughters — I forbid it."

Sarah chuckled quietly. "So am I to understand that you have taken up the high office of determining the gender of our children? I'd say that's a pretty big leap for a mere self-proclaimed pew sitter like yourself, Mr. Darcy."

Together they turned off the lights and left the room in each other's embrace. "So, um, do you fancy a little transgressing, Mrs. Darcy?" he asked as he closed Catie's door softly behind him.

Sarah tilted her gaze up at him with a seductive sparkle in her eye. "I don't believe that is the proper use of that word, Bennet."

"Oh, you're quite right!" he said softly, grinning wolfishly. "There will be nothing proper about it... let me assure you."

Chapter 13

Talking to tombstones had been a long-abandoned, childhood habit of Catie's. But there she was, lying flat on her back on an ornate bench, staring at puffy white clouds, speaking at ease with the dead.

"He doesn't want me to have a mind of my own, Dad. I am never to question his authority or think for myself. He tells me to grow up and then sends me to my room like a child. And Daddy." Catie sat up and looked at her father's headstone. "I am *far* too old to be sent to my room!"

In the first years after her father's death, Catie would seek justice in the Darcy family cemetery. Whenever she and her brother were at odds, she would go to her father and tell her side of the story, just as she had done when he was alive. What brought her there today she couldn't say. Was it the word "burden" Ben used that caused her to seek the comfort of her father? Or perhaps, it was how close she came to joining her ancestors. Whatever the reason, as soon as she reestablished her freedom, the cemetery was her first stop.

After spending an uncomfortable amount of time clutched in Rose's bosom, listening to how she frayed her poor nerves, Catie's reprieve from Rose's hold came in the form of a call from her brother. She had been expecting his summons all morning. Not only had she expected it — she was prepared for it.

In the wee hours before daylight, tossing and turning in her bed, Catie had decided to uphold the proverbial routine they had found so easy over the years. She would tell him what he wanted to hear, not what was in her heart and mind. This was becoming more and more difficult, but her motives were weighty and complicated.

For the entirety of her young life, Catie's love and admiration for her brother were enduring. However, after the ordeal at the Ledfords, the devoted sister added debt to this list. Her indebtedness to him — beyond calculation; she owed Ben.

Not only did he save her life, but when her world caved in eight years earlier, it was Ben who picked up the pieces. Burden or not, he picked them up. His loyalty to his sister was commendable and steadfast, and she, in return, would repay that loyalty. So she went to him ready with an apology and full of the promises she knew would appease him. Catie wondered whether this was how George felt — a life trapped in Geoffrey's shadow, never having the courage to step out and stand in his own light.

"Good form, Catherine," Ben replied softly when she had finished. Of course he realized that she was placating him. He himself had stood on the other side of that desk many times, gut churning before his father or grandfather, employing the same consolatory tactics. But like Catie, he had a strong desire to be on even terms again.

He excused his sister with a brotherly wink, not yet daring to seek affection from the rigid form before him. She hadn't mentioned the heated words they had exchanged the day before, but she was angry. He could feel it like static — unseen but prickly. And why shouldn't she be? Like she said, he wasn't her father. Ben just hoped his sister wouldn't implement a long drawn out installment of the silent treatment as she was known to do after any perceived injustice.

Thankfully, this didn't appear to be the case as halfway to the door she stopped, turned around and addressed him again. "Bennet?"

"Yes, Catie," he answered in a hopeful tone.

"I just wanted to say thank you…you know…for everything." Ben looked oddly at her. But before he had the opportunity to question the reason for such gratitude, Catie turned again and left.

It was then that she took her grievances and complaints to the high court of the departed. Which was most likely what goaded her to the cemetery in the first place, the luxurious freedom to speak freely. Catie placed flowers on both her father's and mother's graves and left.

As she happened by the stables, not completely by accident, her feelings were mixed between whether she wished or feared Sean Kelly to be there. Although the thought of seeing him caused her chest to tingle, she knew avoiding him completely was clearly not an option.

Fortune was finally playing in her favor again. Sean Kelly was not only there but working with the twins, allowing Catie the pleasure of observing him unnoticed. Her fortune was not to be long enjoyed, though. Geoffrey caught sight of his aunt and waved. Catie smiled faintly and returned the gesture, and then turned away for a quick, hopefully unnoticed, escape.

"Catie!" Sean called out.

Her back to him, Catie screwed her eyes shut. She would have preferred Ben lock her in the old bell tower and feed her nothing but stale bread and Mr. Johnston's day old-tasting milk for the remainder of the summer instead of facing him. She took a deep breath, pasted on what she hoped was a natural-looking smile, and turned back.

Her approach lifted Sean's heart, and her smile made him hopeful that she and Mr. Darcy had settled their differences. He took a deep breath, inhaling the heady scents of stable, hay, and horse and cautioned himself. He had tried to pretend it was the warm season or maybe just the romance of their surroundings, any feasible reason that he was frequently and unwittingly lost in thoughts of Catie Darcy.

The night at the pond when he first laid eyes on her was often conjured up in his quiet moments. The moonbeams, filtered by the thick summer canopy, had illuminated her. She had reached to the sky, as if offering her lean, naked body to the gods. He remembered hearing his own heartbeat and feeling the rise and fall of his chest as he watched in the black silence of his cover. He couldn't move or divert his eyes from the beautiful siren that held him rapt. Much like now. *Snap out of it man*, he reproached himself.

By the time Catie reached the three, Sean had taken George off his pony and was handing him over to her. "If you don't mind, hold little Georgie for me. Geoffrey wants to pick up his pace a bit." His smiled at her through a face glistening from exertion.

"No, Mr. Kelly, I don't mind." Catie took George and nestled him on her hip.

Sean grimaced and shook his head. "Could you please stop calling me Mr. Kelly? It makes me feel as old as my father."

"But...I thought you said..."

"Oh, the *mister* thing," he said, waving a dismissing hand. "That was only *craic*. I really never believed you would carry on with it for so long."

"*Craic?*" she repeated questioningly.

"That's Irish for fun. You know, like a good joke." Laughing at the indignant expression that was spreading quickly over Catie's face, Sean took hold of Geoffrey's lead. "How 'bout it, mate, fancy a good go?" Geoffrey nodded gamely, so Sean bellowed with his usual vibrant energy. "Well, man, let's hear an aye, sir, then!"

"Aye, sir!" the child yelled out eagerly.

Feeling bested yet again, Catie uttered smartly under her breath, "Maybe I'll just call you an insufferable ass... *Mister* Kelly!"

The comment was of course meant for her alone, but George, who was still propped on Catie's hip, smiled largely and repeated, "Insus... a... ble ass."

Mouth open in disbelief, Catie gasped dramatically and dropped the boy to the ground. George Darcy had never echoed anyone but his brother. Had it not been for the naughty word he chose to repeat, Catie would have been thrilled. But as it was, she couldn't very well allow him to use such language. "No... no, George, naughty word!" she scolded.

George's chin rose in challenge and he repeated, "Insus... able ass!"

"George!" Catie scolded again, but the child only said the words again, smiling widely as he did so. Apparently he was enjoying himself.

The sight of Catie wagging her finger caught Sean's attention, and he slowed Geoffrey's canter. "What's the matter?"

"Nothing!" Catie grumbled.

"It is something! You are telling off wee Georgie, plain as day."

Instinctively bringing her arms into a huffy fold, Catie replied, "He repeated something I said. That's all."

Sean smiled warmly as he squatted down to George's level. "Good for you, mate! Tell Sean what Auntie said."

Standing above Sean, Catie began a vigorous campaign of head shaking to keep her young nephew from sharing, but George smiled again, almost evilly this time, and pronounced quite boldly, "Insusable ass!"

"George Fitzwilliam Darcy!" Catie shrieked.

Sean stood and faced her. "You know, Georgie, I believe I've heard *that* endearment before."

Cheeks glowing a rosy pink, Catie stuttered, "I... er... I wasn't expecting him... It's just... Well! He's never repeated me before!"

"He has done that a few times with me lately as well." Sean raised a disapproving brow, leaned close to her, and whispered, "But fortunately my language is not *quite* so vulgar."

Catie saw that the corners of his mouth were fighting a considerable grin, and she giggled. Her giggle broke his grin free, and it spread and lit his face.

An hour later as the foursome walked back to the house, George, holding tightly to Sean and Catie's hands, swung out his feet every few steps, begging the two for a high swing. They obliged, but George shook his head with displeasure.

"Sorry, George," Catie said apologetically. "I'm swinging as high as I can."

"Give me your hands, Georgie," Sean offered. "I'll give you a good go 'round."

Catie watched as Sean granted each of the twins several high twirling spins, enjoying their squeals of laughter as their feet left the ground. Although she knew he had the strength, she fought off the improper urge to ask for a turn. Decorum had often been the ruin of enjoyment for Catie Darcy. She knew roughhousing on the lawn with her riding instructor would never be proper behavior.

The sight of the house was encouragement for Geoffrey to run ahead; he knew a snack would be waiting for him, and the boy had the appetite of a man. George, who normally followed his brother everywhere, uncharacteristically lingered behind.

"George," Catie looked down and questioned. "Are you not ready for a biscuit?"

"Insusable ass!" was her nephew's reply. It appeared that these were the only words he was now willing to say.

A concerned look spread over Catie's face, taking her color with it. "George!" she said worriedly.

"Give me a go," Sean said. "The lad listens well to me."

"No!" Catie dismissed. "He is *my* nephew and he will do as *I* say!" She deliberately displayed a very cross look, folded her arms and declared, "George Darcy, if you use that naughty word again, I am going to drag you by the ear straight to your mother!"

To Catie's surprise George mimicked her every movement, including the cross look and said, "Insus-able ass!"

After gasping another fair amount of air for effect, Catie attempted to resolve the problem by worsening George's consequence. This time, however, she placed her hands firmly on her hips and put a more serious tone to her voice. "George! Do *not* say that word again or I shall take you to Rose, and she does *not* allow little children to say naughty words! She'll clean your mouth with soap, and trust me... it isn't pleasant... I know!"

All of Catie's efforts made no difference to George, who again mimicked her every movement and repeated the ill-fated remark.

While watching this display of wills between the two Darcys, Sean snickered annoyingly in the background.

"Will you stop laughing?" Catie turned on him, frustrated. "It isn't helping!"

"Sorry," Sean said, trying hard to suppress his merriment. "You, Catie, are in what I would call a conundrum."

"A what?" Catie asked perturbed.

"A *conundrum*," Sean repeated. "It's a puzzle or problem with no easy solution. You can't very well tattle-tell on Georgie when it was *you* who taught him the naughty word."

Weighing his logic, Catie tapped a deliberating finger on her chin in agreement. "This is true. The first question they will ask is where did he learn such a word?"

At this revelation George pointed gleefully up at his aunt as Sean snickered again. Catie snidely acknowledged, "Yes, George, we know, thank you!"

Although he was quite enjoying himself, Sean once again offered his help. "Would you like me to try, or are you hoping to share a mouth-washing with Georgie? If my aunt is anything like my mam, she'll insist on it. If one of us older brothers encouraged a younger's mischief, we suffered the same consequences — sometimes worse."

There was no deliberating, Catie nodded solidly in agreement. Rose could be a tough old bird when she wanted to be.

Sean crouched down in front of the child and whispered into his ear. Catie tried hard to strain her auditory powers but couldn't hear what was being said.

When Sean was finished, he sat back on his heels and questioned, "Do you promise then, no more naughty words?"

Hands clasped in anticipation, George nodded excitedly as Sean reached into his shirt pocket and pulled out an intricately carved, tiny wooden horse and handed it to George.

George's eyes widened at his reward, and he flipped the carving around in his hand to give it proper examination.

"My brother Joseph carved that horse and gave it to me before I came here," Sean said proudly. "I think he would like you to have it. Joseph named him *Misneach*, that's Irish for courage."

"Oh, no, you mustn't give him that," Catie said. "He has more toys than any child could ever want. George, give that back to Sean."

With a defying glare, the boy tucked the little horse behind his back.

"George," Catie started, but Sean stopped her.

"It's okay, really. George, you can keep it. I have many more at home."

With this assurance, George took off running to the house before his aunt could make any further demands for the little horse's return.

Suddenly alone, several seconds of uncomfortable silence filled the space between Sean and Catie. Fearing conversation, or rather the topic, she thanked Sean for his help with George and started to take her leave, but he reached out and gently grasped her arm. She looked at the point of his hold and raised her eyes to his.

Sean paused. He loved her eyes, the way she looked at him, sometimes over her shoulder, sometimes with a slight tilt to her head. Blue eyes with sporadic bursts of green as if God couldn't quite decide and left them in that ambiguous state. They were enchanting. He released her arm and said a bit awkwardly, "I was just going to tell you…that if…if you want, you could come 'round early this afternoon. You know, to make up for the time you missed yesterday."

She lowered her head and spoke to her fingers that were nervously intertwining themselves in and out of each other. "All right, I can come early."

He struggled not to reach out and lift her face to his once again. "About two o'clock then?"

Catie nodded, so Sean turned and left.

TWO O'CLOCK ON THE DOT Catie arrived. She went straight to the task of saddling Chloe, glancing at Sean often as he settled Thunder in his stall. When finished, she sat in the schooling ring for nearly half an hour waiting on him, beginning to get annoyed. Finally he called out from the other side of the fence. "Come along then, we've not got all day!"

She looked at him puzzled but urged Chloe out of the gate.

Sean hadn't allowed her any serious riding after Catie had refused to share the reason for her fear of galloping. He hadn't told her this exactly, but Catie was keenly aware that she had not been taken out of the schooling ring since.

They walked along in silence as the high grass of summer swayed in the breeze below them, giving Catie a light, floating sensation. She ventured a few glances at him, but their eyes always met. So she tried forcing herself to stop.

"Are we going to practice galloping?" she asked as they rode in the direction of the flats, giving her a slight spark of triumph.

"Yes, I believe if a person is brave enough to turn their back to a gun, that person should be able to pick up a little speed on a horse."

Catie pulled Chloe to an abrupt stop. "How did you know about that?"

"Everybody knows. That story has been told over and over again the last 24 hours." Sean pulled his horse alongside hers. "And by the way, I think it showed real *misneach*."

Stunned, Catie asked, "*Misneach*, courage?"

"Aye." Sean nodded, smiling.

"Maybe you feel it showed courage, but my brother didn't. Ben only sees what I did, or didn't do rather — never mind my reasons. God, I hate that he treats me like a child." It felt good to complain. It felt unshackling, like talking to the tombstones.

A lopsided smile curled up Sean's face, and his Irish accent became heavy. "Oh, stop yer gripin', lass. Me da would have warmed the back of me britches good had I paid him no mind like that. I'd not be sittin' so comfortable in my saddle today if I were you."

"Don't tease me! You said I showed courage. Did you mean it or not?"

Sean thought carefully before responding. "If I said it…I meant it. You did what you thought was right, *but* in the same respect so did your brother."

"You can't have it both ways," Catie argued. "Either I was right or he was right!"

Narrowing his eyes, Sean moved his horse close to hers. He didn't bear the same irritated expression he had the last time he made such an advance, but she eyed him cautiously.

"Catie Darcy, you can*not* go through life on the assumption that, as long as you are doing what is right, there will be no consequences. Not only must you choose your course of action, you must accept whatever comes of that choice. If you knew you were going to upset your brother, would you have done differently?"

"No." She shook her head.

"There you go then."

"Is everything so bloody simple to you…so black and white?" Catie rebutted crossly. "Do you find nothing complicated?"

"Oh, aye!" Sean grinned. "I find many things complicated."

"Name one!" she demanded.

"You."

"Me!"

"Yes, you. When I first met you, I thought you were spoiled, insolent, and selfish. But now... well, now I've discovered that you aren't so selfish after all. It's not very often my first impressions are wrong."

"What about spoiled and insolent?"

Sean kicked his horse into a quick canter and began calling back instructions on the proper seat for galloping. "Remember, forward seat... and *hover* over the saddle..."

Catie rolled her eyes, shook her head, and followed.

Chapter 14

"Bennet Darcy, I have been looking everywhere for you!" Sarah said, walking into the kitchen.

"Well, here I am."

"Why are you down here in the kitchen?"

"I've come to speak with you....and Rose." He nodded to Rose, who was pouring out cups of tea.

"I was looking for you for the same reason." She smiled, delighted. "I have something to ask you."

Twice Ben and Sarah began speaking at the same time, but he finally conceded to his chuckling wife. "Please, go ahead."

"I am having my ladies' luncheon in the orangery on Friday and was hoping you would come down and say a few words. It would be the perfect venue for you to announce the reopening of Pemberley and its gardens to the public next summer."

Ben looked appalled. "You want me to speak at a ladies' luncheon? Indeed not! Feel free to make the announcement yourself, but I have no desire to attend a ladies' luncheon."

"There is no call for such condescension, Bennet! What have the fine women of Derbyshire done to deserve such an adamant rejection?"

"The fine women of Derbyshire have done nothing. I do *not* have the talent of public speaking, Sarah; you know that, *least* of all to a room full of chatty women." Ben pulled at his collar as if it were choking him. "I have agreed to make the announcement at the garden party, nowhere else. On this matter I am fixed," he declared with finality, hoping to avoid any further attempts at coercion.

Avoid he did but not without an exaggerated, "harrumph!" from his wife.

Rose, being the ever so diligent keeper of peace, interjected, "Did you need to speak to us about something?"

"Oh…yes!" He seemed to have lost focus. "I would like to recommend Mark Philips and his wife Annie to fill the Ledfords' place. It would mean both a higher wage and a larger house for the couple. I understand they hope to start a family soon. Of course, it would also mean replacing Annie, but Mr. Reid's daughter, Maggie, is in want of a position, and I believe she could nicely fill Annie's post."

Sarah and Rose immediately locked concerned eyes.

"Is there a problem?"

"No, Bennet, of course Rose and I would want nothing more than for Mark and Annie to take the other position. However…" Sarah paused and glanced apprehensively at Rose.

"However what?"

"Well, Annie attends to Catie when she is home from school, and her success with your sister has been…extraordinary to say the least."

"I can see no reason why Maggie can't attend to her needs just as well," Ben argued. "Catie no longer requires supervision."

"Bennet, need I remind you of the number of different caregivers she has gone through over the years? Granted she is older now, but I fear this change may be a difficult one for her."

"And for us!" Rose chimed in as Sarah nodded a worried agreement in her direction.

"Good Lord." Ben shook his head. "You women do have a tendency to over-egg the pudding!"

"I beg your pardon." Rose sounded as indignant as Sarah looked.

"What I meant, Rose, is…don't worry so…ma'am," he added the "ma'am" for good measure.

"Oh, off with you!" Rose gave Ben a pardoning shoo from the kitchen.

"Er…what shall I tell Mr. Reid?" he turned back from the door and asked warily.

"You can tell Mr. Reid that we women will egg the pudding as we see fit." Sarah's mahogany brows arched expressively.

Ben opened his mouth but then closed it, nodded, and left the kitchen.

PEMBERLEY'S ORANGERY WAS BUILT IN the early eighteen hundreds by Fitzwilliam Darcy for his wife, Elizabeth, on their fifth wedding anniversary. However, by the end of World War II, the building had fallen into disrepair. When Ben married Sarah, he had the dilapidated orangery demolished and a new one built on the sight as a wedding gift for his new wife. Gardening was as much a passion to his bride as horses were to Ben, and he thought the new orangery would be a most befitting welcome for Sarah.

The day before her luncheon, Sarah was in the orangery with two gardeners making the final touches. The long glass conservatory had the appearance of a tropical forest. The sounds of fountains permeated throughout, and a fragrant humidity filled the air. She was pruning one of her beloved lemon trees when Catie entered through one of the large wooden doors.

The girl's attempts to be interested in both Sarah's gardening skills and the upcoming luncheon did not fool her. Sarah was far too wise to be duped into believing Catie's company was only for conversation. But she entertained Catie until the true purpose of her visit surfaced.

"Oh, Sarah!" Catie cried dreamily, hands clapped together in exuberance with an expression to match. "How wonderful it looks in here!"

"Thanks," Sarah replied as she continued to snip branches.

"Though this orangery is not as big as the original one, I do believe it's much more intimate and romantic. Would you not agree?" Catie climbed upon a wrought iron bench and plopped herself onto its backrest.

Sarah, who was more than unconvinced with the wistful speech, dourly responded, "Catherine, please sit on that bench like a proper young lady. There are gardeners about."

"Oh...yes, Sarah, of course." Catie slid obediently to the seat.

This was a bit too cooperative, making Sarah stop her work and stare inquisitively at the younger woman. She couldn't help but think that, if she were a harp, her strings were being deliberately plucked. "All right, Catie, what is it that you want?" she finally asked.

"Want? Whatever do you mean, Sarah?"

"I mean, you are in want of something, so stop trying to butter me up and just ask me whatever it is you came to ask me."

"Well...er...now that you mention it, I was going to ask you something. Do you not think it would be polite to invite Sean Kelly to the garden party? Rose always attends, and I thought he might enjoy a party."

"My, my... this *is* a change of attitude. Last I heard, you considered him to be arrogant and bossy."

"*Weellll*... he is awfully bossy. But then again, Sarah, all men can be rather impossible at times. It really shouldn't be a reason *not* to invite him."

Sarah chuckled. Sean Kelly's youth and rugged good looks hadn't escaped her when he arrived. So much so, she had an initial twinge of worry that Catie might develop a schoolgirl crush on her handsome riding instructor, but the worries quickly subsided with Catie's constant complaining about Sean Kelly's strict manner and superior attitude. These complaints had recently diminished somewhat, however, and Sarah couldn't help but wonder if her earlier concern should now be warranted. She questioned, "Catie, you aren't developing feelings for Sean, are you?"

"Why, Sarah... whatever do you mean?"

"Catie Darcy, your brother might buy that innocent schoolgirl act, but I know better. I was sixteen once myself, and it was *not* all that long ago!"

Catie blushed at the question. "Sean and I are nothing more than friends. You're right. I didn't like him at all at first, but now that I have gotten to know him better... he's... well, he's not so bad."

Being only thirty years of age, Sarah had not completely forgotten the pangs of youthful infatuation. She smiled sweetly, sat on the bench, and nestled Catie under her right arm. "I do think it would be polite to invite Sean. I shall make him out a proper formal invitation at once."

Catie sprang up cheerfully. "Thanks, Sarah!"

"Catie," Sarah said softly, taking the girl's hands into her own. "You know... I'm here if you ever need to talk."

"Yes, I know." She squeezed Sarah's hands reassuringly and rushed off, her mission accomplished. On her way out, Catie broadsided her brother on his way in.

"Catie, watch where you're going!" Ben dislodged his sister from his chest.

"Sorry, Ben," she apologized, giggling, as the two fell into an impassable side step of each other. Ben finally stopped, took his sister by the shoulders, and gently moved her to one side. "Er... sorry again," she said without giggling this time.

"It's all right, Sis, just slow down." Patting her shoulder, Ben sent her on her way.

Catie had been weighing heavily on Ben's mind of late. The afternoon he had left her crying in her room troubled him still. In all of his years as a doting brother never had he been as severe with Catie as he was that day. Not a minute went by that afternoon that he didn't think guiltily of her sitting alone, crying in her room.

The morning she came to him in his study, he would have liked to wrap her in his arms and apologize for being such a brute. But he didn't. "A history of sound discipline has served England for centuries, Bennet Fitzwilliam." His grandfather's voice rang hard in his ears. Ben's life had been one of structure and obedience. Whether at home or school, his father or grandfather, a prefect or teacher, Ben Darcy had had a typical English upbringing. He had learned to toe the line.

His father had been whimsical, followed his fancies and where did it get him? He died, basically killed himself in his recklessness, and left his already motherless children fatherless as well. Ben's jaw tightened as the resentment rose suddenly and then receded, as predictable as the tide.

It wasn't his father's fault, he told himself. Catie's tears had wrenched him since her arrival home from the hospital. Those first days of her life at Pemberley, crying out for a mother who would never come, caused a much younger Ben to heave his supper one night. He had to harden himself to those cries early on. He had to be her rock, not some weakling that spilled his supper over a crying baby. He would make her strong, capable of taking on whatever else this cruel world had to throw at her. He would see to it that she was the Darcy his mother and father would have wanted — would have raised themselves had they lived to do so.

Sarah was right. Catie *was* growing up, becoming a woman. Her very appearance was evidence of it. Seeing her as the perpetual little sister, her brother had not noticed Catie's maturity for the most part until Mr. Ledford's indecent actions made him wake up and take notice.

"What is going on with her hair, Sarah?" Ben asked approaching his wife.

"Whose hair, darling?" Sarah responded somewhat distractedly, never looking up from her work.

"Catie's hair, she wears it down constantly now. Why would she be doing that?" He glanced worriedly in the direction of Catie's departure.

Sarah shrugged. "She probably just wants to look a little older."

He frowned. "Whatever for?"

Annoyed, Sarah again stopped her work and rested her gloved hands on her hips. "Did you come all the way out here to discuss your sister's hair, darling?"

"No, of course not, I came out here to discuss your luncheon."

"Oh…" Sarah cried excitedly. "Have you decided to speak?"

"Certainly *not*, I have come to speak to you concerning Catie."

"*Catie?*"

"Yes…I…I…"

"You what?"

Ben was dead serious. "I believe in the not-so-distant future my sister may start to develop an interest in…in *boys*, Sarah."

She snorted and laughed at the same time, quickly covering her face with a glove in embarrassment.

Ben scowled over the enjoyment being had at his expense. "May I ask what is so amusing?"

Sarah cleared her throat and tried mimicking his sincerity. "Ahem, It's just…I mean…yes, darling, I must concur, *not* so distant at all." Then with some difficulty in keeping a straight face she added, "As a matter of fact it could be upon us before we even realize it."

"Yes, that's exactly what I was thinking," Ben agreed and went into a long explanation about how it was his responsibility to make sure that Catie was well situated in life — that she marry well and, in order for her to do so, needed to be exposed to the *right* group of young men. Gone were the days of ceremoniously presenting England's young — and, of course, well-born — debutantes at Court, announcing their release into society. Therefore, he argued, it was their duty to unceremoniously bring Catie forward. And what better occasion to begin that process than at the garden party.

"But, Bennet," Sarah said. "Catie will have an eighteenth birthday party to come out. And you certainly are no help. You abhor society unless it's the Grand National or a country hunt ball."

"And what, may I ask, is wrong with a hunt ball?"

"You abhor society, your sister abhors hunting, as does your wife," she mumbled the latter quietly under her breath, but he heard her.

"Forget hunt balls." He made a face and shook his head. "It's up to the parents nowadays to manage these things, always has been really. They have the most influence after all. Your comments about the Hirst boy got me to thinking about it all. We need to take the control here, Sarah. You and I need to delicately start the process."

"And what is it you expect me to do?" Sarah asked, alarmed.

Ben leaned in as if he were revealing the plan to some great caper. "During your luncheon use your female tactics to hint that Pemberley would *especially* like to have in attendance the sons, grandsons, and nephews of … well, there's no delicate way to say it…*desirable* families. Make it clear that Catie will be seventeen soon. Old enough to start…you know…socializing with lads." He presented an adamant finger. "Supervised, of course; there'll be no shenanigans to be sure."

Sarah narrowed her eyes. "Should I get references on these *lads* or will any one of England's big-eared, buck-toothed blue bloods do?"

"Sarah Darcy!" he exclaimed. "How could you speak of your fellow country-men in that manner?"

"And how can you put your sister on the block like one of your thorough-breds?"

"I am doing no such thing! I just think it is time Catie started being intro-duced to the *right* pool of young men."

"Catie is a sensible girl, Ben, and perfectly capable of choosing her own suitors. I would hate to think I had picked you out of such a *small* pool of prior chosen eligibles. Her inheritance alone will guarantee that she is well situated in life. Really, Ben, the days of parents intervening in such matters are long gone."

"Let me remind you that Catie doesn't receive a penny of that inheritance before her twenty-fifth birthday. Until then, I hold control of her trusts. Surely, Sarah, even you can see how vulnerable her pending wealth will make her to every blackguard in England." Ben sighed heavily but wasn't to be de-feated. Lowering his voice to a convincing tone, he added, "It is just as much our responsibility to guide her through this as it is to see that she's properly educated, is it not?"

To this Sarah could make no feasible argument. Furthermore, her prior conversation with Catie (not that she would be sharing any of that conversa-tion with her husband) was proof in itself of their young sister's growing need for parental guidance in the social realm. So she agreed.

Satisfied with his success, Ben glanced about to make sure the gardeners were well out of sight and lovingly kissed his wife. "Just out of curiosity, my love," he said, pulling back and flashing a charming grin down at her. "Just how large was that pool of eligible young men you chose me out of?"

To this comment Sarah slowly removed one of her gloves, with care and deliberateness pulled each finger loose, and started whacking him with it. Arms raised in defense, Ben scurried out of the orangery, laughing. He was rather pleased to have gotten the best of her... for once.

Chapter 15

When Maggie Reid received word that Mrs. Darcy would like to speak with her concerning a position at Pemberley, her father was elated. Mr. Reid knew the Darcys to be an exceptional family to work for and was sure his Maggie would be happy with them. Maggie, however, wasn't quite as elated as her father was. A shy girl, Maggie had rarely been out of the county of Derbyshire and never a night away from home.

A learning disability, which went undiagnosed until her early teens, made school almost impossible for Maggie. She could read, but not well, and only when she was forced to.

Just four years old when her father lost his legs, the bulk of Maggie's life was spent caring for him. Her mother worked long hours to provide for Maggie and her younger sister, leaving Maggie to run the house and nurse her crippled father. But she didn't mind this. Like her grandmother, Maggie had an appetite for the craft of healing and spent many hours learning the elderly woman's remedies. She knew that a hot boiled potato would treat corns. She had committed to memory all the medicinal uses of purple sage. Each month when the doctor called on her father, Maggie would fetch instruments from his bag. The black and chrome tools were heavy and solid in her hands. Maggie loved the feel of them. If she'd had the ability to learn properly she would have chosen a career in nursing, but that was a dream she abandoned years ago with the difficult, and sometimes shameful, experiences at school.

Maggie accepted the position. She would be an upstairs maid.

She was apprehensive as she rode her bicycle to the grand manor, which she had only seen from a distance. It wasn't the work that caused her concern.

Margaret Reid had never shirked a chore in her life. It was Catherine Darcy. Granddaughter to the locally hailed Geoffrey Darcy and Lord Byron Sumner, Miss Darcy's lineage was as impressive as the thoroughbreds in Pemberley's stables. To Maggie Reid, Catie Darcy was everything she wasn't — rich, well educated, finely dressed, but most of all...self-confident.

On the day the Darcys came to visit, Maggie had watched Catie Darcy through the window for some time before her father called her. Maggie immediately noticed the girl was very much like her brother, prideful in her appearance with a distinct air of superiority.

Maggie hated to admit it, but she possessed more than a small degree of envy for Pemberley's young miss — not because of the girl's wealth but rather her abundant self-confidence. Maggie had never held herself as straight and proud as Miss Catie did, shoulders back, head up, and looking the world directly in the eye. If she had that level of confidence, Maggie thought, nothing would be out of reach. Possibly not even a career in nursing.

It started to rain, and Maggie pedaled faster.

It was a dreary, wet afternoon in England's midlands. Outside, peonies and roses sagged with the weight of the tiny puddles that gathered on their petals, while inside, Catie sat in her room, answering letters to schoolmates. A small rap on the door interrupted her.

"Yes," she responded, and Rose entered with Maggie Reid.

Catie lifted her head, and her eyes instantly met with Maggie's.

She hadn't been able to stop thinking about Maggie Reid since the day she and Ben rode away from the Reids' cottage. Not only was Maggie Reid in possession of her mother's name, but she had a story that went along with that name. Catie shared no story with her mother, except of course how she died giving birth to her.

Adding to the insult, Margaret Darcy was the first person to ever hold Maggie. Catie had imagined her mother cooing and talking sweetly to the newborn. Maggie had felt Margaret's motherly touch and heard her consoling voice. *God, she resented Maggie Reid.*

"Will it be an inconvenience if we put your clothes away, miss?" Rose asked formally since she was training Maggie.

Giving Maggie a hateful stare, Catie shook her head.

As Rose directed Maggie, she spoke tenderly to the girl, patting Maggie's back and shoulder reassuringly. Catie watched the two intently, and it quickly

146

became more than she could bear. Maggie Reid may have received more attention in life from Catie's mother than Catie was to ever have, but Maggie Reid most definitely was not going to get affection from Rose.

"That is *not* where my socks go!" she said, outraged.

The sudden outburst caused Rose and Maggie to turn to her. "Miss Catie, that is where your socks have gone since you were an infant," Rose replied, trying not to sound too admonishing.

Catie looked Rose squarely in the eye, ignoring the warning look she was receiving. "I don't care where they *have* gone, everything is *most* inconvenient for me, and I plan to rearrange it all!"

"Oh, you do, do you? And when may we expect this rearranging to occur, Miss Catie?" Rose asked, her tone beginning to sharpen.

"When I get around to it, until then she can just place my things on my bed and leave."

Rose didn't reply to this, instead she gave Maggie another gentle tap to her shoulder and sent her to fetch fresh linens for Miss Catie's bed. She walked over and quietly shut the door behind Maggie.

The expression on Rose's face when she turned back made Catie swallow. She had gone too far. Rose came and stood in front of the writing table with folded arms. Catie ignored her, hoping she would simply let it drop, but then Rose cleared her throat, distinctively.

Blast, Catie thought. "Yes, Nan?" She looked up and answered sweetly with a smile to match.

"Let me make something very clear, Catie Darcy. We are *not* going to be unkind to young Maggie!"

"Fine," Catie argued back, her chin raised. "I'll not be unkind, but I don't like her, and I don't want her in my room!"

"And what in the world has that sweet girl done to you, may I ask?" Rose leaned over the desk, causing Catie to sit back.

Maggie Reid may have had my mother but she'll not have my Nan, Catie thought spitefully. "How can you like her better than me, Nan? You have only known her but a few days, and me my whole life."

"What's all this about?" Rose scuttled around the desk and took Catie's face in her hands. "Dearest Catherine, I could never like any girl better than I do you. Maggie is very shy and in a strange place with new responsibilities. I am only trying to help her adjust, make her feel at home."

"Do you mean that?"

"What do you think?" Rose stared down at her.

Shamefaced, Catie lowered her head. "You're right. I'm sorry. I don't know why I behaved that way."

Looking displeased, Rose adamantly concurred, "Nor do I, but I'll not have it!"

"Please don't be cross with me."

"It's all right, child." Rose's motherly scowl softened and she pulled Catie tight against her. She held her there until a faint knock at the door announced Maggie's return.

"Are you okay?" Rose asked.

Catie nodded and glanced at the door. "I'll apologize to Maggie if you say I must."

"We'll not make any more of it this time," Rose said. "But I think Sarah's right. You are starting to grow up."

"Oh." Catie managed a smile. "Tell Ben. Will you?"

Rose rolled her eyes and shook her head despairingly. "He's as thick as any man, Catie. I'm afraid he will have to come to his own realization in his own time. But when he does, he'll puff up and think he's the bee's knees for knowing something we all didn't."

Catie giggled as Rose opened the door and explained nicely that Miss Catie had decided not to rearrange her things.

THE DRESS SARAH BOUGHT IN the spring for that year's garden party was, to her chagrin, amongst the first of her wardrobe to become snug. A trip to London was in short order. She hoped her seamstress could alter it.

Ben was hosting Charles Worthington for the weekend, so Sarah decided to have Catie accompany her. He walked his wife and sister down the front steps of Pemberley and opened the car door. Ben turned to Catie, snuggling her tightly against his chest and giving the top of her head a soft kiss. "Buy a pretty frock now, Sis," he said, grinning. "But leave me a few quid to pay the butcher, eh?"

Catie responded by wrapping her arms around him and squeezing him unusually long and tight. Ben glanced over at Sarah with a slight look of bewilderment. Catie had always been affectionate, but never overly. Ben gently pulled her back and questioned, "Is everything all right, Catie?"

"Everything is fine," she replied, smiling up at him.

Once she was settled in her seat, Ben shut the door behind her to allow him and Sarah a moment's privacy. Nestling her under his chin, he begged his wife to take it easy and not to overdo it. This pregnancy meant so much to them both. Bennet Darcy would have filled Pemberley with fifty children if it were possible. Like his mother, he very much desired a large family. Unfortunately, with the string of heartbreaking miscarriages in the fourteen years between him and Catie, his mother's dream was never to be realized.

"Stop being a fusspot," Sarah said, sensing his concern. "And remember to look in on the children. I know when Charles arrives you will become distracted and forget...so don't."

"Yes, Mrs. Darcy." Ben smiled at her. "Now stop scolding, woman, and kiss me before you miss your train."

"CATIE, DEAR, WE MUST BE off. My appointment with Mrs. Tuttle is in less than half an hour!" Sarah called up the tall, winding staircase of the Darcys' London home as she stuffed a few things in her purse.

"Coming!" Catie appeared, rushing down the steps.

"Is the car ready?" Sarah turned to Wade Radcliff, who was at the door with an umbrella in hand.

"Yes, madam," Wade said, holding up a "one moment" finger to the taxi driver.

The Edwardian townhome, with its impressive Portland stone façade, was purchased in the 1920's by Ben and Catie's grandfather. The home was originally built to host a prominent family through London's Season, but business was the necessity of the day. An investor and financier like his father and grandfather, it was necessary that Ben Darcy be in town several times a month.

Catie never felt at home in Mayfair. Her father had rarely brought her to London with him, as in doing so it would have meant bringing her caregivers as well. The few times she accompanied him to town was when he could devote all of his time to her, which wasn't often. Once Ben married Sarah, Catie came to London more frequently. Sarah, who loved the shopping, entertainment, and restaurants the city offered, enjoyed taking her new little sister to children's boutiques and outfitting her in the latest London fashion. Still, while Catie relished Sarah's attention, Derbyshire and Pemberley would always be home.

Standing in the third floor window of the seamstress's building, looking down on a very busy street, Catie couldn't help but think what a different world the city was from the peaceful serenity of Pemberley Estate. Spotting a fish shop on the corner, Catie's stomach began to rumble, and she walked back across the room to Sarah.

Sarah gazed gravely in the large looking glass as Mrs. Tuttle moved around her, examining the dress and shaking her head. "I'm not sure, Mrs. Darcy," Mrs. Tuttle repeated again as Catie approached.

"Sarah," she interrupted them, "may we have fish and chips for lunch? There's a shop across the street."

"No, Catie." Sarah shook her head, sounding appalled by the suggestion. "I've already made reservations at my favorite bistro for our lunch."

"*French* food! Good Lord, Sarah! I'm starving, and the French hardly put enough on a plate for *half* a person!"

Feeling the binds of her dress tight against her torso, Sarah glanced sourly at Catie. "Catherine, I do not eat fried foods. When a woman reaches thirty and has given birth to twins, it's no longer an option." Catie's shoulders dropped in disappointment. "Plus, I made those reservations for a reason. I have something very special to tell you over lunch."

Catie folded her arms and walked back to the window, grumbling under her breath, "Thanks, Sarah, now I'm starving *and* anxious."

The seamstress chuckled and whispered, "She has personality, that one, and pretty too. Your husband will have his hands full keeping young chaps at bay with that little miss."

Sarah chuckled herself and declared with a hint of pride in her voice, "You haven't met my husband. It is more likely to be the chaps that will have their hands full. Any young man willing to go through Bennet Darcy to get to her, will be worthy of his sister indeed."

Unsuccessful with the seamstress, Sarah and Catie sat at a table by the window and ate their lunch. The two had a long afternoon of shopping ahead of them, as they were leaving town the next day and no new dresses had yet been purchased.

Once they finished at the bistro, Sarah took Catie to one of her favorite boutiques. It was close enough to walk, so they didn't need a taxi. The streets were crowded and busy. Horns blew constantly and sirens wailed in the distance as they slowly made their way.

"Does Ben know?" Catie asked breathlessly, almost doing circles around Sarah as she dodged passersby.

"Of course he knows." Sarah laughed. "Now slow down, you're so excited I can hardly keep pace with you."

"What about Rose?" Catie tried to temper her step.

"Yes, Rose knows as well."

"Have you told everyone? Was I last?" She sounded disappointed.

Sarah stopped and pulled Catie into a shop doorway. "I haven't told anyone my suspicions."

Catie's eyes grew round. "Twins again!"

"Good Lord, no!" Sarah leaned forward and whispered, "I believe it's a girl."

"Oh," Catie squealed, "A girl!"

Sarah gave her head a wary tilt. "However, it may be better to keep my suspicions from your brother as yet."

Catie nodded, glad to be Sarah's confidante on the matter.

Sarah smiled. "All right, let's find us the perfect frocks now, shall we?"

Sarah Darcy was always a welcomed sight inside the small dress shop that catered to wealthy clients. Mrs. Darcy spent freely and was always offered every convenience to keep her shopping. She was generally an easy fit, but today Sarah was to be a more difficult client than usual.

No less than fifteen failed dresses into the afternoon, Sarah was becoming tired. "Maybe madam would like some tea," the shop girl suggested.

"Yes, thank you." Sarah nodded dismally and sat down to wait on the refreshment.

She had just made herself comfortable when Abigail Hirst, Aiden Hirst's mother, came into the shop.

The Hirst family was *nouveaux riche* by Darcy standards. They were long-time dairy farmers south of the Peak District, until coal was found in their grazing fields. The greater part of the Hirst fortune was earned during the Industrial Revolution. They were owners and operators of a Derbyshire colliery, and shareholders in the railway company that carried the coal out of the county. During the mid-1800s, the Hirst family built Ardsley Manor, a Victorian Era country house near Matlock in Derbyshire.

Sarah had done as Ben had asked and "dropped the hint" at her luncheon, casually mentioning to her table that Catie would be seventeen in November and would soon be in want of more socializing. Sarah considered it to be enough to tell Ben she had done as he asked, but certainly not enough to bring about a stampede of England's well-to-do, teenage boys to Pemberley's garden party.

Although she had a very comfortable upbringing, Sarah was raised much more modestly than her husband and was not as well versed in the gossip pipeline of the rich. Unbeknownst to Sarah Darcy, she had said plenty, and Abigail Hirst was first in line to give young Catherine Darcy the once-over.

Sarah was resting in a dressing gown on a small sofa with her feet up when Abigail approached her. Swelling ankles had been a bothersome side effect from her first pregnancy and not a welcomed return. Sarah was never as unsociable as her husband could be, but she was in no mood for conversation.

"Oh…Abigail, how are you?" She pasted on a smile and asked with mock enthusiasm.

"Fine, Sarah, and you're well I see." Abigail took an unoffered seat beside her on the sofa.

"Yes, thank you."

"So…that's William and Margaret's Catherine. My…she *is* petite," Abigail said and looked at Sarah quizzically. "How old is she again?"

"Sixteen."

"Oh, goodness, she's still young, not yet fully grown I'm sure. She could be much taller in a year or so, and a soundly built girl if I ever saw one. And my, she does have a very pretty face. Very much like her mother, that one."

Sarah looked at the chattering Abigail Hirst in disbelief, but the woman took no notice. As if she were shopping for a dress or shoes, Mrs. Hirst sized up Catie's person from head to toe.

"I understand our children have met." Abigail turned back to Sarah with a proud twinkling smile. "Aiden took a real fancy to Catherine I think. He has spoken of nothing else since he returned from the country."

"Abigail…" Sarah tried to speak but the woman spoke over her.

"You do know his Uncle Lawrence and Aunt Eleanor have no children, leaving our Aiden in line to inherit Ardsley. Oh, I know it's not comparable to Pemberley but still a fine house. Will you brunch with us tomorrow?"

Sarah replied shortly, "I'm sorry, Abigail, but Catie and I are leaving town first thing in the morning."

"Oh, no bother," Abigail said, waving off Sarah's less than polite regrets. "We shall see you in a few weeks at the garden party then." Abigail stood but didn't leave. Instead, she glanced around the shop and then leaned close and whispered, "We must be vigilant parents in this less formal age, Sarah. One can never be too careful. Well, cheerio." Mrs. Hirst patted Sarah's shoulder and paraded out of the dress shop, pleased and confident with their little tête-à-tête.

"The cheek!" Sarah hissed under her breath as she watched the woman leave.

The following morning Sarah was quiet during the train journey home, fuming from her encounter with Abigail Hirst. She couldn't wait to have her husband's ear but wait she must. Before she left London, Ben had telephoned her at the townhouse to inform his wife that Charles Worthington was staying on until morning. What Sarah had hoped would be a quiet Sunday family evening was now to be a long drawn-out night of dinner and entertaining. This, of course, did not help the fuming.

Catie was equally lost in her own thoughts that morning. She had missed church, meaning she had missed hearing Sean sing. After his solo he had been unceremoniously put into a choir robe and had riveted the congregation with his voice ever since.

Like the rest of Holy Trinity's flock, Catie waited with anticipation for those cherished five minutes that Sean stood singing with the choir, though for very different reasons. It was only then that she could watch him, study him without drawing attention — his eyes, his mouth, and the way his face grew somber when a verse especially touched him. Although she hadn't yet admitted the truth to her innocent, delicate heart, Catie Darcy was falling in love.

Now in the car and only a few miles from Pemberley, Sarah turned to Catie. "Dress nicely for dinner tonight. Mr. Worthington will be joining us."

"Mr. *Worthington*?" Catie moaned, "Oh, Sarah, can't I please just have dinner upstairs with Geoffrey and George?"

"No one more than me would like to have dinner with Geoffrey and George," Sarah replied without sympathy. "But like you, I have no choice. We have a guest and we must be hospitable to that guest. So when we get home, I want you to go upstairs and get dressed for dinner."

Catie drew in an annoyed breath and breathed out unenthusiastically. "Yes, Sarah." She turned to the window and thoughtfully stared out. *Wesley Howell. Was he the reason for Charles Worthington's weekend visit?* As the car grew closer to Pemberley, Catie decided to take advantage of the rare opportunity of having Sarah alone. "Sarah," she said nonchalantly. "Who is Wesley Howell?"

"How do you know about Wesley Howell?"

"I heard Mr. Worthington mention his name." Catie kept a casual tone.

Sarah gazed at Catie as if contemplating whether she should divulge any information, so Catie thought she would help her along. "Was he related to Arthur Howell or Mary?"

"He was…" Sarah said cautiously. "Wesley is their grandson."

"But how can that be? Mary only had Thomas, and he never married or had children," Catie countered, fearing she had said too much.

Sarah's eyebrows drew close. "How is it you know so much about the Howells?"

Not wanting to share the diary or letters, Catie shrugged.

"Well, I really do not think your brother would want me discussing this with you." Sarah tapped Catie's leg affectionately but dismissively. "It is sordid and complicated, and the less you know about it the better. Your brother has the matter under control and you need not worry yourself about any of it."

Nodding, Catie looked out the window again. *Wesley Howell could not possibly be Mary's grandson*, she thought, but said no more.

Chapter 16

B en felt restless and headed off to the stables for a ride. He had much on his mind and wanted more than anything to push Geronimo and himself, to ride hard and fast until they both were sweating and spent. Since he was old enough to take off alone on horseback, Ben Darcy had found solace in his saddle, galloping over land first settled by his ancestors in the seventeenth century. It humbled him, yet at the same time gave him a sense of power. The land engulfed him with a sense of purpose in a world that so often made no sense.

It was on horseback that he first cried for his mother. He was only fourteen years old and had tried to be a man, to be brave. But once the cold November wind hit him and the repetitive sound of the galloping hooves blocked out all other sound, he crumbled; he wailed and screamed and pushed the horse until neither of them could go on. But he *had* gone on. What was started so long ago would continue through Geoffrey and George and the child Sarah carried.

This was what troubled him about Mary Howell or Aunt Mary as he had known her when he was a boy. How could she have given away her grandson, her flesh and blood, Thomas's child? Penniless or not, how could she have signed over her grandson's inheritance and relinquished his claim on Pemberley? And why had she kept the child's existence from his grandfather? How could he make this right again for both himself and his children … and for Wesley Howell?

When Ben reached the stable yard, he saw Sean Kelly at work in the paddock with Thunder. And, to his surprise, Catie sat watching from the top of the post and rail fence. Curious, Ben glanced down at his watch and stepped back in the shadow of the stable door, out of sight.

Now secure in his surroundings, Thunder was frisky and nibbled at Sean's ear. "We're friends and all, mate, but I don't fancy you like that," Sean admonished the horse who whinnied with great satisfaction, and Catie laughed. Not the girlish sisterly giggle Ben was used to but rather a soft, purposeful laugh that flowed slow and smooth like honey. It suddenly trickled into Bennet Darcy's brain that his little sister wasn't the awkward girl he had thought.

Playfully swinging her legs, she waited until she had Sean's attention and artfully gathered a few windblown tresses and tucked them behind her ear. Her dimples and smiling, half-moon eyes twinkled like gold in water. Ben stood stock-still, shocked to say the least. Surely his sister must know better.

He felt his jaw tighten as he moved toward the two and rested his arms over the fence. Out of the corner of his eye, Ben noticed Catie's teasing expression fade and the playful feet settle firmly on the rail.

She did know better.

"How is Thunder doing, Sean?"

"Feeling his oats today, Mr. Darcy." Sean rubbed the animal's nose. "A bit coltish still but he'll carry a rider soon enough. Some lads take a little longer to learn their manners. Eh, *buachaill*?" he crooned at the horse.

"Excellent, you've done a fine job with him." Ben gave him an approving nod. "I appreciate the hard work."

Seeming flattered by the compliment, Sean smiled. "Thank you, sir."

"Well, we'll leave you to it then, lad; wouldn't want to stand in the way of progress." Ben stepped away from the fence and held out an upturned palm to his sister. "Come along, Catie," he said with a beckoning flick of his wrist.

Looking down, Catie saw Ben's expression, purposefully blank. She hated that look. Reluctantly, she climbed down, glancing uneasily at Sean as she did. He instinctively glanced back, as if offering her some silent encouragement.

Side by side and without speaking, she and Ben walked in the direction of the lake, passing through the long, maple walk where the air was lush and cool under the broad, summer leaves. Ben stopped at the top of the slope and looked out at the scene before him for several minutes. Two ducks waddled into the water in search of an afternoon meal, sending tiny waves to lap against the bulrush.

"It appears as though you have an abundant amount of free time during this part of the afternoon," he said finally, his eyes still cast out over the lake.

"We were only talking, Ben," she quietly clarified.

"With school starting back in a month, I believe this time of day would be much better employed in the music room at your instruments," he replied. Catie exhaled a rush of annoyed air and turned to leave. "Catherine!" Ben stopped her, turning from the water to look at her now. "Dad wouldn't like it. Sean's a nice lad but he works for me. Surely you must see how — "

"Daddy wasn't like that!" she argued back, interrupting him. "He wouldn't care."

"I care!" His eyes darkened with a familiar grief, one Catie knew all too well. "I have an obligation to him. And because of that … *I* care!"

She stared at him, silent, wondering whatever happened to the carefree, little boy who threw cowpats at cars on the highroad. Maybe he died with their mother, she thought, forever replaced by this man who did everything expected of him, and more.

Ben turned back to the lake, as if unable to bear his sister's gaze.

Catie watched him for another moment, then turned and walked away towards the house.

SARAH HAD YET TO SPEAK with Ben about Abigail Hirst. She was waiting for the right opportunity when she would have his undivided attention. Her fuming had given way to concern, and it was her plan to send the children to their rooms early that evening.

The timing was bad, however, as Ben was on edge and preoccupied. He had made a second, substantially larger, offer to Wesley Howell in hopes of settling Mary Howell's debt to the man and was now waiting to hear back from Charles Worthington. But Sarah couldn't keep this to herself any longer, and her husband did seem somewhat relaxed reading his newspaper.

The twins and Catie were stretched out over the carpet as Geoffrey and George listened to their aunt tell the story of when a dragon lived at Pemberley House. Catie loved making up stories — a gift from her father, Rose had once told her. Sarah studied Catie for some time as Abigail's words, "William and Margaret's Catherine," played in her thoughts. She meant no disrespect to Ben's parents, but Sarah just didn't think of Catie as William and Margaret's but rather hers and Ben's. And why shouldn't she? They had brought Catie up, nurtured and loved her, seen to her education, everything a parent is supposed to do.

Sarah had always been Catie's ally, but she had never interfered with her husband's decisions concerning his sister. But this was different. Catie's happiness in life was important to Sarah, and she was resolved to make sure her sister was happy, even if she did have to step on a few of her husband's toes to do so.

As soon as the story was over, Sarah kissed the boys goodnight and gave them over to Mrs. Newell. To Sarah's great relief, Catie claimed to be overly tired and followed, unwittingly completing Sarah's plan.

"Catie was awfully quiet tonight," Sarah observed as soon as she and Ben were alone.

He laid the newspaper on his lap. "She's just sulking. She'll be over it soon enough."

"Sulking? Why?"

He sighed heavily and looked over at her. "My guess would be because her brother refuses to allow her to behave the ridiculous flirt like her friend Audrey Tillman."

"What makes you think Audrey Tillman is a ridiculous flirt?"

With complete confidence, Ben replied, "I have my sources."

"Would this have anything to do with Catie's sudden interest in practicing her piano this afternoon?"

He nodded. "It would."

"Sean Kelly?" Sarah asked with a tone of apprehension in her voice. She had been afraid of this.

"Yes," he answered shortly, his jaw tightening just thinking about it.

"Ben, please tell me you didn't embarrass her?"

"Of course not."

Relieved, Sarah assured him, "It is nothing more than a harmless fancy, very normal and *very* innocent."

"Sean Kelly works for me, Sarah. She shouldn't be so familiar with him. It isn't proper."

"He is Rose's nephew and Catie's friend," Sarah stated firmly.

"That does not make it appropriate for her to behave in such a manner, and I shan't allow it." Ben opened up his paper again and tucked himself behind it, his way of saying that he was finished with the discussion.

Sighing, Sarah didn't press him further. She had more important matters to pursue. "I ran into Abigail Hirst in London."

"Mm-hmm," he uttered, not attempting to hide his lack of interest.

"She seemed to be very interested in your sister."

Ben lowered the newspaper. "Interested...in Catie?"

"Yes, she thought she had a very pretty face, but was a little concerned about her small stature." Legs crossed, Sarah's foot was bouncing to the beat of her apparent resentment towards the woman. "I didn't offer to show her Catie's teeth, as we *were* in a dress shop."

A grin curled up one side of Ben's mouth. Sarah looked like a mother bear ready to fight to the death for her cub. Purely for the sport of it, he bantered back, "Humph...now that *is* a shame, our Catie has good teeth. It is after all one of her best selling points."

"I do not like that humor, Bennet Darcy." Sarah sat up and glowered at him. "And I did not like that old biddy sizing up Catie like she did. Do you know what she said to me? 'You do know our Aiden is in line to inherit Ardsley Manor.' Oh, the cheek of that woman!"

"Take care, Sarah." Ben tried to calm her, barely suppressing what he was sure would be an unwelcomed chuckle. "Abigail Hirst is just a little...you know, old school. She and my mother were presented into society the same year. In those days a young person's mother nudged them a little. And it wasn't always a bad outcome. My parents were nudged toward each other, and they had a happy, loving marriage."

"I'm sorry, Bennet! But I do not see *nudging* any differently than those barbaric, over-the-cradle betrothals of your ancestors," Sarah argued, sitting back in a silent huff. She had accomplished nothing, and worst of all, Ben didn't seem at all bothered by Abigail's actions.

Wisely avoiding the "barbaric" remark, Ben tried to return to his reading, but his wife's humor didn't improve. Putting the paper aside, he patted the spot beside him on the sofa. "Come here," he said apologetically.

She turned her head. Childish, she knew, but effective nonetheless.

"Come here, Mrs. Darcy, or you shall discover just how barbaric we Darcys can be." His voice was throaty but playful.

Against her better judgment Sarah moved over and snuggled under his arm, secretly apologizing to her fellow feminists for caving to such rudimental, masculine persuasion. It wasn't completely without design though. She needed leveraged conversation and knew the closer her soft skin and lightly perfumed scent were to her husband, the better — her own rudimental persuasion. "Oh, Bennet, promise me you'll never nudge Catie in anyone's direction. Maybe she doesn't even want to get married. Maybe she'll run a major corporation or be prime minister. If Margaret Thatcher can — "

"Sarah," he interrupted her, "have you seen the litter of romance novels scattered about my sister's bedroom?"

"A woman can be both a romantic and a successful business woman, Bennet!"

"Did I say she couldn't?"

"No," Sarah said repentantly as she brought his hand to her mouth and brushed his knuckles with her lips. "No you didn't."

"What's all this really about?"

"Bennet, I'm afraid. Maybe we shouldn't interfere so. Surely you can see how she wants nothing more than to please you. I fear if you were to nudge her, she might choose someone to satisfy you instead of herself."

He touched her cheek affectionately. "Darling, no one wants to see Catie happy more than I."

"But that's the problem, Ben, don't you see?" She sat up and faced him. "Your ideal of happiness may not be hers."

"I shan't do anything other than what's in her best interest," he stated resolutely. "Fair enough?"

Sarah nodded halfheartedly, taking note that he made no promises. Her own marriage suddenly came to mind. Sarah had never met Ben's mother — and his father only once. She often wondered if he would have even married her if his mother were alive.

Bennet Darcy was the biggest catch at Cambridge University, and those fishing for him had some rather alluring bait. But he stepped aside from all of the young and pretty socialites who kept a constant circle around him and chose her.

At first Sarah had gone out of her way to avoid him because he seemed conceited. She disliked him really. She was the only person in their World Politics course (including the professor) who challenged his hidebound conservative views with her more liberal ideology. Sarah Mottinger was outspoken and headstrong, the daughter of a nine-to-five father and a school teacher mother, and yet... Bennet Darcy had chosen her.

Would Margaret Darcy, the daughter of Lord Sumner, have approved? Or would Ben have been *nudged* in another direction? It was a question Sarah asked herself almost every time she passed the woman's portrait in the gallery.

NOT REALLY TIRED, CATIE HURRIED to her room to wait. Her bed had been changed and turned down, telling her Maggie Reid had already come and gone. The two were doing an excellent job of avoiding each other, which was just fine with Catie.

She pushed open her window and sat, tucking her knees under her chin, to watch impatiently as night tiptoed slowly in and greedily consumed the sleepy lawns and gardens. Wafting up from the bushes, she could hear the "*crex, crex*" of the corncrakes, screeching loudly to attract a mate. Their rhythm lulled her until the tree tops finally disappeared into the shadows. She turned off all of her lights and took the service stairs down to a side door, praying it wouldn't be bolted when she returned.

Padding mouse-like through the walled garden to the pond, Catie thought of Sean. He had often said he took walks at night to wind down before bed, and she hoped this was one of those nights.

Stepping out onto the small dock, she sat down and removed her shoes to dangle her feet in the cool water. Under a new moon, the still darkness closed in tightly, and she kept her torch light on for comfort, wishing Sean would hurry.

For entertainment, she laid flat on the dock and shone the beam up into the trees, waiting, hoping. Soon she heard the rustling of footsteps, his footsteps. She called softly out to him, "Sean, is that you?"

"Catie?" he said, equally as hushed.

"Yes." She laughed. "Who else?"

Still lying on her back, streaming the light up into the starry sky, she turned the beam to his face when he stepped out onto the dock. As before, he instinctively raised a protective hand to his eyes.

"What are you doing out so late?" he asked.

She turned the beam back to the heavens and exhaled loudly. "Oh, I couldn't sleep."

"You shouldn't be out this late. Go home." Sean gestured toward the manor with his chin.

"And *you* shouldn't be so bossy." She patted the planks invitingly. "Sit."

Sean glanced back towards the house and deliberated. He knew she was too stubborn to leave and decided it was better to stay with her than leave her alone. Kicking off his shoes, Sean rolled up his tattered boot cut Levi's to his knees and sat down beside her. It took several attempts to put his feet in the water, as he winced and sucked air through his teeth.

"Namby-pamby." She giggled.

"Hey! It's cold!" he said defensively. "How do you swim in this?"

"Completely nak — "

"Never mind!" he interrupted her, shaking his head.

"Well, you asked." Still giggling, Catie sat up.

Now side by side and close, the two gently swayed their feet back and forth in the water. Sean seemed so free, so unfettered, and she envied that. It was as if he had no rules, no one telling him how to sit, how to dress, what is and isn't proper. Proper. Sometimes she wished she would never hear that word again.

"So, I hear you've received an invitation to the garden party. Are you coming?" she asked.

"I believe I must. I've never had a cucumber sandwich before."

"Your mother is English and you've *never* had a cucumber sandwich?"

"Aye, but my father's Irish and with five hungry boys to feed, well…cucumber sandwiches would be a bit dainty for our lot. We are more meat and potatoes."

They were quiet for several minutes, listening to the swishing water and the stirring of leaves from a passing breeze.

"What is your father like?" Catie finally asked, already surmising his mother was probably much like Rose.

Sean leaned back on his palms and sighed. "Seamus Kelly…he's a good man, strong and proud but also difficult, bloody difficult. I doubt he and I have spoken ten kind words between us in the last year."

"Why?" Surprised, Catie turned to him.

"Because I made the unforgivable mistake of not choosing the life he had planned out for me. That's why I told you, *all* of the choices you make in life have consequences, some good…some bad. I have been living with my consequences for a while now."

"But…" she hesitated. "It's your life, not his."

"Irish fathers are extremely proud men, Catie. My father owns a good deal of land, a horse farm and livery business. He's Protestant now but he was raised Catholic and poor…*very* poor. My grand-da was a farrier by trade but he found little work. My dad and his seven brothers lived a beggar's life, often went hungry."

"No work for a *farrier* in *Ireland*?" she asked disbelievingly. "I would think there are plenty of horses to shoe there."

"*Northern* Ireland…and yes there are plenty of horses. But most of those horses belonged to Protestants and they'd not have a *taig* shoeing their precious animals if a Presbyterian needed the work."

"*Taig?*" she asked.

"An offensive term for Catholics, like…papist," he explained.

"Oh. So your father…he has suffered a lot during the Troubles then."

Sean nodded.

"Is that why he became Protestant?"

"No. I don't know," he said, shrugging. "That happened before I was born, even before he married my mam. I don't know why he left the church. I've asked him, but he won't talk about it. Like I said, he's difficult at times."

Sean paused and looked away for a moment but then continued. "Anyways, Seamus Kelly was the first in his family to purchase land, to own his own business…to own anything really. It gave him great pride to be able to give me, his first son, an inheritance and an occupation. For me to turn it down, well, it was the same as slapping him in the face. I mean…I love horses, but…it's just…I really want to finish my education. I very much want to teach."

"Teach? *School* you mean?"

Sean laughed. "You sound surprised."

"No." Catie shook her head. "I'm not surprised. It makes perfect sense really. You're certainly bossy enough." She cut a teasing eye at him.

"Evidently *not* bossy enough. You're still not galloping properly, but some students are more thickheaded than others. It's to be expected I suppose." He returned the teasing eye.

"Haven't you explained all of this to your father?" Catie asked more seriously. Sean Kelly no longer seemed so unfettered.

"Da doesn't understand. I don't know if he ever will." He sat back up and brushed his palms. The heaviness of his words seemed to fall away with the debris. Clearly he had a lot of practice shaking off this particular pain. "Now, Catie Darcy," he said with a brightened voice. "I've shared my life story — your turn."

"What do you want to know?"

Sean narrowed his eyes as a devilish smirk creased his lips. "Why do you not like to gallop?"

Rolling her eyes, she slumped back down to the dock. "Oh, all right, I'll tell you. But tomorrow — it's getting late." She pulled her feet out of the water and stood up. Then, using his shoulder for balance, she worked her wet feet into her shoes. "I want to take you somewhere tomorrow, during my lesson…okay?"

"That's fine, but you *are* telling me."

"Yes, I'll tell you." Catie patted him in assurance and started off the dock to home. Getting only a few feet away, she turned and called to him, "Sleep well, *Mister* Kelly!"

She heard him laugh as he called back, "You too, *Miss* Catie!"

Chapter 17

Already awake, Geoffrey and George were playing in their room, waiting for their mother. George liked mornings the best. Mummy came in early every morning to wash their faces and help them get dressed. When they were ready, she would smile, kiss their cheeks, and walk them to breakfast. Mummy was tall and beautiful and looked at him and Geoffrey the same way. Most people looked at George with pity, like there was something wrong with him, but Mummy didn't.

George saw her peek around the door, as she often did. She liked to watch them play when they didn't know she was there, but George always knew. George was an expert at knowing when someone was watching. Still, he waited for Geoffrey to take notice of her first and would only race across the room squealing, "Mummy, Mummy," behind his brother.

George Fitzwilliam Darcy was born four minutes and eleven seconds after his brother, Geoffrey Bennet Darcy. And that day set a precedent. Geoffrey crawled first, talked first, walked first, and often received a smiling look of pride from their father. George had never received that look, but he was content with the way things were. That is until recently.

Living in Geoffrey's shadow was becoming less and less appealing for George. His self-imprisoned voice was beginning to grow restless, struggling to find a way out. He wanted to be heard.

As they approached the breakfast room, George stuffed the little wooden horse Sean gave him deep into his pocket. Daddy didn't like toys at the table, and George was afraid he'd take it away. At breakfast one morning, he confiscated a bouncy ball that escaped Geoffrey's hand, bounced across the table, and landed in Daddy's eggs. George was taking no chances. When they entered the room, Daddy smiled and George waited.

"Well, good morning, Sons!"

"Good morning, Daddy!" Geoffrey yelled boisterously, scrambling over to his father's chair.

George observed closely as Daddy snuggled Geoffrey into his crisp shirt that always smelled like Rose. George liked that smell, the same smell as his sheets with the *D* embroidered on them. Each night he would trace the letter with his fingertips as he drifted off to sleep.

Geoffrey went to his seat, and George carefully mimicked everything he had just observed. "Good morning, Daddy."

AWAKE EARLIER THAN USUAL, CATIE sat in her window seat and watched the sun rise over the hills. She smiled, appreciating the sun more than usual. There was a tingle inside of her — not nervous like butterflies, but happy. She had almost forgotten she could feel so happy.

The smell of bacon drifted up through the house, reminding her that she had only picked at last night's supper. She dressed quickly, frowning at the sight of her ankles peeking from below her cuffs, and hurried down to breakfast.

"Good morning!" she sang merrily as she crossed the room and took her seat. "How is everyone this morning? Sleep well?" When she only got odd looks in return, Catie looked at Ben and Sarah. "What?"

"You are rather chipper for so early in the morning, Catherine," Ben said, somewhat bewildered. The previous evening she had retired to her room, hardly speaking to anyone.

"It's such a beautiful day, Bennet." Catie smiled. "How could one not be chipper?"

Ben looked at her suspiciously and raised a brow at Sarah before retreating behind his morning paper.

"Sarah, are you terribly busy today?" Catie asked as she buttered a muffin.

"No, not terribly busy, dear. Why?"

"I'm afraid I must go shopping. All of my trousers are starting to ride up over my ankles. I can't imagine what they are doing to my laundry."

Sarah smiled. "Catie, no one is doing anything to your laundry. I believe you are just experiencing a little growth spurt. It's normal. I had my last significant spurt of growth at your age as well."

There was a chuckle from behind the newspaper.

"And what's so funny?" Sarah asked her husband.

Ben drew back the corner of the paper, grinning. "I was just wondering, Sarah. Should I report this new development in stature to the old biddy, or shall you?"

Sarah looked back at him blandly, clearly not feeling the comment needed a response. Ben thought it best to go back behind his paper.

Confused, Catie shook her head and didn't ask.

George smiled and with great emphasis repeated, "Old biddy!"

The paper dropped, and Sarah's teacup returned to its saucer. "George," she said gently. "That is not a word of your father's I want you to repeat."

"*My* word!" Ben protested. "It certainly wasn't *my* — "

"Bennet!" Sarah cut him off. "The important thing here is that George not repeat impolite language."

"Impolite, indeed," he agreed, glancing at George. "You know, Sarah, I'm glad he is talking more. But why is it he only repeats words he shouldn't?"

"Yes," Catie chimed in. "I've notice the same thing. And I think he does it on purpose!"

"Catherine!" Sarah exclaimed, as George's face instantly scrunched into a mean look, which he directed at his aunt.

"Well, it's true," Catie argued, glaring spitefully back at her nephew.

George moved his hand to his pocket and felt the little wooden horse, *Misneach* — courage. "I do *not*!" he bellowed across the table at Catie, shocked at his own voice.

Sarah gasped as George's eyes traveled warily from his mother, to his aunt, and then to his father. Then he picked up his spoon and casually resumed eating his cereal.

"George Darcy, look at me." Ben leaned forward.

Putting his hand back over the little horse again, George cautiously lifted his eyes back to meet his father's. The two sat for several seconds in a locked, revealing gaze, making George feel completely exposed, as if all of his secrets were opened up like a window with the curtains flung back for all the world to see. Daddy would know he could talk, but maybe it was time Daddy knew.

"George, my boy," Ben finally spoke. "It sounds as though the women are going shopping this morning. I believe that is our cue as men to go fishing. What do you say to that?"

George gave a slight, hesitant nod.

"Right. Hurry then, Son, and finish your breakfast before it gets cold," Ben urged softly. Then glancing around the table, he added, "Let us all finish our breakfast."

SITTING AT HER PIANO LATER that afternoon, Catie sighed. Her first piano lesson was at the age of four — so small she had to be lifted to the bench. The massive instrument spread out before her, but she wasn't intimidated. It was like coming to a place you have never been before but knowing you belonged. She possessed a musical ear, a gift she shared with her mother and kept hidden like the little locket, always out of sight and close to her heart.

Mariah Jennings was the star pianist at Davenport School. Whenever a pianist was needed to play for a theatrical production or concert, Mariah Jennings was called on to perform. Catie Darcy could play circles around Mariah if she wanted to. But she didn't want to. Instead of flaunting her talent, she used it to torment clueless piano teachers or impress the ones she happened to like.

She didn't need to practice, but practice she must, for the ghosts that dwelled within her brother at times seemed to haunt her as well. Sighing once more, she opened her music and began playing the first movement of Beethoven's *Moonlight Sonata*, which matched her brooding mood.

After only a few minutes, she stopped and looked around the empty music room with a wicked grin. Then she started again, purposefully skipping notes and rearranging bars to lessen the tedium. When she tired of that, she took one particular measure and played it backwards over and over again until Rose had endured enough.

When Rose came to the door, Catie stopped playing and asked, "Did you need something, Nan?" Her voice was as innocent as her expression.

"Enough!" Rose said, bringing her hand to her throat and giving the air in front of it a hard slice.

"Sorry, Nan. Try as I might, I just couldn't make Beethoven proud." Smirking, Catie closed the piano.

Rose narrowed her eyes and pointed a condemning finger, murmuring as she walked out, "I changed your nappies, Catie Darcy, and you've not fooled me for an instant."

OUTSIDE THE STABLES, CATIE NOTICED Sean was already mounted up and holding Chloe's reins. "So I've improved in my gallop so much I am again enjoying the luxury of stable hands, I see," she said smugly.

"Hardly." He grinned, eyes as bright as his face. "It was getting late, so I saddled your horse for you. You're welcome, by the way."

"Thank you, by the way," Catie replied as she stepped up on the mounting block. "Sorry I'm late. I was practicing my piano."

"You play?"

"Yes," she grunted as she adjusted her stirrups.

"Do you play well?"

Sitting back up, she smiled. "Oh, I'm not one for bragging. You must ask your aunt; she was privileged enough to partake of my talents this afternoon."

"All right, I will." Sean's eyebrows, as coal black as his hair, rose in question. "So, Catie Darcy, where *are* we going?"

"Follow me." She urged Chloe into a strong, even gait as Sean followed, smiling proudly at her skilled, easy canter. Catie Darcy was petite, but by no means was she frail. She descended from a long line of hale and hearty Darcys, and Sean saw from the beginning that hers was a physique that could master her mount and become one with the horse.

They skirted around Pemberley to a hidden lea between the dwelling and the hills that rose up behind it. Sean took notice of an old, stone chapel attached to the more ancient right wing of the manor. Probably original to the house, he surmised.

"I was christened there!" Catie called over to him as they rode past stained glass windows, gleaming in the sunlight. "So were the twins and my brother!"

Once they had passed the chapel, Catie pulled Chloe to a stop. "Sarah thinks Ben should let it out — you know, for weddings and such. But he won't hear of it. It's only used for family christenings now." She dismounted and motioned for him to follow. "Come on."

Rising from the ground before them were two stone pillars supporting an elaborate arch adorned with a gilded letter *D*. Attached to the pillars was a wrought iron gate, the only entrance to a flowing iron fence with sharply pointed pales, defending the graves they surrounded. Sean waited as Catie unlatched the gate and pushed it open. The hinges complained loudly and eerily as if warning the dead of their visitors.

Once inside the cemetery, Sean realized the graves were perched high on a knoll overlooking a small glen that was filled with bracken and mournful looking weeping willows. "A lovely view for eternity," he said stupidly. He was nervous but didn't know why.

She nodded back to him in agreement as they continued walking, minding graves with their step.

The age of the cemetery was evident not only by the seventeenth century dates on some of the grave markers, but by the moss and lichen that with time had crept up the stone pillars and discolored the stone.

Catie sat down on a newer concrete bench facing her parents and slid to one side, inviting him to join her. Sean sat down.

"My father," Catie said, giving a nod in the direction of the headstone directly in front of them.

"And your mother?" he asked, pointing to Margaret Darcy's name alongside William's.

"Yes." Catie nodded. "I didn't know her though…she died only minutes after giving birth to me."

"Sixth of November, that's your birthday?" She nodded again. "I'm sorry, Catie. It must be difficult for you without her." A wave of sympathy rushed through Sean as he glanced sideways at her. The bold girl who sat next to him suddenly appeared helpless and alone here amongst the dead. *Thank God Aunt Rose was here for her*, he thought, fighting the urge to take her into his arms and comfort her.

She shrugged. "Not as difficult as losing my dad."

"How did he die?"

"In a plane crash. He had just received his pilot's license. I believe it was only his second or third solo flight." She sighed and looked at him, smiling. "My daddy was always seeking adventure."

"Is your brother much like him?" Sean asked.

"Yes…and no. In some ways he's exactly like him, but Bennet is *not* adventurous. He is more, you know…more…conventional. The most adventure he seeks is on horseback." She stood and walked over to brush a stray leaf from her parents' tombstone. "My brother's life is Pemberley, this house, this land. You know, he was born here in a room just down the hall from mine. And one day he will be buried here." She gestured to a vacant spot beside her parents that would one day hold her brother's remains. "He likes that — his roots, his ancestry — all of it seems to mean as much to him as we do."

"Oh, I see. It's you then." Sean leaned back on the bench and stared up through the trees. The position Catie usually assumed when visiting her father.

"What is me?" She stepped back close to him.

"You...Catie...you are like him, not your brother. You inherited your father's adventurous spirit."

"Yes, I guess you could say that." She picked up a stick and tossed it through the fence. "Daddy and I *were* kindred souls in that manner. Sometimes I think that frightens my brother. You know...afraid I might fly off in an airplane one day and never come back. Sometimes I think he hates Daddy for that...for his adventurous spirit...for dying."

Nudging his feet aside, Catie settled back on the bench so close their thighs were pressed tightly against each other. She had a sudden need to be close to him.

Hoping to lighten the sorrow he sensed, Sean knocked his shoulder into hers. "And yet, Catie Darcy, none of this tells me why you don't like to gallop."

"Oh, yeah...I fell off of a horse."

"Oh, no!" He shook his head laughing. "You aren't getting off that easy. I want the *whole* story."

"All right, I'll tell you." She stood up again and looked down at him. "It was only a month or so after Daddy died. Ben was not himself, mourning probably, but he looked so angry, so...*troubled*, like he could kill someone. He closed Pemberley up like a fortress, even posted a guard at the lodge. As you can imagine, the story of two wealthy orphans was quite the juice." She had been pacing as she spoke but stopped now to smile awkwardly at him. Sean nodded, so she continued, "Well, for some reason, something to do I guess, Ben decided to focus more strongly on my riding. He had given me the odd lesson here and there but nothing serious." Catie stopped again and looked at her father's headstone. Seeing a shudder run through her, Sean got up and took her hand.

"It's all right," he said softly. "You need not tell me anymore. I was an ass for forcing you."

"No." Catie looked up at him, her eyes swimming in grief. "I want to..."

"All right," he whispered. "I'm listening."

"One day...*that* day, he...he smiled. Ben actually smiled. I thought, my God, he's smiling. 'A Darcy born if I ever saw one,' he said as I trotted around the ring, and I thought my guts would burst. He was happy with me, proud. Then it occurred to me, *I* can make him better. All I have to do is please him." Catie paused and smiled lopsidedly. "Stupid, I know, but you must remember I was only eight. Well, afterwards, Ben walked me home. It was the first time since Daddy died that I thought, maybe Ben and I will be all right. When we got to the house, he handed me off to Rose and said, 'An extra biscuit for this champion horsewoman, Rose. She'll be galloping tomorrow and needs her strength.' Well of course, I was too filled with excitement to eat, so I refused the snack and … "

"*And* … you went back to the stables, didn't you?" Sean interrupted.

"How'd you know?"

"My four younger brothers and I grew up on a horse farm, remember. Aside from wee Joseph, each one of us took our turn disobeying Da and heading off alone on our mounts before we had any business doing so."

"You did?"

"Mm-hmm." He nodded. "And each time one of us did, my father tended promptly to our backsides for it."

"So, *wee* Joseph is the brains of the Kelly clan?" she asked, smiling fully now.

"No." Sean shook his head and stepped close to her. "*Wee* Joseph was taught to ride by me, not my father. When Joseph took the notion to mount a horse alone before he knew a head from a tail, it was me he disobeyed." Sean's mouth twitched. "His backside was promptly tended to by me."

"Poor Joseph," Catie said, looking at Sean as if he were some Celtic barbarian.

"Poor *Joseph*!" he exclaimed. "Poor Joseph received a few smacks that stung his pride more than his bum and skulked off to the house. I, on the other hand, sat in the barn and cried like a baby."

"You cried?"

"Aye, I did. I didn't want to swat the lad; me da made me do it." She laughed and he looked offended. "So that's how it is, is it? I expose myself. I tell you about a sensitive, unmanly moment and you laugh. Thanks."

"I don't think it was unmanly … I think it was sweet."

"*Sweet*! Oh, that's *much* better."

"What I mean is … it's nice to see that there's more to you than that rigid exterior of yours." She looked up at him and added softly, "And I happen to like sweet."

Seeing her rosebud lips so close to his, Sean's head instinctively tilted and he lowered his face. He saw her eyes close and her mouth lift upwards. She was accepting him, granting her permission for him to proceed. He could feel her breath on his mouth, he could smell her. God he wanted to kiss her so bloody bad … but he couldn't.

"So, uh…your brother, he…uh, he never found out, eh?"

"Hmm?" Catie opened her eyes and was surprised to see he had stepped away from her. "My brother?"

"Yeah." Sean went back over to the bench and sat down. "He never found out you went back to the stables, never knew you went out riding alone."

"Oh…no, no he didn't." Feeling suddenly vulnerable, Catie folded her arms and looked at him. "The horse — not Chloe," she clarified, "took off wildly when I got her to the clearing. I've never been so afraid in all my life. I didn't think I would ever get her stopped. Then, like she had hit a wall or something, she came to an abrupt halt and I flew out of my saddle like a rag doll."

"Were you hurt?" She nodded. "Badly?"

"No. A few scrapes and bruises. I was lucky. But I couldn't tell Ben. He might have been angry with me, but I didn't care about that. It was because I knew he would be disappointed in me." Her voice lowered to a whisper. "I hate when he's disappointed in me. All I wanted to do was to make him smile again." She fell silent and stared longingly out over the graves.

Watching her stand motionless like the somber marble angels that surrounded her, Sean knew she needed comfort, but he didn't dare approach her. If he ever took Catie Darcy in his arms he might never let her go again. She even looked like one of the angels that stood guard over her ancestors, her cherub-like features in the middle of a beautiful and glorious conflict with her encroaching womanhood. He swallowed the thickness that was gathering in his throat.

"So there," she turned to him and said with a sudden lightheartedness that stunned and relieved him. "I've exposed my most unmanly moment as well. Feel better?"

He chuckled. "Yeah, I feel better. Thanks for telling me."

"You're welcome. But please don't tell Rose." Catie looked at him pleadingly. "When she saw my injuries, I told her I had fallen off my bicycle. I know it was a dreadful lie, but what else could I have done. If she finds out I'll never hear the end of it. "

"It was eight years ago!" he exclaimed.

"It wouldn't matter." She shook her head. "I burned my mouth with hot coffee when I was about ten, and Rose *still* tells me, 'Be careful; it's hot. Remember when you burned your mouth.'"

"Well." Sean got up to leave. "She *is* my mother's sister. Now, shall we have another go at that gallop?"

"Oh, not today, Sean, please." She grasped his forearm, making it tingle from her touch.

Breathing evenly to calm the increasingly growing desire, he mustered a stern expression. "All right, have your way. But this is my last unmanly act for this century."

She giggled, and they walked back across the cemetery. Near the entrance Catie crouched down in front of a large gravestone and brushed clean the soft green grass in front of it.

"Who's that?" Sean asked.

"Fitzwilliam Darcy and his wife Elizabeth Bennet Darcy. My brother and I were named after them. Elizabeth is my second name."

"She died only six months after him." Sean knelt down to better read the headstone.

"Yes." Catie smiled at the names. "The story passed down through the family is that she couldn't live without him, mourned herself to death. Romantic, eh?"

"Ah, true love," he said with mock wistfulness, "a rare find nowadays."

"Rare maybe…but hopefully not *too* awfully rare," she said, brushing her hands clean as she stole a glance at him. "I hope to love someone that much someday…you know…so much I can't bear to live without him."

Sean held the gate for her to pass and then latched it. He gave her a leg-up onto her mount, and they turned the horses back to the house. The rest of the afternoon was spent riding slow and close…talking and laughing, mostly comparing Rose and her sister Emma. Being raised by the sisters wove a common thread between them, lending a kinship of sorts.

It was after five o' clock when they arrived back at the stables, so Sean offered to take care of Chloe for her. "It's late. I'll tend the horse for you."

"Thanks." Catie handed him the reins. "Well, cheerio, then."

He grinned back at her and said, "*Slàn leat,* Catie."

"What's *slàn leat*?" she asked.

"It's Irish for goodbye or cheerio."

"Oh, *slàn leat*, then."

"No." He laughed. "You're leaving, I'm staying. So I say, *slàn leat* and you say, *slàn agat*."

"*Slàn agat*," she repeated slowly.

"That's right! I'll make an Irish lass out of you yet."

She smiled back and left.

Entering her room, Catie stopped short when her eyes met with Maggie Reid's.

"I…er…I wasn't sure if you wanted me to put these things away or not," Maggie stammered as she pointed to the bags from Catie and Sarah's earlier shopping trip.

"No, I'll put them away," Catie replied, removing her cardigan.

"All right, I'll leave you then." The thin timid form started out of the room. "Oh, I almost forgot." Maggie turned around and held out an envelope. "I found this under your night table."

Catie glanced at it. It was the letter Mary Darcy Howell had written to her son, Thomas. The last letter from his mother, the one he had not lived long enough to open and read. Catie had forgotten all about it.

She reached out and took the envelope from Maggie's hand. "Thanks."

"You're welcome," Maggie replied with a gentle smile and quietly left the room.

Chapter 18

For the next several nights, Catie left the house after dark to meet Sean at the pond. These nightly meetings were never planned or spoken of during the afternoon riding lessons, but he was always there, waiting for her. It was exciting and daring, like Mary and Arthur's river rendezvous.

Dangling their legs in the cool pond, they laughed and talked, mostly about the future that was so close at hand, sharing each other's hopes and dreams. Their feet would often touch and purposefully linger. It was like a dream. With Sean by her side, Catie forgot about deceased parents, escaped Ben's overprotective ways, and never once felt lonely. For some strange reason, with him, she no longer felt like an orphan…or a burden.

When he spoke, she studied him intently. She knew the precise spot on his thigh where the muscle contracted when he swung his leg, how a curl behind his ear delicately wrapped itself around the fold just above his lobe, and his night smell — freshly showered and shaven. She loved how the scent of musk from his cheap aftershave would fill the warm evening air and fight for dominance over his breath, which always held a faint tang of the pint he had at the Green Man each evening after work. Everything about Sean Kelly was settling in and taking up residence inside the mind and soul of Catie Darcy.

When alone, she dreamed of him taking her face in his rough, work-calloused hands and kissing her. She envisioned him pulling her into his strong Irish arms and holding her. Although Catie Darcy had never even been kissed, she wanted Sean Kelly to make love to her. Make love to her the way Arthur had made love to Mary. She wanted to go back to her room and her bed with his scent of aftershave and beer on her, and his soft Gaelic words still fresh in her ear. She would give herself over to him, offer him her precious virginity. All he had to do was ask.

But he didn't…he didn't even try to kiss her. Once he reached over to brush a strand of hair from her face, his hand gentle and warm on her cheek. She thought he might kiss her then, but he just stood abruptly and told her it was getting late and sent her home. Catie left more confused than ever.

By the end of the week a band of summer storms moved into the valley, and Catie awoke Friday morning to a hard rain.

Wrapped in a blanket to ward off the damp chill, she looked out the window in disgust. Maybe Sean braved the weather and walked up to the house to have tea with Rose, she thought. She threw off the blanket and dressed.

The kitchen was empty with an odd sense of abandonment that was only exaggerated by the heavy downpour outside. Stepping over to the delivery door, which was wide open to the elements except for a fly screen, she pressed her forehead against the cool metal mesh. Taking a deep breath, she inhaled a mixed metallic tang of sweet summer rain and saturated earth. The noise was deafening as the rain assaulted the gravel and poured off of the house in sheets, smacking down hard on the large entrance stone just outside the door. The soothing, repetitive sound lulled Catie so that she jumped when the motor of the dumbwaiter kicked on behind her, sending the breakfast dishes down to the kitchen. "Relax, Darcy," she teased herself, shaking her head.

She poured herself a tall glass of milk and disappeared into the pantry. After a brief search, she found her loot — three sugar biscuits from Mr. Johnson's stash — and wrapped and stuffed the booty under her arm. On her way out, Catie grabbed the glass of milk and went quietly up the backstairs, hoping to avoid Rose who was like a hound on a fox when it came to sniffing out sugar biscuits.

As she rushed out of the stairway she almost collided with Wade Radcliff. "Mr. Radcliff!" she exclaimed, nearly spilling the milk.

The two had never been particularly fond of each other. Wade cared deeply for the late Mr. Darcy but despised the man's bent on being an indulgent father to Catie. And Catie couldn't stand his persnickety ways.

"Maybe you should watch where you're going, Catherine," he said defensively, making sure no milk had landed on his pristine clothes.

"Radcliff!" Ben called impatiently, causing the man's head to give a sudden jerk.

"Yes…coming, Mr. Darcy."

"Humph," Catie uttered nastily and brushed past him.

Her plan was to spend the morning watching mindless television, but the twins had gotten there first. Catie backed out quietly and headed back to her room, grumbling about Sarah's refusal to allow more televisions in the house.

Sitting at her desk, she unwrapped the cookies, which were crushed in transport, and chewed slowly on the tiny pieces as she sipped her milk. Bored, she flipped through the pages of a magazine until the phone rang.

"Hello."

"Hey, Cate!" Aiden Hirst said. "How are ya, love?"

Cate? Love? Catie grimaced. "I'm fine, Aiden, and you?"

"Couldn't be better! I was thinking of coming out to the country this weekend but the old man needs me in town."

"Sorry to hear that," she lied.

"Oh, be still my beating heart," he said teasingly. "She's sorry to hear she won't be seeing me."

Catie laughed. "Did you only call to tell me you *won't* be seeing me this weekend, Aiden?"

"No, I called to be the first chap to claim a dance with you at your family's garden party next weekend."

"Oh, well…"

"Don't tell me I've been beaten to the punch!" he interrupted her hesitation.

He hadn't, though she had planned on spending the evening with Sean. "No. No one's beaten you to the punch. I'll be glad to dance with you." Her answer was tinged with disappointment. No matter how many hints she dropped, Sean didn't seem the least bit interested in dancing with her.

"Don't burst from excitement, Cate. You're not making a chap feel very special."

"Sorry, Aiden, it's raining pitchforks and hammer handles out here. It's not you, just the weather."

"Pitchforks and hammer handles?" He laughed. "God, I love you shire girls!"

"We *do* own a house in town, you know." Catie's disappointed tone quickly turned indignant. "We Darcys are farmers, Aiden, not country bumpkins."

"I didn't mean…listen, Cate, that came out wrong." He paused momentarily. "Can I still have that dance, even though I'm a daft fool when it comes to women?"

She smiled. Aiden Hirst could be a sweet guy. "Yes, Aiden, we Darcys are also good to our word. You may still have the dance. Though I warn you, out here in the sticks it will be only country waltzes or reels, do-si-do." She couldn't help but chide him one last time.

"Ha...ha. Finished?"

"Yes." She chuckled.

"Good, next Sunday then. I look forward to it. Cheers, Cate."

"Bye, Aiden." Still chuckling, she hung up and happened to notice Mary Darcy's last letter to Thomas lying on her desk. She had never opened it. Catie ran her fingertip under the seal, already loosened with age, and carefully removed the letter.

8th May 1945

My dear son Thomas,

I was saddened and troubled to hear you are feeling unwell. I pray this letter finds you in better health. Thomas, I wish you had not taken your leave so soon after your father's death. I appreciate your calling, but a mother needs her son in difficult times, and these times have been difficult indeed. My son, promise me you will make every effort to be back at Pemberley for Christmas.

On to matters of business; per your consent, by mid-June, I shall sign Pemberley and all of its holdings over to Cousin Geoffrey. He desires to give the home of our ancestors his full devotion; therefore, he will be selling Rosings Park and moving his family from Kent to Derbyshire permanently. His fortune has been great on that front, as Rosings Park became a retreat for officers during the War. A regular visitor, with whom Geoffrey became quite friendly, purchased the home at a suitable price for his future bride. The chap is a dashing and rich American general who took a fancy to an English nurse and plans to make England his permanent home. Rosings Park is most definitely a loss to Geoffrey, especially to a Yank. Thank God he is a heroic Yank, but it is a loss that must be endured for Pemberley's sake!

25th May 1945

My dearest son, I am ashamed to admit it, but I have left this letter neglected for over two weeks. Much has been happening, and the house has been in uproar. With a skeleton crew of servants, my time has been fully employed with recent events. No sooner had I started your letter, than our houseguest went into labor and gave birth. A healthy beautiful boy she named Wesley. According to Rebecca, Wesley was the name of the child's father, whether it be the man's first name or last, I could not say. She told me in confidence he was a close friend of the family, a married man, and a Member of Parliament. Hence, I am assuming the necessity of her remote confinement at Pemberley House.

I can't help but feel a bit sorry for the girl, for she is but fourteen years old and has been quite ill-raised. Your father's cousin sent for her daughter shortly after the birth. A letter arrived today by post thanking me for my "help" with the family's "unfortunate" situation. The only real consolation I have in the matter is that the lady who came for Wesley was a kindly looking woman. She questioned me about his birth record, for Rebecca gave no more than Wesley to the mid-wife, per her mother's direction. Oh, Thomas, I could not very well send the babe into the world with only Wesley for a name, so I offered Howell for his surname. It was the least I could do. The Worthingtons were certainly adamant he wasn't to carry theirs. I bid you pray for little Wesley Howell, Thomas, he will need our prayers indeed.

I shall close now. You are painfully missed by your mother. Please take care my darling, and write soon.
Your Loving Mum

"*Worthington?*" Catie lifted her head from the letter as if questioning the empty room around her. "I *knew* Wesley Howell wasn't Mary's grandson!" As the meaning of what she had just read became clearer, a burning urgency rushed through her ... this was important, it *must* be important. "Worthington?" she repeated. Letter in hand, Catie jumped up and ran to Ben's study, her thoughts racing as fast as her feet.

"Where do you think you're going?" asked Wade Radcliff, stopping her not ten steps from Ben's door.

"To see my brother," Catie answered, trying to step around him.

"No you're not." He stopped her again.

"Mr. Radcliff, this is important. I must see him at once!" she demanded, but Radcliff wasn't budging.

"Sorry, but your brother's on a very important call and is not to be disturbed."

"But, Mr. Radcliff," Catie continued more persuasively. "You don't understand. *This* is important, urgent even!"

"Your brother is in no mood for your childish games today, Catherine. Something big is happening that even *I* am not privy to. He is to leave for London shortly, and hasn't the time."

With folded arms and narrowed eyes, Catie walked past the unmovable man. Oh, how she wished she were six years old again! A vengeful, solid kick to the shin would be overlooked and dismissed as a tantrum. But she had matured and so had her tactics. She stomped loudly down the service stairs, then turned and crept lightly back up. She knew Mr. Radcliff would be making arrangements for Ben to leave, and once he was sure she was gone, he would give up his guard at the door.

"Right as rain," Catie said quietly as she reemerged into the empty corridor, congratulating herself on such a befitting simile, considering the weather.

Now with nothing but a door between her and Ben, she paused. What if the letter meant nothing? Then again, what if the "something big" Radcliff was referring to had to do with Wesley Howell? Either way, she couldn't let Ben go to London without reading the letter. Catie closed her eyes tight and turned the knob.

Suddenly she was standing in the middle of the Persian rug that covered three quarters of Ben's study. His desk chair was turned away from the door and his feet were propped on the credenza behind his desk. Deep in conversation, he knew nothing of the breach into his sanctuary.

"Brother," she said softly, her only endearment for him. When she was small, chubby cheeked and angelic looking, she discovered adding a "my sweet" or in dire situations a "my dear sweet" saved her many dues.

Ben's feet dropped to the floor and his chair turned in her direction. "What's the matter, Catie?" he asked with the phone still to his ear and a confused expression on his face.

"I need to speak with you, it's important," she said, her voice still soft but firm.

"Charles, can you please hold?" Ben said into the receiver and pushed a button for privacy. "Catherine, I am very busy. How did you get in here?"

"I need to show you something. *Now*, Bennet, before you leave for London."

"Catherine, I do not have time for you right now. And furthermore, you know better than to bother me this time of day. Now run along!" Ben said in a shooing tone and swiveled back to the credenza.

Frustrated with his lack of interest, Catie turn on her heel and started out. "I'm sorry, Charles," she heard Ben say as she neared the door. "Please continue."

Charles Worthington... *Worthington*, it meant something, it had to mean something. She stopped, took a deep breath, and turned back. "No, Bennet, I *damn* well *bloody* refuse to run along!" She hadn't meant to accentuate the curse words, but it worked well. She had his attention.

"What did you say?" Ben swiveled back around in his chair, his expression so incredulous she had a painful twinge of regret. "No, Charles, I wasn't speaking to you, but I'll have to call you back. I have a situation here that needs dealing with."

"Catherine Elizabeth Darcy!" Ben stood up as he returned the phone to its base, giving her such a severe gaze that her heart thumped hard in her chest. "You know that I will not allow you to speak to me in such a manner."

Catie looked him straight in the eye. "No? Well, I have something to show you, and how else am I to get your attention when you dismiss me like a child?"

"Catherine —"

"Read this," she cut him off and extended her hand. The letter was crumpled, and she thought it strange that she hadn't even realized she was clutching it so hard.

"What is it?" he asked.

"*Read* it, Ben. It's about Wesley, Wesley Howell. I think it's important... it seems important."

"What do you know about Wesley Howell?"

"For starters, I know he is *not* Cousin Mary's grandson." Catie took another step forward, putting the letter even closer to his reach. "Go ahead, Brother, read it."

With a distinct look of annoyance on his face, Ben took the letter from Catie's hand and unfolded it. His eyes scanned the page, and she could tell he was only skimming the words.

"This is merely a letter Mary wrote to Thomas while he was in Africa, Catherine."

"No, Ben, keep reading," she urged, waving an impatient hand at him.

"All right, all right," he said in a surrendering tone and returned his attention to the letter. Almost immediately his expression began to change, signifying he had reached the crucial excerpt. Frowning, he began to reread the letter.

This time, however, he brought it closer to his face and his lips moved as he read. He felt behind him for his chair and eased himself down. Only then did he look back at her.

"Where in the bloody hell did you get this?"

Catie's eyes widened at his reaction. "In my room; it must've been Mary's room at one time."

"Radcliff!" Ben yelled. "Radcliff!"

Wade Radcliff hurried through the door. "Yes, Mr. Darcy?"

Not lifting his eyes from the letter, Ben demanded, "Ring Horace Harold at once!"

"Horace Harold?"

The Darcy temper was one that reared up quickly. A blotch of red was creeping up Ben's neck and a vein was pulsating. The expression on his face when he raised his eyes from the paper to Wade Radcliff's question needed no words.

"Yes, sir, Horace Harold!" he quickly amended and went straight to the telephone.

Catie understood Mr. Radcliff's need for clarification. Ben and Uncle Horace's business relationship had completely dissolved, and their personal ties had suffered because of it. Still, Uncle Horace was the first person Ben thought to call, and she was grateful for that. Horace Harold was as close to a father as they had.

As Radcliff held the line, waiting for Horace Harold to be pulled from a meeting, Ben began to question Catie. "Where *exactly* did you find this?"

"Behind a panel in my window seat," she told him. "First I found the diary, but I returned it and then I found the letters…"

"There is *more?*" Ben stopped her. "More letters and a diary?"

Instantly regretting the mention of the risqué diary, she hesitantly replied, "Y-yes."

"Catie, hurry off and get everything you have of Cousin Mary's and bring it to me!"

She nodded and left to fetch her little collection of Mary Darcy Howell's history.

By the time Catie returned, Ben's door was closed, and Mr. Radcliff was back at his sentry post. "He is speaking with Mr. Harold and not to be disturbed," Wade said flatly. "I'll take those."

Disappointed, she surrendered the diary and letters to Mr. Radcliff and went to the front hall. She seated herself on the lower part of the grand stair-case to wait. Ben would have to pass her on his way out and maybe he would say something. He might thank her or at least confirm the importance of her find. Maybe, she fantasized, maybe she had single-handedly kept Pemberley from falling into the "wrong hands" again. Or possibly she had finally done something that would make up for being a burden to Ben all these years.

While Catie waited, another storm came upon the manor. It rumbled and howled around the house and against the windows with a threatening strength. Everything felt electric and tense. It was almost an hour before she heard movement and male voices coming from the gallery. Then Ben and Mr. Radcliff rounded the corner and bounded down the staircase with the heavy tread of hurried men. As they neared, Catie stood and moved to the side to allow them to pass, staring hard at her brother in hopes of making eye contact with him. Ben, however, passed by without even a glance. He had a fixed look of contempt on his face, telling her his mind was clearly elsewhere.

She thought of calling out to him before he left. There was time, plenty of time, for he and Mr. Radcliff stopped at the door long enough to don their trench coats and turn up their collars to the wind that was now blowing the rain sideways. There was even a slight delay leaving as Ben waited for Mr. Radcliff to step out onto the portico and raise the umbrella. But Catie remained silent until Ben was outside. Only then did she make her way to the window and watch Ben get into the car. She could see his face through the car window, blurred by the rain as it ran down the glass. "It *had* meant something," she whispered.

She stayed at the window until she could no longer see the black car as it blended into the grey of the heavy rain. For a moment the tail lights were still distinguishable, like two red eyes staring back at her, but eventually they too disappeared into the storm.

Chapter 19

After frantically pacing the hall most of Friday afternoon with a message from Mr. Darcy for his wife, Maggie rushed forward when Sarah entered and exclaimed, "Mrs. Darcy, ma'am!"

"Maggie!" Rose quickly admonished the outburst. "You must never rush Mrs. Darcy and really, child, do allow madam to get a foot in the door."

"Yes, ma'am," Maggie replied, lowering her head repentantly, "I'm sorry, ma'am."

Sarah gave Rose a wink. "It's all right now, Maggie. My foot's officially inside the door. What did you need to tell me, dear?"

"A message for you from Mr. Darcy, ma'am, he said it was to be handed to you the instant you stepped in the house." Maggie glanced warily at Rose, hoping the explanation excused her.

"Thank you, Maggie." Sarah smiled consolingly.

Maggie bobbed her head and hurried off.

"That child's afraid of her own shadow," Rose commented as she hung up her wet coat.

"I like her." Sarah unfolded the sealed message from her husband. "But do remind her Rose, it's madam or Mrs. Darcy. I'm not the Queen for heaven's sake."

Rose chuckled. "Yes, yes, I'll remind her. Now, you must get off of those ankles. I swear the planning for this garden party gets more detailed each year. Where do you fancy having your tea?"

Fully absorbed in reading the missive, Sarah didn't seem to hear the question.

"Sarah." Rose took note of a developing frown and stepped closer. "Is everything all right, dear?"

"I must to go to London, Rose. Please make the arrangements. I shall be leaving immediately."

PULLING BACK THE CURTAIN, ROSE saw the sun streaming through a sparkling mist that had settled over the landscape during the night and breathed a sigh of relief. "Praise the Lord," she whispered and, letting the curtain fall back into place, went to have breakfast with the children. Sarah had vaguely explained the urgency before dashing off to join her husband in London, leaving Rose in charge of Pemberley and its inhabitants — an undesirable task after thirty-six hours of unrelenting rain.

"We are getting out of this house and going on a picnic after church," Rose declared at breakfast Sunday morning.

"We should invite Sean!" Catie quickly suggested.

"Yeah, Rose!" Geoffrey seconded. "We want Sean to come!"

"Yes...yes, Sean's coming. Lord knows, I'll take all the help I can get." Rose sounded exasperated, but in all honesty, she could probably handle the three remaining Darcys as well if not better than Ben and Sarah. She never liked doing so, however, without making a fuss about it.

"Yay! Sean's coming! Sean's coming!" the boys shouted and banged their utensils on their plates. Clearly the Darcy twins intended to take full advantage of being temporarily parentless.

Catie laughed as Rose scolded, "Children, really!"

The Darcys' preferred picnic spot on Pemberley Estate had been a favorite for many generations. Located along a particularly still, shallow part of the river, the surroundings created a perfect place for children. There was a large fallen tree, uprooted during a storm, which lay midway across the water at an ideal height for climbing. In an old, well-spread oak, Catie's father had hung a sturdy, flat-board swing from a tall branch that carried its riders soaring over the water and velvety grass. Shade trees lined the banks of the river and beckoned picnickers to lie back as the swaying limbs rocked them into a tranquil afternoon nap. It was a peaceful spot full of happy memories, and Catie loved it. Many a summer Sunday afternoon she had spent here, and just the smell of the place evoked visions of her father pushing her on the swing, cautioning her to hold tight.

Today however, she was here with Sean, watching him look around and take in the beauty. Seeing him breathe deep and smile, she could tell he appreciated the naturalness of it — nothing altered; nature at its best. This had always been the way of the Darcys: less formality to the land, let nature be the artist, and enjoy what God has created.

"Beautiful, isn't it?" she asked as they walked to the clearing.

"Oh, aye, it's almost as picturesque as County Down." He took the picnic hamper from her hand. "Here, allow me."

"Thanks." She smiled up at him as the twins ran up to them.

"Come push us, Sean." Geoffrey tugged on Sean's arm.

"Sorry, lads, I'm being a gentleman at the moment. Away off to the swing with you, I'll be there directly." The boys took off squealing, racing to be first to the swing. "And don't go near the water!" he called after them.

"So, only almost?" she asked.

"Well." He grinned and cut his eyes at her. "No true Irishman would ever admit to English soil being lovelier than his own. It's *bròd*, you know."

"It's what?"

"*Bròd*... pride, but I reckon you English feel the same way. What fills the eye fills the heart, eh?"

She nodded. "I'd say that's very true."

He set the hamper down where Rose had spread the blankets. "Hope that's as good as it is heavy, Auntie," he said. "I'm starving!"

"You go amuse the twins." Rose shooed him away. "We'll have your lunch ready soon." Sean lifted a cloth that covered a tray full of biscuits. "Off!" She slapped his wrist.

"Sorry, Aunt," he said as crumbs dropped from his lips. Having obtained one tiny biscuit in the skirmish, Sean popped it in his mouth like a defiant little boy. "I did say I was starving." He winked at Catie and ran off to push Geoffrey and George on the swing.

"Lord, my poor sister never can keep her lot fed. With five boys, someone's always hungry." Rose shook her head as she and Catie began unloading the food.

They worked in a silent chorus of preparing the meal as Rose glanced at her helper. She had intended to speak with Catie before bedtime tonight but decided to go ahead and have a word with her now. She appeared to be in an unusually good mood, and the distraction of the picnic might ease the necessary reproof.

"Catie," Rose said casually as she unwrapped the sandwiches.

"Yes, Nan?"

"Stop ringing London, dear. You're driving poor Mr. Radcliff mad."

Catie slammed the picnic hamper closed. "No one tells me anything except *stop* or *no*! I'm the one who found the bloody letters after all."

"Catherine, child, you must — "

"I'm not a child!" Catie interrupted. "He treats me like I'm still eight years old. I'll never be anything but the *little* sister to him. If Daddy were alive — "

"Daddy, Daddy!" Rose scoffed. "Your memory of your father, Catherine, is rather distorted, coming from the vantage of a little girl…his pet no less. How do you think your brother came to be the man he is? I knew William Darcy well, Catherine. I cared for him — you know that — but he was *not* an easy man. His expectations for you would have been as high if not higher than your brother's; make no mistake about it." Looking a bit shamefaced, Catie began smoothing wrinkles in the picnic blanket. "Stop telephoning London," Rose said again in a gentler voice, pulling Catie's chin up. "He'll explain all this business when he's ready and not a minute before."

"If at all," she whispered doubtfully.

"Then that's what you must accept."

Catie stared at Rose. Even under a wide-brimmed hat, her high cheekbones were slightly pink from the sun, flattering her soft grey eyes. "Yes, Nan," she answered softly.

"There's a good girl." Rose smiled. "Now fetch our men; they'll be starved by now."

After lunch Sean again occupied the twins, chasing and splashing them. So early in his manhood, there lingered still some little boy at heart.

"He misses his brothers," Rose said to Catie as they watched from the blankets.

"What are they like?"

"Just as good hearted and just as handsome." Rose grinned. "Then again, I am a bit partial. But Sean…he has always held a special place in my heart. I went to stay with my sister when he was born. It was right after I lost my Henry and just before I came to Pemberley."

Catie had never thought of Rose's life outside of Pemberley. She only knew of a Pemberley with Rose. Rose *was* Pemberley to Catie; Rose was home. "Promise me you will never leave me, Nan." Catie nestled her head in Rose's lap.

Rose gently pulled her fingers through Catie's hair. "I'm sure it will be you that leaves Pemberley before me, child. Some very lucky — and I pray, patient — man will one day take you away from your ol' nanny."

"Never!" Catie vowed. "I shall stay with you forever, my dear, sweet Rose."

Grabbing Rose's hand, Catie cradled it at her cheek.

Rolling her eyes, Rose shook her head and shooed Catie away with a scold. "Oh, go on with your silliness and let a poor woman rest while she can. Lord knows, I'll not see another minute's peace until your brother and Sarah return home."

Giggling, Catie narrowly escaped a good snap of Rose's tea towel as she ran to join Sean and the twins at their play.

Rose drifted in and out of sleep in the cool shade. As midday surrendered to afternoon, the sun was beginning to get hot and the cooler air near the river was appreciated. An hour or so later, she sat up and watched the frolicking foursome playing in the river. Jeans rolled up to their knees, Sean and the twins were scouring the river's soft silt floor for treasures while Catie treaded the waters and headed downriver. The current was rushing from the storms, and Rose began to worry she had wandered too far.

"Sean!" she shouted, pointing in Catie's direction as she got up and hurried over to the riverbank.

Seeing the source of his aunt's concern, Sean nodded. "Catie!" he called out, cupping his hand around his mouth. "The water is too dangerous there, come back this way!"

"Oh, I'm fine," Catie dismissed him. "I've played in this river all of my life."

"Catherine Elizabeth Darcy, you will mind what Sean says and turn back this instant!" Rose demanded. "I'll not have your brother returning home to a cracked skull!"

With an indignant expression Catie propped her hands on her hips and declared, "Mind *Sean*? Please, Rose, I know this river far better than he does. If anything he should heed what I say. I am perfectly safe where I am."

"Oh, I'll heed what you say all right, Miss Catie." Sean always called her "Miss" when she spoke like royalty. "Do you wish to come back on your own two feet or shall I carry you sacked over my shoulder?" He bowed grandly and added, "I humbly await your command, m'lady."

Catie's hesitation was evident only by the dropping of her hands from her hips. Her voice kept its conviction. "I will come back when and *only* when I am ready, *Mister* Kelly!"

Sean smirked in a pleased sort of way. "You know, Miss Catie, I had a feeling you were going to choose over-the-shoulder."

"Sean! Mind your temper," she heard Rose warn as he started towards her in fast deliberate strides. Catie's eyes grew wide as she hastily surveyed her surroundings. Behind her was the little drop off waterfall she had meandered down river to look at, and the embankment on both sides was far too high to climb. She was trapped, and with the flow of the current working in his favor, Sean was fast upon her.

"No!" she screamed as her feet were pulled from the water with such ease, she almost hadn't realized he had picked her up. Finding herself suddenly upended, Catie could feel him struggling with the extra weight as he carefully navigated the large slick river stones. "Put me down!" she screamed.

"Be careful, Seany!" Rose called out fretfully.

"Relax, Auntie, all's well; just toting the wee vixen back to safe waters." He stopped long enough to shift his load and give Rose a reassuring smile.

"Vixen!" Catie repeated, beginning to flail in protest. "Who are you calling a vixen?

"Stop kicking, lass, or we'll both be swept down the river. My aunt will be none too happy with me if I accidentally drop you over the wee falls there."

"Over the falls?" Catie cried, nervously grabbing hold of his waistband to steady her jostling from his wobbly unpredictable footing.

"Oh, stop your whining. You've only your stubborn self to blame!" he huffed, stepping slowly and carefully.

Once back in the calm trickle of the wading pool, Sean stopped to catch his breath and utter a few choice words in Gaelic.

"Put me down!" she demanded. "And stop saying things I don't understand!"

"You want down, eh, lass?"

"Yes, and *now*!

He winked at her nephews who were looking up at him wide-mouthed. "She wants down, boys. What do you say?"

The two heads nodded in unison.

Effortlessly, he hoisted his victim off of his shoulder and caught her cradled in his forearms. Looking down at her, his head flew back with laughter. Catie's face was a deep red from anger and humiliation.

"Put...me...down!" she said slowly through closed teeth, her temper now at its pinnacle.

"As you wish, m'lady," Sean said obligingly and gave her a gentle toss into the deeper waters of the pool.

Rose gasped, but Sean just walked casually out of the river and sat down on the bank while Catie floundered and slapped at the water to get her footing.

"Sean Kelly!" Rose gave him an insistent shove. "Get up from there and help her."

"But, Auntie," Sean argued, grinning. "She knows this river far better than me. How could I be of any help to her?"

Soaked from head to toe and coughing, Catie finally dredged herself from the river's bottom. Her face was still scarlet, indicating the cold water had not chilled her fury. Sean tossed back his head and laughed again, making her glower as she sloshed towards him.

"No one…has ever…*manhandled* me that way before!" she shrieked, stopping in front of him. "You…you…"

"Insufferable ass," he finished for her as a wicked gypsy grin spread over his face.

"*Arrgh*!" Catie screamed and kicked a large amount of water in his direction.

Rose grabbed a blanket and wrapped it tightly around Catie. "Go sit in the sun, child, so you'll not catch cold," she insisted. Then she turned to her nephew and gave the back of his head several smart clips.

Walking away, Catie smiled with appreciation as Sean cried, "ow…ow…ow," in between each smack.

In the bright sunshine, away from the water, she spread out the blanket and lay down. Wet or not, it was a perfect day for sunbathing, and the late afternoon heat worked instantly to warm her skin. Back at the river, she heard Rose instructing the boys to collect their spades and buckets, her voice an equal mixture of aggravation and affection. A mother's voice, Catie thought. A few seconds later a tall, shadowy figure took her light, and she opened one eye to a slit. Sean loomed overhead, the sun at his back like a great firestorm he had left in his wake.

"Aunt Rose said I had to apologize." He sat down on the blanket next to her. "So?" he asked, still grinning. "How's your pride? Still red and stinging?"

She glared at him. "Faring as good as your head I'd say. Is it still stinging?"

"Aye." Sean rubbed the spot gingerly. "A mean arm, that woman. I reckon I deserved it though. A man should mind his elders whether he agrees with them or not."

"Is that your idea of an apology?" she asked sharply.

Sean leaned over, rested his chin in his palm, and gazed at her.

"Well, are you going to apologize or stare at me?"

"You're a very pretty girl, Catie Darcy, but when you're spitting mad and soaking wet you're downright beautiful. How's that for an apology?"

Speechless, Catie rose up on one elbow and stared into his eyes, soft, blue, and sincere. Their faces were close, kissing close. But they weren't alone.

"Seany!" Rose called. "Where's George's right shoe?"

Sean got up from the blanket, slowly, without releasing her eyes. "Coming, Auntie," he called back. Then he turned and walked away.

ON WEDNESDAY MORNING IT WAS approaching ten o'clock before Catie made her way down to the kitchen for breakfast. While waiting for her toast to pop, she noticed Mr. Johnson unwrapping a large beef tenderloin from white butcher's paper.

"Are we having roast for dinner tonight?"

"That'd be why I'm unwrapping it, Miss Catie," Mr. Johnson replied.

Catie knew Mr. Johnson would never make a tenderloin roast just for her, the twins, and live-in staff. "Is my brother coming home today?"

"Should be here any time now; the missus called early this morning to order supper...said they were leaving then."

Leaving her toast, which popped as soon as she bolted from the kitchen, Catie ran to the front hall. Both large entrance doors were opened wide in anticipation of Mr. and Mrs. Darcy's return, a centuries-old Pemberley tradition. If weather was at all permitting, the doors were propped back, fully open as a welcome home gesture to the master and mistress of the house.

The morning sun was spilling into the hall, bringing with it the smell of freshly cut grass. Catie stepped outside to sit on the steps — sit and wait as she had done as a small girl, waiting on a big brother who had been too long away at school. She would spend hours on those steps, watching the drive for any sign of him. Both her father and Rose had learned there was no cajoling her back inside if Ben was expected, so they gave up trying and instead made sure she was dressed properly for the weather.

It was only minutes before she saw her brother's car and stood as it rolled smoothly over the gravel drive and stopped in front of the house. Ben stepped out and came around the car to give Sarah a hand, and Catie was sorry to see that he wore the same hard expression with which he had left.

He walked Sarah up the steps with his hand to the small of her back as Catie hurried down to meet them. "You're home!" she said unnecessarily.

Sarah smiled warmly; she knew how worried and curious Catie had been. "How about this, Bennet, we have ourselves a little welcoming party. I do believe we were missed." Sarah pressed her cheek to Catie's in welcome. "Everything is fine," she whispered softly into Catie's ear.

Catie looked beyond Sarah to her brother. He didn't look as if everything were fine.

"Is that true, Sis? Did you miss us?"

She nodded as he leaned over the top of her head and gave her his usual brotherly peck.

Catie walked alongside them up the steps and into the hall, studying Ben for a sign, a clue that he wanted to tell her something... but nothing. He simply kissed Sarah and told her he would be in his study the rest of the afternoon if she needed him.

Disappointed, discouraged, and longing for his attention, an explanation, something, Catie padded softly behind him down the long corridor to his study. Reverently, she stood and watched him fumble through his pockets for the key to unlock his door. Once he found it, he slid it into the lock and glanced back at her. He knew what she wanted, but he just couldn't do this right now. Ben's head fell back as a long heavy sigh left his lungs through puffy cheeks. "Not now, Catie, please, dearest... not right now."

Not responding, for his words required none, Catie watched as he turned the key and disappeared into his study. She never blinked until the door closed behind him.

Perfumed arms wrapped her from behind, as Sarah's whisper tickled her ear once more. "He needs our patience right now, dear. He has been betrayed by someone he thought was a close friend."

Catie gasped and turned to face her. "Mr. Worthington!"

Sarah nodded and added, "And his own good judgment."

"But he's not at fault. How could he have known?" Catie protested.

Sarah's eyes moved to the closed study door. "Try convincing *him* of that." Catie's own gaze followed Sarah's, her throat suddenly thick with emotion. "Give him some time, a little space."

"Is he all right?"

"He will be." Sarah smiled. "Are you all right?"

She nodded, so Sarah patted her arm and started to walk away. "Sarah," Catie stopped her. "Uncle Horace?"

"He's been with us constantly the last few days, and a great help and comfort he has been, I might add."

"Do you think…" Catie hesitated.

"I know," Sarah replied with smiling conviction.

Catie nodded again. "That's good."

Chapter 20

"Not right now," must have meant not today, not tomorrow, or the next day either. Catie's eagerness to know what had happened in London sat too long, like bitter, overly steeped tea. She told herself that she didn't even care any longer, but that wasn't the truth. She did want to know, but evidently Ben wasn't going to tell her. All summer it seemed, brother and sister had been at odds over something, as if they had been slowly climbing opposite peaks and now stood high and at such a distance, they might never meet again in the valley below. He was seemingly unwilling to take even a step in her direction, and she was giving him his space as Sarah had advised. So much space you could hear an echo between them.

By Friday evening, even Sarah, who had the patience of Job when it came to her family, was losing her usual fortitude. The time for her to implement some clever scheme had come.

It was shortly after the boys had gone to bed that Catie stood to excuse herself for the evening. "I think I'll turn in early tonight," she declared through a fake yawn.

"That's a good idea, dear. You shall need your rest," Sarah replied.

"Rest? Rest for what?"

"To practice your galloping tomorrow," Sarah stated with sureness as if it had been planned for weeks. "Your brother will take you out to practice after lunch."

With an abrupt snap, Ben's head flew up from his newspaper. "Sarah, I am very busy tomorrow. The garden party is on Sunday, and I'll be needed here." He cast a wary glance at Catie. "And anyway, why the sudden urgency?"

"I am sure the setup will go just as smooth, if not smoother, without all of your grandiose supervision and finger pointing," Sarah said. "And…seeing that you refuse to allow her to ride alone, it is you who must take her to practice." She skillfully raised her hammer and with one sharp blow drove in the last nail. "I was speaking with Sean Kelly in the kitchen earlier today and he claims he has never seen such reluctance in a student. He thinks our Catie may just be incapable of galloping."

"Incapable!" Ben exclaimed. "I'll have him know that a Darcy isn't *incapable* of anything, at least not when it comes to horsemanship."

"Yes, darling, that is exactly what I told him, and therein lays the urgency. Sean will only be here another week."

Catie listened to the exchange with quiet alarm, trying in vain to catch Sarah's eye with an expressive plea. *What is she thinking? The man has hardly strung three words together the last few days.*

"*Incapable*…Catherine, be dressed and ready to ride after breakfast. We shall settle this matter early. Grandiose or not I *will* be overseeing the setup tomorrow afternoon." Ben shot Sarah a daring look.

"But…I…" Catie fumbled for a way out, but he cut her off.

"And you might as well leave all of that reluctance here. There'll be no need for any of that."

Sighing huffily, because that was all she could think to do, Catie turned and left.

"Incapable," he scoffed one last time as he shot Sarah another look and snapped open his newspaper. "Indeed."

Sarah smiled.

"*Gerrl*," Catie tried mimicking Sean's accent to the voiceless shadows of her room. "You're a very pretty *gerrl*." She blew out a big breath and turned on to her side. The summer had gone by so quickly, the long afternoons with Sean, the nights she tempted fate and met him at the pond, that moment by the river.

Lying there in the dark of her room, Catie began to feel like the past few weeks were a dream that may or may not have happened. From her bed she stared out of the large window. The wind was still and the stars hidden. Was she reluctant? She most definitely wasn't afraid. So why was she crying?

SARAH'S PREGNANCY HAD HER UP all hours of the night. At five the next morning, she was wide awake and fighting a nagging motherly instinct that something was wrong. Not a completely uncommon occurrence for her, but profoundly worsened by the growing life inside of her. By five-thirty the feeling had not left her, so she resolved to appease it in order to get some sleep.

Easing herself up so as not to disturb Ben, Sarah crept softly out of the room and down the corridor. Pemberley's centuries-old floorboards had a tendency to cry out at the first early morning riser who dared cross them.

Within seconds she was standing at the foot of Geoffrey and George's beds, smiling and relieved. Their doll-like faces were serene in the depths of their dreams…just as she had presumed. For fear of waking them prematurely, she fought the motherly urge to kiss and tuck and instead stepped quietly out of the room. Before returning to the warmth of her bed, on a whim, she walked the long length of the hall and gently pushed open Catie's door. The first trickle of early dawn was beginning to leak a grey hue into the valley, lighting Catie's room just enough to reveal an empty bed.

Trying to control the panic that was quickly overtaking her senses, Sarah rushed back to wake Ben, letting the floorboards cry at will. "Bennet!" she cried, shaking him firmly "Bennet, wake up!"

"What is it? What's the matter?" he asked groggily, not opening his eyes.

"It's Catie. She's not in her room. She's *missing*, Ben!" She emphasized the *missing* to startle him into understanding.

His eyes popped open. "What do you mean missing?"

"She's not in her room."

"Have you checked the house?" he asked, clumsily trying to pull on his trousers.

"I came straight to wake you. I have a bad feeling, Ben. It's five-thirty in the morning. Where else would she be?"

A quick search of the house turned up nothing, so they woke Rose and dressed to search the grounds. A low, thick fog greeted them as they rushed down the front steps, and Sarah touched her husband's arm. "I don't like this, Ben."

He put a hand over hers. "There has to be a logical explanation. Look." He pointed to the carriage house where Catie's bicycle leaned against the garage door, slightly obscured by the mist. "If she came out of the house, she must be on foot."

"What about the stables? Maybe she took Chloe out?"

"No." He shook his head. "From the first time I lifted her into a saddle, I've warned her never to ride alone. She knows better." Sarah saw a subtle but definitely budding doubt in Ben's expression as he rubbed wearily at the back of his neck. "Then again," he amended, "it's better that we should look than not."

Sarah had to double step to keep up with her husband's long, hard strides, but she could see the worry lines creasing his brow and didn't request that he slow his pace. At the end of the path, they saw the stable door was open and a dim light shone out through the heavy fog. "Thank God," Ben murmured and ran across the stable yard, yelling, "Catherine!"

"Mr. Darcy?" Sean stood and turned just as Ben came in the door.

"What are you doing here this early in the morning?" Ben asked, surprised and firmer than was necessary.

"Wrapping Thunder's legs for his morning exercise." He pointed to the animal's partially wrapped leg as if to verify. "Is something the matter, sir?" Without answering, Ben hurried past him, so Sean looked to Mrs. Darcy for an explanation.

"We can't find Catie," Sarah told him. "Have you seen her this morning?"

"Chloe's gone!" Ben called out before Sean could respond. "Sarah, go back to the house. I'll find her."

"No, Ben, I'm coming with you."

Ben was already leading Geronimo from his stall but paused long enough to give his wife a calculating glance. "Horseback — in this fog and in your condition? No, Sarah, I'll not have it, and I haven't the time to quarrel with you. So please, do as I say and go back to the house."

"I'll go, Mrs. Darcy," Sean offered, already gathering tack.

Sarah thanked him and stood by feeling utterly useless and underfoot watching the men saddle their horses. "Oh, do hurry," she said anxiously for lack of anything constructive to do.

First to mount, Ben instructed Sean to fetch the two-way radios out of the tack room. "If you see her, radio me immediately," he advised firmly.

Sean couldn't tell whether Mr. Darcy was more afraid or angry. Probably a bit of both, he surmised, like himself. "Yes, sir." He mounted and rode out of the stable with a look of unreserved determination that took Sarah by surprise.

She had been aware for some time that Catie had developed a schoolgirl fancy for her handsome riding instructor, but it had never occurred to her until now that young Sean Kelly might have reciprocated those feelings.

"Don't worry, Sarah." Ben stopped on his way out of the stable. "We'll find her directly. Now go to the house where it's warm."

She nodded soberly and watched as Ben and Sean rode off in opposite directions.

Ben had not gone far when he brought Geronimo to a halt and looked back over his shoulder. It suddenly occurred to him that the young Irishman might have a better idea of where Catie was than he. "Damn and blast," he said guiltily to himself. He had been so consumed with his own bloody pride that Catie's own brother and guardian, the only person she had left in the world, had no idea where she was going — or why. He turned Geronimo about and kicked him hard in the flanks.

SEAN THOUGHT OF LUAS, HIS sorrel-colored Irish Hunter back home as he pressed the good-natured but slow gelding that had been provided for him. Frustrated, Sean pulled a branch from a passing tree and switched the horse's hide for encouragement.

Luas, the Irish Gaelic word for speed, was a gift from his father on Sean's thirteenth birthday. "You're a man now, Seany," Seamus Kelly had said as he gave his son's back a hearty slap. Sean remembered digging his toes deep into his shoes and using all his might to keep his footing. He didn't want to stumble in front of his da.

Sean had trained Luas himself and had often wondered how his Irish Sport horse would match up against Mr. Darcy's Geronimo in a race. He proudly wagered that even if Luas didn't win, he would surely give the thoroughbred a fitting competition. That morning, however, he needed Luas' agility and speed to get to Catie, and he knew Luas would get him there fast.

Sean knew she was at the flats trying to gallop, and he was to blame. He had been harder than usual on Catie the last few days because of her stubborn refusal to let her horse run. If she was hurt, he would never forgive himself. He had pushed her — pushed her to overcome whatever she was holding in. Maybe he had pushed too far. What was he thinking? Catie was young and naïve, and although his years on her were but a few, Sean was wiser, and he understood the world better than she did. He knew she was falling in love with him, but their families, their backgrounds, their worlds were so different that no amount of fondness, affection... or love for that matter could ever make them right for each other.

Descending down into the lowlands by the river, Sean rode out of the fog. The mist hung over the fields like the earth's ceiling, making him feel as if he was atop one of the county's highest peaks. He gave a grateful sigh of relief at the sight of her. She was safe, sitting atop Chloe and as hesitant as she had been all summer.

The sound of beating hooves caused her to turn slowly, clearly not expecting anyone. As she came into focus his heart gave a hard thump, and he had to remind himself to breathe. Her face, still bearing a bit of puffiness from sleep, told of her youth. Her lips and cheeks were rosy red from the chill of the morning and looked as if they had been painted on her soft, fair skin. She had the appearance of a beautiful ghostly child surrounded by the thickness of the morning around her. "Keep your senses, Seany!" he reminded himself.

When she recognized the approaching rider, her eyes lit, and a sweet tender smile spread across her face so broadly that it dimpled her cheeks. Her obvious delight in seeing him caused the knot in his heart to tighten. While his first impulse was to be cross with her for going out alone in the fog, he couldn't help but smile back.

"Sean!" she called out as he neared. "What are you doing here?"

"*Me*? Catie Darcy, I've a good mind to — " He stopped. There in her eyes was that damned sorrow he'd seen so many times before. She wasn't just being reckless by riding alone in such weather. There was something else. There had always been something else, but try as he might Sean had been unable to put his finger on it. "Why are you out here, Catie?" he asked gently, hoping to find the answer that had escaped him all summer.

She shrugged and gazed down the long, grassy field as Chloe pranced about underneath her.

"She wants to run." He moved closer to her. "She knows that's why you brought her here."

"I know," she said so softly it was almost a whisper.

"Then let her. She's waiting for you. She won't go until you tell her it's okay. You have all the power, Catie."

To calm the anxious horse, Catie reached out and patted Chloe's neck. "Easy girl." Then she looked at him and asked, "Will you run with me?"

"If you'd like." He eased his horse alongside Chloe. "But you must start."

She nodded, her eyes fixed on the land that lay out in front of her, but Catie's hesitation did not ebb. "I am not afraid, Sean. You were right...what you said at the cemetery. I am more like my father when it comes to seeking adventure. It isn't fear."

"Then what...what is it?"

She released a shuddered breath. "I've been awake all night trying to figure that out. All I know is...I must..." A burst of tears strangled her words, and she buried her face in the crook of her arm to hide her emotion.

Sean reached out and clutched her shoulder. "God, Catie, what is it? What's the matter?" She sniffed but didn't answer. "Come, lass, you need to go home. Your family is looking for you."

Tears streaming, Catie turned to him. "Looking for me? My brother is looking for me?"

"Yes. They're worried about you."

"No, Sean, I refuse to leave. Not until I do this, I *must* do this."

"Then stop all the bloody theatrics and do it," said a deep voice from behind them. The two had been so caught up they hadn't heard Ben draw near but turned with equal swiftness to the sound of his voice.

"Well...what's it going to be, Catherine? Are you going to cry about it or are you going to do it?" Ben asked.

Sean looked back at Catie. Her gleaming eyes showed clear apprehension in meeting her brother's, and Sean understood. He above all others understood. Sean Kelly was well versed in the pains of disapproval from the one person in the world from whom you needed approval. He understood perfectly. She had slipped back to the stables that day eight years ago for him, for her brother. She had hoped to impress him, please him when grief had consumed their hearts. This was between brother and sister, it always had been. Sean moved his horse away from Catie's side as he glanced back at Ben.

"Mr. Darcy, she wants someone to run alongside her. I believe she would prefer it be you."

Ben urged Geronimo forward and looked down into his sister's wet face. "I'm not so sure she will like my instruction. She's well aware of my expectations." Ben gave his sister his usual brotherly wink. "Is that what you want, Sis? Do you want your brother to gallop with you?"

Catie finally let her eyes meet his. "I would."

"All right, but there will be no more of this crying!" Ben stuck up an adamant finger. "And none of this reluctance I've been hearing about." He shook his head. "You're a Darcy born if I ever saw one, Catherine. And we Darcys are anything *but* reluctant." He gave Sean Kelly a sidelong glance and straightened himself tall in his saddle. "Now then, there will be no reining in, and you will maintain your position. Do I make myself clear?"

Now beaming, Catie squared her shoulders soldier-like and shouted, "Aye, sir!"

Sean chuckled and Ben shot him another glance, sharper than before, and continued his instructions. "And as for your seat, you must — "

"*Tch, tch.*" Two loud clicks stopped him mid-sentence as Catie tore off running across the grasslands.

Staring at Chloe's hindquarters, Ben heard young Kelly chuckling again. "Beg pardon, Mr. Darcy, but it seems you've lost your student." Grinning widely, Sean gestured down field.

"Yes, Sean, thank you," Ben acknowledged and kicked Geronimo into a fast gallop.

"You're welcome, sir," Sean called out as he watched the thoroughbred quickly make up the distance. Like her brother, Catie Darcy was one with her horse, rider and animal working in perfect harmony as they galloped solidly and smoothly down field. Sean knew she could do it. The girl had the build of a rider; it was in her blood. He watched for another moment and then turned his horse and headed back to the stables alone.

When Catie reached the end of her run, she let out a proud whoop and turned Chloe about so fast she was nearly jostled from her saddle.

"Be careful, Catie," Ben cautioned.

"But...where's Sean?" she said, squinting into the bright break of day burning through the mist. "Did he not see me? Where did he go?"

"He saw you," Ben confirmed, as he dismounted and took hold of Chloe to steady the horse. "Dismount, Catie; you and I need to talk."

Catie gave the field she had just crossed another victorious gaze. Then, swinging a leg over, she carefully navigated the long slide to the ground. Ben left the horses to graze on the sweet, dew-soaked grass as they walked toward the river. He stopped beside a large flat tree stump. "Sit down, Sis."

Catie sat down and took off her riding hat. She placed it in her lap and looked up at him, sure she was in for a sermon for the trouble and worry she had caused.

He stared at her for some time and then turned away, towards the river. When he finally spoke, he did not look back at her. "Your brother has been played for a fool, Catie."

"What?" she asked, surprised by his words.

"I know you have wanted to know...to understand the circumstances surrounding Cousin Mary and Wesley Howell, but I have been too ashamed." He paused for another moment and then faced her. "Catie, had you not found those letters, I would have been swindled, duped by a con artist, a man no better than a common pickpocket. Our father advised me — warned me many, many times — that if anything were to happen to him, to put my trust in Horace Harold. But...I followed a path of my own conceited confidence. I wanted to run Pemberley and my business affairs my way, not Dad's. Horace Harold scolded me like a child when I brought Charles Worthington on board, and I shut him out." Ben took a deep breath. "In arrogance I turned from what I was taught by our father, letting him down — and all those who depend on me."

Catie couldn't stand the speech any longer. Staring up at Ben, she saw what she always saw: strength and confidence. "No, Bennet, you have let no one down! What have you done wrong but trust a friend? The only person to blame is Mr. Worthington, not you! You could never be to blame for anything. You always know what is right, and you always do what is right."

"No, Catie, I don't!" he snapped at her. "I am just as fallible as any man, and your perception of me is far too unrealistic!" The sharp response made Catie lower her eyes and fiddle with her hat straps. Ben grimaced regretfully. "Sis," he said softly, kneeling on the wet grass in front of her. "You're not a child anymore. It's time you grew up. You have to stop romanticizing the world around you. You idolized Dad when he was alive and have set him upon a pedestal and worshiped him since his death." He placed a warm hand on Catie's knee. "He was human, dearest, just as I am. The truth is, I, like our father, have made many mistakes in my life and will make many more. I'm honored by your admiration, but it's difficult to live up to. It was for that reason that I've put off coming to you. How do I tell my little sister, who looks to me for guidance and security, of my own carelessness? I never wanted to let you down, Catie."

Catie stared at him. "You haven't."

He marveled at how her eyes were just like their mother's eyes, and smiled. "Still...you are at an age now that you must understand...I don't always know what is right, and I *certainly* don't always do what is right."

"But you do." She sniffed back both the chill of the morning and her increasing emotion.

"No, Catie, I don't."

"Yes, you bloody well do! I *am* grown-up, Ben; grown-up enough to understand what you did for me, the sacrifices you've made for me. I know what a burden I've been and — "

"*Burden*!" he interrupted. "How could you say such a thing?"

"It was you who said it, Bennet, not me."

"I said it?" He stood and looked down at her. "I never would have — "

"Yes, Bennet, you did. When you put me in my room, remember?"

His expression showed his disbelief, but inside he didn't question the truth of it. "My God, Catie, I was out of my mind with worry that day. Please know — whatever I said, I didn't mean it. You have been anything *but* a burden."

Ben motioned for her to make room for him on the stump and sat down beside her. "Do you not understand why I was so upset that day?"

"Because I didn't leave the Ledfords' when you told me to."

"No." He shook his head. "That's not it. Catie, I almost lost you, and that would have been like losing our parents all over again. God, Sis, every time I look into your face, I see our mother. And you are overflowing with Dad's personality, his determination, his sense of humor. You aren't a burden; if anything you have been a gift. You're all I have left of them."

"I'm so sorry they died." Catie's voice broke, but she was determined not to cry.

Ben swallowed hard. "I'm sorry too. But you and I... we've done all right, eh?"

She nodded as her bottom lip trembled, and she bit it fiercely.

"It's all right, dearest." Ben pulled her into his chest. "Cry if you must... God knows I'm about on the verge myself."

He held her as she cried. When she had finished, he helped her dry her face, and they walked back to the horses. "Cold?" he asked, noticing a shiver.

"A little," she admitted with a half smile.

Following her to Chloe's side, Ben took off the pullover he had grabbed before leaving the house and gave it to her. "One, two, three," he counted and hoisted her into the saddle. Then he mounted Geronimo and the two headed back to the house, riding slowly and evenly.

As they made their way home, Ben finished unburdening his soul. He told her how he had trusted Charles Worthington, their casual friendship going back to Cambridge. He and Horace Harold had been knocking heads for some time, and although it wasn't an excuse, Worthington was in the right place at the right time, so to speak. Once Horace Harold was completely out of the picture, Worthington had put his plan firmly in place to extort an inheritance for Wesley Howell.

Ben said he'd been made to believe that impregnating young Rebecca was the primary reason Thomas Howell had left the country and gone to Africa. And following the birth of her grandson, Mary Howell had paid the girl off and sent the baby away so as not to cause any complications with Grandfather Geoffrey's takeover of Pemberley. In actuality however, Rebecca was Rebecca Worthington, Charles Worthington's aunt and a distant cousin to Arthur Howell. Ben had no clue of the kinship between the Howells and Worthingtons until Horace Harold discovered it in his investigation.

Mary Darcy Howell, he told Catie, had been nothing but generous by allowing Rebecca to spend her confinement in the privacy of Pemberley. She only gave Wesley Howell her husband's surname out of kindness — not familial obligation.

"I believed Worthington, Catie. He promised to deal with the matter swiftly. He hired a phony private investigator who produced a falsified birth record naming Thomas Howell as Wesley's father. I saw the bloody thing myself and believed it."

"The man named Sams in front of the house?" Catie asked, and Ben nodded.

"I should have sent you out to kick him in the shins, Sis." He smiled finally, remembering the times she had done just that. Once he was in a heated dispute with a traffic warden over a parking ticket in London, and she slammed her little Mary Janes in the poor man's leg so hard, he was sure he was going to prison. "It was a well designed plot, Catie — one that would have worked had it not been for the letter you found and the quick work of Horace Harold's staff.

"So… where is Mr. Worthington now?"

"Fled the country most likely. No one has been able to locate him. Bloody blackguard somehow knew Horace and I were on to him." He looked over at her with the glimmer of a smirk on his face. "But don't worry, your Uncle Horace is seeing to him."

"Poor Mr. Worthington," she said with a chuckle.

"Indeed," her brother agreed gravely.

Catie looked serious again and asked, "What about Wesley Howell?"

"Mr. Howell, or whatever his name really is, claims to be a victim of Worthington's as well, and with Worthington nowhere to be found…" Ben shrugged. "Who's to say otherwise? I'll admit it was a fair mess I fell into, Sis, but thankfully I'm no worse for having been so foolish."

They reached the lake and pulled the horses to a halt to gaze upon the grand home of their ancestors. "You know, Catie, Grandfather once told me, 'Bennet, my boy, if you love and care for Pemberley, Pemberley will love and care for you in return.' Never have I believed that statement more than when you burst into my office that morning with Mary's letter in your hand, taken from Pemberley's very walls." He shook his head disbelievingly. "You had no way of knowing this, but I was just minutes away from leaving. I was headed to London to sign over a very large sum of money to Wesley Howell."

Upon their return to the house, Rose took Catie to the kitchen for cocoa, while Ben went to the nursery where Sarah was readying the boys for breakfast. Sean had called the house as soon as he returned to the stables, letting all know Catie was safe and with her brother.

"You're back," Sarah acknowledged, handing him Geoffrey's shoes and gently pushing the child in the direction of his father.

Ben took a seat and pulled the boy onto his lap. "Yes, we're back."

"*And*?" Sarah's tone was anxious.

"And…she galloped," Ben replied, as he tried to wriggle Geoffrey's shoe onto his foot. "Are you sure this shoe fits this boy?"

"Of course it fits him, I just bought it. Though it wouldn't shock me if it didn't; the poor dears have their father's feet. So where is she now?"

"Who, love? Ah…there you go, Geoffrey!"

"*Catie!*" Sarah exclaimed as she gestured to George, who stood waiting, shoes in hand.

Ben patted his knee and the boy climbed upon his father's lap. "She's in the kitchen having cocoa with Rose."

"Cocoa!" she exclaimed again. "Is *that* your idea of a proper consequence?"

"Consequence?" His brows knitted and he paused to look up at her.

"Yes, Bennet, a consequence!" she answered tersely. "Have you forgotten how she left this house before dawn without telling anyone, how she went out riding her horse in that dreadful fog...alone?"

Visibly fighting a grin, Ben argued, "Really, Sarah? Is punishment your only recourse? I have found that it is much better to *talk* to her, to *reason* with her."

Sarah stared at him. "You'll not use my words against me, Bennet Darcy! That was before she scared me half out of my wits this morning."

"Well, Sarah," he offered, the grin now spreading. "She's in the kitchen. If you feel she needs to be punished, go to it. I'll certainly not stop you."

Arms folded and lips pursed, Sarah tapped a contemplating foot. "And I would too," she declared, chin thrust up. "Had this not been such a trying week for us all, but seeing that it has, I feel the matter is probably better dropped."

Still grinning, Ben finished tying George's shoe and helped him off of his lap. "There you go, Son."

"Thank you, Daddy," the little boy said, looking up at him.

The grin transformed into a proud beam as Ben replied, "You're welcome, George."

Sarah's face softened at the sound of her little boy's voice. Although still slow in coming, George's independent speech had markedly improved after his little fishing trip with his father. "Oh, Bennet, whatever did you say to that child to encourage him so?"

"That, Sarah, is between father and son." He stood, wrapped her in his arms, and kissed her.

Sarah pulled back and smiled at him. "Catie is galloping; George is speaking. Shall I expect any further parental miracles this summer, Mr. Darcy?"

He sighed musingly. "No, my love, I believe my work is done. Except, that is, for the garden party." Ben turned to his sons. "Come, lads, we must break our fast. Your father needs his nourishment. I have a long day of grandiose supervising and finger pointing ahead of me."

Cupping her hand over her mouth, Sarah laughed softly into her palm. The return of her husband's teasing and playfulness said more than any words ever could have. He was finally himself again.

Chapter 21

From the formal Italian terrace to Sarah's less symmetrical English cutting garden, the park surrounding the house by mid-August had matured into absolute perfection. The grounds were a sight to behold, and for over a century, Pemberley's annual garden party had been timed accordingly. As tradition mandated, the tables would be adorned with only the cuisine the valley had to offer. The fare was arranged on silver trays lined with doilies and placed amid elaborate ice sculptures and floral displays. There would be lawn games and Pimms, face painting and pony rides. And finally, to top the festivities off properly, guests would spread picnic blankets on Pemberley's large front lawn and watch fireworks as soon as the sky was dark enough to act as a canvas.

On Saturday, the set-up was busy and hurried. In a faded Cambridge University tee-shirt, Mr. Darcy worked alongside the men all day to ready the lawn and gardens, placing chairs and folding tables at Sarah's direction. Rather grandiose direction, Ben thought, but was wise enough to hold his tongue on the matter. When the work was completed, an exhausted Mr. Darcy tapped a keg brought up from the Green Man, and Mr. Johnson lit a large grill to cook generously cut steaks for the workers. This evening feast was as traditional as the garden party itself. It was a time for Mr. Darcy to eat and drink with them, to socialize and thank them for their help.

By dusk the men were so full they had begun to recline in order to drink more, as no self-respecting Derbyshire man would let the remnants of a keg go to waste. Like the others, Sean had worked hard all day, impressing those who had fancied him for nothing more than a university boy who never got his hands dirty. He now sat picking his old guitar and singing pub songs. For pure sport, the men had dutifully kept his mug full and laughed heartily as they saw him beginning to feel the effects.

Well before midnight, he stood and announced, "I think I'll be off to my bed, mates."

"An Irishman that can't hold his stout?" a fellow called out.

Sean smiled. "Aye, a disgrace to my fellow Ulstermen, eh?"

"You'll no sing for us anymore, laddie?" another said but was quickly interrupted by the former. "Leave the boy be, Tom! His auntie will skin 'im if he's up past his bedtime!" An uproarious laugh followed, but Sean took their tease in jest. He had seven uncles on his father's side and had suffered his fair share of ribbing before.

"Aye, she will at that," he agreed good-heartedly as he threw his guitar over his shoulder and started off. "Good night, mates."

"Sean!" Hearing his name, Sean turned to see Mr. Darcy following him.

"Yes, Mr. Darcy."

Ben extended his hand. "I just wanted to thank you for today."

Sean gave his employer's hand a firm shake. "Don't mention it, sir. I didn't mind helping set up, and I rather enjoyed this evening."

"No." Ben shook his head. "I was referring to this morning. What you did for Catie; I want you to know it was very helpful and most appreciated." Laughing softly, Ben rubbed wearily at the back of his neck. "My little sister... well... she's none too easy to manage at times as I'm sure you've noticed."

"She's... I mean... it was no bother..." Sean's voice trailed off. Even through the slight buzz of beer, he was mindful enough not to expose his affection for the girl he knew he could never have. It was best to say no more. "Good night to you, sir." Sean gave a single nod and departed.

WITH ONLY A SHORT TIME before the guests were expected, Ben gave another knock at his sister's door and yelled for her to hurry. Although Catie never would admit it, she was at a loss getting herself ready for such an event without Annie. Even though Maggie had pressed her dress, Catie chose to do her own hair and makeup. The sprigs of baby's breath that Sarah insisted she tuck in her hair were giving her the most trouble.

After fumbling with the tiny flowers for some time, her impatience was hurled at the next knock at the door. "Bennet, please!" she shouted. "I'm hurrying as fast as I can!"

"It's Maggie, Miss Catie, may I come in?" a timid voice called back from the hall.

Seated at her dressing table, Catie scowled at her reflection in the mirror but answered pleasantly, "Yes, come in."

The door opened slowly, and Maggie Reid took a few cautious steps into the room. "Mrs. Darcy sent me to help you."

Meeting Maggie's eyes in the mirror, Catie sighed. "Yes fine, if I can't make these flowers work, Sarah will make me wear one of those ridiculous, wide-brimmed hats."

"Oh, I can help with that," Maggie said and rushed to stand behind her. "I am really good at doing hair. Everyone says so. Do you have curling tongs?"

Catie pointed to the drawer and for the next half hour intently watched in the mirror as Maggie worked industriously with her hair. Though only fifteen months Catie's senior, the girl had much more womanly features, which Catie envied. Maggie was beautiful, not in a polished way, but a rather wholesome beauty that Catie imagined would be quite attractive to a man.

When Maggie finished, Catie looked at herself. Maggie had done a good job, an exceptional job actually, and she had no choice but to compliment her. "It looks very nice, Maggie, thank you."

"So you like it?" Maggie asked with childlike enthusiasm.

"Yes, Maggie, I like it very much," Catie responded, mirroring Maggie's kind smile.

Waiting for Catie in the front hall, Ben and Sarah looked up when she appeared at the top of the staircase. She was wearing an ivory, tea-length party dress that dropped just off the shoulders and flattered her maturing form, presenting her brother with the sight of a beautiful young woman, not a little girl. Slightly taken aback, Ben stared at her in wonder. Had she truly blossomed so rapidly or had this change been coming over her for some time? Had she concealed it from him or had he just refused to see it?

His contemplation appeared to Catie as her brother's usual taciturn demeanor, and she countered it with sisterly playfulness. "What's the matter, Bennet?" she asked. "Do you not think I look pretty?"

Barely softening his expression, Ben answered, "I was thinking quite the opposite, dearest."

Taking Ben's proffered arm, Catie teased back, "Well, Sarah, I guess we can safely say it wasn't my brother's dazzling talents in the art of flattery that won you over."

On the other side of her husband, Sarah gently tossed her head back and laughed. "Hardly, Catie…but I did feel rather sorry for him!"

Catie giggled. "Sorry for him!" she repeated. "Are you going to take that, Brother?"

"I believe I must. I'm clearly outnumbered at present," Ben replied dryly as Catie nuzzled close to his arm. "You haven't lost her yet old man," he quietly assured himself as they walked.

Tedious is the only way to describe the start of any party when you are the host and hostess. The repetitive act of welcoming each guest and trying to find something remarkable or interesting to say to each one becomes an outright chore. Catie's task however was simpler, she only had to smile and offer a white gloved hand to each person in turn, while accepting winks from older gentleman. But she was accustomed to being the belle of Pemberley and enjoyed charming the older chaps.

This year, however, was markedly different. Catie could not help but notice that she had already been introduced to more than eight young men, and a very distinguished group they were indeed. One young lad was the grandson of a baroness, another, the nephew of an earl, and all equally touted by their mothers or grandmothers for something amazing or noteworthy in their person.

Catie had listened to praises ranging from horsemanship to penmanship and everything in between before finally turning to Sarah and asking, "Is it just me or are there an unusual number of lads here this year?"

"It is more likely, my dear, that you are at an age where you're taking more notice of *lads*," Sarah whispered in response

"I can assure you, Sarah, that I am not taking notice of any *lad* who speaks through his nose and whose mother can find nothing to recommend him beyond his exceptional penmanship."

"*Catie!*" Sarah quietly scolded. "Not so loud."

"Sorry." Catie laughed softly but then saw Horace and Diana Harold and ran squealing to her godparents. "Uncle Horace, Aunt Diana, how have you been?"

"We have been missing our goddaughter, that is how we have been," Horace Harold responded, swallowing her in his arms.

"There now, see, Diana," Horace said to his wife, pulling Catie back for inspection. "She has not changed all that much since Easter."

"Oh, how could you say that, Horace?" Diana said contrarily. "She is much grown, and her face is so changed I should hardly recognize her." The woman glanced sharply at Ben, clearly still possessing a tinge of bitterness over the events of the past year. "Never shall so much time pass without laying eyes on her again, never I tell you!"

Although it normally fell to Sarah to smooth the wrinkles in conversation when it came to her husband, Catie understood the implication for her brother and felt for him. "No you shan't, Aunt Diana!" Catie confirmed. "I insist on spending my next holiday from school with you and Uncle Horace. Maybe I could persuade you both to take me to Scotland again. I have such fond memories of our trip to Edinburgh, and I promise…no hospitals this time."

Diana warmed with Catie's charm. "No hospitals indeed!" She laughed, readily agreeing to take her goddaughter anywhere of her choosing.

As the couple moved on to mingle, Catie caught Uncle Horace giving Ben's shoulder a fatherly pat and was glad to see it.

Next in line was the Hirst family, each in turn greeting the Darcys, Lawrence and Eleanor Hirst of Ardsley Manor, his brother, Walter and his wife, Abigail and lastly their son, Aiden. There was a great hubbub of welcoming before Aiden finally reached Catie. She smiled and offered him her hand. He took it and squeezed it gently in affection. Aiden Hirst's stature and appearance was one that neither his horsemanship nor penmanship was needed in order to gain the attention of a young girl.

"How are you, Cate?"

"Fine, thank you." She smiled.

"If you're finished here, would you like to give me that dance you promised?" he asked, not yet letting go of her hand.

"I…" Catie blushed and glanced at Ben. She'd all but forgotten about the dance with Aiden.

Seeing the root of her hesitation, Aiden drew himself up with a playful but sincere formality and asked Ben, "If Mr. Darcy sees me as a suitable dance partner that is? Sir, may I?"

"Of course," Ben replied with a chuckle. "I have a high regard for country manners, Hirst. You are granted the first dance with my fair sister."

Aiden laughed. "Thank you, sir," he said and offered Catie his arm.

Catie stole a glance at Sarah as the two strolled off; she wasn't laughing either.

"You must never encourage my brother's peculiar wit," Catie admonished.

"He's a funny chap," Aiden replied. "I like him."

Catie cast a warning eye at her dance partner. "If you ever find yourself on the wrong side of him, you'll quickly see he's not a man to be trifled with."

"Then I shall take care not to find myself on the wrong side of him." He turned to her and they fell into a quick, easy rhythm. Each had been educated in schools that put a finishing touch on a student's education, meaning they were comfortable on a dance floor.

"You're not bad," Catie said.

"Is that a compliment, Catie Darcy?"

"Not really. At school our dance class is all girls."

"Thanks." He chuckled. "So I'm not bad compared to a room full of giggling fifth formers."

"Exactly." She laughed softly.

They danced for the next few minutes in silence, his hand pressed firmly against the small of her back. When the music stopped, he led her from the dance floor and asked, "Would you like something to drink?"

Catie looked past Aiden and noticed Sean standing next to Rose, looking around as if in search of her. "I...I'm sorry, Aiden," she said apologetically. "I really should mingle for a little. Maybe later?"

"I'll hold you to it." His eyes lingered on her as he released her hands with an obvious reluctance.

Approaching Rose and Sean, Catie saw he wore a pair of khakis, a banded collar shirt, and a waistcoat that was left open until his aunt took notice and gestured for him to button it up. As she drew closer, she noticed his thatch of black hair was a bit more tame than usual and smiled. She liked his ruggedness, his commonness. Like Pemberley's grounds, Sean Kelly was also untouched and left as God created.

Rose was dressed for the party, but she most definitely wasn't taking a leisurely afternoon off. She could request that a tray be refilled or a guest be offered a drink with no more than a glance or a slight nod to her serving staff. She had an exceptional knack for making a party go off without a hitch. Grateful for Catie's arrival, Rose scanned the tables and hurried off, leaving Sean temporarily in Catie's care.

"So, Mr. Kelly, did you finally have your first cucumber sandwich?" Catie asked.

"Aye," he answered with a grin.

"*And?*"

"And, I found them exactly as I expected I would, dainty and not at all filling."

"Well, maybe we can spear a wild boar for you." Catie's teasing eyes met his. "Or maybe you would like to kill the poor thing with your bare hands."

He laughed. "Wild boars roam the gardens of Pemberley, do they?"

Before Catie could retort, Audrey Tillman rushed over to them. "There you are!" she panted. "I've been looking everywhere for you."

"Aud, how are you?" Catie asked as they hugged.

"Wonderful. Hello, Sean Kelly," Audrey said over Catie's shoulder.

"Hello, Audrey Tillman," Sean replied. "Have you had a nice summer?"

She had had a very nice summer indeed and wasn't about to let Catie off without telling her everything. A vacation to Paris with her father, travelling to Turkey with her mother… Audrey went on for some time before Sean stopped her.

"May I?" He gestured towards her punch glass.

"Hmm? Oh, yes, thank you." She handed him the empty glass.

"Catie?" Sean turned in her direction, raising one shrewd brow.

Catie grinned in understanding. He had interrupted Audrey Tillman's ramble to spare Catie any further talk of white sand beaches and Parisian boutiques. "No, Sean, thank you… really."

"Thank God! I thought he'd never leave," Audrey blurted as soon as Sean stepped away. "So tell me… why all the young chaps this year? This is usually a ripe old geriatric event."

Catie shrugged. "Maybe England's young male population has abandoned Black Sabbath for orchestra music and finger sandwiches."

The two girls looked at each other and burst out laughing.

"Speaking of young chaps, you and Kelly seem to be rather chummy. Anything you wish to tell me, Darcy?" Audrey nudged her friend with an elbow.

"No, Tillman." Catie saw Sean returning and put a finger to her lips. "Now *shhh.*"

The girls talked for a few more minutes as Sean sipped nervously at his drink and scanned the crowd. Catie sensed he might be feeling a bit out of place and was glad when Audrey parted their company in search of more flirtatious conversation.

"See that gentleman over there with the bad hairpiece," she whispered when they were alone again, hoping to make him feel more at ease.

"Um-hmm." He cut his eyes down at her. "What about him?"

"See the older woman with him?"

He nodded. "His mother?"

She shook her head and mouthed, "His nanny."

"No way!" he hissed disbelievingly. "What is he doing with his nanny?"

"Married her...after his mum died, seems they never *really* parted ways, a secret affair for almost thirty years."

"How could he be with a woman who had wiped his arse...er, sorry...bum for him?"

Catie shrugged, giggling.

"The rich are an odd lot, eh?" Glancing at her, he instantly realized his error. "I mean...not you..."

"No," she stopped him. "I'm just, what was it...spoiled and insolent?"

"Well." He smiled. "You *are* to be sure, Miss Catie. But that's just the opinion of a very poor insufferable ass."

"An ass maybe, but not so insufferable," she said softly as their eyes met and held for several seconds. Conversation between them began to flow more easily, and Sean seemed more relaxed...almost enjoying himself.

As the afternoon wore on, the Darcy twins were brought from where the children were being entertained to make an appearance. They entered holding hands, curls plastered to their little heads, and wearing navy blue blazers with white short trousers. There was a collective gasp, followed by ooh's and aah's as the crowd parted so the boys could make their way to their parents. Sean chuckled.

"What's so funny?" Catie asked.

"Do you have any idea how embarrassed they'll be when those pictures are pulled out ten, twelve years from now?"

"I think they look cute!" Catie argued.

"No boy of mine would ever be dressed that way," he solemnly stated.

"They will if their mother has anything to say about it. Sarah bought those outfits herself, and I helped her pick them out."

"I'm sorry." Sean laughed. "But they look like miniature waiters. Put a tray in their hands, and your guests will stop *oohing* and *aahing* and ask them for more champagne."

Giving him a playful elbow, Catie protested, "That's cruel, Sean."

"No, cruel is putting them in those little monkey suits..." Sean started, but was interrupted by the sound of a silver fork clinking lightly against a piece of crystal stemware.

Donald Tillman stood up to say a few words. He and the late Mr. Darcy had been good friends and had worked together for many years on behalf of Derbyshire to boost the county's tourism. He spoke of the beauty of Pemberley House and grounds and expressed his gratitude that the grand old manor would once again be open to the public, explaining that the centuries-old family home had always been a favorite of tourists.

Pemberley had opened its doors to holiday travelers since its beginning. It was tradition, and Ben was unquestionably a traditionalist when it came to the running of the estate. However, the circumstances surrounding the loss of his father had gained so much public attention that Ben couldn't bear the thought of tour guides retelling the tragedy to nosy sightseers in his very own drawing room.

"An estate is no different than your money," Grandfather Geoffrey had told Ben numerous times. "Make your estate work for you...*Never* work for your estate." Geoffrey Darcy knew how to run an estate and, even in some of the most difficult economic times, to keep it running. Before he died, he taught his grandson everything he knew. Ben was not ignorant to the amount of income he was forfeiting by closing the house and grounds.

At Mr. Tillman's introduction, Ben got up to speak. He was opening Pemberley again. Enough time had passed. He and Catie had healed. He spoke of his father's work in the county's tourism industry and stated his eagerness to reestablish Pemberley among the ranks of Derbyshire's list of "must sees." His announcement caused an eruption of toasts and cheers that lasted several minutes.

After the speeches the party quickly returned to the low hum of conversations. Ben took a glass of champagne from a tray and began to search for his sister. He was not in the least bit thrilled to see that she remained in the company of Sean Kelly. Sarah caught her husband's expression and excused herself to go to him.

"Something is troubling you?" she asked and affirmed in the same breath.

"Catie," Ben said with a little nod in her direction. "She has not left Sean Kelly's side all afternoon."

"She is just being polite. He really knows no one beyond her and Rose."

"Well, I for one think she has been polite long enough. She is just as obligated to the rest of the guests."

Sarah glanced again at Catie and Sean; she knew it was not just politeness. She was rather sure that the two preferred each other's company. Sarah began to fear that if it hadn't already, their close friendship could easily turn into a dangerous liaison... especially where Bennet Darcy was concerned.

"You could diplomatically, and I do mean *diplomatically*, Bennet Darcy, request she circulate with you for awhile," Sarah suggested, cringing inside as she tried hard to convince herself that she was in no way behaving like Abigail Hirst.

Ben nodded in agreement, handed her his glass, and slowly made his way through the crowd to Catie. No easy task, as he was stopped every few feet and had to respond appropriately to each interruption, not wanting to appear as if he were on a mission and draw undue attention. Finally he approached Sean and Catie bearing a very diplomatic and uncharacteristic smile.

"Sean, are you enjoying yourself?" he asked pleasantly.

"Yes, very much so, thank you, Mr. Darcy."

"Grand." Ben's smile widened as Catie looked at him strangely. "If you wouldn't mind," he continued, "I was hoping I could steal my sister. I have been so preoccupied this afternoon I'm afraid I haven't been able to show her off properly."

Now she understood. Like the day at the paddock, it wasn't proper for her to be standing with her riding instructor all afternoon. People might talk.

"No," Sean replied hastily, as if he had done something wrong. "Please, sir."

"Thank you. Please enjoy the rest of your evening." Ben turned to Catie and offered her his arm. "Sis?"

Reluctantly, Catie took hold of Ben's arm and walked away with him, glancing over her shoulder at Sean as they departed.

Chapter 22

For the next hour, Catie looked Sean's way every so often. Sometimes he would notice her gaze and return it. Other times he was busy, engaged in conversation with various, curious guests. More than once she tried to be excused from the mind-numbing discussions of shooting and fishing, politics and farming, but wasn't successful. Ben, it seemed, was determined to keep her by his side. Eventually she was asked to dance by a boy whose name she couldn't recall, but jumped at the chance of escape from her brother.

From the dance floor, she inconspicuously but frantically searched the crowd for Sean but could no longer find him. Several different dance partners later, she assumed he had left.

As afternoon gave way to dusk, Sean headed back to the cottage. His headache from the morning had returned and the lackluster party could no longer hold his interest. On his way he passed several guests, who clearly preferred the outskirts of a party rather than the midst.

Only yards from his door, Sean heard a noise that brought him to an abrupt stop. He was still close enough to hear the orchestra and first assumed that was probably what he had heard. But in just a few more seconds of listening, came a distinctive, "No!" Sean changed course and hurried in the direction of the voice.

On a bench, tucked under a vine laden arbor, Sean found Audrey Tillman and a young man he had seen her with at the party. Audrey looked away at the sight of Sean and began buttoning her blouse, while the young man stood as if protecting her.

"This is a private party, mate," he declared, thrusting out his chest like a peacock.

218

Ignoring him, Sean looked around to Audrey Tillman. "Audrey, your father is looking for you. It would be best that you go to him now."

"He is?" She got up and moved around her would-be protector. "Thank you," she said quietly to Sean as she brushed past him.

"Audrey!" Sean called out to her, and she stopped to listen to him. "I'd suggest you stay close to your father the rest of the evening." She nodded and went on.

"You know, Paddy. It is Irish, eh, your accent?" the young man said.

"It is. Ulster, not that it's any of your bloody business."

"Right. Well, I don't know how it is in Ulster but around here *no* oftentimes means *yes*…with the birds anyway. You follow me, mate?"

"No, I was taught to mind my manners, especially when it comes to respectable young women. Follow me…*mate*?" Sean crossed his arms and set his jaw firmly.

The moon was waning but bright enough for Sean to see his adversary's face. A sneering smile showed the young man's white teeth in the grey darkness. Apparently he was amused by Sean's comment. "Well, that's the nice thing about being rich," he said, raking his fingers through his hair. "You really don't have much need for manners."

"Then you must be a man of wealth," Sean countered, growing tired of the conversation. "Because when it comes to manners you certainly have none." He started to leave, but the young man wasn't finished.

"Ulster, eh, so tell me, Paddy, are you Catholic scum or loyal to your Queen?"

Sean spun about and took a couple of hard steps in the Englishman's direction. "My religion and my loyalties are none of your bloody concern."

"Calm down, Paddy. I only asked because I noticed that you enjoy the company of Catie Darcy."

Sean's fists balled but he forced them to remain at his sides. "Don't say her name," he murmured low and hoarsely, taking another step forward.

The young man moved back, almost into the arbor, clearly unsure of his chances if the altercation came to blows. "I was just going to offer you some friendly advice, mate."

Narrowing his eyes, Sean took a deep, calming breath, which seemed to encourage the young man to continue.

"You see, Paddy, that brother of hers will never approve of her going to the stables to fetch her gentleman friends. It matters not how much she fancies you; big brother makes the decisions for her."

"Humph," Sean uttered spitefully. "That only tells me how very little you know of Catie. She is strong-minded and strong-willed and very capable of making her own decisions."

"Now that's where you are wrong, Paddy. Strong-willed she may be, but old Mr. Darcy made sure if anything ever happened to him, his son would have complete and absolute control over his sister. *By way of her money*," he said the latter in a whispered voice as if it were a well-kept secret. "You see, Catie Darcy is to inherit a fortune, but not until she is twenty-five. Until then, brother Bennet holds her purse strings, and she'll not see a penny that hasn't passed through his hands first." He grinned meanly. "I guess her daddy wanted to deter any youthful impulsivity in his absence. You know, like dallying around with stable workers and no-good Irishmen living on the English dole."

Sean could feel his pulse quicken as he drew himself up and squared his shoulders for battle. His balled fists clenched tighter, so tight his nails dug into his palms, but then he turned and walked away. He wanted more than anything to punch the boy in the mouth, but of course he couldn't. For the sake of his Aunt Rose, he had to keep his cool. Any trouble caused by him could and probably would put her in a bad light with the Darcys. He didn't want to be the cause of problems for her. There was a parting remark from the arbor, but Sean was too caught up in his thoughts to hear it.

His mind raced as he walked back to the cottage. It occurred to Sean that his presence at the party had been the hushed talk of the afternoon, ripe gossip like the man who married his nanny. Catie in his company had been noticed, and was most likely the reason Mr. Darcy walked over and took his sister from Sean's side. He wasn't good enough for Catie Darcy, not as far as her brother was concerned. Of course Sean knew that already. Bennet Darcy would prefer someone with wealth, someone well-bred. Someone — Sean shuddered at the thought of it — someone like the blackguard Audrey Tillman was wresting off her. This made Sean sick. He had thought Mr. Darcy to be a man of character, a man Sean respected.

At the stables several weeks earlier, Mr. Darcy had encouraged Sean to continue his education, assuring him his father would eventually respect him for it. He even increased Sean's wages for his work with Thunder, securing the last of the funds Sean needed for tuition. Feeling he had earned Mr. Darcy's esteem, Sean had considered speaking to him about Catie and asking his permission to write to her or call once he was no longer an employee of the estate. Clearly that would have been foolish. He was just a charity case to Bennet Darcy. Sean stopped before reaching his door and cast his eyes to the black heavens. He had to get her off his mind and out of his heart. She could never be his, no matter how much he wanted her.

Flinging back the door, Sean couldn't open the bottle of aspirin fast enough. Cupping his hand under the tap, he quickly washed down three little white pills. Then, for good measure, he popped another in his mouth and washed down a fourth just as a ground shaking explosion made him jump. "Fireworks, Seany, stop being so jumpy, man," he said to himself and stepped outside to watch.

By the third bang, Sean saw someone approaching and sighed hard as soon as he was able to distinguish his visitor. "Catie." His tone was annoyed. "What are you doing down here?"

When she came into the yellow light of the small porch lamp, he could see her broad, dimpled smile. God she's beautiful tonight, he thought. Sean's heart had thumped so hard in his chest when he first saw her that afternoon — he could have counted the beats through his shirt.

"You left without saying goodbye," she said. "I was just wondering if everything is all right."

"Everything is fine. I just had a headache and came down to take some aspirin. You need to go back; your brother will be looking for you."

"No." Catie sat down next to him on the stoop. "He's watching the fireworks with the twins and Sarah. So... did you enjoy yourself?"

The sky lit again before he could answer, and they both looked up into the bright red and blue explosion.

"I guess," he said passively. "I've certainly been to more lively festivities, but the fireworks are a nice touch."

They sat in silence for several minutes as the sky continued to light and rumble. Catie watched him rather than the show. She watched the bright, colorful explosions spread over his blue eyes and enjoyed his faint smile as they fizzled and dropped from the black smoky heavens.

"What!" Sean exclaimed laughingly, taking notice of her inattentiveness.

Slowly, tenderly, awkwardly, Catie leaned forward and pressed her lips against his. Sean grabbed her by the shoulders and pulled her close to him, almost into him. Then his grip tightened and, with every bit of will he had, he pushed her away.

"Catie, what are you doing?" He stood abruptly and stepped away from her.

"I'm sorry. I…I like you, Sean. I…I th-thought you felt the same way," she stammered nervously.

Sean closed his eyes and turned away. He couldn't bear to see her face. "You're wrong, Catie. I do *not* feel the same way. I came here to give you riding lessons…nothing else. I'm truly sorry if I've said or done something to make you think otherwise."

"Nothing else! I thought we were at the very least friends, Sean." She came to her feet. "You're sorry if you said or did something? What about all those nights down by the pond and last week at the river? What was that about?"

Sean's face tightened as the last firework fizzled and enveloped them in darkness. "Go back, Catie," he said evenly. "Go back before someone comes looking for you. It's not proper for you to be here."

"But…Sean." There was a catch in her voice that caused a cold stab in his stomach.

"Go back, Catie!" he swung around and shouted, his voice hoarse with pain and anger. "Go now, damn it, or I shall drag you back myself!"

The yellow lamp washed her face just slightly, but enough, enough to see how much he had injured her. "Catie," he whispered, but it was too late. The night, the trees and shrubs and shadows had already swallowed her departing form.

LIKE A VOLCANO, THE SWELL in her chest burst suddenly, forcing Catie into a thicket of rhododendron. She could hear voices and laughter all around her, restricting her release to a squeezing, binding silence. Her chest tingled with sparks and heat like the fireworks, making her want to wail, moan, and scream — but she couldn't. She wished she could just run to her room, but the guests were leaving and her absence would be questioned. It took several minutes, but she was finally composed enough to make another brief appearance. Drying her eyes with her lace-gloved hands, Catie took a deep breath and returned to the dwindling party.

Her plan was to find Rose and feign illness, knowing Rose would insist she go straight to bed. She spotted her, only a few steps away. *Thank God.*

"Cate, I have been looking everywhere for you." Aiden Hirst was suddenly upon her, blocking her path to Rose.

"You have? Why?"

He smiled. "I was hoping to finish our conversation, *and* I wanted to invite you to my birthday party. It's the first weekend in October. My uncle and aunt are throwing the bash, and I hear they've hired a pretty good band."

Catie's head was swimming. *Why can't he just leave me alone?* "I can't give you an answer, Aiden," she responded politely, glancing longingly at Rose. "I'll have to speak with my brother first. Just send 'round the invitation, all right?"

"Why not ask him now?" Aiden said, taking her by the arm and marching her over to where Ben and Sarah were seeing their guests out.

Catie's precarious emotional state left her incapable of protest. She felt detached as she let him lead her, hoping Ben would decline the invitation for her.

"Mr. and Mrs. Darcy," Aiden said enthusiastically.

"Aiden," Sarah said warmly, still possessing her hostess air. "I hope you've enjoyed yourself this evening?"

"Yes, Mrs. Darcy, very much so, but I'd like to ask a favor of you and Mr. Darcy."

"Of course," she said.

"I've invited Cate to my birthday party on the first Saturday in October, and we've come to ask your permission."

Catie searched Ben's face for his usual vigilance on her behalf, but he simply smiled at her and granted Aiden's request, "Of course she may attend. I'm sure she looks forward to it."

"Great!" Aiden turned back to Catie, brimming with excitement. "I'll be in the country for a few more days. I'd like to see you again."

Catie simply nodded. She didn't know what else to do.

It was then that Sarah noticed the pallor in Catie's complexion, the emptiness in her expression. She waited anxiously while Aiden finished saying his goodbyes and then asked, "Catie, is something the matter? You look as if you aren't well."

"Actually, I'm not feeling well. I'm rather light-headed. I think I need to lie down."

"Have you eaten anything this afternoon?" Ben asked worriedly, taking a gentle hold of her elbow.

"No, with all the excitement I must have forgotten. Sorry." She glanced timidly at him, grateful to be given a reason to be excused.

"It's all right," he said in a comforting whisper. "Let's get you to Rose."

OUT OF HER DRESS AND into her nightgown, Catie waited with Rose for a tray to be brought to her room. When it came, Rose stood over her like a prison guard until she drank all of the orange juice and ate the small snack. "Into bed with you now." Rose tucked her tightly under the covers as Catie smiled faintly to hide her breaking heart. "Don't smile at me, missy. I'll serve you a proper tongue-lashing for neglecting your nourishment in the morning. I'm too tired tonight."

"Yes, Nan," Catie replied softly as tears prickled at her eyes.

Rose's brow furrowed with concern. "Are you all right, child? You look as though you might cry."

"Just tired," she whispered.

"All right." Rose smiled. "I'll stay with you until you fall asleep."

Catie rolled onto her side to hide her tears and, after a few minutes, pretended to be asleep. Rose patted her hip affectionately, walked softly across the room, and quietly closed the door.

As soon as she was alone, Catie scooted out from the covers and went to her favorite perch in the window. Tears flowed freely down her cheeks as she stared out into the night, listening to the sounds of the fading party drifting up from the garden.

COVERING HER HEAD TO ESCAPE the bright light that suddenly filled her room, Catie groaned at Rose who had pulled the curtains open. Her head ached, and her eyes were still puffy from crying.

"Are you going to sleep all day, child?" Rose stood over her.

"No," came the muffled reply from under the covers.

"Are you feeling better?"

"I don't know."

"Well, I have some news for you, dear. Sean had to leave this morning. He wanted to say goodbye but was in a rush to get home. He received a call from his father very early, expressing an urgent need for his return. I am not sure of the particulars, but it had something to do with their horse farm." Rose was now sitting next to the small mound that was Catie.

In the safety of cover and darkness, Catie eyes instantly streamed again as she held tight to her bedcovers to keep them from being pulled away. *He's gone. He's really gone.* It was with skilled control that she spoke through her sorrow. "I'm not feeling well, Rose. I must have a touch of something. Please just leave me for a while longer."

"I'll do no such thing!" Rose demanded, tugging at the blankets. "Now come out immediately and let me feel your head."

Left with no alternative, Catie sat up, exposing her tears and blotchy red face.

Rose immediately took Catie into her arms. "What is it, Catherine? Tell me, love; tell Nan!"

"I can't!" she sobbed. Had it been any other man in the world, Catie would have latched onto Rose and cried her heart out — spilled her soul — but not Sean. She couldn't tell Rose. "Please, Nan … please d-don't make me," Catie pleaded. "Please leave me."

"*Shhhh*, child." Rose pulled her tighter, her heart now breaking as well. She knew. She had seen Sean that morning, and he wasn't faring much better. "Stay in your bed and rest. I shall have tea and toast sent up to you directly." Rose kissed her and left.

A few minutes later, there was another knock on Catie's door. "I'll be out later!" she called, but Sarah entered anyway.

"I know what's upsetting you," Sarah said, approaching the bed and sitting down. "Do you want to talk about it?" Remaining silent, Catie looked at her with evident skepticism. Sarah went on. "Catie, I know your feelings for Sean have grown beyond friendship, and his leaving so suddenly has grieved you tremendously."

Catie's eyes widened with concern. "Are you going to tell Ben?"

"No." Sarah shook her head compassionately. "It is my belief that the fewer people who partake in a young girl's first broken heart, the better." She smiled. "Especially where *that* gender is concerned."

Catie's throat tightened. She hadn't sought comfort; she was used to soothing her own pain. But when Sarah's arms opened to her, she fell into the solidness of her bosom. "Oh, Sarah," she cried, "I loved him."

"I know." Sarah stroked her hair.

"No." Catie shook her head. "I *really* loved him! I know you think I'm too young to know what love is, but I do know! I do, Sarah!"

Sarah felt a sudden innate feminine understanding and wrapped the younger woman tightly in her arms. "Let it out, Catie. I'm holding you, dear … just let it out."

Snug in Sarah's embrace, Catie unburdened her shattered heart and wept for a long time.

IN HER LAST WEEKS OF holiday, Catie made every effort not to mope around the house. Sarah was ever ready with a reassuring smile, and Rose fussed much less when she picked at her food. With her improved riding skills, Ben now allowed her to take Chloe out alone, and she had enjoyed several long afternoons of solitude by the river, thinking of Mary Howell's summer romance — as well as her own.

As promised, Aiden Hirst dropped by a couple of days after the garden party and stayed for dinner. Although she was polite, Catie tried fervently to discourage his attentions, but unfortunately, her efforts failed.

"I want to see you again soon," he had said when she walked him out.

"I don't know, Aiden. I'm back at Davenport next week," she responded tactfully as she opened the door, willing his departure.

He smiled and brushed a stray hair from her face. "Leave it to me. I shall work something out...you'll see."

She sincerely hoped he wouldn't.

Time moved rapidly, yet somehow drearily and monotonously, but eventually Catie was packing to return to Davenport. Occupied with her task, she started at a soft knock at her door.

"Come in," she called.

The door opened, and Ben stepped inside, closing the door behind him. "Almost finished?"

"Yes, sixth form, *finally*." She smiled.

"*Sixth* form?" he repeated, his look incredulous.

"Yes, Ben, you knew that."

"Ah, yes, of course...I knew that." He paused, looking at her. "The...uh...time has moved quickly, eh?"

Catie shrugged. "Not really."

"No, I guess not," he said quietly. "Anyway, I wanted to give this to you. I think she would have wanted you to have it." He held out Mary's diary.

Hesitantly, Catie took it from his hand. "Thank you."

"Have you read that diary?"

Trying hard not to visibly cringe, for she could think only of Mary's overly explicit writings, Catie blushed and hesitated. "Um..."

"It's okay, Sis." He chuckled. "I'm glad you've read it."

"You are?" She finally looked at him.

"Yes." Ben put a hand on her shoulder. "Catie, Mary Darcy was young, beautiful, and heiress to a fortune. It's what made her vulnerable to a man like Arthur Howell. Mind that you heed the valuable lessons that diary has to offer. Not every man is what he claims to be, dearest."

Catie nodded softly as Ben gently stroked her cheek with the back of his hand. "Well, I'll not disrupt your packing further."

"Bennet," she called after him as he crossed the room.

"Yes, Sis?" He turned back.

"Did you know Mary?"

"I not only knew her, I loved her very much. She died when I was twelve. You can't imagine my shock and pain when I was made to believe she had abandoned her only grandchild. I should have known she would never do such a thing."

"Was she happy? Did she find peace after the loss of Thomas?"

Ben's expression lit with remembrance. "She was very happy and, along with our grandmother and mother, spoiled me horribly when I was a little boy. So much so, Dad and Grandfather refused to allow me to be alone with them."

Catie giggled. "That's not true!"

"You ask Horace Harold; he'll tell you the truth of it."

"I will." Catie grinned.

Before closing the door, Ben winked at her. "Love you, dearest."

"Love you too, Ben."

Catie looked at the diary for several minutes before walking over and removing the panel. Carefully, she placed it back where she had found it.

Chapter 23

Sitting alone in the library at Davenport, Catie spent the morning at her studies. Her return to school had helped. Unlike Pemberley, school held no reminders of Sean. Thoughts of the stables, the pond, the river — even George's little wooden horse — brought on surges of sadness. Sarah's consolation and comfort was appreciated by Catie, but as for Sarah's understanding, Catie knew it was anything but complete. She was sure Sarah in no way grasped the depth of her real emotions: how truly strong her feelings were for Sean — and, she believed, how strong his were for her.

The kiss, which at first had caused her unbearable humiliation, when replayed over and over in her mind brought back a memory of a fleeting moment of being pulled closer to him. It wasn't her imagination. She had felt it. Sean desired that kiss as much as she did. His smiles and stares, his behavior altogether had inadvertently revealed his growing affection, even to a girl as naïve and inexperienced as Catie.

His sudden departure was difficult for her, but his reason was even harder for her to bear. His urgency to return home, Catie knew, was a ruse to avoid her, not only her but his feelings for her. *"Bròd."* His raspy Irish came to her in a whisper…she understood. She was born to the manor, the daughter of a wealthy man, while Sean, the son of a horse farmer, struggled to finance his education. That damned Irish pride of his. "Bloody insufferable ass," she grumbled under her breath as a tear raced down her cheek and dropped onto the page of her textbook.

Realizing that her mind had wandered from her French lesson, Catie packed her satchel to return to her dorm. The late September afternoon was cool and the thought of a brisk autumn pleased her. The day was so lovely and crisp that Catie hurried her pace, hoping to convince Audrey to take a walk with her before dinner.

Entering their shared dorm room, Catie was struck still by her dorm mate's appearance. It being Saturday, the girls were not expected to be in school uniform, but Audrey Tillman was quite obviously dressed for more than the dining hall at Davenport. Her tight designer jeans and low cut blouse were accentuated by a pair of heels, and her makeup was far beyond Davenport standards.

"Is your father or mother coming to take you out?" Catie asked.

Still brushing powder on her over-made face, Audrey evasively responded, "No."

"Then why are you dressed like that?" Catie pried.

"I have a date," Audrey answered nonchalantly as if it were common practice, which of course it was not. Dating was strictly prohibited at Davenport. Leaving campus with anyone other than a parent or guardian was grounds for expulsion.

"A *date*! Aud, what are you thinking? What if you get caught?"

"I'll be back before lights out. No one will miss me before then."

Catie looked at her anxiously, but Audrey seemed resolved to her plan.

"Stop looking at me like that, Darcy! We can't all be Miss Goody Two-Shoes. Anyway it's worth the risk. He's the most wonderful, amazing guy I've ever met." She stared off dreamily for a second. "We were getting to know each other quite well at your garden party until Sean Kelly interrupted us."

"Sean Kelly!" Catie repeated, astonished.

"Yes," Audrey replied, adding sarcastically, "You know the two of you would be perfect for each other, you both possess the high moral standards of a clergyman." She walked past Catie but stopped on her way out to assure her friend. "Don't worry! I'll be back in a few hours, and no one will be the wiser." The heavy oak door closed loudly and echoed as Audrey's high heels clacked hurriedly down the steps.

The afternoon waned and dusk came quickly. Darkness engulfed the fields and walks of Davenport's campus as security lights flickered on and windows glowed orange with lamplight. Yet Audrey had still not returned. Catie took one last look out of her window and saw nothing but the empty courtyard. It was chilly out and well past curfew. Thankfully the housemother, Mrs. Jenkins, was later than usual on her rounds, but that didn't ease Catie's anxiety.

Eventually, Mrs. Jenkins was heard making her way down the hall, saying good night and talking sweetly to giggling girls. Catie lay reclined on her bed in closed-eyed apprehension of the inevitable.

Her eyes opened at the small rap on the door and she answered softly, "Yes?"

"It's time for lights out, girls," Mrs. Jenkins announced as she poked her grandmotherly face inside the room.

"All right, Mrs. Jenkins," Catie replied, unintentionally glancing at Audrey's empty bed.

By instinct, Mrs. Jenkins' eyes traveled to where Catie's had, and her smile receded. "Where's Audrey, Catherine?"

"She's not here," Catie answered stupidly, realizing she was stating the obvious.

"Do you know where she is?"

"No, Mrs. Jenkins." Catie shook her head.

Clearly concerned and a bit annoyed at Catie's apparent lack of cooperation, Mrs. Jenkins came fully into the room. "Catherine Darcy, you must tell me what you know at once!"

Reluctantly, Catie closed the book she was aimlessly flipping through and sat up. Having no real choice, she relayed what little she knew. She had to. Not only was she worried about Audrey, for she should have returned over an hour ago, but she certainly wasn't going to tell a lie, friend or not.

Mrs. Jenkins took in the information with a growing alarm. "And you're sure you don't know where she has gone or with whom?" the woman asked frantically.

Catie shook her head adamantly.

With an expression that seemed to bear anxiety for her own fate as well as Audrey's, Mrs. Jenkins hurried out of the room, muttering, "I must inform Miss Spencer at once."

Tossing about her bed most of the night, Catie waited and worried, but Audrey never returned. As she readied for breakfast the next morning, her room filled with curious teenage girls wanting in on the story. Audrey Tillman leaving school to rendezvous with a boy she had met at Pemberley's garden party was not only a serious breach of Davenport's rules, but ripe, scandalous gossip as well. Not wanting to betray her friend any further than she had already been forced to do, Catie was vague and claimed to know no more than they.

"You're holding out, Darcy," a girl said accusingly.

"Yeah, we all know Audrey tells you everything. Come now... tell," another added.

"Break this up at once!" Mrs. Jenkins' shrill voice stopped the inquisition, and her clapping hands scattered the senior sixth form students like kindergarteners. The nosy crowd was fast to disperse but lingered in the hallway to listen. "Catherine, Miss Spencer has sent me to summon you to her study."

"This morning?" Catie asked as a knot formed in her stomach.

"This very minute," Mrs. Jenkins said simply and left. "To breakfast, girls!" she was heard calling out curtly as her footsteps faded down the long dormitory hall. Mrs. Jenkins was obviously not her usual kind self that morning.

Sliding on her school blazer, Catie took a quick look in the mirror before the walk across campus. Her shirt was properly tucked and her skirt was straight, so she buttoned her blazer and nervously set out. Though her pace was swift, it certainly wasn't fast enough to account for the sound of her heart beating in her ears, and she would have given almost anything for a swallow of water as she climbed the steps to Daven Hall, Davenport's administration building.

Daven Hall was a large Jacobean structure with great mullioned windows. At one time the family seat of the Davenport family, Daven Hall was converted into a school in the 1860's by Evelyn Davenport. Never married and Anglican in faith, Evelyn was a prudish Victorian woman who wore plain black dresses and never smiled — at least not in any of the multitude of pictures that lined the way to Miss Spencer's study. Standing tall and angular alongside Davenport's earliest students, who looked equally as miserable as their headmistress, Miss Davenport's disapproving eye seemed to follow Catie's progress. The pictures conjured up memories of Miss Scatcherd flogging Helen Burns with a bundle of twigs at the Lowood School in Charlotte Brontë's *Jane Eyre*, making Catie feel as if her veins suddenly had ice water running through them. No, Miss Spencer would never flog a student today, but she *was* a formidable woman nonetheless.

Since it was Sunday morning, the building was quiet, amplifying the slight sound of Miss Spencer's small movements behind her large, antique desk. Unnervingly, this quiet also amplified the creak of the door and the sound of Catie's shoes as they struck the marble floor.

"Miss Darcy?" Miss Spencer called from her office. If she knew the first names of her students they were unaware of it, for she only addressed them formally. Miss Spencer, never being married or having a family, didn't have the nurturing faculties of women like Mrs. Jenkins.

"Yes, Miss Spencer," Catie answered and waited to be called in.

"Come in, Miss Darcy." Catie stepped inside the room and, at Miss Spencer's instruction, closed the door behind her. She was directed to sit, which she did, legs crossed at her ankles and back straight. Miss Spencer had no aversion to correcting inappropriate posture, causing a squirm of straightening backs whenever she appeared. "I am sure that you are aware of the reason I have called for you this morning."

"Yes, miss," Catie replied, her tongue so dry her words scraped the roof of her mouth. She cleared her throat.

"I shall start by telling you that Miss Tillman was recovered last evening and is currently in the custody of her father. I cannot begin to tell you how grieved Mr. Tillman was at his daughter's conduct, which I might add has only been worsened by Miss Tillman's refusal to reveal the name of her companion. Mr. Tillman, I understand, is a dear friend of your family."

Audrey's all right. Catie gave an inward sigh of relief. "Yes, miss, he is."

"Then you can understand his desire to know *who* would take his daughter from school without his permission."

"Yes, miss." Catie nodded. "But I'm sorry to say that I don't know his identity either."

An indignant, unconvinced expression overtook Miss Spencer's countenance, highlighting her sharp features even more. "Do not mock my intelligence, Miss Darcy," she said sternly. "I have been equally privy to the rumors that this young man and Miss Tillman became acquainted at Pemberley a little more than a month ago. You are her closest friend, her dorm mate, and I have no doubt her confidante on matters such as this. Perhaps I can persuade you to convey all you know of this affair by telling you that the young man in question treated your friend quite poorly."

Catie shifted in her seat as her blood started to warm. She was essentially being accused of lying. *"Honor," her father said, lifting her up to the tall stained glass window in Pemberley's gallery, allowing her tiny fingers to trace the lead between the brightly colored panes of her family crest. "Being a Darcy is about honor," he continued. "It's what has delivered our good name through all these centuries. It is what we have that no one can take from us. It is more valuable than anything in this house. Without honor you have nothing. Whatever you do in life, Catherine Elizabeth, be honorable."* Catie's teeth connected in an uncomfortable grind as she composed her words carefully. "Miss Spencer, please know that I wasn't brought up to mock the intelligence of a respectable woman like yourself. Yes, Audrey and I are the closest of friends, but she did not share with me any more than I have already told you. I am not covering for Audrey nor do I condone her actions last evening. If you doubt the truthfulness of what I'm saying, then I will beg you call my brother. He, better than anyone, can speak on my behalf."

Miss Spencer's eyes narrowed in contemplation, but she had no intention of tangling with Bennet Darcy. A highly respected man, it was a credit that Ben Darcy entrusted Davenport with his sister's care and education. The late Margaret Darcy was a graduate of Davenport and served on the school's governing body until she passed away. In addition, a great many of the school's alumni and contributors were close friends of the Darcys. No, questioning Catherine Darcy's honesty without foundation was plainly not an option. It probably would bring a darker cloud over Davenport than Audrey Tillman's little escapade could ever do.

Clearly, Miss Spencer thought resentfully, *young Miss Darcy understands her family's elevated position and is taking full advantage of it.* This did not please the headmistress, but she most certainly understood. Playing the centuries-old game of, "The One with the Most Money Wins," was part of obtaining and keeping a position like Headmistress of Davenport. Left with no real alternative, she coolly thanked Catie for her cooperation and excused her to the dining hall for breakfast.

Later that morning, after church, Catie walked alone back to the dormitory. She didn't want company, didn't want to talk to anyone. When she opened the door to her room, Audrey's things were gone, her bed and desk as bare as the day they moved in. Expelled, Catie thought as she closed the door behind her. Audrey wasn't coming back to school.

ON FRIDAY AFTERNOON BEN DARCY drove his black sports car among the stone walls and hedgerows of England's countryside, ignoring posted speed limits. The car always gave him a sense of invincibility. The 1977 Porsche Carrera was a gift from his father on his twenty-first birthday. That was ten years ago now, but he couldn't part with it and probably never would.

"She needs to come home this weekend," Sarah had said to him a few nights ago. "She sounds terribly downcast." Ben knew Audrey's expulsion had taken its toll on Catie. He felt sorry for Donald Tillman. *Thank God his sister had never been so imprudent.* Not that Catie was immune to the charms of such a man...any young girl might be. His jaw tightened at the thought of it. Girls their age were inexperienced and vulnerable. He had seen it enough in his younger days. Most men were gentleman, but some most certainly were not.

He settled his sister in the car and tossed her bag in the boot. She could have taken the train, but Ben usually preferred to drive her. The hour-long trip back and forth gave them a chance to be alone. Sometimes they rode in silence with only the hum of the engine between them, and sometimes she talked all the way home. Today she hadn't uttered a word, just stared silently out of the rain spattered window, leaving Ben with only the dragging wiper blades as company.

"They're sheep, Catie." Ben's voice jarred her from her thoughts.

"What?" Her head turned to him, her eyes as blurry as the window.

"Sheep...you've been looking at sheep for half an hour."

"They look sad."

"It's raining, Catie, everything looks sad. Do you want to stop? Have a drink?"

"No, I just want to go home."

When they arrived at Pemberley, Catie ran to see Sarah. It had been a month since she last laid eyes on her, and she was anxious to inspect Sarah's expanding girth. As Ben watched them hug, a smile creased his mouth. And when Catie cupped Sarah's round belly and spoke in a sweet singing voice to the future member of the family, he laughed softly, glad she was home.

"Has she kicked yet?" she asked, ear pressed against the bulge.

"She?" Ben repeated. "That's not a she."

"And how do you know, Bennet?" Catie asked.

Shaking her head, Sarah explained, "Your brother has forbidden me to have a daughter."

The two fell into hysterics at the stupidity of such a ridiculous demand.

"Why would you forbid Sarah a daughter, Ben? Just think — she might be like me. Would that not be grand?"

Sarah laughed even harder at the look of alarm that crossed her husband's face. "Yes, Bennet," she asked, her eyes bright with her laughter. "Wouldn't that be grand?"

The following evening the Darcys were invited to Ardsley Manor for dinner, an invitation they felt imposed by social grace to accept. As Ben drove, Catie rode quietly in the backseat, unable to force Audrey from her thoughts. "That *dreadful* boy," Sarah had hissed angrily when they were finally alone and able to talk freely. "He took Audrey to a shabby roadside inn and, after having his *expectations* of the evening met, put her out almost a mile from the school. Poor girl was discovered walking back on the road to Davenport in a drizzle of rain, cold and soaked." Sarah shook her head sorrowfully and repeated, "Poor girl."

Catie shuddered as if cold and soaked herself, and gazed out at the horizon which had gone black, giving her nothing but her own reflection to stare at. Sarah had assured her that according to Mr. Tillman, Audrey was all right, if a tad dispirited. Next term she would be attending a school in Northern England, and Catie could write to her in a few weeks.

Catie was so lost in her distraction that their arrival at the gates of Ardsley went unnoticed. Sarah's voice startled her. "Catie! Goodness, dear, where were you?"

Catie shrugged. "Daydreaming I guess." She smiled faintly and got out of the car.

Ardsley Manor wasn't as grand as Pemberley, but Catie appreciated its more intimate and welcoming size. As they climbed the steps to the entrance, the door was opened and Lawrence and Eleanor Hirst stood ready to greet them. "Halloo, Darcys!" Mr. Hirst welcomed boisterously. His thick, black eyebrows were groomed to a fine point and bobbed with excitement. "Welcome, welcome."

Aiden appeared as soon as they were in the hall, smiling cockily. She despised his pretentiousness. Sean Kelly was a proud man to be sure... but never pretentious.

"Hello, Cate, allow me." Aiden removed her coat. "I told you I would see you soon. Sorry to hear about Audrey Tillman though," he whispered from behind her.

Catie's head turned abruptly to him. "How — " she started but stopped. Aiden had friends at Davenport; of course he would know. "So you assumed I would be home this weekend?"

He nodded. "Hence the sudden invitation. My uncle and aunt were thrilled with the idea. They like you very much, Cate... as do I." Aiden winked and offered her his hand. "Now, let's get through dinner with the old folks, and then maybe we'll have a few minutes to ourselves."

The meal was long, and the conversation had Catie counting window panes to pass the time. The subject of tennis alone occupied the whole of the second course. Naturally, Aiden played the game and played well. It seemed that Aiden did everything well, according to his uncle. Politics came next. Mr. Hirst knew he and Ben shared political views. Sarah, however, did not. Her Labour party had recently suffered its third consecutive loss in the general election, but she politely endured, only challenging occasionally as Ben patted her hand under the table. Mr. Hirst wasn't trying to be impolite or insensitive; he was just rather old school. Born in the thirties, he still assumed the wife supported the political affiliations of the husband.

By dessert, everyone was equally suffering from the discomforts of having sat too long, and it was unanimously decided to adjourn to the drawing room. Seeing his opportunity, Aiden whispered into Catie's ear, "Would you like to get some fresh air instead?"

Glad for an escape from the dull conversation, she nodded eagerly in return.

"I'd like to show Cate more of the house if that's all right," Aiden said to the group, but his eyes rested on Bennet Darcy.

"Fine, just don't wander too far," Ben answered, glancing at his sister. "We must be leaving for home shortly. The twins have been promised a tuck-in by their mother."

"Yes, Brother," Catie replied softly.

"You've done a fine job with her, Bennet," Lawrence Hirst said to Ben as soon as the young couple left the dining room. "Your father and mother would be proud. Aiden tells me that Councilman Tillman has had some difficulties with his Audrey. A shame that. I understand the girl was a talented violinist."

"She still *is* a talented violinist, Lawrence," Sarah countered.

"That may be, Sarah," Eleanor said. "But I understand Donald had aspirations of Newnham, and I daresay an expulsion from Davenport will not bode well."

"Had much sport this season, Hirst?" Ben tactfully redirected the conversation.

"Not one grouse yet this year but I did..." Lawrence began a detailed rundown as Ben gave his wife's thankful expression a discreet smile.

THE LARGE HALL WAS MARKEDLY cooler than the dining room, but Catie warmed as they climbed the carpeted steps to the upper floors.

"The ballroom is over there." Aiden pointed across the landing. "But there's a nice view of Matlock from the terrace." He pulled open the large French doors to the crisp October night.

"Ooh," Catie said softly, hugging herself. "It's brisk, eh?"

"Oh, right." Aiden quickly removed his dinner jacket and draped it over her shoulders.

236

"Thank you." She accepted the offering. "But I wasn't being a flirt."

"You never are." He raised his brows at her. "Not that I would mind the encouragement."

"Do you visit your aunt and uncle often?" Catie inquired, leaning over the cold balustrade, not so subtly changing the subject.

He chuckled, not seeming offended. "Yes, as often as I can. They are like a second set of parents to me. You can't imagine the nuisance of having two mothers coddling and fussing over you."

Catie glanced away from the remark. "No, I suppose not."

"God, Cate, that was horribly insensitive of me." Aiden reached out and turned her to face him. "It must be awful not having your mum."

She politely stepped out of his hold. "There's no need to pity me, Aiden. I may not have been fortunate enough to enjoy the attentions of my own good mother, but I've had Sarah for the last eight years and my Nan for the whole of my life."

"Nan?"

"Yes…Rose, Pemberley's housekeeper. When my mother died, my father turned my care over to her. She's like family to us."

"*Family*?" Aiden repeated mockingly. "Cate, she's the help."

"Rose Todd is anything but *the help*." Catie glared up at him. "She has loved and cared for me like a mother."

"Sorry." Aiden raised his hands in surrender. "But in truth…she *was* being paid for all that love and care, no?"

Catie pulled his jacket from her shoulders and held it out to him, clearly ready to go back inside. "Rose Todd is very dear to me, Aiden — not only to me but Ben and Sarah as well."

"I see," he conceded, suddenly unassuming. "But…please don't go back inside, not while you're cross with me."

Catie sighed. He couldn't have known and wouldn't understand anyway. Rose's relationship with the Darcys was the result of circumstance and rather unusual. "I'm not cross with you," she said in a forgiving tone. "But I really should go to my brother now. He isn't overly fond of long dinner parties and is probably ready to leave."

"All right, as long as you aren't cross." Aiden slid his jacket back on. Then he leaned down and kissed her lightly on the lips.

His mouth was warm with the taste of dry red wine. "Aiden," she started, but he kissed her again, stopping her words.

"Don't speak," he whispered, pulling her close to him. "Let's end the evening there. Eh?"

Thankfully, Ben and Sarah had donned their coats and were giving their parting adieus to the Hirsts when Catie and Aiden returned.

"Ah, Aiden, there you are," Mr. Hirst said playfully. "Thought I was going to have to have a stern word with you, lad."

"No, Uncle, we were just on the terrace." Aiden smiled. "I apologize if we've kept you and Mrs. Darcy waiting."

"Not at all," Ben said, holding out Catie's coat for her.

"Good." Aiden turned to Catie with a pleased look. "I look forward to having you at my birthday party in two weeks. Shall I pop over and give you a lift?"

"That won't be necessary, Aiden," Ben answered for his sister. "I shall drive her myself."

"Yes, sir, of course," Aiden consented gracefully, glancing warily at Ben. "In two weeks then, Cate."

"Yes…two weeks," Catie replied, her words lacking the luster Aiden would've preferred. "Cheers, Aiden."

Chapter 24

"Catie, there is no way out of it..." Sarah paused as Ben eavesdropped on her telephone conversation from behind. "Yes...I do understand, but the invitation has been accepted and you..." Sarah paused again to listen, and Ben stepped forward. The sight of her husband made Sarah's expression change from startled to a masked smile; she hoped he hadn't noticed. "Yes, Catie, I look forward to seeing you too, dear. Bye-bye now." Returning the receiver, Sarah turned to her husband. "And how long have you been lurking about, sir?"

Not being able to stifle a soft chuckle at Sarah, standing there with her mound of a belly and fuzzy slippers, Ben raised his brows reproachfully. "Long enough to know that a feeble attempt is being made to deceive me and...for future reference, madam, Darcys do *not* lurk."

Sarah picked up the book she had been reading before Catie called and opened it with feigned attention, a futile effort to avoid the foreseeable discussion. Ben sat down in a restless manner and gave his chin a thoughtful caress between his forefinger and his thumb.

"I just don't understand, Sarah. She is less than a month from seventeen. What girl that age doesn't want to attend a party with other young people?"

Not looking up from her book, Sarah replied, "Well, darling, she *is* a Darcy. And, in my experience with *that* family socializing ranks right up there with lurking." She cut her eyes at him with a satisfied smirk. "They simply don't do it." She lowered her voice and mumbled, "Least not without a fair amount of kicking and screaming."

"Humph," he uttered, looking at her over his cupped hand. "Well, she can kick and scream all she wants, but my sister *is* going to the lad's birthday party."

Sarah closed the book. "Why is it so important to you that she like him? You can't very well force Catie to develop feelings for someone. And...to be honest, there is something about that boy...something about the Hirsts altogether that I just don't care for."

"This isn't about the Hirsts! And, if I were to be totally truthful...well...I find them a bit...a bit..."

"Beastly!" Sarah filled in.

"Pretentious, I was going to say, but that's not the point. I would never try to force Aiden Hirst on Catie. Surely you have noticed how low in spirits she has been of late. If anything, I'm trying to snap her out of her gloom. It's not normal for her to be so moody."

Sarah laughed. "I cannot speak for seventeen-year-old boys, but girls of that age can be quite moody. I can assure you, darling, it is *very* normal."

Ben reached for his newspaper. "Normal or not, come Saturday night Catie Darcy *will* be at Ardsley Manor. No matter what frame of mind she is in." He opened the paper and disappeared into its fold.

"Sorry, Catie," Sarah's little internal voice echoed regretfully. "I tried." Though in truth, she hadn't tried too awfully hard. She never would "nudge" (as Ben had put it) Catie in the direction of Aiden Hirst, but he *was* a boy. Not just a boy but a nice-looking boy who seemed fond of Catie. Being a woman, Sarah knew that the best medicine for a broken heart, especially at the tender age of seventeen, was the attentions of another. Although she sympathized with Catie's foot-dragging protest of social activities, Sarah had to agree with Ben. It was best for her to be "nudged" a little — to attend the party at least.

CATIE STARED OUT OF THE window for the better part of the drive to Aiden's birthday party. She tried to convince herself that she wasn't sulking, but she was. The exaggerated sighs that she exhaled every few minutes gave her away.

"You are aware, Sis, that I am taking you to a party...not the dentist."

Turning from the window with a little smile at his joke, Catie sat back and focused on the road ahead.

"Was Sarah your first love, Bennet?" she asked, breaking the silence with what felt to him like a wrecking ball.

"I..." Ben stammered as a quick flash of his university years passed through his brain. Not a part of his life he had *ever* planned on sharing with his little sister. "What exactly do you mean, Catie?"

"I *mean*...did you love anyone before you met Sarah?" She turned in her seat to face him. "Really love them, I mean."

Ben cast a nervous glance in her direction and then quickly back to the windscreen. "No," he replied simply.

"So, she *was* your first love?"

Very much wishing his sister was still silent and sulking, Ben stammered again, "No...I mean...yes...yes, she was." Admonishing himself for being so inept in this particular area of parenting, Ben gave the accelerator a little push to pick up speed.

"How did you know?" she asked.

"Know what, dearest?"

Catie's tone became frustrated. "Know that you loved her...you know, fancied her above all the others! Lord, Bennet, are you daft?"

"No, I'm not daft!" he said crossly. Then, after a moment's silence, he added quietly, "I knew because...because I could be myself around Sarah. She enhanced my qualities while accepting and balancing my faults. I loved her for that. I still do. And." He smiled at her. "She's beautiful...very beautiful."

"Ah, that's sweet, Brother." Catie reached over and patted his shoulder. "Almost romantic."

"Oh, only *almost*!" She laughed, nodding, and he was pleased with his success. Nevertheless, Ben gave a look of gratitude to the heavens as they passed through the gate at Ardsley Manor. He escorted his sister inside and with a kiss to her cheek, turned her over to Aiden Hirst.

Knowing no one else except Aiden, Catie stayed close by his side for the better part of the evening. He attended her every need for refreshment and graciously introduced her to all of his friends, all the while keeping a gentle hold on her elbow. Catie eyed the large clock in the hall and rejoiced each time ten whole minutes passed. Scanning the crowd, she suddenly caught sight of Jenna Makepeace, Aiden's former girlfriend. It was with Jenna that Catie had first met Aiden in London last spring. For whatever reason, Jenna had not returned to Davenport that year, and Catie had been so caught up, she hadn't telephoned her friend to find out why. Catie smiled, but Jenna gave her a spiteful look and turned away.

A cluster of Aiden's mates — his pack as he called them — succeeded in coercing him away from Catie. "Chap talk." Aiden smiled down at her. "I'll be right back. Will you be all right?"

Catie nodded and said, "Aiden, did you and Jenna part on bad terms? She's here you know."

"I know." He kissed her forehead. "Don't worry, love, she's yesterday's news."

"I wasn't worried," Catie corrected. "But she would hardly look at me."

"That's because she's jealous of you. Like most of the girls here tonight." He smiled again, smugly this time, and walked away.

She flushed with indignation as she watched him disappear into the gent's smoking room. During the nineteenth century such a room was for gentlemen only, adorned with hunting trophies, and not very inviting to a woman. Pemberley also had several rooms that boasted a more masculine décor for the sake of history and tradition. Tourists loved to hear how differently men and women lived a hundred years ago. Standing alone, Catie realized how little things had actually changed.

Making her way to the refreshment table, she glanced out over the room. Boys and girls danced or stood in small huddles talking and laughing. The band was decent but loud, and caused an irksome echo in the old room meant for a stringed orchestra, not heavy metal. The band members, tattooed and shaggy headed, were a stark contrast to the clean cut tennis- and polo-playing partygoers.

Enjoying her moment's solitude, Catie sipped slowly at a glass of punch. She had promised Ben no alcohol, not even a small glass of wine while he wasn't present. "Too many chaps for you not to be thinking with a clear head," he had said firmly. Shaking her head at her brother's relentless safeguarding, she noticed Jenna approaching, still bearing the spiteful look. Catie glanced away, hoping she was only in search of a drink. This soon seemed unlikely however, as she was eyeing Catie directly and heading straight for her.

"Hello, Catie," Jenna said shortly.

"Jenna," Catie replied equally as curt.

"I see you have taken a fancy to one of my toss-aways."

Catie didn't answer the snide comment, so Jenna moved closer, uncomfortably close. So close she could feel the girl's breath on her cheek. Not caring for the intimacy Catie turned her head, but Jenna took this as an invitation to whisper into her ear.

"Just giving you fair warning," Jenna hissed. "Aiden will forget he ever knew you once he has enjoyed your *company*, if you know what I mean." She pulled away and gave Catie a meaningful look.

Catie set her glass down, her pulse quickening with offence. She met Jenna's eyes directly. "I don't foresee that being a problem as I never intend on allowing Aiden Hirst the pleasure of my *company*, as you call it. Now, if you'll excuse me." Catie brushed by her and rushed for the doors to the terrace. She needed air.

It was with an angry, heaving chest that Catie inhaled the cold October night. She was not well seasoned to catty, backbiting females, but she had held her own. She was glad for that. Her pulse calmed as she leaned on the thick stone balustrade and stared up into the starry night, wishing it was time for Ben to come take her home.

Aiden appeared suddenly. "I thought I would find you out here."

Startled, Catie turned to him. He sauntered over to her and gently lifted her chin with his fingers. "Now look, young lady, I'll allow you to duck out of my party now, but once we are married — " He stopped to cluck his tongue with disapproval. "You will have to suffer and smile through the whole soirée. Do I make myself clear?"

Catie's expression was such a mixture of uncertainty and puzzlement, it forced Aiden to laugh. "It was a joke, Catie — lighten up." He leaned over the railing beside her. "But…one day you will be the lady of a house, not so unlike this one, I'd wager. And you will have to assume that responsibility — mistress…hostess."

Catie's eyes scanned the large stone home as he spoke and then rested on his profile. "That is, of course, if I marry a man of wealth. Maybe I'll shock all of Derbyshire — all of England for that matter — and marry a pauper."

"And deny all of those future socialites in there the opportunity to pant at your feet like neglected dogs? Come now, Cate! You're a Darcy — a beauty." He shook his head and stroked her hair. "The society columns will always carry your name, and not only will you be invited to every social event, but women will pace their homes in wait of an invitation to yours."

"My future sounds bleak indeed by your account. I would hope to accomplish more in life than reigning over panting socialites."

Aiden laughed again, not the hearty, head-tossing laugh of Sean Kelly, but rather a low, not really amused laugh. He brought his face close to hers. "May I kiss you, Miss Darcy?" he whispered.

Without knowing why, Catie granted him a slight nod of agreement and tilted her head. The kiss was long. He bit gently on her bottom lip and slid his warm tongue inside her mouth. Although a bit stunned, Catie was rather enjoying it. She wrapped her arms around his neck; his hands were pressed against her back. Then, they pulled away to gaze upon each other. That was when she realized his wasn't the face she expected to see, or the lips she imagined she was kissing. *Sean*, she thought as her chest exploded with that painful spike of longing yet again. Catie took in a breath of clean autumn air to suppress the sting and turned away from him.

"Shall we return to the party?" Aiden rasped in her ear, vainly mistaking her emotion. "You mustn't keep me to yourself all evening."

Chapter 25

S tumbling into the kitchen around nine, Catie sat at the long wooden table with the hopes of leisurely nursing a hot cup of coffee. Rose made her a plate from leftovers and placed it in front of her.

"I haven't the time, Rose. I must ready for church." Catie pushed away the plate.

"Geoffrey and George have a slight case of the stomach virus that has been spreading around the parish school. No one is going to church this morning."

"Oh, thank the Lord!" Catie moaned and plopped her head into her hands.

"Catherine Darcy! Did you just thank the *Lord* that you do *not* have to go to church?" Rose scolded harshly.

Catie sat up straight. "No, Nan...not that...I didn't...I mean — "

"My ears may be old, missy, but I know what I heard. That was nothing short of sacrilege, and I'll not hear you speak that way again!" Rose's lips were pursed firmly.

Taken off guard by Rose's sharp tone, Catie glanced across the large kitchen at Maggie, who was making her own breakfast. Maggie shrugged, so she looked back at Rose and slowly pulled the plate back in front of her. "Yes, Nan," she said and obediently picked up her fork and started to eat.

Rose sat down opposite Catie with a hand at her chest and grimaced. Catie noticed beads of sweat breaking on Rose's brow and she sounded out of breath. "Are you okay, Rose?" she asked, shoveling scrambled eggs in her mouth.

"I'm fine. Maggie...child, please drop me a couple of fizzy tablets in water. I have a mighty case of indigestion this morning." Rose gave her chest another pat, her discomfort evident in her tightly closed eyes and clamped mouth.

Maggie rushed to Rose with the tablets already dissolving in the water and, holding out two aspirin, practically ordered Rose to take them as well.

"I think you should see a doctor, Rose," said Catie worriedly.

"A doctor would only tell me..." Rose's words were interrupted by another piercing pain. "Ohhh," she cried.

"Get my brother and Sarah!" Catie said to Maggie as she rushed to Rose's side.

In less than a minute Ben and Sarah trailed Maggie's hurried pace into the kitchen. "Is it the stomach virus that the boys have had?" Sarah asked anxiously, taking Rose's hand.

Rose shook her head, her eyes closed tight against another stabbing pain.

"Rose." Ben knelt down beside her. "Talk to us."

"Should I ring for an ambulance, Mr. Darcy?" Maggie asked, the panic in her voice matching the look on her face.

"No! No ambulance!" Rose said, but Sarah nodded to Maggie behind Rose's back and kept her distracted while the girl made the call.

"They're on their way, Mrs. Darcy," Maggie said as she hung up the telephone.

"I said no ambulance, no hospital, and no doctors!" Rose paused to gasp for air. "It's only a dreadful case of heartburn!"

"You're going to the hospital, Rose Todd. And I'll hear no more about it!" Ben said firmly.

Rose turned a motherly eye on Ben. "You think I'm going to take orders from a man whom I have known since he was in knee trousers?"

"I mean no disrespect, Rose, but yes...you are," he replied with certainty.

Another pain, the worst yet, amplified their mounting alarm. "Call for a car to be brought around back, Maggie! I'll be damned if I sit here and wait any longer!" Ben shouted as Rose collapsed against him. A man accustomed to doing rather than waiting, his patience was gone. At the very least he could meet the ambulance at the end of the drive.

BEN REPROACHED HIMSELF FOR NOT making Catie stay at home. She had jumped in the backseat with Rose so fast that he didn't stop to argue with her. He had been so careful when their father died. As soon as he heard that his plane was missing, he telephoned the house and demanded Catie be taken to her room and kept there until his arrival. "She isn't to know anything before I've had a chance to speak with her," he had warned.

How would Catie weather another loss? Rose was the only mother she had known. What kind of cruel god would expect someone so young to endure two tragedies in the short span of only eight years? Ben breathed deeply and murmured another silent prayer. Rose's condition had worsened drastically before they reached the bottom of the winding road. He knew she was having a heart attack and prayed for the sound of a siren. The piercing wail finally reached them well ahead of its source, allowing Ben the time to pull off of the road and wave it down. He, Sarah, and Catie followed the ambulance to the hospital, watching the medics through the small windows in the back as they worked to save Rose's life.

In the waiting room, Catie stared out of a small slit in the blinds and cried quietly. Sarah flipped through a magazine so fast she couldn't possibly have read a single word.

"Good Lord, what's taking so long?" she exclaimed, tossing the magazine aside and pacing the room again. "We have been waiting for over an hour! Ben, can't you do something. Haven't you made enough blasted donations to this hospital?"

"At your request, Sarah, I've already spoken with the nurse twice, and both times she assured me the doctor would come to speak with us as soon as he could. Now sit down and stop pacing. You're making me nervous."

As if on cue, the door to the waiting room swung open, and an older, stocky man entered, his balding head shining against the harsh hospital lighting. He wore wire-rimmed glasses, a white coat and a tired expression.

Seeing the doctor, Catie bolted from the window but was stopped by Ben, who pulled her close against him while they waited for the man to speak.

"Mr. Darcy." The doctor extended Ben his hand. "Dr. MacAndrews."

"Dr. MacAndrews," Ben repeated cordially as he shook the doctor's hand and introduced Sarah and Catie.

The doctor took a seat and opened a folder. "Please," he encouraged them to sit, giving Sarah and Catie a friendly nod.

Once they were all seated, he took off his glasses and went straight to the matter at hand. "Mrs. Todd has suffered a mild heart attack. Though minimal, her heart has suffered some damage and her recovery, I expect, will take four to six weeks."

"But she's all right?" Catie asked anxiously.

"Oh, yes, I believe she will make a complete recovery. However," he looked at them gravely and explained, "She will have to make some serious changes in her lifestyle. Her diet, exercise, all now will have to be considered."

"She will do whatever you say. I shall personally see to it," Catie stated with conviction.

The doctor smiled at her. "Well, I can see she will be in competent hands. Has anyone contacted her next of kin?"

"Yes," Ben said. "I've called her sister, Mrs. Kelly. She lives in Northern Ireland and is on her way here now. I am afraid though, that my heightened concern for Rose's prognosis has put her in a highly distressed state."

"Actually, Mr. Darcy." The doctor took on a serious air. "Mrs. Todd's condition could have been much worse. Who, may I ask, had the good sense to give her the aspirin?"

"It was Maggie," Catie told them. "She insisted Rose take aspirin."

"Well, this Maggie," Dr. MacAndrews said, closing the folder, "quite possibly saved Mrs. Todd's life. At the very least she significantly minimized the damage to Mrs. Todd's heart."

"When can we see her, Dr. MacAndrews?" Sarah asked.

"She is resting quietly now. A nurse will come for you soon."

BEN LEANED ON AN OUTSTRETCHED hand and watched the last rays of the autumn sun disappear behind the hills. It wasn't even six o'clock yet, and dusk was already hard upon them. He looked over at his sister. Catie had not left Rose's side all day, determined to be there when her Nan woke up. But Rose hadn't even stirred, not once. Not unusual, according to the doctor; her body was weak and required the rest. The nurse didn't know when Rose might wake, and Catie refused to leave her side until she did. Ben sighed. The close of daylight and a tired, pregnant wife presented him with the unpleasant task of forcing his sister to do just that — leave.

"Before she wakes?" Catie cried. "No, Ben, someone must be here when she wakes up."

"Catie, dearest, I'll bring you back first thing in the morning," Ben whispered insistently. "Be reasonable, she might very well sleep all night. Sarah is exhausted, and you and I fare little better. Now please don't quarrel with me further."

"Brother, please." Catie's eyes were as imploring as her voice. "I can't leave her alone."

"Oh, for heaven's sake, child, mind your brother," Rose grumbled, struggling to sit up.

"Nan!" Catie gasped. "Oh, be still, Nan. You shouldn't try and — "

"Oh, stop fussing over me so." Rose grabbed the covers Catie was trying to straighten. "You didn't think you were getting rid of me that easy did you?" With considerable effort, she managed a weak smile across her ashen face.

"We thought no such thing." Ben took one of her hands and rubbed it gently between his. "How do you feel?"

The faint smile receded as Rose's eyes traveled from one worried face to the other. A tear broke free and raced to the pillow. "Oh, my, dearest children, I was so harsh with you both this morning. To think I might have gone to my eternal reward, leaving your last memory of me being…being…"

"Crabby," Catie finished, grinning. Her own tear-filled eyes sparkled as she leaned down and kissed Rose's cheek.

"Rose, you weren't well. We all have far too many pleasant memories to remember anything of the sort." Ben's voice was gentle and loving.

"Ben's right, Rose," Sarah said. "No one cares about what happened this morning."

"Plus," Ben added, teasing his sister. "I'd wager twenty quid that Catie rightfully deserved it."

"I did not!"

Rose laughed and then groaned, her face drawn in agony.

"See what you did, Ben!" Catie said. "Are you all right, Nan?"

"I'm just sore, child. I must be all right if I'm still listening to the two of you squabble."

A great deal of fretting and pillow fluffing ensued, as the three tried to get Rose into a comfortable position. The door opened and they turned, expecting the nurse who had come around all afternoon. Instead, a woman, looking very much like their patient, came in hesitantly and was followed by a solid, broad man with wavy black hair and piercing blue eyes which Catie recognized immediately — Mr. and Mrs. Kelly.

Disregarding the other occupants of the room, Emma Kelly rushed to her sister's bed and grabbed Rose's hand, pressing it hard against her cheek. Tears streamed freely down her face, her emotion so strong she couldn't speak. Mr. Kelly took a handkerchief from the inside of his coat pocket and held it out to his wife. "Mother," he whispered hoarsely.

Sensing the woman's distress, Ben apologized profusely for having caused her anxiety and gave her a quick but detailed account of Rose's diagnosis. "The doctor," he finished, "has left for the night, but I'll ring him directly if you desire to speak with him."

Mrs. Kelly smiled up at Ben with a relieved expression. "You, young man, must be Bennet Darcy." Emma Kelly had spent the last eighteen years hearing weekly accounts of the Darcy children, the overachieving, perfectionist Ben, the bold and spirited Catie. Mrs. Kelly's eyes brightened as they fell on the girl across from her. "And you…you are Catherine, eh?"

"Forgive me," Ben said. "My sister Catherine, and my wife…"

"Sarah," Mrs. Kelly filled in for him. "It's a pleasure to meet you, Mrs. Darcy. I have heard so much about you all. It's as if I know you already. Please forgive my outburst, but it was an answered prayer to see my sister awake when I came into the room."

"No forgiveness is necessary. Prayers were answered indeed."

Catie barely heard the passing conversation as she was thoroughly distracted by Sean's parents. Mrs. Kelly had given Sean her smile, full-faced and warm, but Mr. Kelly had given his son everything else — his thick black hair, sparkling blue eyes, and a sturdy physique. Mr. Kelly looked as if he had sprung directly from the earth itself, like a hearty oak tree.

The door opened again and Catie turned around. Suddenly unable to breathe, she moved away from Rose and closer to Sarah. Sarah reached for her hand and gave it a comforting squeeze.

Mrs. Kelly's smile widened at the sight of her children filing slowly into the room, led by their eldest brother. The youngest, Joseph, was crying as he came to the side of his aunt's bed. "Auntie…" he whimpered.

"Come here, Joseph, my boy." Rose reached out for the child, no more than twelve, and pulled him to her cheek. Catie noticed the boy's sorrow lighten as Rose whispered some sweet assurance into his ear. "You hear me now?" Rose asked, releasing him.

Joseph Kelly bobbed his head and then sought the consoling embrace of his mother.

With his family now intact, Mr. Kelly offered his own string of introductions: "My sons, Mr. Darcy…Sean, I believe you already know." Ben nodded. "Next to him in age are Gabriel, then Ronan, Cian, and the wee lad there with his mammy is our youngest, Joseph." Although Catie longed to scrutinize every Kelly face intently, her eyes would not allow her to stop fixating on the one that had monopolized her thoughts each night before surrendering to sleep.

It had been over two months since she had last laid eyes on him, and she was pleased that her memory had preserved every detail of his face. His hair was all that had changed, much longer than when she saw him last.

Sean caught her gaze and smiled faintly, but Catie looked away.

"Rose, dear," Ben leaned down close to her and said, "I must get Sarah home. We'll be 'round to see you in the morning. Let me know if they don't take good care of you, because — "

"I shall be fine," Rose stopped him, patting his hand.

"Say your goodbyes now," he said to Sarah and Catie, and turned to the wool-coated Irishman. "Mr. Kelly, where is your family staying?"

"I'm not sure yet, Mr. Darcy. We came straight to the hospital, of course." Mr. Kelly looked weary as though he hadn't thought that far ahead yet.

"Grand! Then you will stay at Pemberley," Ben declared, putting up his hand, fully prepared for Mr. Kelly's rejection. "I am sure your sister-in-law has sufficiently portrayed my deficient character to you. I have a stubborn-lacking ability to take no for an answer. It is an infamous trait."

"And my husband does have a reputation to uphold, Mr. Kelly," Sarah added with a convincing smile. "Please stay with us. We have more than enough room, and any family of Rose's is family to us."

Mr. Kelly looked at his wife and then made a passing glance over the faces of his children. His eyes lingered on them momentarily. "Mrs. Kelly and I will accept your gracious offer, but the boys will stay in the cottage our Seany lived in over the summer."

"But, Mr. Kelly," Sarah exclaimed. "That cottage is so small; your sons will be much more comfortable in the house."

"Mrs. Darcy, I mean no offence to your kind offer, but I have spent the last twenty years raising this lot and I can guarantee you that your fine home is no place for my rowdy cubs."

Appraisingly, Sarah scanned over the sturdy teenage boys. "As you wish, Mr. Kelly. Visit with Rose as long as you like. Your rooms will be ready for you when you arrive."

As Catie followed Ben and Sarah out, she could feel Sean's gaze on her, willing her to turn to him. She desired more than anything to once again meet his eyes with hers, but she never looked up. He had broken her heart, and for that she couldn't forgive him.

The ride home was silent, the trials of the day having finally caught up with each of them. Once back at Pemberley, they climbed the stairs like shire workhorses that had been in the fields since dawn. When they reached the top of the landing, Ben gave Catie a peck on her head and sent her to bed.

"Bennet, Sarah, I need ask you something," she announced, stopping them. "I want to stay home until Rose has recovered." Catie's eyes darted from Ben's to Sarah's and then back again.

"No, Catie, you will return to school tomorrow afternoon as planned," Ben said gently. "Now go to bed. You must be as exhausted as we are."

Her body might have been exhausted, but her determination was wide awake. "But, Ben, I will only be distracted worrying about Rose. It isn't fair that I must be over an hour away. What if she needs me? What if she gets sick again?"

Catie's eyes had a willful gleam that told Ben how important this was to her. In his heart, however, he didn't feel it was for the best. He reasoned, "You will get behind on your work, Catherine, and I can't allow that."

"But that's easily solved. You can have my lessons sent from school, and I can do my course work here at home until Rose is better."

"Without instruction?" he asked. "Catie, it's not feasible. I do not have the time to interview and hire you a tutor, and your schoolwork will suffer. I shall come for you on the weekends and that is the end of it." Ben swept his hand through the air, a gesture meant to end the discussion.

Sarah, who wasn't required to submit to such gestures, took this as her cue. "Of course, I could instruct her." Ben gave his wife a look so incredulous, it forced Sarah to retaliate. "Don't look at me like that, Bennet. My teaching credentials may be dusty, but I do not think them obsolete."

"Now there's a grand idea if I've ever heard one!" Catie exclaimed, smiling broadly.

Ben looked from sister to wife and knew his only hope was to divide and conquer. "Catherine, go to bed. Sarah and I need to discuss the matter privately."

Unable to stop herself, Catie asked, "And may I expect an answer before I go to sleep?"

"You can expect an answer when I have one. Now go to bed."

Without so much as a nod to her brother, Catie spun around on her heels and went to her room. Only a mild defiance, considering she had the will to argue the matter till dawn.

SARAH EXHALED A RELAXING BREATH as the caressing silk of her nightdress made its way down her body. She slid on her dressing gown and crossed the corridor to check on her sleeping sons. There had been no more signs of stomach upset since late last evening, and their heads felt cool to the touch. She bestowed a kiss on their cheeks and quietly left the room.

Ben was lying on the sofa of their sitting room with an arm draped over his eyes. "Rose gave me quite a scare this morning," he said as she came in.

"The scary part will be getting her to follow the doctor's orders once we get her home." Sarah loaded her hands with lotion and smoothed it down her arms, with extra effort at the elbows. Then she sat on the sofa and leaned against his legs to apply the remainder to her shins. "Did you have the cottage readied for the Kelly boys?" she asked casually.

"Heat and lights have already been turned on," he replied lightly.

"Well, goodnight, darling." Sarah leaned over to give him a kiss but was halted by Ben raising his arm and revealing his eyes.

"Goodnight? What do you mean *good*-night?"

"Its meaning, I believe, is universal, Mr. Darcy. A polite parting till morning, wishing the person you are offering it to a restful sleep."

"You know what I mean, Sarah. Are you not going to try and convince me to allow Catie to stay home for the duration of Rose's recovery?"

"Why would I do that, darling? The decision is yours after all."

Ben leaned up on one arm. "It isn't that I don't want her here. It's just, what if Rose does get sick again? You heard the doctor. She's not out of the woods yet."

"Catie is capable of enduring more than you give her credit for."

"I knew you were going to say that." He smiled at her.

She smiled back. "Well, it's true. Plus having her here might be beneficial to Rose."

He sighed thoughtfully. "But will having her here be beneficial to you. Sarah, I need not tell you that my sister is not the most attentive student to her studies."

"You may not believe this, Bennet Darcy, but when I was still teaching, the children referred to me as Miss Meanie." He chuckled. "But you're right." She twitched her mouth ruefully. "With Rose recovering I *will* be stretched to my limits."

"Exactly," he concurred.

"Though with Catie's elegant hand, she would be very helpful with my secretarial duties in Rose's absence. I mean the Christmas invitations will be coming in starting this week, and they must be attended to. And the — "

"All right…all right, she can stay! I'll be damned to misery if she doesn't!" Ben sat up and was met with a satisfied shine in his wife's face. "Miss Meanie."

Sarah laughed and tried once again to kiss him, but he stopped her.

"Oh, no, I'm not finished. There will be rules."

"Like?"

"Like…if I see that she is falling behind in her studies, she will be at Davenport before the day is out. And furthermore, she *is* returning to school at the start of the next term…*even* if Rose isn't one hundred percent!"

"Anything else?"

"Not that I can think of at the moment." Ben fell back on the sofa and threw his arm over his eyes again.

"I do love you, Bennet Darcy." Sarah lifted his arm and finally kissed him.

"Yes, yes," he replied and waved her away.

Smiling, Sarah got up and headed towards the hall. "I shall be back directly."

"Where are you going now?"

"Why, to tell Catie she can stay home for a few weeks."

"Please tell me, Sarah Darcy, was the ink dry on our marriage certificate before the two of you began to conspire against me?"

"Oh, Bennet, we weren't even engaged when your sister and I began conspiring against you." She disappeared around the corner and then popped her head back into the room. "Ben, would you please go down and fix me a sandwich? I'm starving."

"*Starving*? Sarah, we just ate an hour ago."

"Well, I can't help it!" she exclaimed. "This child of yours has the appetite of a horse."

"I knew it," he whispered elatedly as soon as she had disappeared again. "A boy! Mr. Kelly and his five strapping sons, ha! I'm not far behind you old man — not far at all."

Chapter 26

Catie looked up from her reading as the sound of footsteps approached her door. Anxiously, she put the book aside and waited. "Come in," she called out to a soft rap, as her little internal voice repeated, "Please don't say no, please don't say no." Sarah's smiling face gave her answer, and Catie's relieved words came in a rush. "He said yes! How did you do it? He seemed as unmovable as a mountain."

"Even mountains can be persuaded to move, Catherine — with the proper delicacy of skill, that is." Sarah winked at Catie as she eased onto the bed beside her. "I am worried about you though, Miss Catie Darcy."

"Worried? Why?"

"A certain young gentleman . . . S . . . K," Sarah said, tapping Catie's knee affectionately.

"Oh, there's no need to worry about him." Catie reached for her book. "Surely you don't think I'm still in love with him. That was months ago! Anyway, I gave him a good look over at the hospital tonight and decided he's really rather ugly." Catie opened the book and furrowed her brow in feigned concentration.

"*Cath-er-ine*," Sarah drawled out for effect.

"What?" Catie asked innocently.

"I am very tired and in no mood to deliver a lecture."

"There's no need, Sarah!" Catie snapped the book closed. "I already know what you would say. And, yes . . . I understand. I understand perfectly . . . all right?"

"All right." Sarah, put her hands up in surrender. "I'll say no more. Goodnight."

"Goodnight." Catie watched Sarah cross the room, her usual graceful stride was made even more so with the swelling life inside of her. The younger sister instinctively touched a curious hand to her own flat stomach. "Sarah," she said.

"Yes."

"Thanks."

"You're welcome."

"MISS CATIE…Miss Catie," Maggie whispered loudly, moving hurriedly around Catie's room, opening curtains and laying out fresh towels. "Miss CATIE!" she finally shouted.

"What!" Catie sat up straight. "Is it Rose? Did the hospital call?"

"No." Maggie shook her head.

"Then why are you waking me up?" Catie asked. "What time is it?"

"Half past seven," Maggie replied.

"It's too early." Catie slumped back down and pulled the covers over her head. "Come back and wake me in an hour. We aren't leaving for the hospital until nine."

"But, Miss Catie," Maggie persisted, standing over her now. "Mr. Darcy expects you to be at breakfast this morning. You have guests, and he said if you weren't there…he said…"

Catie lowered the covers and peered out at her. "He said what?"

"Oh, please don't make me repeat what he said," Maggie pleaded, wringing the towels she was holding.

"Let me guess." Catie pulled the covers back and rubbed her eyes. "Something like…having me hung up by my toes and beaten like a dusty old rug."

Maggie nodded.

"Oh, all right!" Catie slipped down to the floor and took a towel. "You need not look so worried, Maggie. He was only joking."

"How am I supposed to know? He always looks so stern and sour, just like your ancestors in all those paintings. Lord, some of their faces give me gooseflesh."

"My ancestors look dignified, Maggie, not sour."

Trying her best to look contrite, Maggie said, "If you say so, Miss Catie."

"I do."

When Catie came into the breakfast room, she drew up short and her eyes widened. Thank God she didn't gasp. There, sitting on one side of the table, were the Kelly brothers. Of course they would have to have breakfast in the house. But it hadn't occurred to her they would be in her breakfast room. They saw her too and stood with such haste there was a thunderous sound of chairs scraping the floor. Rather discomfited by their display of manners, Catie looked at Sarah and went awkwardly to the only empty seat, which was unfortunately next to her brother and directly across from Sean. Smiling his signature broad smile, Sean came quickly around the table and pulled out the chair for her.

"Good mornin', Miss Catie." His thick Irish brogue brushed against her neck as he settled her in her seat.

"Thank you," she replied quietly, giving his brothers a bashful nod.

The boys noisily sat down.

"It's not that I don't appreciate the show of ceremony, lads," Ben said, raising a witty eyebrow to his attentive audience. "But if you insist on standing every time my sister walks into a room, I'm afraid you will find yourselves quite light-headed. She buzzes around this house like a horsefly trying to find an exit."

The lads roared with laughter.

"Brother!" Catie hissed, her face growing scarlet. She turned again to Sarah for support but found her line of vision blocked by a mass of a man. Mr. Kelly was as broad as he was tall and hovered over his plate in a way that would have earned him a sharp reprimand had his last name been Darcy. Irritated, Catie lowered her eyes and silently ate her breakfast.

Talk of horses, horses, and more horses came from each side of her, as she listened faintly to Sarah and Mrs. Kelly dote over the three littlest boys at their end of the table. Left with no companionship, Catie performed the much anticipated task of scrutinizing the four younger Kelly brothers seated across from her.

Gabriel looked to be about eighteen and was every bit as handsome as Sean, though slightly taller, which gave him a lankier appearance. Cian and Ronan were very close in age — early teens, Catie surmised. But unlike most boys, who are all limbs and feet at that age, the middle Kelly brothers seemed to be faring a little better. Both had dark, wavy locks and those trademark Kelly blue eyes. The two appeared to be somewhat rambunctious, making her wonder whether they alone were the reason the brothers were exiled to the cottage. Wee Joseph, as Sean so often called him, was a definite favorite of his mother's: a beautiful child, quiet and watchful, much like the Darcys' George. Catie couldn't suppress a smile as she thought of Sean looking much like him not so long ago.

The tedious, sluggish conversation of getting to know one another drew out what should have been a short meal. Sitting across from Sean, Catie's eyes met with his often, and each time they did there was another stab to her already brittle emotions. It was almost as if some unknown force pulled them into each other's gaze. The sting of his stare was so excruciating that she tried not to cast even a glance his way and breathed a prayer of thanks when the meal finished.

"Catie." Sean caught up with her in the hall, glancing back nervously to see if anyone was listening.

"I haven't the time to speak with you. My brother and I are leaving for the hospital shortly." She started away from him.

"Listen to me." His voice was low but insistent.

Catie spun around to face him. Her heart was racing, and she was sure her cheeks blazed as hot as they felt. "Do you really think I have any desire to hear whatever it is you have to say?"

He stared at her for several breaths.

"Comin', Seany?" one of the brothers asked.

"Aye, Cian, I'm coming," Sean said to his brother. Both his tone and expression were dejected, but Catie refused to feel sorry for him.

The morning visit to the hospital was an unsettling one. Rose had a long night of reactions to some of the medicines she was taking, and her weak and ashen appearance from the previous day was worsened by a cold sweat and fever. Seeing the woman she loved so dearly looking so feeble, shocked Catie and she crumbled in her brother's arms. Ben comforted her with the gentle words their mother or father might have given her, all the while praying for Rose and praying his sister would be spared this grief. When her tears dried, they sat holding hands without speaking, listening to the repetitive song of hospital monitors until it was time to leave.

"Is Nanny Rose going to die, Bennet?" Catie asked in the car on the way home.

It was the first time Ben had heard his sister call Rose that in years. "I don't think so, Sis, but I'm praying all the same."

She brushed away a tear. "Me too."

Consumed with the dreadful "what ifs," Catie had to force herself to do something constructive and decided to devote an hour or so to her piano. The music room was the one place she was sure she could be alone. She especially liked to play when she was down. The somber resonance of a poignant sonata was like a comforting embrace to her. Rose knew this about Catie. Rose knew everything about Catie. If Rose were home, she would come to her and ask,

"What's weighing so heavy on your bosom, child?"

In the music room she was surprised and somewhat annoyed to see Seamus Kelly reading the newspaper and having his tea. *Were the bloody Kellys everywhere?* He looked up when she entered.

"Excuse me, Mr. Kelly, I didn't mean to interrupt your solitude. I'll come back later."

"Catherine, please stay," Mr. Kelly's deep voice gently requested.

Catie took a tentative step closer. Because of Sean's description of the man she was hesitant, and he did have an intimidating presence with his large barrel chest and bushy eyebrows.

"I–I was going to practice my piano, sir, and I fear the noise will be a nuisance to your reading."

"Nonsense, I could use a bonny song to balance the melancholy of these past two days." Mr. Kelly's large smile swelled even his broad chest, and Catie relaxed a little.

"If you'd like," she said and took her seat at the piano.

Mr. Kelly stepped over to the instrument and asked, "I don't suppose the little miss knows any Irish tunes?"

"Yes." Catie gave him a brief smile. "I know a few. How about 'When Irish Eyes are Smiling,' Mr. Kelly?"

He expelled a guttural sound of displeasure. "Not Irish, lass. The song was written in America for a musical production."

"Oh." Catie winced apologetically. "Sorry."

"But why not!" Seamus Kelly bellowed so sudden and loud she jumped. "It was meant as a tribute to the Emerald Isle after all, and it is a lively tune. 'Irish Eyes' it is, Catherine!"

Catie took up the song with alacrity, and within seconds the Irishman began singing along in a rich baritone voice. His deep timbre reverberated throughout the halls of Pemberley, bringing Ben and Sarah to act as audience. When finished, singer and pianist bowed to claps of praise.

"Bravo!" Sarah cried. "You've a beautiful voice, Seamus."

"Thank you." Mr. Kelly bowed slightly and turned to Ben. "I don't reckon you'd want to show me your fine stables now. I could use the air."

"I would be delighted!" Ben smiled.

"May I join you?" Catie asked. "I'd love to introduce Mr. Kelly to Chloe."

"I believe, Sis, that your music awaits you," Ben said, squelching Catie's enthusiasm.

"To be glued to an instrument, drudging over sheets of music on such a day as this one?" Mr. Kelly made another gruff sound of displeasure. "The child best take in all of the fresh air she can. Winter will be upon us before we know it, and..." He turned and gave Catie a conspiring wink. "And when there are no more pretty days as we have before us now, the instrument and music will get more than enough attention. Eh, Catherine?"

"Aye, Mr. Kelly," Catie answered in her best Irish accent, giving her brother a vindicated smile.

If Bennet Darcy was anything he was a gracious host. He inclined his head in acceptance and gestured the unlikely cohorts to take the lead. "Sarah?" he said to his wife on his way out. "Would you like to join us as well?"

"No. I think a warm cup of tea will suit me instead." She chuckled softly and added in a hushed tone, "But keep an eye on the two of them. They could become dangerous allies."

He pointed to his eye, telling her he would, then stepped close and whispered, "Any word from the hospital?"

"No." She shook her head. "But that's good news. Emma said she would ring us if Rose's condition worsened. It was nice to see Catie smile for a change, was it not?"

"Yes," he said. "Yes it was."

Talk of breeding had Catie walking a good pace behind the men, and she fell back even further when Mr. Kelly broached the topic of mounting difficulties. Horse husbandry, it seemed, was absorbing conversation. Trailing at such a distance, she was the first to notice Sean's approach.

"Da," he called out to his father. "Have you seen the boys?"

Mr. Kelly stopped. "What do you mean have *I* seen the boys? Didn't I tell you to keep them out of trouble?"

"Well, you did, Da." Sean glanced around as if hoping to spy them somewhere. "But I had a wee bit of studying to do and let Gabe take them to the river. But they should've been back by now."

"I think I hear them!" Catie pointed to the sound of yelling coming from the stables. She noticed Sean and his father exchange sidelong glances as they hurried off in the direction of the uproar.

"Oh, my." Catie came to an abrupt stop. Cian and Ronan were on the dusty ground of the stable yard, apparently trying to rip each other to shreds while

Gabriel stood over them laughing and egging them on. The observer, Joseph, was sitting on top of a fence rail, safely out of harm's way.

Mr. Kelly drew in a deep breath and let out a piercing high-pitched whistle that made Catie cover her ears, but the two boys didn't seem to hear him.

Gabe reached down and pulled them apart. "Stop!" he shouted, holding them by their collars, still kicking and swinging at each other.

"Gabe, Cian, Ronan," Mr. Kelly bellowed. "I'm fair disappointed in youse. Goin' at each other in front of a nice, wee lass. Where's your manners, lads?"

"Sorry, Da," Gabriel said, grinning. "Just settlin' a minor difference of opinion, that's all."

"He started it, Da!" Cian yelled to his father, pointing an accusing finger at his brother.

"Did not, you arsewipe!" Ronan broke free of Gabe's hold and tackled his adversary. The two hit the ground with a thud and began walloping each other with equal force as before.

Catie glanced over at Sean. The tips of his ears burned red with humiliation. "I'll take care of this, Da," he said, visibly fuming.

With one ferocious yank, Sean separated his brothers. "Stop it!" he shouted. "Stop it now or I'll beat you both senseless."

Still grinning, Gabe took one of the miscreants by the arm. "Shouldn't take long to beat a couple of buck eejits senseless! Eh, Seany?"

Sean lifted Joseph off of the fence and motioned his brothers back to the cottage with a menacing bark, "Away off!"

The three youngest Kellys ran ahead of their irate brother. Gabe, however, turned to Catie, removed his flat cap, and held it against his heart as he batted his eyes boyishly. "My apologies, miss, that must have been a most disturbing scene."

"Now, Gabriel!" Sean shouted.

"Sorry…must be off!" Gabe plopped his cap back on and pulled himself away by his collar, making a silly strangled face. Catie giggled.

Once they were gone, Mr. Kelly broke into a hearty laugh and ran his thumbs down the inside of his bright red bracers. "I'll bet the farm you would've put your money on Ronan the older one, wouldn't you, Mr. Darcy? But that Cian, he's strong as a mule. Pinned Gabriel down just last week; had to take him by surprise, but he did it, by George!"

Looking as if he didn't quite know what to say, Ben's mouth twitched several times before he spoke. "You must be extremely proud," he said finally and walked away.

Catie felt a warm glow fill her face as she looked up at Mr. Kelly, but the man didn't seem at all offended. "Shall we, Catherine?" He smiled down at her, his usual jovial self.

"If you'd like, you can call me Catie, Mr. Kelly," she said as they walked. "Everybody does."

"Me ma was named Katherine, lass," Mr. Kelly answered, softer than she had yet heard him speak. "I fancy the name, like hearing it spoke out loud again. So I'll stick with it if it's all the same to you."

Catie nodded.

ON TUESDAY AFTERNOON ROSE WAS showing the first signs of improvement, and there was talk of her coming home by the weekend. The news made Catie give an audible sigh of relief, slightly relaxing the tight ball that had formed in her stomach the morning they took Rose to the hospital. "Thanks be to God!" Ben said when Sarah hung up the telephone, and Catie nodded, unable to speak.

The Kelly brothers also seemed in better spirits knowing their aunt was finally on the mend. Catie watched from the window as they played football on the lawn. Although they taunted and teased each other relentlessly, there was a real sense of family among them. It occurred to Catie that the brothers might very well fight to the death for one of their own. Mr. Kelly soon joined his sons, bringing Geoffrey and George along. Fresh air, the man believed, was the key to health and long life. Mr. Kelly definitely put more value on a game of football than schoolbooks, just one of the many areas in which he and her brother didn't see eye to eye. Catie caught herself laughing out loud at her nephews and would have given almost anything to be outside with them. But instead she sighed away her wishful thinking and returned to her schoolwork.

Because Catie was nearly two days behind in her studies, Sarah sent her back to the library after supper to finish an essay on the French Revolution. Having Sarah for an instructor was not the cakewalk Catie had thought it would be, but she knew her sister had done her a favor and didn't complain. An hour into her assignment, the library door opened, and Sean walked in. She took an uneasy breath. Had he come to try and talk to her again, she wondered. She wasn't sure she'd have the strength to deny him a second time.

"I don't mean to bother you," he said, "but Mrs. Darcy told me I could look for a book to read to Joseph before he goes to sleep. I believe he's missing his mam at bedtime."

"Help yourself," Catie replied and returned to flipping aimlessly through an encyclopedia.

"Uh…" he uttered, and she looked back up. "Children's books?"

"Under the window, so children can reach them." With the end of her pen, Catie pointed to the low sitting bookcase.

"Ah, makes sense."

As he crouched, searching the shelves, Catie watched him. Watched his fingers trace the book bindings, watched his brows knit as he pulled one out, looked it over and slid it carefully back into position.

"What do you think of *The Jungle Book*?" He looked up suddenly.

Embarrassed, she dropped her head. "Hmm?" she murmured, never lifting her eyes.

"I said." He came closer to her, chuckling. "What do you think of *The Jungle Book*?"

"I think it is perfect," she said smartly. "Wee Joseph will no doubt associate with Mowgli quite well."

Sean leaned over the table and flashed that wicked gypsy grin of his. "Are you saying he has wolves for brothers?"

"Not necessarily. I'm sure any wild animal would sufficiently describe his brothers."

In retaliation, he snatched her paper and perused it with a professorial stroke of his chin. "Humph, seems to me you have forgotten a very important battle, young lady."

"I have not!" Catie took the paper defensively.

"You most certainly have! The Battle of Lodi on May 10th in 1796. You mention Napoleon's marriage to Josephine on March 9th of that year but omitted Italy."

"I did not *omit* Italy! Napoleon wrote Josephine some very romantic love letters from Italy."

Sean's face scrunched. "And what does *that* have to do with the Revolution?"

"Everything to Josephine, I would presume."

"Josephine was ruthless. She only married Napoleon to keep from being tossed out in the streets and regularly entertained other gentlemen while he was in Italy. The Battle of Lodi on the other hand was pivotal to Napoleon's career. If I were your teacher, I would hand that essay back to you in shreds!"

"Well, fortunately, you aren't!" She met his eyes straight on and then looked hastily away.

Taking his book, Sean strutted from the library shaking his head. "*Love letters?*"

WHEN NURSES BEGAN TO COME away from Rose's room rolling their eyes, it became clear the woman was rapidly on the mend.

"This is the most uncomfortable bed a body has ever been forced to lie down in!" she declared to Dr. MacAndrews on more than one occasion, along with similar complaints about the food, dust on the blinds, temperature of her room and so on and so forth. In response, Dr. MacAndrews finally came to the conclusion that releasing his patient to the comforts of home would be most beneficial to her recovery.

A chilly, autumn drizzle fell lightly on the house Friday morning, but it couldn't dampen the spirits of Rose's homecoming. With great anticipation the Darcys and Kellys waited on the steps under umbrellas to welcome her, waving and cheering at the approaching car.

"Look at all of you out in this weather!" Rose fussed, though she was smiling ear to ear as Ben helped her out of the car.

"As you see we've kept Pemberley standing in your absence." Ben gestured to the house. "However we're bloody well glad you're back!"

"And I'm bloody well glad to be back!" She stopped and took the time to look around at each of their faces. "Well, are we going to stand out here in the cold and rain and catch our death or shall we go inside?"

Catie laughed. Her Nan was home for sure.

It was inevitable, however, that this good fortune would mean the departure of the Kelly family. It was like waiting for a balloon to pop, and Catie didn't have to wait long. At supper Mr. Kelly took his last bite and folded his napkin. "The boys and I are booked on the ferry home tomorrow." Sarah made a move to argue, but he put up a hand to stop her. "I'm more than appreciative for the gracious hospitality you've shown my family, but I must get back to Kells Down. There's hay to store and..." he paused and smiled at Ben. "Well, as I'm sure you understand...the *ands* go on and on."

"I understand completely," Ben said. "It has been a pleasure having you...all of you."

"Yes," Sarah seconded. "The house will not be the same when you are gone."

Catie felt her heart thump hard in her chest as she listened. *Sean was leaving again.* Of course she knew he was going to leave, eventually. But she wasn't ready... not yet. When he went away so unexpectedly last summer, they never said goodbye. How could she tell Sean Kelly goodbye? He was leaving tomorrow, and she would probably never see him again.

"Emma," Mr. Kelly continued, "would like to stay on for a couple more weeks to see her sister through the remainder of her recovery, if that's all right with you, missus?"

"Emma is welcome for as long as she wishes to stay," Sarah assured him.

"Aye, then our Seany will stay too and see his mother home. It wouldn't be possible for me to come back and fetch her meself."

Catie released a breath, not realizing she had been holding it. Not tomorrow... not yet.

A toast was offered to Rose's improved health. Forsaking their usual "cheers," the Darcys called out the Gaelic *"slàinte"* in respect of their Irish guests, and with glasses raised, the Kellys boisterously rang back, *"slàinte!"*

In honor of Rose's homecoming, the two very different families celebrated together that evening. Rose was made comfortable on a sofa in the music room as she listened to a performance by Catie and Mr. Kelly, and then laughed until it hurt when the Kelly brothers joined their father in singing "The Star of County Down."

Catie noticed Ben took out his finest Scotch, by far the best means for gauging his feelings towards someone. She knew her brother didn't share all of Seamus Kelly's opinions, but Ben Darcy had come to like the Irishman. Mr. Kelly was an honest, hardworking man, and Catie knew Ben respected that.

When she finally went to bed that night she was still wearing a smile. She would miss the rowdy Kelly boys with their untamed ways. Never had Pemberley been so alive with music and ruckus. As she lay in what seemed like deafening silence, waiting for sleep, her mind did what it so often did... recalled the soft blue eyes of Sean Kelly.

Chapter 27

As Sarah predicted, Pemberley took on an eerie quiet after the greater part of the Kelly clan departed. Catie was up early each morning to visit with Rose before starting her schoolwork. The sisters had their breakfast in the sitting room of Rose's apartment, and Catie found great enjoyment in sipping coffee as she listened to Emma and Rose reminisce. They told tales of childhood antics and youthful romantic courtships that kept Catie both laughing and gasping in equal turn. The two, it seemed, had been quite the favorites among the young gentlemen during their heyday.

Even Sarah, after getting Geoffrey and George off to school, would frequently get caught up in a tale of a former lover. Then she would notice the time and hastily shoo Catie to the library before Ben noticed that his wife and sister had whiled away a whole morning over coffee, tea, and female prattle.

Not being able to stand the idleness, Sean helped at the stables or did other odd jobs to keep busy. It was the least he could do for the kindness the Darcys had shown his family. He had heard his father make numerous offers to compensate Mr. Darcy for his generous hospitality. Seamus Kelly was in no way ignorant to the cost of hosting such a large family for a week, and his sons' healthy appetites only increased what was already an undue burden. Bennet Darcy, however, refused any offer of reimbursement, explaining that no amount of money could ever repay the loyalty and devotion Rose had given his family.

"My father relied greatly on Rose after my mother died," Ben had told Seamus one evening, chuckling in his remembrance. "Catie wouldn't allow anyone else to feed her when she was a babe, and 'Nanny Wose' were the first words the little moppet spoke. And I dare say…" Ben's expression grew as grim as his

266

voice. "Rose Todd was the glue that held Catie and me together after Dad died."

Sean saw that Mr. Darcy's words were sincere, and he began to reconsider his judgment of Bennet Darcy last summer. He was just a man after all; doing what all men did — what he thought best for his loved ones.

The night under the fireworks stayed with Catie like a nagging, lingering cough, but at least the distress she felt in Sean's company slowly eased as the days lined up behind them. She often joined him and his mother in Rose's sitting room after supper to play cards, work a jigsaw puzzle, or watch television by the glow of a warm fire. No, she hadn't forgiven him, but her desire to be close to him was stronger than her resentment. If she were to be honest with herself, she still loved him, might always love him. It occurred to Catie that, like Rose and Mrs. Kelly's stories of lovers past, she might one day sit and tell her daughter about the summer she fell in love with her riding instructor, the summer of her first broken heart.

She mused over these thoughts as she and Sean struggled over the last pieces of a one thousand piece picturesque scene of England's coastline. In the puzzle the sun was shining and teams of sea aster bloomed on the shore, while outside a driving October wind circled the house, creating a sorrowful howl that rattled windows.

"Gracious, what a night," Emma said, tightening the sash and drawing the curtains. She leaned over her son's shoulder and pointed to a prospective puzzle piece. "Try that one, Seany."

He shook his head. "I did."

"Try turning it, Son." She patted him and sat back down beside her sister.

"Ah." He smiled over at his mother. "Thanks, Ma."

From the music room, the old grandfather clock chimed the nine o'clock hour. Its late eighteenth century mahogany case was inlaid with musical instruments, a reminder for children not to neglect their practice. The nine solid gongs echoed throughout the house like the familiar voice of an old friend. On the final bell Maggie came in to collect the tea things, as if the old clock had summoned her.

"Oh, Mrs. Todd!" Maggie cried out as she put away Rose's medicines.

"It's Rose, Maggie. I've told you a hundred times," she admonished.

"Yes, ma'am, but Mrs. . . . er . . . Rose."

"Yes, Maggie."

"Please tell me you didn't take this yellow pill after you ate."

"I'm not sure, Maggie. I reckon I did. Emma?" Rose turned to her sister.

"Um-hmm," Emma said, giving Rose an accusing eye. "She was supposed to take it earlier but forgot. So I just put it out with the evening pills."

"But, Mrs. Kelly, this pill has to be taken on an empty stomach. Mrs. Todd must take the yellow one at least two hours before she eats." When Maggie finished speaking it was as if she just took notice of her own voice. She blushed profusely and returned to clearing the teacups, which clanged unmercifully under her trembling hands.

"Thank you, child," Rose said kindly, trying to ease Maggie's anxiety. "Emma and I will be more careful."

Maggie's concern over Rose's medicine made Catie remember the aspirin. "Nan, did you know that Maggie practically saved your life? Dr. MacAndrews said so. I had completely forgotten about it until now."

"That's impressive, Maggie," Sean said.

"Rather," Catie agreed. "How do you know so much about medicine, Maggie?"

Keenly aware of their eyes upon her, Maggie set the tray down noisily and murmured so quietly they could barely hear her. "Me dad takes those yellow pills too. I wasn't sure if Mrs. um…. if Rose was having a heart attack, but she had all of the symptoms. That's how I knew she should take the aspirin."

"You should be a nurse or a doctor," Catie declared, making poor Maggie blush again only deeper. "Do you not think she would make a fine nurse, Nan?"

As if Catie's words offended her, Maggie snatched up the tray and scuttled for the door. "Will there be anything else tonight?" she asked Rose.

"No, child, you be off to bed now."

Maggie nodded and was gone.

"That poor child," Rose said, shaking her head. "She's had enough hardships in her eighteen years for a lifetime."

"Did I say something wrong, Nan?" Catie asked.

"Not purposefully, Catherine," Rose told her. "Don't let it worry you. Now to bed with you. It's getting late."

Catie unconsciously looked at Sean before getting up, and he instinctively looked back.

"Good night, Catie," he said softly.

"Good night," she replied equally as hushed.

Catie stopped at the door. "Please tell me what I said that upset Maggie, Nan."

"Didn't I say not to let it worry you?" Rose gave Catie a pointed look.

"Yes, but it will."

Though she bore a slight look of annoyance, Rose motioned Catie to her side and affectionately took the girl's hands in hers. "Maggie was upset because she would like more than anything to be a nurse, but she can't."

"Why?" Catie asked.

Rose tapped Catie's hand meaningfully. "Because, Catherine, we don't all have the same opportunities in life."

Catie's cheeks colored. *How could she have been so insensitive?* "Because she's poor?"

"Yes, she's poor, and her family needs the money she earns here, and she has a learning disability. Maggie's life is full of reasons she can't, Catie."

"I should apologize," Catie said.

"I think it would be better if you didn't." Rose patted her hand once more. "Go to bed, Catherine. Not everything in this world can be fixed."

When Catie left the room, Emma said to her sister, "She's exactly how you described her all these years, Rose. Fresh baked bread, hot and crusty on the outside but soft and warm in the middle."

"That's my Catie." Rose chuckled lightly.

"Well, I should be off to bed meself." Sean stood and stretched. "You women don't stay up too late now."

"We managed more than twenty years before you came along," his mother crisply informed him, and he laughed.

"So you did, Ma. Well, good night."

Finally alone, Rose looked at Emma with a rueful grimace. "You do know that those two children of ours are extremely fond of each other."

"That's putting it mildly." Emma drew a deep breath then blew it out slow and resigned. "But when worlds as different as theirs collide, it's like a train wreck; lives become derailed. My Seany knows better. He couldn't live Catie Darcy's life any more than she could live his."

"It hurts me, Em. I can't bear seeing them both so unhappy. And there is such a thing as a happy medium."

"Stop worrying, Sister, no one has ever died of a broken heart," Emma said as the shadow of a frown came over her face. "But I do hope that whoever does marry my son looks at him like Catherine Darcy does."

WHY IS SUCH ABUNDANCE ALLOTTED to only a selected few, while the rest suffer through life with very little? The age-old question troubled Catie's sleep. Rose was right; not everything in the world can be fixed…but some things can. By suppertime the next evening, Catie Darcy had accomplished "fixing" at least one: a promising future for Maggie Reid. All she needed now was her brother's consent.

Ben put down his fork, wiped his mouth, and sat back in his chair. When his sister wasn't nervously picking at her food, she was staring at him with that look in her eyes. Clearly she had something important to say. And knowing his sister as he did, a relaxed position was in all probability going to be needed.

"What's on your mind, Catherine?" He swirled and drank his last swallow of wine.

"My mind?"

"Yes, your mind, that constantly overactive area between your ears. I can tell when you're conspiring, so out with it. What do you want?"

Taking an uneasy sip of water, Catie glanced over at Sarah and then back to Ben. "Actually, I was wondering if I might speak with you in your study after supper."

Ben's eyes instantly traveled to Sarah's but were met with an expression that said, "don't look at me."

He looked back at his sister. "About?"

"A private matter."

Ben nodded worriedly. "After supper then."

With no real work at hand, Ben paced from his desk to the window, while, unbeknownst to him, his sister paced the gallery.

Finally resolved in her strategy, Catie made the short walk to Ben's study. The door was partially open, so she pushed it a little further. "Brother," she said to his turned back.

Glad to get the matter under way, Ben motioned her in and settled behind his desk. Catie sat down in the chair across from him, purposefully not making herself comfortable. "Bennet," she said with a businesslike air. "I need to discuss a financial matter with you."

"Financial matter?" he asked. "What sort of financial matter?"

Catie swallowed down her nervousness and continued, "My money. I know that Mother and Dad both left me an inheritance, and I'd like to use some of that inheritance."

"For?"

"A gift," she said. "I want to give someone a gift."

Ben's brows lifted. "And may I ask to whom you plan on giving this...gift?"

"Maggie Reid."

"Maggie Reid?" Ben repeated.

"Yes." She nodded.

Ben got up and came around the desk to sit in the chair next to his sister. "Catherine." He leaned on his knees to be level with her. "I think you'd better explain."

"Will you listen to me as a woman coming to you with a request, and not as your baby sister?"

He considered this for several blinks and then said, "I will."

"All right. Maggie Reid, I believe, has a calling to the field of medicine." She paused to see if he was taking her seriously.

"Go on." Ben sat up, offering her his full attention. "I'm listening."

"Well, she has nursed her father most of her life, ever since his accident. I know for a fact that she would have pursued a career in nursing but unfortunately wasn't able to finish school because of a learning disability."

"I see." Ben tapped his steepled fingers contemplatively. "What is it that you wish to do for Maggie?"

Catie felt a slight jolt of excitement. She hadn't expected this to go so smoothly. "Well," she continued, beginning to relax. "This disability of hers is called dyslexia. It makes reading difficult. It can't be fixed, but with the help of a specialist her reading skills could greatly improve. Specialists cost money, money the Reids don't have. Maggie must learn to read. None of her dreams can be achieved until she does."

"Catherine." Ben leaned close to his sister again. "I think the idea you have come to me with is very noble, but Mr. Reid is a proud man. You heard him yourself. He won't accept charity. I fear he may look upon this gift of yours as just that...charity."

"No." Catie shook her head. "Mr. Reid is pleased that Maggie will be taught to read properly. I rode out today and spoke with him myself. That's how I found out that Maggie has dyslexia. Mr. Reid told me all about it."

"You've already spoken with Mr. Reid about this?"

"Yes, but please don't be cross with me for not coming to you directly. I wanted to learn more about Maggie's disability before I spoke with you."

Ben released a short disbelieving laugh. "He was pleased, you say."

"Yes, Brother, quite pleased."

"Catherine, do you have any idea how many years I've been trying to get that man to take my help? And you just waltz into his little cottage and offer his daughter a specialist and he accepts it? No… is *pleased* to accept it?" Ben stood up and Catie stared up at him watchfully. "So you told him you wanted to give Maggie a financial gift, and John Reid was *pleased*?"

"Not exactly." Catie looked away, cringing.

"What do you mean, not exactly?" Ben asked, lowering his voice.

"Well…" she hesitated.

"Sis." Ben sat back down. "I think you'd better tell me."

"Well, you're right; at first he wasn't so keen on the idea. Not so keen at all."

Ben inclined his head. "Then how the devil did you convince him?"

Catie cringed again. "I'm afraid I lost my temper."

Ben sat back and closed his eyes. "Catherine, you didn't."

"I did."

Not opening his eyes, Ben said, "Well, best get it over with. Tell me what you said."

Catie bit her bottom lip in apprehension. "I called him a ripe old curmudgeon and told him that he should stop being so bloody pigheaded."

Speechless, Ben expelled a small moan and began to massage his eyes with his thumb and forefinger.

"It's okay, Ben; Mr. Reid just laughed."

Ben's eyes popped back open. "Laughed?"

Catie nodded. "He laughed harder than I've ever heard anyone laugh before and said I was the spit of my mum inside and out."

"And this, I assume, is when he agreed to allow Maggie to see the specialist?"

"Yes. He said the decision was Maggie's of course, but that she would have his blessing. So what do you say, Ben? Can I have the money for Maggie?"

Ben stared into his sister's eager face, while in his mind his father's voice came to him: "Benny, the real treasure of a man's wealth is in the good he achieves with it."

"Or a woman's, Dad," he whispered.

Chapter 28

The colorful reds and golds of autumn had been generously dispersed and scattered over the harvested valleys of Derbyshire. The mornings were brisk and glistened with frost. The days, however, were unusually sunny and mild and were frequently topped off with the fanfare of a red October sky, a deceptive splendor that usually ushered in a cold windy night.

Saturday morning had been a tedious one for Catie. She had helped Sarah with secretarial duties by addressing correspondence for the first half of the day. The midday sun, aided by a soft autumn wind, put a dance in the vibrantly colored leaves, making concentration difficult. Catie's eyes wandered to the window and lingered there with an unmistakable longing until her reverie was broken by the clearing of Sarah's throat.

With a pitiful sigh, Catie resumed her task, only to be interrupted minutes later by the playful laughs of her nephews, running about the garden with a new puppy. The dog was a gift from their father for reaching the ripe old age of six. She could hear Rose and Mrs. Kelly heartily laughing at the spectacle, and the window was once again enjoying a concentration the envelopes were obviously not going to receive. Sarah, the indulgent soul that she was, finally caved in.

"Oh, go on! Lord knows half of those letters will end up in China somewhere if you don't relieve your fidgets."

Catie grinned as she bolted from the confines of the small, lady's study, making Sarah call after her, "I saw that smirk, young lady! And put on a coat!" Giving her head a defeated shake, Sarah walked over to the window and watched for a few seconds until she was likewise summoned by the call of a pretty day. Unable to resist the sight of her adorable twins in pursuit of their equally adorable four-legged playmate, she gave her desk a regretful glance and reached for her jacket.

As soon as Catie stepped out of the house, the sun hid behind an unpromising cloud. Tightening her fists at her sides, she gave the earth a stamp in protest as she turned an angry eye to the heavens. The sun reappeared instantly, as if in fear of her wrath.

Fearing the worst for the afternoon weather, Catie passed up the lure of the puppy and decided to give Chloe some exercise before the rain set in.

"It's not a good idea, missy," Percival replied gruffly to her request to have her horse saddled. "That mare of yours no more likes the rain than my ol' bones."

"Then I'll turn back at the first drop." Catie smiled sweetly at him and added, "I promise."

No more able to tell Miss Catie "no" than he was able to fly, Percival went off grumbling to his task.

As Catie approached the mounting block, pulling on her gloves, Sean rode into the stable yard.

"Are you just now going out?"

"Yes."

"Alone?"

"As you see." She cut her eyes at him and mounted.

"The weather could turn any minute. It is already quite dark less than a mile from here," he warned. "It's why I came back."

"Then my ride shall be unfortunately short." Catie gave him one last glance, clicked her tongue, and cantered away.

Percival came to take Sean's horse but he waved him off. "No, thanks, Percival, I believe I'll keep a watch over Pemberley's resident pain in the arse."

"You said it, mate, not me!" Percival said, laughing.

Catie immediately detected her trail and picked up her pace to force Sean out of his secretive stalk. A devious grin and an aggressive pump of her heart sent a surge of blood rushing through her veins, and she was at a full gallop well before she reached the river with Sean hard on her heels and gaining. In seconds they were at an even gallop, nose to nose. Catie's heart was beating as hard as the pounding hooves below her. In her mind's eye she had been here many times, running across the fields of Pemberley with Sean galloping at her side.

Forgetting the impending weather, she continued carefree and fast, and far from home. She didn't want to wake up from the dream again and have him stolen away. But this wasn't a dream. It was real. Sean was there, galloping beside her with that lovely smile on his face and that desperately missed twinkle of challenge in his eyes.

Then, from out of nowhere, they crashed into a driving rain. Catie pulled Chloe to a stop and looked over at Sean. He motioned for her to follow him, and they rode away from the river and into the farmlands. They found a small shed, empty, to their good fortune. The lean-to had only three walls and a tin roof that exaggerated the weather to a deafening degree.

While Sean settled the horses, Catie removed her coat to shake out the wetness. "Steady on, girl," she heard him say soothingly to a very anxious Chloe. "It'll be over soon." She watched him ruffle Chloe's ears and smiled that he remembered how the horse liked that.

"When it lets up some we'll head back," he said, peeking out from under the roof. Then he looked over at her. "Are you warm enough?"

"I am... thanks."

Truly alone for the first time in months, she felt there was still something between them, something unresolved.

"You seem to have made amends with your father," Catie said.

"Aye." He smiled. "Me da has turned his aspirations to my brother Gabriel. It's for the best; he's better suited for the horse business than me."

"Is he supporting you in your education then?"

"Morally, yes, but then again that's all I've ever asked for."

Silence took hold again, and Catie prayed for a break in the downpour. Having already given her best effort, she leaned against the closest wall. They could stand there stupidly mute until the rain stopped for all she cared.

"I heard my aunt and mam talking about Maggie," he said finally. "I think what you did for her was kind, *very* kind."

"Maggie's quick thinking gave Rose a second chance. For that I could never repay her." Not wanting to look at him, she scuffed her boot on the dirt floor.

"Catie," he said after a few moments, raking his fingers through his wet black hair as if mustering up courage. "I... I owe you an apology. If you only knew how many times I sat down to write to you, to explain myself, to ask your forgiveness." He glanced at her to see if his words were having any effect, but she had turned away from him. Sean came up behind her. He reached out to touch her, but with an expression of sheer agony, stopped himself. "Please say you forgive me, Catie," he whispered.

"There is nothing to forgive, Sean," she said, keeping her back to him. "I behaved like a silly, foolish schoolgirl. Clearly, I misunderstood the attention you were giving me. So, please...let us both forget it."

"You didn't misunderstand anything, Catie; my — "

"I said forget it!" She spun around, her eyes blurry with emotion. "Please, say no more."

"Damn it, Catie! I must say this." He took a step closer, and she lowered her head. "Please, look at me." Sean reached out and pulled her face up, but she stared past him, not trusting herself to meet his eyes. "I said look at me." She obeyed him then, her eyes glistening with the pain of her broken heart. "Christ, Catie, you're tearing me apart."

Her tears broke free and streamed down her face, and he gently wiped them away with his thumbs. "Say what you must say." Her words and face were like stone. "Say it now, Sean, or you may never again have the chance."

He swallowed and his throat rippled with the effort it took to do so. "I lied to you that night under the fireworks. I had to; there was no other choice. Catie, I come from a poor Irish horse farmer. I know what it's like to do without, to want something you can't have. I could never give you the life you're accustomed to. Look what you did for Maggie. Look around you! What could *I* possibly ever offer you? That's why I left, because I'm a coward. I left rather than face you and the truth."

"What is the truth?" she asked, still looking him directly in the eye.

"The truth is that my feelings for you are stronger than I have ever felt for any other human being. The truth is...I love you, Catie Darcy. But I mustn't — *we* mustn't. You deserve better than me. I'm no good for you, and I never can be. That's all."

A torrent of emotion rushed over Catie and she plowed her face into her hands and wept.

"God, Catie, please don't cry," he whispered into her hair, pulling her tightly against him. "Please, don't."

His embrace was like a soothing ointment on a festering sore. As if she'd been given a tranquilizing shot, Catie relaxed into a calm serenity in his hold. The coming together of their two souls seemed to be a destiny far out of the realm of their understanding, and they held each other silently, afraid to let go...afraid to speak.

At last Catie whispered, "I don't care about the life I'm accustomed to, Sean."

276

"Catie —" he started, but she cut him off.

"No, Sean, now you listen." She pulled back but held his gaze as she spoke. "I have been a selfish being my whole life. My behavior at times has been unpardonable. But what no one really knew was…I pitied myself. Pemberley's orphan, no mum, no daddy, feel sorry for her like she feels sorry for herself! But you never felt sorry for me. You made me look at myself. You made me look at everything and everyone and see, *actually* see. Even with Ben, for the first time in eight years I realized that I wasn't the only person who lost their father when that plane crashed."

"But none of that changes anything. I'm still the son of a horse farmer."

"Sean." She leaned against him again, her voice as tender as the easing rain. "A very wise person recently told me that the *right* person enhances your qualities while accepting and balancing your faults. Don't you understand? Where we come from doesn't matter. All that matters is where we go from here."

For the first time without fear, they freely stared into each other's eyes. Then the pull they both had been so ardently fighting brought them slowly together, savoring every second. Their lips touched. Tenderly, she felt his mouth caress hers. He took her face into his hands, forcibly holding their union. He kissed her tears, kissed her closed eyes, and then her mouth again. He kissed her like he might never have the opportunity to kiss her again. He kissed her until the last drop of rain fell on the tin roof over their heads.

Reality took hold when the rain ceased and brought them back to an understanding of what lay ahead. "Your brother," Sean said, those two words being enough for them both to understand.

"At the end of the day, Bennet Darcy is his father's son. What Ben respects in a person is integrity and character." She finally smiled at him. "Both of which I believe you possess, Mr. Kelly."

"That's flattering, Catie, but — " he hesitated.

"But what?"

"But, he'll want only the best for you, and I am sure my integrity and character will not be enough, at least not where you are concerned."

"Well, there's only one way to find out, isn't there?" The certainty in her voice gave no hint to the apprehensive knot beginning to grow in her stomach.

Back on their horses, the two urged their mounts in the direction of their unknown future, a future that now lay in the hands of Bennet Darcy. They didn't know whether or not he would allow them to embark upon the beginnings of a relationship, but they had to try. Their feelings for each other could no longer be denied or concealed, and the worst outcome now could only be shadowed by continuing to keep those feelings hidden and painfully locked inside.

After they had settled the horses, they gave each other a reassuring smile and started the short walk to the house. *Stronger than I have ever felt for any other human being.* Sean's words echoed in Catie's head. It felt as if nothing could come between them now, nothing except for...Aiden Hirst. Catie looked up and came to a dead stop. Aiden was coming towards them with hard, determined strides.

"Aiden!" she said, sounding surprised. "What are you doing here?"

Giving Sean no more regard than a cutting look, Aiden rushed to her with exaggerated concern and grabbed hold of Catie's hands. "I heard about your housekeeper from my uncle and came to you straight away. I remember you telling me how much she meant to you."

"Means to me," she corrected. "Rose is going to be fine, and so am I." Uncomfortable with Aiden's intimacy, Catie inwardly cursed herself for ever allowing him to kiss her. Glancing sideways to determine what Sean might be making of Aiden's familiarity, Catie surprisingly found an unnerving glower that went far beyond jealousy. She curiously looked back at Aiden and asked, "Have you two met?"

"Oh, yes." Dropping Catie's hands, Aiden finally gave Sean an acknowledging nod. "Paddy and I met at your garden party. Good times, eh, Paddy?"

Aiden's words did not ease Sean's expression. If anything, his eyes piercingly narrowed and he visibly stiffened.

"Sean," Catie asked. "Do you know Aiden?"

Softening his face just enough to look at her, he answered through a clenched jaw, "I know all of him I care to know."

All at once, Catie was struck by a revelation. Before Audrey left school that night, she had said, "Sean Kelly interrupted us." Sean Kelly knew who took Audrey from school. He had seen them together at the garden party. "You!" she turned squarely on Aiden Hirst and shouted accusingly. "You took Audrey from school and then put her out to walk back. She was expelled because of you. How could you, Aiden?"

Aiden looked spitefully at Sean and back at her as a lopsided smirk crept up one side of his face. "Audrey and I had a few laughs, but she was willing. No one forced her from school that afternoon."

"Save your excuses for her father, Aiden," Catie said in a threatening tone, seething from his arrogant nerve. "He has wanted nothing more than to know who took Audrey from school, who took advantage of her. I'm sure he will be glad to give you the opportunity to say your peace."

Gone quickly was the charming boy Catie had met last spring. Aiden's face suddenly blazed with a violent anger. Seeming to forget Sean, he grabbed her under the arm and jerked her up onto her toes. "You'll do as your slutty friend did and keep your bloody mouth shut!" His face was less than an inch from Catie's, and his throaty voice spat in her eyes.

"Take your filthy hands off of her, you bloody bastard." Sean's Ulster accent was suddenly deep and gruff.

In the brief fleeting stillness, Catie watched Aiden's bulging eyes cut sharply over her head at Sean. "Bugger off, Paddy — " he started, but color drained from his face as his eyes traveled slowly back to Catie's. The sharp pain in his leg, caused by her riding boot that had just slammed solidly into his shin, made him release her. "You bitch!" He hobbled delicately backwards.

As soon as Aiden was a few safe steps away from Catie, Sean stepped between them. "It's time someone taught you a little respect for women, mate," he said as he drew back and crushed the finely chiseled nose with a well-landed fist. Aiden's eyes went wide with surprise, and he staggered backwards.

Charged with rage, Sean made up the space Aiden had put between them with two quick steps and then dealt another blow into his midsection. Aiden folded in half and then fell to the ground with a dull thud. Gasping, he instinctively curled into a protective ball. Sean stood over the coiled body, casting a lengthy shadow from the late afternoon sun that had reappeared after the rain. "Do not ever touch her again." Sean's tone had an eerie casualness to it.

Aiden moaned softly.

"I said." Sean reached down and pulled Aiden to his feet by the front of his shirt and shook him fiercely. "Don't ever touch her again!"

"All right," Aiden croaked weakly. "All right!" Now standing, he coughed and wiped the blood pouring from his nose on the sleeve of his jacket. He ventured a glance at Catie and then turned and limped back up the path.

"Are you okay?" Sean turned to see her rubbing gingerly at her arm. "Did he hurt you?

Catie shook her head. "I'm all right."

He came over and pulled her under his chin. "Look, if you're going to be my girl, you must let me fight the men, aye?"

"Aye," she said back, unable to repress a faint smile. "Sorry."

"It's all right. Sorry about the language. Me da taught me never to curse in front of a lady, but I was a wee bit riled."

"Forgiven," she said.

"You know, Catie Darcy," — they had begun walking towards the house again — "you kick with the force of a mule."

STANDING ON THE FRONT STEPS of Pemberley, Ben watched Aiden's little, red sports car peel out of the drive, sending gravel flying in its wake.

"What the devil is the matter with him?" He looked at Sean and Catie.

"I hit him," Sean said bluntly.

"You *hit* him?" Ben looked at Sean disbelievingly.

"Aiden took Audrey from school, Ben," Catie hastily clarified. "He admitted everything."

"Aiden Hirst?" Ben repeated skeptically. "Are you sure?"

"Yes, Ben, I'm sure. Sean even saw him with Audrey the night of the garden party."

Ben's steely eyes turned back to Sean. "Is that why you hit him?"

"No, sir." Sean shook his head. "I hit him because he hurt Catie."

"Hurt Catie?" he exclaimed, quickly descending the steps to examine her. "Catherine, are you all right?"

"I'm fine," she said. "He just yanked my arm rather hard, that's all."

Wrapping his sister protectively in his arms, Ben looked over at Sean. "Did you hit him hard?"

"Aye, Mr. Darcy." Sean grinned. "I believe I broke his nose."

"Good man, Kelly!" Ben said and gazed again in the direction Aiden had sped off. "Aiden Hirst," he murmured. "Who would have thought? Well, come, Catie, you must get indoors and out of that wet coat. I need to telephone Donald Tillman. I'm confident he will want to make a call on Ardsley Manor this evening, and I think I might just join him."

"Mr. Darcy," Sean said, halting Ben. "May I first have a few minutes of your time…in private?"

Ben instinctively glanced at his sister. Meeting his gaze, Catie's expression revealed her comprehension of Sean's request, and her eyes beseeched him to listen. Ben stepped aside and said, "Come through."

Ben took Sean into the front parlor. Hearing the heavy door click shut, a shaky sigh left Catie's lungs. She didn't like this, but Sean had insisted on speaking to her brother man to man. At least they weren't in the territorial grounds of Ben's study.

Preparing for the worst, from a conversation that was probably going to be short and to the point, Catie stationed herself at the bottom of the grand staircase to wait. Not expecting a miracle, her mind began planning her next course of action when Sarah, Mrs. Kelly, and Rose happened upon her on their way to the orangery.

"Catie, what's the matter? Why are you sitting there like that, dear?" Sarah asked.

Closing her eyes despairingly, Catie dropped her head into her hands. Then she peeked through her fingers, but the three women were still circled around her with puzzled expressions on their faces.

"Catherine Darcy," Rose said fussily. "What is going on?"

Giving the double parlor doors a wary glance, she said, "Bennet and Sean are talking."

"Talking? About what?" Sarah asked.

Nervously glancing at Mrs. Kelly, Catie lowered her eyes and said, "Me."

"Oh," Sarah uttered. Then comprehending fully she repeated with more emphasis, "Ohhh!"

Quick to understand as well, Rose and Emma gave their own concerned pass over the doors and sat down beside Catie on the wide flare of the staircase.

Almost an hour later there was still no word from the parlor, not a voice had been heard nor a sound been made. Restless, Catie stood and paced the hall.

"Good Lord, what is taking so long? They have been in there nearly an hour." She looked at Sarah pleadingly. "Maybe you should go in there?"

"No, dear," Sarah refused, shaking her head definitively. "I'm a progressive woman, Catie, but there are still a few areas where women should not tread. This is between your brother and Sean."

Sarah was getting concurring nods from Rose and Emma when the parlor doors opened, and the women came rapidly to their feet. Sean came out first, followed by Ben. The two men looked rather astonished seeing the four anxious faces that were fixed upon them.

Sean grinned boyishly as he walked over to the most eager of all. "Catie

Darcy, would you like to have dinner with me in the village this evening?"

Eyes glowing brightly with excitement, Catie first glanced to her brother for approval. Standing as tall as he could make himself with his arms in a formidable fold, Ben gave her an ever so slight nod of his head. "I'd love to!" she answered.

"Seven?"

"Seven's fine."

"Seven then," Sean confirmed and started for the door but turned back as if he had forgotten something. "Ma, Auntie, could you fetch some scissors and come down to the cottage?"

"'My Seany knows better,' eh?" Rose raised a brow to Emma.

"Oh, hush and get the scissors," Emma fussed back as they hurried off together.

Catie rushed to the window to watch Sean descend the stairs as Sarah went to her husband. "You're a good brother, Ben Darcy," she said, as he unfolded his arms to gather her into his chest.

"Well, she's ready." He smiled down at her. "And since I made you a promise, I thought I'd better keep it."

Sarah smiled back. "Sean is a fine boy. I don't believe even Bennet Darcy could find a fault with him."

"His hair is too long," Ben replied flatly.

Sarah pulled back abruptly. "Is that why he asked for the scissors? *Bennet Darcy*," she cried incredulously. "Please tell me you did *not* tell that boy he had to cut his hair before he could take your sister to dinner."

"I most certainly did," Ben said with conviction. "If he wishes to dine with my sister he is going to go about the business respectably."

Shaking her head, Sarah gave her bulging belly a discreet but reassuring tap.

Afterword

Four Years Later

Standing in front of her full-length mirror, Catie Darcy gazed intently at her mother's beaded and lace wedding gown. It had just arrived back from the seamstress, and she was quite engrossed by her own image. Taped to her mirror was a photograph of her mother wearing the same dress on her wedding day, and Catie was carefully comparing her likeness to the picture of Margaret Sumner Darcy.

Behind her, the sound of pounding little feet grew increasingly louder. Suddenly a small child with a mop of strawberry blond curls darted through her door and slid quickly out of sight under her bed. A heavy footstep followed close behind.

"Did Eliza Jane come in here, Catie?" Ben asked firmly.

Her brother's brow told Catie it would be better for Eliza Jane to prolong her father's search. "What do you think, Brother? Will I make you proud next week?" she asked, successfully diverting him.

Ben beamed at the sight of her. "Very proud, Sis." He warmly embraced her. "Sarah and I will be as proud as Dad and Mum would have been." Ben gave Catie a wink and resumed his search for his daughter.

"If you see Eliza Jane, tell her that her father wishes to have a word." Ben stopped at the door and added, "And he is *not* happy."

"Whatever did she do, Bennet?"

"Geoffrey said something she didn't like so she poured a whole glass of milk over his head."

Catie bit her bottom lip to keep from laughing. "I can't imagine where she gets that temper from."

Ben stared at his sister blankly and then walked away.

Her father's fading footsteps stirred the fugitive, and an angelic, full-cheeked face popped out from under the bed. "Thank you, Auntie Catie," Eliza Jane whispered.

Sarah's voice calling for her daughter was heard from the hall, and the child quickly vanished.

"Catie." Sarah appeared at the door. "Have you seen Eliza?"

With a subtle cast of her eyes to the bed Catie revealed the child's whereabouts, and Sarah nodded understandingly.

"Oh, Catie…your dress is back!" Sarah carefully inspected her seamstress's work with a discerning eye and satisfied, brought her clasped hands to her cheek. "You are going to be the most beautiful bride, Catie, but…" Sarah broke off with a sigh. "I'm afraid we shall have to find you another flower girl. Our little Elizabeth Jane has run away from home, never to return."

"I have not," said the bed.

Smiling, Sarah walked over and crouched down beside the bed. "Elizabeth Jane Darcy, come out from under there this instant." Though the tyke obeyed her mother, she was dutifully hard at work defending her actions by tattling on her milk-laden brother as she did so.

"Yes…yes, save it for your father," Sarah gently advised and, finally having the tiny miscreant in hand, gave Catie one last admiring gaze.

"Auntie Catie." Eliza Jane tugged on her wedding gown. "When can I get married?"

Catie leaned down and gently tapped Eliza's nose. "When your prince comes riding in on a horse to take you away with him."

"Is that what happened to you?" The child's eyes went round with amazement.

Catie laughed. "It is, Eliza Jane."

"Come, Elizabeth Jane." Sarah lifted her little daughter into her arms. "You must first square things with your father over the milk incident before asking his permission to marry."

Alone again, Catie turned back to the mirror, smiled at her reflection and said, "It *most certainly* is."

On the morning of Catie Darcy's wedding, Pemberley's seventeenth-century chapel never looked more regal. The old stone church was alight with candles and adorned with greenery and bouquets of flowers from the estate's own gardens. At the altar her future husband waited. He turned to her the moment she entered with a look that teetered somewhere between panic and complete bliss, and she couldn't suppress the little hiccupping laugh that escaped her at the sight of it. She understood his sentiment. After all, they were practically children when they first fell in love. Indeed, she and Sean had traveled a long and difficult path to get to that moment. But despite the travails of a drawn-out courtship, which often had the cold Irish Sea between them, and families that were rarely in accord, Sean Kelly came riding out of a foggy morning up to Pemberley House to claim Catherine Darcy as his bride. Inspired by Catie's love of romance novels, he galloped in on a white mount wearing a top hat and morning coat. He wanted the moment to be better than any she would ever read in a book, but most of all he wanted her to accept his proposal.

"Ready, Sis?" Ben stood at her side, and she nodded.

Eliza Jane led her father and aunt to Sean Kelly over a path of pink rose petals, taken from a rose bush planted by Catie's mother. At the end of the aisle, Ben gently lifted his sister's veil and kissed her cheek, and then graciously put her hand into her soon-to-be husband's.

After a traditional ceremony that brought them from man and woman to husband and wife, the newlyweds danced late into the night surrounded by their closest family and friends. At Catie's request, fireworks lit the sky as the couple prepared to leave the cheering crowd to spend their wedding night in remote rooms of Pemberley, which had been especially prepared for the occasion.

"At last!" Sean said, scooping his new bride into his arms. "You are finally mine, Catie Kelly, to do with as I please."

"Perhaps you did not listen to the vicar, Mr. Kelly," Catie replied with a clever lift of her brow. "I believe he said it is the husband's duty to do his wife's bidding."

"He did?" Sean looked down at her skeptically. "I must say, Mrs. Kelly, I don't remember that part of the ceremony. What say you then, my love? What is your bidding?"

Catie leaned up and whispered softly into his ear.

"Here? Now?" he questioned.

Impishly biting her bottom lip, she nodded.

"As you wish, m'lady."

Catie Darcy Kelly lay back in her husband's arms and stared up into an explosive, sparking night as her husband twirled her on the front lawn of Pemberley.

The End

CPSIA information can be obtained at www.ICGtesting.com
Printed in the USA
LVOW041159120412

277326LV00002B/7/P